To those we lost along the way,
who stay beside us, day by day.
To those who always will remain;
our source of strength, our source of pain.

THE DAMAGED

The Damaged

Simon Law

THE DAMAGED

THE GREAT STORM
1987

The glorious summer had long since receded in Sussex, south of England, and the autumnal colours of amber and red had rapidly spread through the leaves of the trees. The evening weather report by Michael Fish had blissfully laughed off any rumours that a hurricane might be on its way to England that night, and assured viewers that aside from a little rain, the evening would be most uneventful. Meteorologists would later argue that Michael Fish was technically correct in his deliberation, as the term 'Hurricane' actually referred to a storm that originated from the tropics, and 'The Great Storm' of '87 had not. The impending storm had actually developed in the Bay of Biscay, and was originally predicted to reach no further north than France. They were wrong, so very wrong.

Disagreements over mere terminology, however, could never detract from the damning failures of the met office that night, leaving the population completely unprepared for the carnage and bloodshed that would awaken them from their cosy slumbers.

A storm of such strength and ferocity not seen in England in almost three hundred years was now on a direct collision course. It was a storm that was destined to rip the south coast to pieces, to send over fifteen million trees bellowing to the ground below, to cause over fifteen billion pounds' worth of damage to buildings and cars, and to take the lives of nineteen unsuspecting people.

The peaks of technology in 1987 comprised of basic 8-bit gaming systems, compact disc players, and soda streams. It was a world without mobile phones or iPods, and the 'World Wide Web' was nothing more than a concept that appeared on shows like 'Tomorrow's

THE DAMAGED

World'. Advanced weather predicting software was still in its infancy, and access to instant information was completely unheard of.

Margaret Thatcher (known to many as the 'Iron Lady') had just celebrated the win of her third term election, and although seen by her followers as a modern-day feminist hero, many considered her to be the devil incarnate. This stemmed from her apparent uncaring self-preservation attitude towards society, as she set out to demonise the 'welfare state', and those who had fallen on hard times.

The truth to many, was that she was no feminist at all, having never done a thing during her time in office in support of women's rights. She was an 'accidental feminist' in the sense that she just happened to be a woman, and her journey to power inspired other women to fight for their own successes too.

Sandra Mason, a self-proclaimed 'Thatcherite', was a woman who also felt inspired to further her career. She had first begun working just three years prior when her son Matthew started primary school, starting off as a bank cashier and quickly working her way up to assistant manager. Like many 'Thatcherites', Sandra had styled herself in Thatcher's image, wearing frumpy beige suits with oversized shoulder pads, a permed brown bob, and a string of pearls to finish off the look. Her husband, George, had worked for the past twenty-seven years as an architect for a top London firm, commuting back and forth each day in his prized black Ford Capri.

Together, the happy couple had paid off the mortgage on their spacious three-bedroomed detached house – complete with a vast cellar underneath to store their growing collection of vintage wines and ports. They had decorated their house in typical eighties-style, with floral wallpaper with bland shades of cream and brown, garish pub-style floral carpets on the floors, sharp mahogany furniture in the lounge and dining room, and a frilly white doily under each and every vase and ornament. Life was good for the Masons; that was, until the storm ripped their family apart.

October 15th started off as any normal Thursday did for the Masons. Sandra walked Matthew to primary school for eight-thirty before making her way to the bank, and George set off on his daily commute to London. Matthew spent the morning learning his times tables, followed by sports and games. This was followed by school dinner of bangers and mash, and then an afternoon of rehearsing his part in the school's upcoming production of Noah's Ark.

At three o'clock the school bell rang and Matthew was greeted at the school gate by his Aunt Julie, the elder sister of his mother Sandra. Julie, a recent divorcee with no children of her own, met Matthew from school every day. She would walk him home to her sister's house and assume the role of babysitter until Sandra got home from work around half five. Julie and her sister were close and babysitting felt like her honourable duty, as it would allow Sandra to have the career that she had recently become so obsessed with. Julie hated children, but it would have been churlish of her to refuse the task on these grounds alone.

The wind had already started to blow quite hard by this time, but this did not seem in any way unusual for a mid-October afternoon.

The front door opened and Matthew made his way straight into the lounge, switched on the television, and slumped himself onto the sofa just in time for the afternoon cartoons.

"Matthew! Shoes, please?" his Aunt Julie yelled at him from the hallway. "Off!"

"Sorry, Aunt Julie," he replied, as he pulled apart the laces and reluctantly returned to the hallway, placing his size three school shoes down upon the wooden shoe rack next to his aunt's cream suede high heels.

"Now try and keep it down a little, your aunty has a headache, okay?" she told him as she rubbed her head.

"Yes, Aunt Julie," Matthew replied with an innocent smile.

He was trying to be as good as possible for his aunt today, as yesterday he had upset her by playing in the swamp out the back and getting his school clothes caked in mud. As punishment, she had stopped him from watching his cartoons and had sent him straight up to his room. This was not something that Matthew wanted to repeat again today. The cartoons were the highlight of his day.

It was just at that moment that Matthew began to hear the opening title music to 'Thundercats' from the TV set, and immediately bounced back to his position on the sofa with the joyous glee and enthusiasm that only a child could experience from the sound. Julie shook her head in bewilderment, seemingly ignorant to what it was once like to be a child.

Julie made herself a coffee and lit a cigarette (a forbidden pleasure in her sister's house), and gazed from the kitchen window for a while, watching with curiosity as the wind rustled through the leaves of the fir trees that bordered each side of the back garden. Balancing her cigarette carefully upon the ledge of the kitchen windowsill, she then began to rummage around the drawers in search of some headache tablets.

'Thundercats' was followed by 'Transformers', and then 'He-Man', all of which were Matthew's favourite shows. Once the cartoons had finished he proceeded to plug his games console into the aerial port of the television, and spent the next hour saving the universe from an alien invasion. It was at this point that Sandra arrived home from work, to the relief of Julie, who had spent the last two hours staring numbly at the daily crossword in the newspaper and chain-smoking cigarettes out of the kitchen window.

"Hey!" Sandra called from the hallway, closing the door again and shaking out her windswept hair.

"Hey, Mummy!" Matthew quickly called back from the lounge, still eagerly engaged in killing aliens.

"How was school today, Matthew?" Sandra asked him, as she unstrapped her black stilettos and stepped into the lounge.

"Today was good Mummy, we...we had sports and maths and then... then we did err...err...we did rehearsals for the... err... the school play, and the teacher said I was really good mummy!" Matthew stuttered out in the way an excited child would talk quicker than his brain could keep up. "Are you coming to see my play, Mummy? It's next Friday after school," he continued, placing the computer game on pause and staring up at her with his big blue eyes, eagerly anticipating her approval.

"Of course I will, sweetheart. I wouldn't miss it for the world!" she replied with a loving smile, before leaning down and placing a kiss upon his forehead.

"...And Daddy? Is Daddy going to come too, yeah?"

"Yes, and Daddy too. Do you have any homework to do today?"

"Err...Yeah," he replied with a lethargic change of tone. "I got spelling and times tables."

"Okay, Sweetheart. Well why don't you get started on it now while Mummy starts the dinner, alright?" she asked, ruffling up his blonde hair with her hands, and giving him another smile and a nod.

"...Okay then," Matthew agreed reluctantly. "What've we got for dinner today, Mummy?"

"What would you like?"

"Err, I want... Err... I want chicken nuggets with err... spaghetti letters and chips!"

"No worries. I'm sure I can manage that!"

Matthew smiled in approval, before switching off the television and dragging his school bag past her, up the stairs, and into his bedroom, where instead of doing his homework as told, Matthew got out his pencils and began to draw.

"Good day then Sandy?" Julie asked, placing her Biro back down onto the crossword puzzle again.

SIMON LAW

"Well, could've been worse I guess, Jules," Sandra replied, letting out a long sigh and placing her handbag down upon the kitchen side. "He's still being an arsehole to me though," she continued.

"Your boss?"

"Yep, who else would I be talking about?" she replied with a hint of annoyance, as if she hadn't complained about him a million times already.

"So, what's he done today then?"

"Oh, just the usual, staring at my arse when he thinks I'm not looking, talking to me like a child, making me do the most menial tasks imaginable. Just another day in the office!"

"Well, he's a *man* isn't he? What do you expect? They're all the damn same if you ask me."

Sandra paused for a second and looked at her sister with frustration, wondering when her indiscriminate man-hating would ever end.

"Not *all* men are the same, Jules. You can't paint them all with the same brush you know."

"I can, and I will," Julie replied defensively. "I'm yet to be proven differently about them."

"And what about George then? He's not the same is he?"

"I dunno, do I? He's your husband, not mine."

"Well, he's not. You might meet a nice one too if you dropped the attitude a little!"

"Hey! I thought we were talking about your problems anyway?"

"We were!"

The two of them then shared a smile of surrender and shrugged off the argument.

"Coffee then?" Julie offered.

"Yes please."

Julie left shortly after, and made her way through the blustering winds to her small two-bedroomed bungalow a few streets away. She was greeted like usual by her two hungry Persian cats that jumped at her legs excitedly in anticipation of food.

"Alright, girls, calm down!" she told them, as she quickly poured some cat crunchies into a bowl. She then sparked herself up another cigarette and sat herself down on the sofa to watch television.

The welcomed sound of the engine from George's Ford Capri roared above the noise of the wind and bounced through the walls of the house. Sandra was just sliding a tray of chicken nuggets into the oven when she heard a key turning in the lock.

THE DAMAGED

"Hey, Darling," she heard from behind her, and turned to give him a smile.

"Hey, Hubby!" she replied, walking over to land a kiss on his perfectly clean shaven right cheek.

"Good day?" he asked, removing his leather driving gloves and hanging his tweed jacket upon the coat hook.

"Yeah, not bad, thanks," she told him, deciding not to burden him with the saga about her boss quite yet. "...And you?"

"Yeah, it was really good actually! We seem to have solved that problem we were having with the drainage designs, and it looks like we're going to have the plans all finished ahead of schedule," he told her with a slightly smug grin, oblivious to the fact that the details of his job did not excite her in the same way.

"Ah, well done Love!" she replied, faking an appropriate amount of enthusiasm.

"What's for dinner?"

"Just nuggets and chips, it was Matthew's choice today, remember?" she told him, hoping not to arouse too much disappointment.

"Nuggets, hey? Well why didn't you say we were going all gastronomical today?" he replied with a little chuckle. "I presume a fine Chardonnay would suffice then?" he continued, brushing gently passed her towards the cellar door.

"Yes, George. That should be fine. Thank you Sir," she replied, poorly trying to mimic her husband sarcastically posh tone.

Shortly after, they gathered around the mahogany dining table and ate their dinner to the sound of Vivaldi's 'Four-Seasons' which George had recently re-purchased on a shiny compact disc. This was followed by a round of neapolitan ice-cream before then resigning to the lounge with the remainder of the Chardonnay wine. Sandra and Matthew shared the two-seater sofa as usual, while George sunk himself down into the deep red leather of his Chesterfield armchair, which sat with accompanying side table – complete with lamp and television remote, all sat gently on top of another white laced doily. Within a brief thirty minutes or so, both Matthew and his father had fallen gently into a state of unconsciousness.

They both continued to snooze for the next hour or so, while Sandra's attention flittered back and forth between the television screen and the growing noise of the wind from outside the window. The hypnotic noise seemed to morph back and forth from the deep grumbles in the sky above to the high pitched whistling through the branches of the trees below, and seemed to grow stronger with every passing minute. The television then cut to commercials and Sandra noticed the clock striking nine-thirty. She turned to her son beside her, sleeping peacefully and curled against her in a foetal position with his thumb firmly inside his mouth. It almost seemed wrong to wake him up, but she knew he had to.

"Matthew? Matthew?" she gently whispered into his ear, giving him a little nudge. "Wakey Wakey!" The boy started to grumble back at her, and his sleepy eyes began to open.

"Come on son, time for bed, yeah?" she told him with a smile. Half awake, Matthew gently shook his head and closed his eyes again.

"No, come on, up you get now," she said more sternly. He opened his eyes again, wider this time, and looked around to his sleeping father on the armchair. He then looked back at his mother with a look of disapproval, as if to say – "Well, what about him then?"

"Don't worry, I'll be waking him up as well in a minute," she confirmed, as if having read his mind. Matthew finally released a sigh of surrender and pulled himself from the sofa. He scratched his head and let out a yawn, before stumbling over to the stairs and flipping on the landing light.

"Remember to brush your teeth, and I'll be up in a minute," she called over in a half whisper.

"Okay, Mummy," he replied, just managing to get the words out before another yawn took control of his jaw. He turned, and started ascending the stairway.

Sandra pulled herself from the sofa too, took the empty wine glasses into the kitchen and returned to the lounge again. She reached over to draw the curtains closed for the night, but found herself staring worriedly into the turbulent night. The sun had set a long time ago now, and the darkness completely masked the angry black clouds that had consumed the night sky. She watched as the trees shook violently from side to side in the orange glow of the street lights, and started to feel an eerie sense of malevolence all around. The feeling grew stronger and stronger, and started to run down her spine with a tingling chill. A distant crackle joined the roars of the wind, as rain began to fall from the sky, bouncing from the window and gushing along the guttering. Her feelings of anxiety then started to peak as she felt herself suddenly twitch. She closed her eyes and rubbed her face, quietly telling herself to "Get a hold of yourself woman!" She shook herself free from the consuming hypnotic state, and pulled the curtains firmly shut.

"Alright, love?" a voice suddenly called from behind. Sandra immediately jumped a foot into the air with shock and turned to face her husband.

"You scared the hell out of me!" she blurted angrily.

THE DAMAGED

"Hey. Hey! What's wrong with you?" George replied in confusion, rubbing the sleep sediment from his eyes and staring back at her with a look that demanded an explanation.

"I'm sorry George, you just startled me. You've been asleep for over an hour!" she explained, her apology only sounding half sincere.

"Guess I was tired, my love. You're not angry at me for that, are you?" he asked with the look of confusion still apparent upon his face.

"No, no of course not."

"Is Matthew in bed?"

"Yeah, I'm just about to go check on him," she replied, reaching down to switch off the television set. "You coming to bed too?"

"Err..." he replied, turning his head to focus on the tall grandfather clock as it ticked over to nine-forty. "Yeah, I guess," he continued. "I'll only fall asleep in the chair again otherwise!"

She smiled back at him and laughed, before offering her hand out to him and helping him up from his comfy chair. It was at this point that George finally tuned in to the noise of the weather outside, and the look of confusion returned to his face once more.

"God, it ain't half blowing hard outside tonight!" he announced.

"You can say that again, start of another long winter I guess."

They turned off the rest of the downstairs lights, pulled the rest of the curtains shut, and made their way upstairs. They brushed their teeth and changed into their matching set of silk pyjamas before meeting again outside Matthew's bedroom door.

"Goodnight, Sport. See ya in the morning," George called from the open doorway.

"Goodnight Daddy," replied a muffled voice from underneath the bed sheets.

George retired to the master bedroom and got into bed. Sandra, still hovering in the doorway, looked down at Matthew in the bed, wondering why he had felt the need to pull the sheets over his head and hide himself underneath. She stepped further into the room and sat herself down gently on the side of the bed.

"Matthew?"

"Yes Mummy?"

"Why are you hiding?"

"'Cos I...I don't like the wind, Mummy. It's scary!"

"Oh, it's only wind, Matthew, it can't hurt you," she told him, refusing to acknowledge her own moment of anxiety only minutes earlier. She reached over and gently pulled the covers down below his head. "Well you can't sleep like that!" she continued.

"Okay, Mummy."

SIMON LAW

"Have you brushed your teeth like a good boy?"

"Yes, Mummy."

"Okay, Sweetheart. Sleep tight, and don't let the bed bugs bite!"

"And if they do?"

"You bite them back!"

Sandra stood from the bed and turned to leave.

"...Mummy?"

"Yes Matthew?"

"Can you put my night-light on, please?" Matthew asked, leaning forward in the bed.

"Sure thing," she told him, bending down and flipping the switch on the small plastic box on the wall. Matthew smiled as the calming blue light began to radiate into the room, giving everything in its path a faint blue hue.

"Thank you" he called out, snuggling back down in the bed again. Sandra blew him a kiss and closed the door again, calling "Love you, Sweetheart," as she left.

The wind and rain rumbled into the night, growing stronger and fiercer with every passing moment. The southern coastline of England was the first place to feel the full brunt of 'The Great Storm'. It flipped over cars in the streets, it toppled over trees, and it sent caravans skidding down the hillsides. By 11pm the storm had already taken the lives of three people, all crushed to death by falling trees and collapsing rooftops. By midnight another three had been killed, including a fire-fighter who was crushed to death by a falling oak tree. By 2am the full force of the storm had reached twenty miles inland, and was blowing at over ninety miles per hour. It roared and cackled from the sky with deafening volume, like a demon ripping its way out of hell. It whooshed down into the streets, lifting every leaf, twig, and piece of rubbish, and filling the sky in a flowing sea of debris. Trash cans, bicycles, and plant pots all lifted from the ground and flew through the air as if the laws of gravity no longer existed.

An enormous shattering of glass suddenly woke Matthew in his bed. A loose roofing tile from a nearby house had come free and smashed through both panes of his double glazed bedroom window like a speeding bullet from a gun. It shot across the room and crashed into an adjacent bookcase, sending his collection of 'Transformer' action figures plummeting to the ground. He sat bolt upright, trembling with fear and petrified stiff. The fearsome wind gushed mercilessly through the open hole and engulfed the entire room in a whirling vortex, sucking every book and toy into it.

THE DAMAGED

Matthew soon became aware of the throbbing pain down the right side of his neck. He nervously reached up to touch the area, and gently brushed his fingertips against the tiny shards of glass that now protruded from his skin. He looked down at his hand, gently glowing blue by the light of the bedroom night-light, and fixated upon the tiny cuts upon his fingers. He took a deep gulp, as he began to feel the blood gently trickling down his neck.

His attention then returned to the whirlwind of books and toys in front of him, as they span closer and closer to his face. He felt his teeth begin to chatter and his toes begin to curl.

"Mummy! Mummy!" he screamed into the air, finally managing to free himself from the static freeze of shock. "-Mummy! Mummy!" he quickly screamed again, hoping that his little voice would somehow rise above the roaring gusts of the wind and reach his parents in the next room. Within seconds the bedroom door flew open and Sandra and George appeared at the doorway, mixed looks of frantic panic and confusion upon their faces.

"Oh God!" Sandra exclaimed, as her eyes tracked the whirlwind of debris around the room. She placed her arm up in front of herself to shield her face from the projectiles and the wind, and began to force herself into the room.

"It's okay, Sweetheart, Mummy's here," she called reassuringly, making her way closer to the bed and setting eyes upon Matthew's wounds. She helped Matthew out of the bed and shielded him with her arm, as she guided him back to the doorway. George immediately grabbed the door handle again and pulled with all his might against the force of wind, until finally the door was shut again, trapping the whirlwind inside the room and immediately reducing the noise of the deafening roars.

"Are you alright, Son?" he asked, panting from the strain.

"My neck..." Matthew whimpered gently. "What's going on?" he continued with a confused and pained grimace.

"It's just a bad storm, Sweetheart," Sandra interrupted, taking Matthew's hand and leading him towards the stairs. "George, can you grab me some pliers, please?" she asked.

"Yeah, sure," he quickly replied, following them as they dashed down the stairs.

"It's just a few little cuts, Matthew, it's nothing to worry about," Sandra told him with a forced smile, flipping on the light switches and setting him down upon a dining room chair. She gave him a loving kiss to the forehead and peered down again at the glass that was protruding from her son's neck, trying her best to suppress any looks of concern. She turned into the kitchen and started searching the drawers and cupboards for some anti-septic and plasters. George quickly brushed past her, pulled open the wooden slatted door to the wine cellar, and descended down into the darkness in search of his tool box.

Matthew sat quietly on the chair, patiently waiting for his parents to gather up the supplies. He closed his eyes, took a few deep breaths, and tried to slow his heartbeat from its racing pace.

The wind outside continued to bellow from the sky with accompanying whistles and hisses through the trees. The window panes of the house rattled vigorously with thumping and chattering in all directions. Matthew placed an index finger in each ear to block out the sound, and began to hum a nursery rhyme in his head to distract himself from it. He opened his eyes again a few seconds later to find his parents back in front of him again, looking down at him with false smiles which momentary fooled him into feeling safe once more.

"Okay, Sport, just come into the kitchen where we can see you." George encouraged him, gesturing for him to stand under the light. Matthew stood, and gingerly did as he was told. George knelt down beside the boy, pliers ready in his right hand, and gently tilted Matthew's head to expose the tiny shards to the light. The shards twinkled and sparkled, as George quickly counted each piece and prepared himself to extract them. Sandra nervously stood by, antiseptic, plasters, and cotton wool pads ready to hand, as she stared down at the blood-stained fragments and grimaced as George began to open the pliers.

"Now keep still Matthew, this may hurt a little bit, okay? – But try not to move," he told him, as his forehead creased up in concentration, and he closed the pliers down on the first piece. With one fluid motion, George ripped the glass fragment clean from Matthew's skin and gently released it onto the kitchen sideboard.

"See, that wasn't too bad, was it?" he asked with a smile, looking up to see a single tear running down Matthew's cheek. Matthew gritted his teeth and nodded gently, trying to hold back the rest of the tears which were starting to brew. "Okay, Kid, you're doing great, just a few more to go now." He continued, deciding it was probably best to get the rest of them out as quickly as possible.

George wrenched out the second and the third pieces in quick succession, placing them both down with the first one on the sideboard. He then prepared to take out the last one, the biggest one of them all. He quickly ripped out the last piece and the gaping hole immediately erupted with blood which gushed down the boy's neck. George threw the pliers to the floor and quickly grabbed a cotton pad from the side, slapping it straight onto the wound and pressing with as much pressure as he could.

THE DAMAGED

"You okay, Son?" he asked in a worried, shaky tone.

"It hurts, Daddy!" Matthew whimpered in response, tears now flowing freely from both eyes.

"I know, Son. I'm sorry," George told him.

George released the pressure a little, and started to tease the cotton pad back off again. He then let out a long sigh of relief to see blood flow receding back to a gentle trickle.

"All done now, Sweetheart," Sandra told him with a look of relief, as she knelt down to join George on the floor. She opened up the bottle of antiseptic, soaked one of the cotton pads in it, and began to clean up the boy's blood-drenched neck. George reached for the pliers, stood, and released another long sign of relief. He dropped the pliers back in the toolbox, and gazed from the kitchen window as the gusts continued to batter the trees and bushes back and forth.

"I bet that tile was from Edgar Brown's house!" George mumbled in a bitter growl. "He's been losing roof tiles for months now. I told him about them too! Lazy Git!"

"It's not his fault, George, come on. Matthew's fine, and that's all that matters now."

"I guess," he replied bluntly with a tut. "Did you see the weather report today?"

"Yeah, they didn't say anything about this though."

"Nothing at all?"

"Nope."

"Strange. I've not seen a storm like this since...Well, for ever to be honest."

"Me neither. We are safe though, aren't we?"

Their brief moment of calm then came to a sudden end with the almighty sound of a shatter and thud which pierced clean through the groans of the wind and sent vibrations throughout the house. The three of them suddenly froze in their positions and turned to the direction of the noise. They had expected to see another shattered window or door, but there was nothing obvious to be seen. "What the hell was that?"- George muttered to himself, as he gingerly began to pace towards the lounge windows. Sandra and Matthew looked on in eager anticipation, as George drew back the curtain slightly and peered through the gap.

"My car! My ruddy car!" he screamed in shock, as he looked at his prized Capri, crushed and crumpled beneath a fallen tree.

"What's happened?" Sandra quickly piped in, shocked to hear her usually well-mannered husband's expletives.

George did not respond. Instead, he put on his shoes and coat and reached for the door handle.

"George!" Sandra called again, stern and assertive. "It's too dangerous outside!"

"I'll be fine, my love. I just want to check the damage."

"It's just a car, George. Leave it!"

"I'll just be a second!" he told her, equally as stern.

He turned the door handle ninety degrees, and before he had even started to pull it a gust of wind took control of it and blew it clean from his grasp, sending it swinging around on its hinges and embedding the handle deep into the plaster of the inside wall. The wind blew George back into the coat hooks and he struggled to keep his footing. It gushed into the house, sending picture frames flying off the walls, along with papers, magazines, and white cotton doilies.

"For God's sake, George!" Sandra screamed at him, wrapping her arm around Matthew to protect him from the debris.

Again, George did not respond to his wife. He grabbed the door handle with both hands and wrenched it out from the wall, before fighting his way outside and wrenching it closed once more.

Sandra tutted and shook her head in disapproval, as she cast her eyes over the broken frames and debris that now covered the lounge floor.

"Where's Daddy gone?" Matthew asked her with a scowl of confusion.

"He'll be back in a minute, Sweetheart. Don't worry," she told him as she mopped up the last of the blood and started applying plasters to his wounds.

George held up his hand to protect his eyes from the gusts, and looked down disappointedly at his poor Ford Capri. A thirty-foot long oak tree lay embedded across the windscreen and roof. He followed the trunk along with his eyes to where it divided into branches, and then into leaves and twigs, which ended a mere four-foot from his house. It was at this point that he realised how lucky he had been not to have lost his house too, and although the Capri was a prized possession of his, the situation could have been worse. He brushed his hand tenderly along the bonnet of the car and gave it a smile of surrender.

His attention then turned to the sound of smashing glass in the far distance, and he turned to look. A shadowy silhouette then appeared on the horizon, illuminated only by the flickering orange lights of the distant street lamps. He put both hands around his brow and tried to focus in on the figure. The figure staggered from side to side, meandering down the street, desperately fighting to keep his footing. The figure got closer, and closer, until finally George could distinguish it as a man, but not a man he knew. George knew everyone who lived in the small affluent cul-de-sac and most of the neighbourhood's regular visitors too, but this man was none of them.

THE DAMAGED

The man then stepped directly underneath one of the street lamps and the orange glow illuminated one side of his rugged face. It was a tramp.

George stared in confusion for a while, wondering how the tramp had stumbled his way into *their* street. There were plenty of shelters for the homeless near to the town centre, along with many secluded alleys and hidey holes that would have been far more befitting of him. George almost felt a moment of anger that the man had even dared to step foot in *their* street, but the feeling was quickly blown away as a strong gust of wind almost blew George off his feet.

The man suddenly stopped in his tracks and looked straight over in George's direction. He called over to him and waved his arms about in the air for attention. A brief moment passed, but that was all it took for George to dismiss the man's calls for help. His fear and ignorance immediately overwhelmed any part of his conscience that would tell him to help the man. He turned his back, and headed straight back to the house again.

George closed the door to his house once more and immediately the balance of guilt started to shift. *What if the poor man died outside because of me?* he started to ponder.

"Is everything okay? George?"- Sandra called out in a mildly unimpressed monotone.

"Yeah, everything's fine, Darling," he replied unconvincingly, hanging his coat back upon the hook and walking through to re-join them.

"Cup of tea?" she asked with a look of resignation.

"Yeah, okay."

George rubbed his face and ears that had frozen numb in the wind, and looked down at his son. Matthew looked back up at him with his big blue eyes, both hands wrapped around a warming cup of hot chocolate, and gave him a smile.

Sandra had turned to re-boil the kettle when she was startled by a loud knocking at the door. George closed his eyes in an attempt to wish the situation away, but the knock repeated, louder and harder.

"Who the hell's that...? George?" Sandra asked, scowling at him accusingly.

George let out a long breath, as his guilt finally toppled the scale.

"It's okay, my love. I'll sort it out," he told her begrudgingly, and started making his way to the door again.

Sandra, perplexed by the apparent visitor, gestured sternly to Matthew to stay in the kitchen, before side stepping into the dining area to get a clear view of the door.

George turned the handle and opened the door once more, instantly allowing the monsoon of wind back into the house again. Standing before him was a scruffy man, dressed from head to toe in layers of filthy brown rags which rippled in the wind like waves. The man had long greasy brown hair and a scraggy brown beard that was stained yellow from nicotine. His big Roman nose was bent to one side and the left side of his face was smothered in wind-smeared blood from a recent fall. The rancid stench of stale beer and urine emanated from every inch of cloth, and as the wind blew into the house it carried the vile smell with it. The putrid smell wafted into their nostrils in the wind, causing their stomachs to churn in revulsion. They couldn't help but gag.

"Oh thank God!" the man panted in a gravelly rasp. "You have to help me. It's hell out there tonight, I...I can barely stand!"

"Are you alright, fella? Do you need an ambulance?" George shouted through the wind.

"No, I just need somewhere to shelter, please, can I come in?" he asked, trying to step further into the house.

"I..." George hesitated, searching for the best way to respond. "I'm sorry, fella, but you can't stay here...You'll have to find somewhere else."

"Please! I'm gonna die out there!" he shouted sharply, offended and frustrated.

"No. I'm sorry, fella," George told him sternly, starting to push the door against the wind.

"You selfish, self-centred son-of-a-bitch!" he hissed at George like a snake, bouncing each word from his tongue with a projectile of spit. "Who do you think you are? Huh!" he continued, pushing the door fully open again. He then peered up at Sandra, watching from afar. "Who the *fuck* do you think you are?" he screamed again, giving her an angry snarl.

Sandra looked away from the angry man and back around to Matthew, who stood out of sight of the man in the corner of the kitchen. Matthew looked up at his mother with a worried frown, eager for words of reassurance, but they didn't come. She looked around to the open cellar door, and then back at Matthew again.

"You think you're so much better than me, don't ya? In your big expensive house?! Huh?" the man raged on.

"Just get out, now!" George yelled back, tussling to close the front door on him.

THE DAMAGED

"Everything's okay, Sweetheart." Sandra gently whispered to Matthew, ushering him into the cellar and closing the door. "Just stay here a minute," she continued.

Matthew began to tremble again, as he stared back at his mother longingly through the gaps in the wooden slats of the cellar door, chewing anxiously upon his thumb nail.

"You snobby-stuck-up fuckwits!" the man continued to hiss, projecting his stale breath right into George's face, pushing harder and harder against the door.

In a brief moment of fear and adrenaline, Sandra quickly snatched a long knife from the kitchen side, holding it firmly behind her back as she slowly stepped back into view again. She edged closer and closer, her eyes fixated on the man and her teeth grit tight.

Another huge gust of wind then exploded into the house and blew the door clean from both of the men's grips, sending it hurling back into the embedded groove in the wall. The man lost his footing in the gust, knocking George into the coat hooks behind him and sending himself plummeting head first onto the lounge floor. The gust engulfed the entire house again, sending the lamps and vases smashing into a thousand pieces.

The man began to pull himself to his feet, when he was met by the sight of the kitchen knife in his face. Sandra's eyes fixed firmly upon his with a bitter scowl upon her face.

"Get the *hell* out of our house!" she screamed down at him with aggression.

The man's eyes followed the length of the blade as it glimmered underneath the shine of the lounge light. He slowly stood back up, gingerly backing away.

"You crazy fucking bitch!" he muttered to her, as he projected a globule of phlegm at her feet.

"Now!" she insisted, gesturing to the door with the knife.

The man slowly turned to the door again to see George looking back at him from the hallway, his eyes nervously flittering back and forth between him and his knife-wielding wife. The man glared at George with bitterness, and watched as a single bead of blood began to roll down from the coat hook sized hole in the side of his head. George looked back at him, and watched as a sadistic grin started to form in the corner of the man's lips, as if the sight of the blood had excited and pleased him.

In a split second the man lunged at Sandra unexpectedly and grabbed both of her wrists with his hands. He pushed and struggled with her, and forced her backwards to the kitchen, where he thrust her against the kitchen side. He pulled and pushed again with all his weight, crunching her lower spine repeatedly into the sideboard. She cried out in anguish as the pain shuddered through her body. He increased the pressure on her wrists and squeezed until her fingertips started to go blue, sending the knife descending to the lino floor.

"Get off my wife!" George growled at him, as he dashed though the lounge to help. He leaped onto the man's back, wrapping both arms around his neck in a headlock. Starting to choke, the man finally released Sandra's wrists from his grip and sent a flying elbow into George's face, cracking the bridge of his nose and sending him crashing to the floor. He quickly swooped down and grabbed the fallen kitchen knife from the floor, immediately thrusting it against Sandra's throat.

"How do *you* like it, bitch?" he screamed at her. "Ain't nice having a fucking knife in your face, is it?!"

"Please stop, please!" she begged with him, her spirit finally broken.

"Oh I'm sorry, have I interrupted your perfect fucking lives, have I?" he snapped angrily, pressing the knife harder into her throat.

"Please!" Sandra repeated, as she started to tremble and cry.

"Look, fella... Please. Just take what you want and leave us. Please don't hurt my wife." George pleaded with him desperately, as he slowly stood from the floor and wiped the blood from his nose.

"Oh, so now you wanna help me, do you? You didn't give a shit five-fucking-minutes ago though, did you? Huh?" he snarled, turning his attention to George.

"Please, just put down the knife and we'll talk, alright?" George pleaded again, edging closer and closer to the man.

"Take one more step and your bitch-wife's gonna get it!"

Sandra then caught the sight of a saucepan out the corner of her eye, and gingerly started to edge her trembling hand towards it.

"Look, what's your name, fella?" George asked calmly, trying his best to pacify the crazed man.

"...My name? What the hell do you care what my name is?"

"My name's George and this is my wife, Sandra," he calmly continued, discreetly edging forward still.

"*George*? What a snobby-fucking name too!" the man replied with a snort, starting to ease the pressure off the knife.

THE DAMAGED

"So what's your name, fella?"

"You can call me King-Kong for all I give a shit!"

Their conversation was then interrupted by another enormous crash from outside, as another tree plummeted to the ground, taking out another car with it. The house shook with the impact, and in the brief moment that the man was distracted, George reached forward to grab the knife. The man quickly reacted, and swiped the knife at George, slicing deep into his open palm with a splattering of blood against the tiled kitchen wall. Sandra gulped with the knife finally away from her neck. She saw her opportunity, grabbed the saucepan, and swung it ferociously against the man's head. The pan cracked hard into the man's skull and sent vibrations all the way back up her arm. The man growled in pain, but did not fall to the floor as hoped. He snapped his head at her, clenched his teeth, and plunged the kitchen knife deep into her jugular.

"Sandra!!" George shrieked in horror, as he watched her gargling blood from her mouth. "No!" he cried again, as he ploughed his clenched fist into the side of the man's head. The man clenched his teeth again, retracted the blade from Sandra's neck, and furiously embedded it into George's ribcage. George fell to the floor again in agony, clutching at the bloodied wooden handle of the knife.

Sandra reached for her throat with both hands, desperately trying to ease the gushing blood flow, as it sprayed from her neck like a burst fire hydrant. She gagged for air, unable to breath, frantically shaking and convulsing on the spot.

"Sandra!" George called out one last time, sobbing and panting on the floor. He motioned to cry again, but the energy had left his body.

"You see! You see what *fucking* happens! You stupid fuckwits!" the man roared at them in frustration, watching as George drifted into unconsciousness. "You did this to yourselves!" he continued defiantly, as he turned and ran out the front door of the house, into the street, and off into the distance.

Sandra slowly stopped convulsing and her lifeless body finally collapsed into a heap on the lino, as her throat continued to expel the rest of the blood in her body. The growing pool of blood around her rippled and bubbled in the wind, as it slowly engulfed the entire kitchen floor and started to trickle down between the gaps of the wooden slatted cellar door.

Matthew stood motionless and traumatised, his jaw frozen open and his eyes glued upon the lifeless corpse of his mother. His pyjamas were soaked through in his own urine and his feet were immersed in a growing pool of his mother's blood which flowed down the concrete steps.

Matthew was alone, with only the sounds and sensations of the blistering winds for company, tingling icily over his goose-bumped skin. The power then vanished from house, extinguishing all the lights and plummeting him deep into the unforgiving darkness.

THE DAMAGED

THE DEMONS OF TAMMY ATKINS
2012

Tammy Atkins curled up alone in her queen sized bed, praying that her nightmares would not return. Praying not to god, to whom she held no belief in, but praying to her own subconscious to allow her a little respite from the horrors.

The little red sleeping pills that the doctor had prescribed were due to kick in at any moment, as she lay naked underneath the black silk bed sheets. She stared numbly at the fresh coat of black paint on the bedroom wall, listening to the rhythmic ticking of her bedside clock. Her heavy eyelids fell and slowly she drifted away, but her prayers were not to be answered.

The nightmare started as it always did, with raindrops beating mercilessly against the windscreen of her silver Renault Clio. The blurry sight of glaring car headlights splashed past her in the road. Her visibility was no more than a mere few metres ahead, and was impaired even further by the swaying giddy blur caused by the ten vodka shots that she had downed in the bar while formulating her plan. It was a mistake for her to be in the car and she knew it, but her emotions were running high that night and her decisions were impaired. An even bigger mistake than drunk-driving in the middle of a torrential downpour was doing so with her sleeping five-year-old daughter on the back seat, having snatched her from her ex-boyfriend in the middle of the night. Keith *really* should have taken back the spare key to his mother's house.

The drone of the engine and windscreen wipers were numbing and hypnotic to her, and it wasn't long before she began to feel her eyelids beginning to drop. This had been the worst decision of her life, and she knew it, but it was too late to turn back now, too late to try and return the girl to her safe warm bed again. She forced her eyelids back open again and gave her face a vigorous rub. She reached over to let a little cool air into the car, not so much as to cause a cold draught that might wake her sleeping daughter from her slumber, but just enough so that she could feel the crisp sensation upon her face.

A road sign shortly came into sight and Tammy squinted to try and read it through the smeary windscreen. 'Crawley – 10 Miles' it read. *Nearly home, keep it together girl*, she thought to herself. She then cast her eyes up to the rear view mirror of the car to catch a glimpse of her daughter in the back, curled up asleep and wrapped tightly in her Snow White duvet. *Still asleep – this is good. Hopefully she won't wake at all and mummy can explain it all in the morning.*

Tammy's eyes returned to the road, but her attempts to try and keep them open were futile. Her dizzy head began to slump forward and rest gently upon the steering wheel of the car as if in her mind it was a soft warm pillow. The road ahead then began to gently curve off to the left, but the car did not. It gradually began to drift over the centre line, inch by inch. Inches soon turned to feet when Tammy was startled awake again by the piercing screech of the horn from an oncoming truck. Its headlights were blinding and mesmerising. The truck slammed on its brakes and began to swerve, as did Tammy in return, but it was too late. The huge truck clipped the rear of Tammy's Clio with such force that it sent the car into a spin. The Clio hurtled out of control and spun across all lanes of traffic as Tammy desperately tried to regain control of the wheel. The tyres screeched and skidded, filling the air with the smell of burning rubber and exhaust smoke. The car then came to a sudden crumpling halt as it collided head first with a tree. The bonnet of the car caved in and hugged itself tightly around the trunk of the tree; Tammy's face hurtled straight into the steering wheel with a bone breaking crack, and the windscreen exploded into a million pieces as Tammy's daughter was sent flying straight through it.

"JESSICA!" she howled hysterically, spitting a mouthful of blood and broken teeth onto the dashboard.-"NO!"

Tammy threw open the car door and stumbled drunkenly into the road as a sea of headlights and buzzing horns whizzed all around her. She dashed to the bushes and frantically began searching the grasses.

"JESSICA!" she screamed again, as blood and tears poured uncontrollably from her face.

She dropped to her knees and rummaged desperately through the wet leaves and twigs with her hands until finally brushing against the girl's body.

"My baby... MY BABY!" she cried, as she brushed away the leaves and twigs to reveal the battered and bloodied corpse of her once beautiful daughter.

THE DAMAGED

"What have I done!?" she shrilled, as her eyes passed over the huge bleeding crack in the girl's skull and crooked, broken angle of her neck.

The sound of screeching tyres and car horns began to merge with the sound of the rain to form a numbing drone which grew louder and louder in the background, becoming rhythmic and echoic like cackles of sadistic laughter that mocked and taunted Tammy as she cast her eyes to the sky and screamed.

She turned back down to her daughter and wept with sorrow, as she stretched out her trembling arm to tenderly stroke her fingers over the dead girl's cheek. Her fingers ran gently along the girl's skin when suddenly they sunk deep into the girl's flesh as if it were made of jelly, rotten and putrefying. Tammy retracted her hand in shock and disgust and inadvertently ripped the girl's lower jaw clean off with a sticky squelching sound. The gaping hole immediately erupted with ravenous maggots that wriggled down from the girl's throat and bored further into her rotting flesh with an incessant rustling sound.

Tammy sat bolt upright in bed in the midst of a full blown panic attack, dripping in pools of cold sweat and hyperventilating for air. The dream would have been distressing for anyone, but for Tammy Atkins it was worse, as she knew that it was only partial fiction. In fact, it wasn't a dream at all. It was an embellished memory from six months prior. The embellishing factor of the dream being the girl's death, when in reality she had survived the accident with barely a scratch. It seemed that reality had spared Tammy from the horrors that her own guilty conscience would not, and had continued to torment her ever since.

Tammy rocked back and forth gently in her bed, trying to calm herself down with the breathing exercises that her therapist had taught her. *Breathe in, count to five. Breathe out, count to ten*, she told herself while applying the actions. She then repeated the motion again while staring down at her bedside clock. The ten-minute dream had taken almost eight hours to dream it, and she felt more exhausted now than she had when she first went to bed. The doctor had promised her that the pills would stop the nightmares and that she would finally get a refreshing night's sleep, but he was wrong.

Her heartbeat raced away with her and her head felt like it would explode at any minute now. It was no good; the '*Breathing Crap*' wasn't working at all. She threw the silk bed sheets to the floor and dashed through to the bathroom where she ransacked the medicine cabinet for her trusted Wilkinson razorblades.

Sitting on the edge of the toilet seat with one leg resting on the edge of the bath, she reached down to caress the ensemble of scabs and scars upon her inner thigh. Finding an empty space, she positioned the razor in place and sharply perforated it through the skin. She looked down as a single droplet of blood seeped to the surface and a flooding wave of pain pulsated through her body. Immediately she started to feel relaxed again. Her tense muscles started to ease, and her heart rate began to fall. She then clenched her teeth as she dug the blade deeper into her flesh and dragged it down her thigh, carving a gouging wound that ran parallel to the others. She dropped the blade to the bathroom floor and released a long satisfying exhale.

Gently leaning back on the toilet seat, Tammy closed her eyes again, enjoying the release and tranquillity of the feeling for a few moments longer. Her ears tuned in to the dripping of the blood as it gently trickled down her bare skin and fell upon the cold tiled floor of the bathroom, and she felt at total peace, if only temporarily.

After a while the feeling started to fade away, as it always did, and the feeling of release was replaced by numbing apathy and exhaustion once again.

Opening her eyes, Tammy glanced down with a look of melancholic defeat at the pool of blood she had created. There was once a time that the sight of blood may have repulsed her, even turned her stomach maybe, but that time had long passed, and now all she saw was a sticky mess that needed to be cleaned up.

She leaned over, grabbed the bottle of green antiseptic that stood on the shelf beside her and braced herself; unscrewed the cap, and poured the fluid generously into the gaping wound, immediately sending another intense wave of pain to surge through her body. She exhaled again, enjoying the second wave of pain as she had the first, before dressing the wound in a fresh white bandage.

Wiping the tears and sediment from her eyes, Tammy gave her face a gentle rub, releasing a groan of discontent and thinking *God I could do with a drink!* She quickly shook off this feeling and banished it to the back of her mind. She then stood, and began searching the bathroom for a cloth to clean the pools of antiseptic and blood before they started to congeal.

Tammy had been dry from alcohol now since the night of the accident back in February, but not a day had passed since that she hadn't felt close to a relapse. Alcohol had become her only loyal companion over the two years prior to that and had stuck by her when everyone else had not. Her unhealthy relationship with alcohol had first started when Tammy lost her mother to cancer back in 2011, and Keith had been too emotionally retarded to comfort her. She turned to it to help numb her guilt, her pain, and her sorrow, and soon became dependent upon it. It was there again to comfort her through her

THE DAMAGED

breakup with Keith, when he left her saying; 'He could no longer cope with her drinking and her erratic behaviour any more'. When the courts awarded Keith full custody of their daughter Jessica, it was there to comfort her again, and when all of her friends had turned their backs on her, it was still there, loyal and accepting of all her faults.

Alcohol had been more loyal and dependable to her than anyone else in her life had been, but even though it had seemed like a devoted friend to her in the midst of her drunken blurs, only now was she starting to realise the truth, that it was no friend to her at all. It was a selfish friend with no regard for her well being, and with no concern for its consequences. Yet, like any disassociated friend from the past, she was still nostalgic for its companionship.

The razorblade had soon become her new best friend, and although she knew that it was nothing more than a rebound relationship, something that could never last, she still needed it, at least for now. It was her one means of release, something that she was in control of, something she could rely on again. As long as she could keep her new best friend a secret from the courts then they would think she was making progress. They would be convinced that her problems were now all behind her, and they would continue to let her see her beautiful daughter.

There were just six months left of her driving ban now, six months left of her condescending AA meetings and breathalysers, six months left of her counselling and parenting classes, then she would be done. She would be free from everyone's judgemental eyes and condemning stares once again; she would be free to fight for her daughter. Even if she could only get joint custody it would still be worth the fight, just to hug her beautiful daughter again without the presence of social workers with pens and clipboards that watched her every move. That was her plan anyway. It was something for her to aim towards, and it was the thing that kept her going. Without hope there would have just been despair, and the razorblade would cut much deeper.

Tammy's only saving grace had been the fact that she had already passed her criminal records check long before the conviction, and the care company that she worked for were unlikely to conduct another any time soon. She just hoped that nobody would turn her in, someone like Keith who would protest under the guise of morality when in reality it was mere vindictiveness that drove their motives.

Her boss had been completely unaware of her conviction or the accident so far, and that was the way that Tammy wanted to keep it. If the company were to discover that she was actually travelling to her clients by taxi and bus then that would surely mark the end of her career. Tammy had been lucky to have gotten away with it so far, and even luckier that none of her clients had ever reported her for turning up to work with the stench of alcohol on her breath, which she was sure she must have. Maybe the clients had remained quiet out of pity for her, or maybe it was because they had grown attached and didn't want to see her go. Either way, Tammy had counted her blessings gratefully.

It had become apparent to Tammy in the two years that she had worked for them that training and qualifications were almost irrelevant requirements to the company, as apart from a basic NVQ in health and social care, Tammy had none. It seemed that all that was required was a clean criminal record and a driver's licence, and Tammy now had neither.

Tammy threw the blood-stained floor cloth into the bin in the kitchen, grabbed her packet of cigarettes from the counter, and sparked one up. She took a long deep drag and released a large satisfying cloud of smoke into the air. She then returned to the bathroom again and took a long look at her naked reflection in the full-length mirror. She looked into her face and watched as the reflection stared back at her, but Tammy didn't see herself any more. It was the reflection of a stranger, a doppelganger, a body-snatching clone who to the untrained eye would have definitely passed for her, but it wasn't her. The life had somehow disappeared from behind her eyes and had left them dark and empty. The bags under her eyes were getting darker each day, the lines on her forehead were getting deeper, and her skin was becoming blotchy and tired. She looked up and down at her gaunt looking body and ran her fingers gently along the deep ridges of her ribcage. She *really* needed to start eating properly again.

It would be Tammy's twenty-fifth birthday in a few months' time, but she was convinced she looked more like forty-five, as if the stress of the past two years had taken the toll of twenty.

Tammy took another long drag from her cigarette and blew the smoke at her reflection in protest, before throwing the rest of the cigarette into the toilet and walking back to the bedroom again. She slipped on some knickers and a bra, and found some dense black tights that would hide the white bandage on her thigh. She completed her attire with a white blouse and a knee length black skirt and sat herself down in the lounge, leaving the baby-blue carer's T-shirt that she was supposed to wear hanging dustily in the cupboard.

Tammy's wardrobe comprised of many tops and skirts in a variety of different bright shades of pinks, blues and greens, but none of which felt appropriate to wear any more. The vibrant colours would imply a happy outgoing nature that simply wasn't a part of her anymore and wearing them would be nothing but a lie. She wished she could just rip them out and paint them all black, as she had done with her bedroom's walls, but a small part of her still held hope that the day would return when they felt comfortable once more. Tammy had once owned a full range of dark colourless attire back in her rebellious teen days of Goth-Rock. It was during this stage of her life that she first started to cut herself, although at the time it was nothing more than teenage attention-seeking behaviour. It wasn't until meeting Keith, and falling in love, that she finally started to snap out of it. It seemed ironic therefore, that he was now the reason that she felt a return to old ways.

Tammy took a slurp from the remnants of an old can of energy drink and flipped on the television for a look at the day's morning news. She sat back and groaned as the TV bombarded her once again with the never-ending highlights and menial interviews from the previous day's events of the 2012 Olympic Games. She immediately turned the channel, but there it was again, and again. It was as if the world had unanimously decided to put everything else on pause for the games, and she hated every minute of it. She hated the sunny bright colours, the sea of happy cheering faces in the crowds, the perky optimistic attitudes, and the general feeling that the world's darkness and horrors could be quietly swept under the carpets for a few weeks while the world bathed in the glory of its own meaningless achievements. Her hatred was also compounded by the fact that she knew Keith would be enjoying every moment of it. She quickly turned the telly off again and threw the remote onto the coffee table.

The sudden ringing of a telephone then startled Tammy. She looked around confused for a second, as the sound was not familiar to her. She continued looking around, half convinced that it must have been a neighbour's phone that was just really loud, before suddenly realising that it was the sound of her house phone. The house phone had come as part of her broadband and television package, but she never used it, and no one ever rang it either. The only two people that even had her home phone number were her boss and her mother, and unless her mother had somehow come back from the dead to call her, it only left the one option. *Why on earth would that old battle-axe be calling at this time of the day?* she asked herself, peering up at the wall clock. It then dawned on her that maybe she had found out about her conviction from the police, or maybe someone had turned her in. *But who could have told her? – Keith? It must have been Keith! That son of a bitch!* she told herself as paranoia began to set in.

Tammy leant forward and began rummaging through the piles of empty cigarette packets and drinks cans that lay spread upon the coffee table until finally finding the cordless phone at the bottom of the heap. She picked it up, composed herself, and pressed the answer key.

"Hello?" she answered with trepidation.

"Hi, Tammy? It's Maureen," the voice replied sharply.

"Hi Maureen, how are you?"

"Yeah, I'm fine; I'm just calling about Mrs Langley, your nine-o'clock?"

"Oh, is she okay?" Tammy asked, finally releasing the breath she had been nervously holding.

"I'm afraid not. An ambulance was called during the night and, well, she didn't make it." Maureen told her in an emotionless sterile tone.

"Oh, I see. What happened to her?"

"I don't know, her heart went or something... You know how it is with these old folk. I'm just letting you know so that you don't attend this morning."

Tammy paused for a second to take it all in. She was relieved that the call had not fulfilled her prediction, but the death of Mrs Langley was still sad news. Mrs Langley was a sweet old lady who lived alone in a warden-patrolled flat a few miles away. She was always thrilled to see Tammy and greeted her every day with a cup of hot chamomile tea. She had been alone since her husband died of emphysema and didn't have much left in the way of family, none that bothered to visit her anyway. She had spent her retirement collecting miniature porcelain dogs that she kept on display in an old glass cabinet in the lounge. She had been her fourth client to die now in the time that Tammy had worked for the company, and she had begun to get used to the idea of them dying, but it was still upsetting. Mrs Langley certainly deserved a little more emotion than Maureen's bland clinical delivery.

"No, okay. I understand," Tammy finally replied.

"Yeah, so that'll be why your pay's a little shorter this month, so don't be calling me up to query it," Maureen continued.

"Yeah... Fine."

"I might have something to replace the slot though if you're interested?"

"Yeah, okay."

"I won't know for sure until later though. I'll give you a call tonight and let you know, alright?"

"Yeah. That'll be fine, thank you."

"Okay, bye."

Maureen then hung up the receiver before Tammy could respond, leaving a dead tone buzzing in her ear. Tammy looked down at the phone and shook her head in disbelief. "Heartless-fucking-bitch!" she muttered to herself, and threw the phone back into the mess on the

THE DAMAGED

coffee table. Mrs Langley may not have meant anything to her, but she sure meant something to someone. Tammy then started to think about her own mother again, and how frail and withered she had looked towards the end. She started to wonder if the nurses and carers that had looked after *her* had been so blasé and heartless about her death too. The thought quickly started to make her feel angry and bitter about the situation and so she immediately shook it off.

She leant back and peered back up at the wall clock again, 'Ten to Eight' it read. It then dawned on her that she now had nowhere to be until midday. The routine of her days had become a good distraction from her problems and helped to pass the time, but now she found herself at a loss. She then started to debate calling Jessica before Keith took her to school. Technically she was not allowed, and she definitely didn't want to do anything to damage her chances of getting her back, but the sound of her sweet voice would have been comforting. Maybe it was the dream or the death of Mrs Langley, but she just needed a reminder of what she was fighting for again.

Tammy grabbed her iPhone from her handbag and scrolled down to Keith's mobile number. Keith's picture popped onto the screen and she gazed upon it with mixed emotions of nostalgia and hatred. Keith had been a good boyfriend to her at the start of the relationship and she couldn't have faulted him at all. He was caring, attentive and generous. He used to take her out to expensive restaurants and spoil her rotten with presents and flowers whenever he could. Life was perfect, but now she hated him, she hated him with every inch of her being. Tammy found it hard to understand how someone could become so emotionally numb and distant in just a few years, and how they could turn their back on you when you needed them the most. Bitter thoughts began to ruminate in her head until they started to make her feel dizzy and anxious and she could feel another panic attack starting to brew, as it often did when her thoughts turned to Keith.

The mere sight of his face on her phone made her flustered and angry to the point that her pale cheeks began to burn red with rage. She closed her eyes and began to recite her breathing techniques again, remembering the importance of being calm and courteous to Keith, if only for the sake of their daughter.

She pressed the green call button and placed the phone to her ear. It rang, and rang, but no one answered.

"God damn it Keith, answer the phone!" she grumbled into the handset.

It continued to ring.

She started to feel the uncontrollable urge to yell something obscene at him that she would later regret, and so decided to hang up quickly before he answered. She threw the phone back into her handbag and sparked up another cigarette, slumping back into the sofa with her feet upon the coffee table and her eyes reverting back to the ticking clock once again.

Tammy stubbed out the cigarette a few moments later and walked to Jessica's bedroom door, smiling sadly as she ran her fingers gently down the wood, before reaching for the handle. She was immediately bombarded with the sight of bright pink walls and happy soft toys which stared up at her, forcing a bitter-sweet tear to roll down her face. Jessica's bedroom was the only room in the house to have remained clean and tidy since her daughter had been taken away, and Tammy took great care to keep it that way. She wanted it nice and welcoming for Jessica, ready for the day she would come home to her again. She stepped inside and quickly closed the door again, as if the mess from the rest of the house might somehow contaminate the room if she left the door open for too long. She turned on the light and perched down on the end of Jessica's bed, gently breathing in the air and wiping away the tears from her face. Turning to the bedside cabinet, she stared deep into a framed photograph that sat upon it. She reached over and picked it up, gently caressing the frame. The photograph had been taken when Jessica was just two years old and depicted the girl along with Tammy and her mother before she became ill. It was Tammy's favourite photograph, and reminded her of a time when all was good in her world. She kissed two fingers and placed them tenderly onto the photographic cheeks of her mother and daughter, before slowly placing the photograph back down again and picking up Jessica's favourite stuffed toy – a giraffe that Tammy had bought for her from the London Zoo's gift shop. She hugged the toy tightly and lay down with it on Jessica's bed, snuggling up into her pillows and trying to smell for any remnants of Jessica left behind.

Despite her hatred of him, she knew that Keith was a good father and that he would be taking good care of her precious little girl. Keith's mother would be spoiling her too, with new toys and sweets and cuddles. She knew Jessica was safe, maybe even safer than she was with *her* during her drunken peak (if Tammy was being honest with herself), but visitation days seemed so far apart, and Tammy feared that Jessica would forget about her. She feared that Keith and his mother would be filling her head with hateful thoughts about her, and would remind her what a bad mother she had been to her. Tammy knew that she had failed her daughter, but just longed for the chance to make it up to her again, and show her how much she really loved her.

THE DAMAGED

Tammy soon fell asleep again upon Jessica's bed and to her relief her dreams were uneventful. She woke up again just after eleven o'clock and scrambled to the bus stop to catch the number five to visit her first client. She sat herself at the back of the bus where she felt safe that people wouldn't see her, or judge her, and placed her iPod headphones into her ears to the numbing sound of loud heavy metal.

Tammy arrived at Mr Carlson's house just before twelve, where she teamed up with her Polish colleague Agnieszka and assisted in giving Mr Carlson a sponge bath, all the while trying to ignore his belligerent comments and repugnant attempts to fondle her behind.

Returning to the bus, Tammy then travelled to her next clients. She had spent the last six months studying the bus times intently, and now knew them all off by heart. She was now able to time her journeys each day as to arrive on time to the majority of her clients, fully aware that a late arrival would more than likely result in the clients calling the company.

After Mr Carlson, Tammy tended to three old ladies in a purpose-built block of retirement flats, where her senses were filled with the scent of old lavender and the sound of Vera Lynn on seemingly infinite repeat. She changed colostomy bags and adult nappies, and dished out various different pills and potions. She then visited an elderly couple with dementia who lived together in a quaint little bungalow on the outskirts of the town, before finally returning to Mr Carlson's house to prepare his dinner. By this time it was just coming up to five o'clock and it was time to return to her empty flat once more.

It was often a long and tiring day for Tammy, but an empty day would have been worse as it would give her too much time to think. The fact that maybe she had made a difference, no matter how small made her feel somewhat redeemed for the less amiable things that she had done. Most of the people that she visited each day had very little family that visited and their poor health meant that it was hard for them to get out and about. So, for many of them, Tammy was the only person that they saw on a regular basis, and she could tell by their smiles at her arrival how much it meant to them; all but Mr Carlson that was.

She dismounted the bus at her home and was greeted by the friendly face of a homeless man whom she had befriended. The man sat at the bus stop with a happy contented smile on his face, stroking the head of his scraggy-looking dog. He'd named him 'Bronco' after the American football team. The man was old and tatty and sported a long dirty beard, but had somehow retained a look of dignity and pride. He reminded Tammy of a jolly old granddad who now spent his retirement playing Santa Claus at the local shopping mall once a year.

SIMON LAW

"Hi James, you had a nice day today?" she asked with a welcoming smile.

"I mustn't grumble, thank you Tammy. How are you?" he replied in a deep American twang.

"Same ol' same ol'... At least the weather's quite nice at the moment."

"Oh yes, it's been lovely today. You can't take this good old British weather for granted ya know!"

"You're not wrong there! We wouldn't want it to rain down on our Olympians, would we?" she replied, keeping her intended sarcasm carefully masked. "And how's Bronco doing?" she continued, bending down to scratch the dog behind the ear.

"He's fine, ain't ya boy?" James replied, patting the dog affectionately on the head. The dog looked up at him in return and barked as if he understood.

"Have you eaten today, James?"

"Yeah, I had a lovely cup of soup down at the shelter earlier. Tomato, my favourite!"

"Well that's good then," she replied with a nod, reaching into her purse for some change. "Well take this anyway, and make sure ol' Bronco gets something too yeah?" she told him as she placed the loose coins into his tatty glove.

"Bless you my dear. Bronco says thank you too."

"You're welcome. See you tomorrow?"

"Sure will."

Tammy gave James a smile and turned away in the direction of her flat. She had greeted him every day now for the past six months and had gradually learnt the story of his descent from grace. James was an American citizen who first flew over the pond back in the early nineties. After his wife left him for another man he decided to get away and make a fresh start somewhere new and exciting, choosing the United Kingdom as his destination. James lived off of his life savings for a while but they ran out quicker than he had expected, and without a steady income he quickly found himself homeless and begging for money to survive. It was at this point that a stray dog began to follow him around, begging for food the same as him. James spent much time trying to give the smelly old dog the slip, but still he kept on coming back. He eventually gave in and accepted his new companion, naming him 'Bronco" as a reminder of home. James knew that the American embassy could repatriate him at any point, but there was nothing left for him back home any more, and his pride and dignity prevented him from admitting defeat.

THE DAMAGED

Tammy wondered to herself how a man who clearly had nothing, who had been forgotten by all his friends and family, could possibly display such a genuine smile. She knew the smile was genuine too, as it displayed all the traits that her own smile did not, despite the many hours trying to perfect the forgery in the mirror. There was once a time that Tammy wouldn't have even acknowledged James; she would have turned her back in disgust and hurried back to the flat in fear that his rancid presence might somehow infect her with something, but not now. Maybe it was just her loneliness or her newfound craving for human interaction, but her revulsion had long since disappeared.

Opening the front door and picking up the pile of mail that had accumulated in her absence, Tammy was greeted by the cold sterile glare of emptiness once more, a feeling that hit her like an icy brick wall. She sighed and headed to the kitchen, peering into the fridge for inspiration. Her stomach had been making the most horrid rumbling sounds all day long, but while the fridge was full of food, there was just nothing she wanted to eat. She rummaged around regardless, hoping to find something that may tempt her, but nothing did. After a while of futile searching, her eyes settled upon a fruit yoghurt, deciding that it was probably the most inoffensive item. She resigned to the sofa with her yoghurt in hand and fingered through the pile of crumpled white and brown envelopes, undeluded that they would be anything but bills and spam.

Returning her attention back to the yoghurt again, she ripped off the lid with apathy and scooped her index finger into the pink viscous gloop, before staring at it a while in contemplation. Finally releasing a sigh of surrender, she sucked the gloop from her finger and forced herself to swallow it. The sensation felt odd and out of place, as she felt the cold gooey substance travelling down her oesophagus and into her stomach. It had been days now since she had consumed anything even semi-solid. She brought the tub to her lips and quickly poured half of its contents into her mouth, swallowed, and placed the tub back down again. She then immediately lit a cigarette in an attempt to make her body forget about the odd sensation, and proceeded to use the half-empty yoghurt tub as an ashtray. It was at this point that her home phone rang for the second time that day, but unlike the first she recognised the sound immediately. She reached forward to where it lay upon the table and answered it.

"Hi Maureen," she said.

"Hi... Tammy, how did you know it was me?" Maureen replied, sounding mildly perplexed.

"Either I'm psychic, or you're the only one that calls me!" Tammy told her, sounding unintentionally facetious.

"Oh, I see," Maureen replied, clearly irked with Tammy's attitude. "Everything alright?"

"Fine, just calling about the new client I mentioned earlier. If you're still interested that is?"

"Yeah, definitely."

"Okay, well it's just a meds round, twice a day, nine and five, fifteen minutes. I'm sure you can handle that, right?"

"Yeah, sounds simple. You got their details?"

"Yep, just gonna email them over to you now. Let me know if you have any issues with it, it's not exactly your normal type of client."

"Oh, what do you mean?"

"It's an ex-psych patient on release, but you're just doing the meds so I can't foresee a problem."

"A psych patient?"

"Yes, is that a problem?

"Well no, but I...I haven't really been trained on mental illness..."

"No, I'm aware of that Tammy, but this will give you some experience, won't it?"

"Yeah I guess so, I'm sure it'll be fine. They're not...dangerous or anything?"

"No, of course he's not! They wouldn't have released him otherwise, would they?" Maureen told her sharply.

"No, I guess not."

"Besides, I already met with him today and he seems harmless."

"Oh, okay then."

"You don't sound convinced Tammy. I can always give it to Aggy if you don't think you can manage it, it's not a problem for me."

"No, it'll be fine, I'm sure.

"Okay. Well I've just sent you over his release notes and medical history, so have a good look through. Okay?"

"Okay."

"He already has a supply of his daily meds at his home, but you'll also need to pick up some extras from the chemist, he has a prescription at his home. His anti-psychotics are to be taken twice daily, nine and five. These are the ones that he has at his home. Now, the doctors have said that you need to watch him take them because apparently he can be averse to taking them. If at any point he refuses and you can't get him to take them you need to call either me or the hospital immediately, okay?"

"Right..."

"...The prescription he has is for Diazepam – which he is only to take when he needs it, and he's only allowed a maximum of two per day. These are to be kept with you at all times. Okay?"

THE DAMAGED

"Okay."

"Are you going to remember all that, Tammy?"

"Yeah, I think so. Can I ask a question?"

"Yes?"

"What exactly happens if he doesn't take his anti-psychotics?"

"Well I imagine he goes a little psychotic! The clue's in the name really, isn't it?"

"I thought you said he wasn't dangerous?"

"He's not so long as he takes his meds, and if he doesn't you're to call me!" Maureen snapped abruptly. –"Besides, the drugs have an accumulation affect and he would need to be off them for at least a week for it to make a difference."

"Okay then. Nothing else? No personal needs?"

"No, Just the meds. Physically he's in good shape so he should be able to take care of other things himself, but if you think he needs anything else you can let me know and we'll assess it."

"Okay. When do I start?"

"Well social services have been over there with the doctors tonight, so you'll be needed from tomorrow morning."

"Okay and what's his name?"

"Err... It's Matthew. Matthew Mason."

THE HOUSE ON OAK STREET

Tammy spent most of the evening reviewing the notes of her new client who now seemed so daunting to her. She knew what to expect from the elderly, their needs were all much of a muchness, but a 'psych' patient was a brand new kettle of fish to her.

It seemed to Tammy that if Maureen actually cared for the welfare of her staff, or clients, then surely she would have ensured that appropriate training was supplied. Tammy hadn't even cared for someone with learning difficulties, let alone someone who was fresh out of the loony bin. It was therefore clear that Maureen *didn't* care for either of them, but this revelation came as no surprise to Tammy.

Many of the words in the single-page document didn't even make sense to her, and she spent much time 'Googling' their meanings on her laptop; obscure words like 'anemophobia', which she presumed was some type of phobia, but later learnt was the abnormal fear of wind. She wondered to herself how anyone could develop 'an abnormal fear of wind', then she also remembered the words 'post-traumatic stress', 'delusions' and 'violent tendencies' from the document too, which made her anxieties over the situation even worse. She really should have just told Maureen that she wasn't comfortable with the situation, but she hadn't, and now it was too late.

Tammy slowly accepted her fate with some trepidation, knowing that she had very few alternatives. Despite her uncertainties about the new client, she knew that it could only be a good thing to have one of her morning slots refilled. Without it, she would have the entire morning to herself each day, and far too much time alone to think. The client would give her motivation and a reason to get up, and would also increase her experience for any future clients of that *type*.

Tammy released a long yawn, before looking up Matthew's address on Google maps and planning the best bus route to his house for the following morning. Before she knew it, the clock had struck midnight and so she hurried herself to bed, took her sleeping pill, and returned her gaze back to the black painted walls of her bedroom.

She woke from her slumber eight hours later, dream-free and refreshed for the first time in months, as if the anxiety of her new client had somehow distracted her mind from its usual recurring guilt. She washed and dressed herself before swallowing two vitamin tablets with a can of energy drink and leaving the house.

The bus arrived at the top of Oak Street at a quarter to nine that morning as she stepped off into the bright warm sunshine that surrounded her. She slowly walked down the long street, keeping her eyes peeled for number eight, and looking with awe at all the expensive houses that surrounded her on either side of the road.

A house then came into sight in the distance that took her by surprise, and her steps quickly came to a halt. The house looked old and decrepit and completely out of place in the expensive and pristine looking street, like a tramp slopping back caviar at a black-tie dinner. The grass in the front garden was a good two-foot tall and infested with dandelions and stinging nettles. The windows were all boarded up with thick hardwood which had been spray-painted with the tags of youths and vandals, along with various profanities and lewd suggestions. She grimaced at the sight and continued walking down the street, counting down the numbers on the houses and hoping that this was not the house she was heading for. She got closer and closer until the number eight hanging loosely from the wooden door was undeniable.

She stopped in her tracks at the foot of the pathway and double checked her documents once more, just to check it wasn't number eighteen, or twenty-eight that she was really looking for, but it wasn't. She then became aware of the eyes that were burning a hole in her, not from number eight, but from the neighbours, including an older, and now greying Edgar Brown, all of whom had seemed to stop what they were doing to have a good look. She turned to them to smile, but the smile was not returned. Instead, looks of confusion and disapproval were all that she received, as if being there had been forbidden. She immediately started to feel uncomfortable and her original anxieties all returned in full force. She turned her back on the crowd and gingerly began to edge towards the door, fully aware that the stares behind her were increasing by the minute as the neighbours all whispered to each other "Hey! Look over there!"

Reaching out her trembling arm, Tammy knocked on the door three times. Stale dust immediately showered over her from the porch roof above, causing her to sneeze and itch as it settled down upon her skin. The sound of the knock echoed eerily through the house, but there was no reply. She waited a few seconds longer before then reaching up to wipe away some of the dust from the frosted glass of the door, leaning forward and trying to peer in. As she squinted to see through the glass, she suddenly felt something crawling up her leg, as if something had leaped at her from the long grasses of the lawn. She immediately flinched and shuddered from the sensation, as images from her dream of wriggling burrowing maggots shot back into her anxious mind again. Frantically she patted herself down, and it was at this point that the front door finally creaked opened, but Tammy was too distracted to notice. A figure then appeared in the shadow of the doorway, watching her as she span around patting herself.

"You alright there?" the figure asked in a pleasant and friendly tone.

"Oh God, I'm sorry, I..." she started to blubber with a look of embarrassment upon her blushing face.

It was then that she finally stopped itching herself and looked up at the man. She had expected to see someone old and decrepit to match the state of the house, someone dishevelled and smelly and possibly a little odd-looking. What she actually saw came as a pleasant surprise. The man was tall and well-built, with a smooth clean-shaven face and well groomed blond hair. His smile was welcoming and friendly and his eyes were the deepest shade of blue that she had ever seen. He was dressed in sharp pinstriped suit trousers with a perfectly creaseless shirt and a smart black jumper to finish it.

"Hi... I'm Tammy, *The Carer,*" she finally told him, realising that she had probably been staring at him for an unnatural length of time.

"Hi Tammy, I'm Matthew. I've been expecting you."

"Nice to meet you Matthew," she replied, offering out her hand to him. He reached out in return and shook it gently. His hand felt surprisingly soft and smooth to Tammy, like a man who had never used a tool or worked outside a day in his life, but strong and firm at the same time.

"You're much younger than I was expecting," he told her.

"Oh?"

"Yeah, I'm not sure what I was expecting really. Most of the nurses at the hospital are a lot older."

"Oh, I see. You're not what I was expecting either to be honest," she replied. 'Much more attractive' was what she really meant, but she kept that to herself.

"You coming in then?" he asked, stepping aside.

"Yes please," she replied, stepping inside the house and shutting the door behind her.

THE DAMAGED

"I think they said a handy man would be out in a few days to help take down the boards and stuff." Matthew told her, as he gestured for her to sit upon the sofa.

"Well that's good then."

Tammy sat herself down upon the two-seater sofa in front of her, and as she cast her eyes around the room she immediately felt unnerved once again. Every window on the lower floor of the house was boarded shut and it felt like she was sitting inside an enclosed wooded box, and it was slowly closing in on her. All natural light had been completely banished from the room, except for the single ray of sunlight which pierced through the glass of the front door, cutting through the room like a laser beam and illuminating the flickers of dust that gently floated through the stale musty air that surrounded her.

Tammy started to notice all the dated eighties furniture and ornaments around her. Her eyes passed over the old fashioned television set that sat in one corner of the room, then to the wallpaper that curled and flaked from the corners of the cobweb-filled walls. Her eyes finally settled upon the old grandfather clock that sat in the other corner of the room, its dusty pendulums silent, and grounded. Tammy's skin quickly started to crawl again, as if she were covered in thousands of tiny creeping insects that tickled and itched her all over. She felt her toes starting to curl as she began nervously fidgeting side to side on the sofa.

"I do apologise for the state of the place. I did start vacuuming last night, but I guess I still have some way to go!" Matthew explained, finally interrupting the eerie silence.

"It's not a problem, Matthew," she assured him, trying to subdue the look of growing fear from appearing on her face. "Do you need someone to help you with the housework?"

"No, I can manage it, thank you. I'm not sure how long the old vacuum is gonna hold out though!" he told her with a smile. "I can make you a cup of tea if you like? The social worker did do a little shopping for me."

"No, I'm fine thank you. Actually, could I please use your toilet before we get started?" she asked, feeling the pressure in her nervous bladder starting to build up.

"Yeah, of course you can. It's up the stairs, second door on the left."

Tammy nodded and immediately stood from the sofa, scurried past him, and ascended the stairs. She reached the top, counted the doors, and dashed into the bathroom to relieve herself.

The upstairs of the house was in a similar state to the rest, with all the windows boarded shut and wallpaper peeling from the corners, but Tammy had been too focused on her bladder to even notice. She placed her head in her hands and felt her heart beating away in her chest like she had just run a marathon. *Just be professional, everything's fine*, she thought to herself. She took a few long deep breaths, stood, and flushed the toilet.

Tammy's attention turned to the putrid pea-green ceramic bath and sink, wondering to herself – *how could anything so vile have ever been in fashion?* Her eyes then cast over the black mould that grew from between the off-white tiles that covered the bathroom walls, and then to the plastic toothbrush holder that housed three old tatty toothbrushes, all different colours. She turned on the tap and splashed a little cold water in her face, straightened herself up and practised a smile in the mirror before composing herself and returning to the lounge.

"It feels strange to be back here after all this time," Matthew told her as he stood patiently awaiting her return.

"Yeah, I can imagine," she replied with a nervous smile.

"I remember it being a lot bigger to be honest," he continued, as he looked around nostalgically. "But I guess everything looks bigger through the eyes of a child."

"It's a lot bigger than my little place though. Do you own it?" she asked him, trying to engage in light conversation.

"It was my parents'. No one else wanted to buy it, so I guess it's mine now."

"Oh I see ...and where are your parents now?" she asked as she sat back down again. Suddenly she knew that she had made a mistake.

Anyone with half an inkling would have known the answer to that question would not be a happy one, but Tammy was still too unnerved to think straight. She had been telling herself all morning to try and avoid any awkward questions but had failed almost immediately.

The room quickly became silence and a sad look started to diffuse across Matthew's face. She offered an apologetic smile and turned her eyes away in an attempt to atone for her loose tongue, but it was too late to now un-pose the question or to stop the memories from circling Matthew's head.

"They...They died," he told her with a look of remorse as he gently sat down upon his father's Chesterfield armchair.

"I'm sorry Matthew, I shouldn't have pried," she blurted abruptly, desperately wishing that she could take it back.

"No, it's okay, Tammy. I assumed that the hospital would have filled you in on everything."

"I wasn't told anything about you really, confidentiality I guess."

"Confidentiality or not, it seems quite pertinent to my situation! They... They were both murdered when I was a kid, so it's just me now."

THE DAMAGED

"Murdered? Oh god, that's awful. What happened?" she asked, quickly wishing again that she had more control over her tongue.

"They..."

"...I'm sorry; it's none of my business Matthew. We don't have to talk about this," Tammy interrupted again, worried now that the conversation would trigger something off – an 'incident' perhaps.

"I don't mind talking about it, Tammy. I mean, it's still painful of course, I guess it always will be."

"Yeah, I bet..."

"It happened during 'The Great Storm'... "

"...The storm of eighty-seven?" she interrupted again.

"Yeah that's right, do you remember it?"

"Not exactly, no." she replied ambiguously, before quickly explaining. –"It was the day I was born."

"Oh, really?"

"October sixteenth, nineteen eighty-seven."

"Yeah, that's right," he replied with a nod. "What a strange coincidence," he continued with a look of contemplation.

"I wasn't actually due until closer to Halloween, but I think the storm triggered it off. You know... with the stress and stuff. I was born at home in the end 'cos all the roads were blocked and the ambulances couldn't get through," she rambled, her voice still shaky and uncertain.

"I see. I bet your mum sure remembers the storm then."

"Yeah of course, she spoke about it all the time."

"*Spoke*?" he asked, noticing the past tense.

"Yeah. I... I lost her recently."

"I'm sorry to hear that," he told her, but his voice lacked the sincerity of his words.

"Me too."

"How did she go?" he asked without hesitation.

"It was the big 'C'."

"Cancer?"

"Yeah."

Matthew nodded solemnly, wondering to himself why people affected always referred to it as 'the big 'C'', as if saying the name in full might bring a curse upon them or something.

"Did she suffer for long?" he then asked, seemingly enthralled by the conversation.

"It was about a year or so from diagnosis," she answered uncomfortably.

"I'm not sure which is worst really."

"...Between what?" she asked sheepishly.

"Cancer and murder. I mean, they both have their merits and disadvantages."

"Excuse me?" Tammy protested.

"Well, cancer is drawn out and demoralising, yes, but at least you have time to say your goodbyes. Murder is so quick that you barely realise what's going on."

"I don't know. It's not much of a choice," she replied with clear discontent in her tone.

"No, I guess not," he replied dismissively.

"I don't like to think about death."

"No, well most people don't, but sometimes you can't help the things that you think about, can you?"

"No....I..."

Tammy quickly became too creeped out by the conversation to continue. An uncomfortable shudder passed through her. Aside from Matthew's initial reaction to the mention of his deceased parents, his thoughts around death seemed completely unemotional and strangely detached.

Tammy looked away and took a breath, as she felt her heart begin to race again, but as she looked back she found herself lost in the deep blue oceans of Matthew's eyes again and any fear or trepidation quickly dissipated, at least for the moment.

"Do I make you nervous, Tammy?"

"No, of course not," she told him, but it was clearly a lie.

"I didn't kill them, if that's what you're thinking?"

"No, I...I didn't think you had. I just..."

"Shall we talk about this another time?" he asked with a sympathetic smile.

"Yes please," she replied with a mild grimace and a nod. –"So, I understand you met with my colleague Maureen yesterday?" she continued, quickly changing the subject.

"I did indeed, a delightful woman," Matthew responded with the mildest hint of insincerity in his voice, a hint that would have probably gone undetected had Tammy not known what she was *really* like.

She looked at him and smiled to acknowledge the unspoken allusion, and he smiled in return.

"Did she leave you a care plan?"

"She did," he told her, and nodded to the kitchen.

Tammy stood from the sofa and slowly made her way through to the kitchen, where she found the familiar-looking clear plastic folder upon the worktop. Her eyes were then drawn to the wooden knife block on the counter, housing five blades of varying length and shape, with the sixth slot empty. The mere sight of the blades made Tammy start to

THE DAMAGED

worry again, as she pondered whether it was safe for someone like him to have access to them. Her eyes settled upon the empty slot, and the thought briefly crossed her mind that Matthew had it stashed, ready to stab her in the back the moment that she wasn't looking. She quickly labelled her thoughts as ridiculous and shook them off, unaware that the missing blade itself was the very one used to murder his parents, and was most likely still smothered in their blood and locked away in an evidence bag at the back of the police archives.

Tammy's attention returned to the folder and to the refillable plastic pill box that sat next to it, pre-filled with a week's supply of pills. She opened the folder and took out the prescription, which she slipped into her handbag, before flicking through a few of the notes in the pack before returning her eyes to the medication again. She read through the contents on the sleeve of the pack, and proceeded to empty the pills from the 'Morning' compartment of the current day into her hand. Company rules stated that pills should never be handled, but directly tipped into a serving tub; but this, along with her uniform and various other things, was merely another rule that she casually flouted. She returned the plastic pack to the kitchen side again and looked down at the assortment of pills in her palm – two small blue capsules (the anti-psychotics), and a slightly bigger yellow tablet (a vitamin D supplement). She reached for a glass, rinsed it out and filled it half way with water, and then returned to the lounge again.

"Right, so we have three pills now and another two this evening," she told him as she placed them down with the water upon the little side table next to him.

"Yeah, that's right," he told her with a sombre nod and a look of disappointment.

She sat down again and looked across at him expectantly.

"I'll take them when you're gone Tammy, don't worry," he told her begrudgingly, fully aware that his response was unlikely to be accepted.

"I'm sorry Matthew; I'm on strict instructions to watch you take them."

"Oh, is that right?"

"Yep."

"The doctors told you I didn't like them, didn't they?"

"Kind of, yeah. It was pretty much the only thing I *was* told."

"Did they tell you *why* I didn't like them?"

"No, they didn't."

"Do you care why?"

"I care, sure, but you still have to take them."

"Have to? I thought I was a free man now?"

SIMON LAW

"You are. I mean, I can't force you to take them, it's up to you. But if you don't then I have to report that back to the doctors."

"I see. That probably wouldn't be good for me, would it?"

"I don't think it would, no."

"They couldn't re-commit me now? Surely?" he asked in disbelief.

"I don't know Matthew, but it was my understanding that you were out on a trial basis, so it probably wouldn't be good to give them any ammunition."

"No, you're probably right."

"Besides, you wouldn't wanna get *me* in trouble, would you?" Tammy asked light-heartedly.

"I'll take the vitamin, how about that?" he asked with a cheeky child-like grin.

Tammy shook her head with a smile.

Matthew nodded in surrender and the grin quickly sunk from his face. He turned his eyes down to the little blue pills and looked at them with contempt. He picked them up, threw them into his mouth, and quickly washed them down with the water.

"Better?" he asked dejectedly.

"Yes, thank you."

"Are you off to your next patient now then?"

"No, I don't have another *client* now until midday, so I'm gonna pop into town for a few bits and to pick up your prescription. Do you need me to get anything else for you?"

"No, I don't think so, thank you," he told her, his words starting to slur a little.

"No? Nothing at all?" she asked again, as she noticed a glazed blank expression starting to appear on Matthew's face.

"I...."

Matthew tried his best to keep focused on the conversation at hand but soon enough Tammy's words became nothing more than muffled pockets of sound that floated through the air in vague murky bubbles. He quickly felt his articulate brain engorged with a thick dense fog that turned all of his thoughts to mush. Love and hate and every emotion in-between all merged together into meaningless zombified numbness and nothing remained important.

He slumped gently into his father's Chesterfield armchair and his vision slowly focused in on a spindly black spider as it scurried out from underneath the cobweb-filled recess of the TV stand, stopped to look around, and slowly crept towards him across the lounge floor.

It immediately became obvious to Tammy, who had watched the metamorphosis take place, as to why Matthew was so resentful of the

THE DAMAGED

pills. But whilst she regretted the need to subject him to such a state, she knew she had to. The doctors surely knew best anyway.

"I'll see you at five then Matthew?" she called as she made for the door, but there was no reply.

Tammy left the house and the sunlight embraced her like a warm shower of liquid light. The dark gloom of the house had made her forget what a bright and vibrant day awaited her outside, and the light stung her unprepared eyes. When her vision finally returned she was greeted by the sight of prying neighbours once again, all staring at her intently like news reporters at a press conference. She decided that another smile or a wave would achieve nothing and so just ignored them all instead, turning away and making her way back up the road again to the bus stop.

Tammy was glad to be leaving the house, as the awkward first meeting was now over and done with. It was undeniable that Matthew's references to death on their first meeting were deeply unsettling to her, but it was also undeniable that her own misconceptions and ignorance were vastly to blame for her nerves and for her anxieties. In reality, despite the awkward conversation, Matthew seemed like a perfectly pleasant man; he was friendly, soft-spoken, handsome, and not at all like her idea of a 'psycho', although she was well aware that her skewed perception was based solely upon figures from the movies. In fact, he seemed to have a very innocent and endearing nature which she felt quite drawn in by, maybe even attracted to. It was possible that the house itself had made the situation worse too. It had an eerie malevolence about it, a funny smell in the air, and a lingering resonance of something seriously wrong. Maybe she would feel better after the handyman had taken down all the boards that blocked the windows. Maybe the sunlight and fresh air would banish the eerie feelings and bring the house back to life again. Either way, she could hardly tell Maureen that she had now changed her mind about the client based solely upon the unsettling nuances of the house, not if she expected to be taken seriously anyway.

Tammy had tripped over her words in the house too many times already, and although she desperately wanted to avoid any further awkward conversations with him, part of her was deeply curious to hear the rest of his story. *Had Matthew been locked away since the storm of eighty-seven?* she pondered. *That was nearly twenty-five years ago! And if so...why? Had the incident with his parents messed him up that bad?* Tammy had many unanswered questions, but none of which were easy conversation starters. *Maybe I would be better off just not knowing,* she contemplated. *What if he was lying about not killing them? – that would explain why he had been away for so long, or maybe he*

had a split personality and couldn't actually remember killing them? –
That would make even more sense. She quickly confirmed in her head
that in fact she did not want to know the answers. If the doctors had
established that he was not a danger any more, then she would just
have to trust them on that.

The stress and anxiety that Tammy had needlessly put herself through
had completely devoured the little energy that she had, and five
minutes later she found herself fast asleep on the back on the bus. Her
head pressed firmly against the glass of the window and dribble slowly
emerged from the corners of her open mouth. She remained asleep for
the duration of the journey, until the bus was boarded by a gang of
obnoxious teenagers dressed in back hooded jumpers. They
immediately made their way to the back of the bus.

"Wahey! Well what do we have here then eh?" one of them jeered as
they all sat down around her.

"Wakey-Wakey sleeping beauty, your prince charming has arrived!"
called another one, as he lapped his tongue at her.

Tammy awoke to the sight of spotty faces, greasy hair, and to the
overpowering stench of sweat and cannabis that emanated from every
fibre of their clothing. She jumped from the seat, clutching tightly at
her handbag and began scurrying away.

"Oh, where ya going? I got something for ya' here!" one of them
called, as he grabbed his crotch and gestured at her.

The teens all laughed and whistled at her as she turned and dashed
for the exit, reaching the door just before the driver started to pull away.
She stood at the bus stop and felt her heart starting to race away as
adrenaline pumped through her body. The bus pulled away, and as it
passed she could see the youths staring at her from the back seat
window, pointing and laughing. She scowled back at them and raised
her middle finger, as she watched them disappear into the distance.

Tammy's heart continued to race and she felt her head beginning to
spin with anxiety. She took a breath, closed her eyes and pinched her
fingernails fiercely into the flesh of her hip. The pain she could inflict
with her nails alone was a far cry from the comfort and satisfaction of
her trusted razorblade, but it would just have to do.

Tammy spent a few moments longer trying to calm herself down, and
thinking about the reason she had come to town. Aside from collecting
the prescription, Tammy omitted to tell Matthew the real reason that
she was heading into town that morning. It was Monday, and that
meant she was due to attend the 10 o'clock Alcoholics Anonymous
meeting at the town hall with the other dregs of society.

THE DAMAGED

Tammy released her nails from where they embedded her skin, checked the time on her phone, and sparked up a cigarette. She took a long deep drag and orientated herself resentfully in the direction of the town hall.

Arriving with a brief few minutes to spare, she sat herself down upon one of the plastic school-like chairs, and she watched as the other 'alcoholics' all started to arrive. The plastic chairs were all aligned in concentric semi-circles that faced a tatty-looking wooden podium at the front of the hall, along with a long laminated list of the clichéd twelve sacred steps to sobriety. The list, which apparently had no direct correlation to God or to religion, mentioned 'God' in almost every step. Tammy had arrived at the conclusion very early on in her meetings with the group, that she didn't need the list; she didn't need the twelve steps, she didn't need the group, and she certainly didn't need 'God'. The accident itself had been more than enough to make Tammy realise the error of her ways, and her daughter was more than enough encouragement to get her life back on track again.

She looked around at the sea of faces around her, wondering how many others were there by court order too, and how many would actually still be there if they didn't have to be. The stench of stale alcohol in the air was proof enough to her that the twelve steps were clearly not working for some of them, not so far anyway.

She endured the class for the sixty long minutes that it ran, listening to people stating their names and admitting their addictions, as she had done too on her first appearance, and listening to the stories of those who had managed to remain dry. The group clapped and applauded every minor achievement that transpired with seemingly genuine enthusiasm, until finally it was all over with, and Tammy was free of them all for another week. She hurried out through the double doors as quickly as she could, desperate not to be approached and forced into meaningless conversation with any of them, and stepped out into the street.

Tammy had grown grateful of almost all human interaction since the accident, but these were not the people she wanted any association with, partially through disgust, but mainly through the fear that she would see herself in them. Deep down she knew that she was no better than them, maybe even worse. Her own mistakes and addictions had been just as bad as theirs, but she refused to admit it and insisted in drawing a line between them and her.

With her earphones firmly back in place, and the music turned back to full volume, Tammy headed through the town centre to the pharmacists. She bought herself two bottles of 'Slim-fast' milkshake, which she hoped would take away the painful growling in her stomach, and drank them both down while she waited for the assistant to prepare Matthew's pills. She then hopped back onto the bus and made her way to her 12 o'clock client.

From that point onwards, the day seemed to fly by with very little conscious effort, as if she had somehow reverted to autopilot mode. She gave Mr Carlson his bath and medication, then to the cheerful Ethel, Florence, and Agnes at the flats before attending to Mr and Mrs Holmes at their quaint little bungalow. All the while her thoughts meandered back and forth between her beautiful daughter and the unsettling house on Oak Street.

She arrived back on the street at five-fifteen, and was greeted once again by the prying eyes of nosey neighbours, all eager for round two of gawking. Tammy by this point was far too tired to pay them much attention, and strolled passed them without any acknowledgement. She knocked on the door and waited for Matthew to answer. A few moments passed before Matthew finally opened the door to her, topless and dripping with sweat. Tammy was taken with surprise, and when the shock started to dissipate she found her eyes wandering longingly around his toned body as she watched a single droplet of perspiration slowly running between his pecs and down through his chiselled six-pack. She found herself both aroused and embarrassed at the same time, like a schoolgirl accidentally walking into the boys' changing rooms. She shook her head and quickly looked away as her cheeks began to blush.

"I'm sorry, I was just working out a bit and I forgot what the time was," he quickly explained to her, oblivious to his inappropriate appearance.

"Oh, no, it's fine," she blurted out with an awkward smile, averting her sight nervously.

"Come in," he told her, as he turned his back and grabbed a towel that lay upon the lounge floor. "So how was your day?" he continued.

"Yeah, it was fine. Thank you," she told him as she stepped into the house and closed the door.

"Good good," he replied, as he patted down the sweat and pulled a T-shirt over his head.

"..And you?"

"Quite productive, I think. I got most of the housework finished anyway."

"Good."

"Yeah, but then I realised the TV didn't work anymore."

"Oh, really?"

THE DAMAGED

"Yeah, I can't seem to get a signal. Any ideas?" he asked, as he leant forward and switched it on.

The television faded in from black to fuzz and the room was filled with white noise. Tammy took a look at the old tatty box in the corner and had to restrain herself from making any 'antique' comments that might offend him.

"Oh, it's probably the digital switch-over," she explained to him, seemingly proud that she actually knew something for a change.

"The *what*? Sorry?" he replied with a perplexed frown.

"You know, when they converted to digital signal?" she told him, somewhat confused as to why he didn't understand.

"That means nothing to me, Tammy. I'm not exactly up-to-date with current affairs really," he told her, sounding mildly frustrated.

"Oh, right. Sorry, I forgot," she replied, her proud voice now levelling off at a more sombre tone. −"Well they turned off the analogue signal a few months back now. The old TVs can't receive digital. You need a Freeview box, or cable these days."

"Oh, I see. Guess I'll have to do without then," he replied with a nod, as he leaned back in and turned off the switch.

"I can pick one up for you, if you like?" Tammy offered, seeing the disappointment in Matthew's face.

"No, it's alright, thank you. I might as well just get a new television. It's seen better days, that thing," he told her with a mild grin. − "Besides, I'm still waiting for the banks to release my money. The accounts were all frozen when I was committed."

Tammy pondered her next question for a few moments before deciding to remain silent. Her unanswered questions were all on the tip of her tongue, but she was still not brave enough to ask them.

"You're not missing much," she finally responded.-"It's all coverage of the Olympics at the moment."

"You're not a fan then?"

"Not at all!" she told him with a dismissive shake of the head. "Are you?"

"Not really, no. My dad used to watch a lot of sport. I just miss my cartoons. They were pretty much all we were allowed to watch at the hospital."

"Really? Why's that?"

"Just policy I guess. I imagine because they're friendly and non-offensive. They wouldn't get the residents worked up. Most of the residents had a mental age of a child anyway, and the others were so drugged up that they had no idea what they were even watching."

"Oh, I see. So what's your favourite cartoon then?"

"Transformers!" he immediately told her with childish enthusiasm, his blue eyes suddenly widening at the thought. –"They played re-runs almost every day! *He-Man* was good too," he continued.

"I used to like Winne the Pooh!" she told him with a nostalgic grin. –"My daughter likes that *Peppa-Pig* thing. Cartoons just aren't the same anymore!" she continued, clearly starting to feel more at ease in Matthew's company.

"Oh, you have a daughter?"

"Uh-huh" Tammy replied with a nod, wondering whether it was a good idea to mention it or not. –"She's five."

"What's her name?"

"It's Jessica."

Matthew acknowledged this with a nod and a smile before pausing for a second, looking at Tammy with a curious expression upon his face.

"You've... never had a client like me before. Have you?" he eventually asked.

"Is it that obvious?" she asked with a guilty frown.

"Well, yeah. You seem surprised by a lot of things."

"I normally deal with the elderly."

"Oh I see. Well you can always give me a sponge bath if that makes you feel more comfortable?" he suggested with a flirtatious smile.

Tammy immediately started to blush again and looked away with an embarrassed smile.

"I'm joking!" Matthew quickly added, though Tammy half wished that he wasn't. "You fancy a cup of tea then? Before you turn me into a zombie again, that is?" he continued, the levity and jest in his voice clearly laced with a subtle layer of resentment.

"Yeah, alright then, thank you," she replied, trying to keep her smile from slumping to a mournful look of regret, as she too remembered the true purpose of her visit.

Matthew nodded and smiled as he turned his back and made his way to the kitchen. Tammy sat down upon the sofa and waited for his return. The eerie feeling of the house was still lurking, and would still have sent shivers down her spine if she were to let it, but the impact that it first had was now lost on her, as if she was now becoming desensitised to it. The fresh scent of furniture polish and air freshener had now replaced the stale must in the air and the deathly silence had now been replaced by the comforting rhythmic ticking of the grandfather clock, polished, wound, and brought back to life once again.

"...Milk and sugar?" Matthew called from the kitchen.

"Yeah, milk and two, please," she called back.

THE DAMAGED

It was at this point that Tammy noticed the photo album that lay open upon the side table next to the Chesterfield. She nervously leant forward for a better view, twisting her neck round and peering down awkwardly. The photograph on display was old and faded, but its depiction was clear, even from her skewed angle. The photo was of a young couple on their wedding day, happy and smiling with the sun beaming down on their faces. *Was this his parents?* she wondered. She heard a footstep from behind her and quickly returned to her original position, worried that Matthew would be angry if he caught her prying into his business again.

"It's okay, you can look," he quickly reassured her, as he appeared with two cups of tea. He placed one down on the large coffee table in front of the sofa, and the other down upon the side table next to the album.

"Are you sure?" Tammy asked, aware that she was quickly stepping into personal territory.

"Yeah it's fine, I was just having a look earlier. I haven't seen these photos in a very long time now," he told her as he sat back down into the armchair. –"Here you go," he continued, as he picked the album up and gently passed it over to her.

Tammy smiled and took the album from his hand, gently placing it down onto her lap for a closer look.

"That's them. My parents, that is. Nineteen-seventy-nine I believe," he told her with a smile to mask his sadness. "It's a good photo, isn't it?"

"Yeah, it's beautiful," she replied, as she looked down in admiration at the intricate flowing white dress and the sparkling crystal tiara that sat gently upon his mother's head.

"I was thinking of getting a print of that one, putting it in a frame or something?" he told her, his voice sounding vulnerable and fragile.

"Yeah, you should," she told him with a tender smile.

She reached down and gently flipped the page to the next photo, revealing a woman in a long blue dress and holding a bouquet of flowers.

"And who's this?" Tammy asked.

Matthew looked over and tilted his head to the photo, and his look of sadness immediately turned to anger. Lines appeared on his forehead, his nostrils started to flare and his teeth grit together tightly. Matthew's eyes continued to fixate upon the offending image with an intense piercing stare as a vein down the side of his head began to pulsate.

The transformation was dramatic and scary, and Tammy immediately found herself uncomfortable and genuinely frightened by Matthew's reaction, convinced he was about to snap.

A few more seconds passed, as Tammy's nerves began to peak and manifest themselves in the shaking of her hands and the beating of her heart, until Matthew finally released a breath and looked away from the photo. Tammy released a breath too, and tried to restrain her shaking limbs.

"That's... That's my Aunt Julie," he bitterly spat out, reaching forward and taking the book back from Tammy. –"We didn't exactly get on," he continued, forcing a smile upon his face.

"Oh, I see," Tammy replied nervously, matching Matthew's forced smile.

"I'm sorry, I...I didn't realise that photo was in there," he told her, his voice starting to return to its usual tone.

Matthew closed the album and placed it on the floor.

Tammy knew she would regret it, but couldn't stop herself from asking. "...Why didn't you get on?"

"She's the reason I got locked up. Fifteen years in that damn hell-hole because of her!" he told her despairingly, but desperately trying to keep his composure.

"Why was that?" Tammy asked, still afraid of Matthew's temperament but too intrigued now to let it go.

"Because she hated me, that's why. She hated the fact that I got all their money, and she didn't!"

Matthew stood from the chair and turned to face the boarded window opposite. He stood quietly, thinking, breathing deeply. Tammy looked up at him, still shaking with nerves, but now with more empathy and understanding than before. Something then occurred to her that didn't make sense.

"Wait, fifteen years? I thought it happened in eighty-seven? – that's twenty-five years?"

The room briefly turned to silence with the exception of the ticking of the grandfather clock in the background. Matthew honed in on the sound and listened to the pendulum swing back and forth, hypnotic and soothing to him.

A few more moments of uncomfortable silence passed until Matthew finally turned back around to find Tammy sheepishly looking up at him. He smiled in return, seemingly calm again, and sat himself back down again upon the rustic red leather of the Chesterfield. He then took a sip of his tea.

"It wasn't the murders that caused me to be sectioned, not directly anyway. It was because of that evil woman. She... She hated all kids, not just me," he began, offering Tammy another smile and a brief glimpse of his deep blue eyes again.-"I don't know why. They just grated on her, I guess. I spent a few nights in child services after the storm, after my parents were killed, and then I was told she had agreed to take me in, to be my legal guardian. So this house was boarded up and I went to live with her and her two cats."

"Well, that seems like a nice thing to do," Tammy interjected.

"Yeah, it seemed that way and maybe it did start off genuine, but you should have seen her face when the lawyer read the will; the house, the bonds, the shares in the company, everything went to me. She was horrified, betrayed, like she had spent all those years babysitting me for nothing. She contested the will, obviously, but she couldn't get it changed. I was too young to inherit at the time, so probate took their percentage of the money and the rest of it went into a trust fund until I was eighteen. She treated me like dirt ever since that day. I think she only ever kept me because the courts had granted her a small allowance from my inheritance in order to look after me."

Matthew paused for another sip of tea.

"You really think she had you just for the money?"

"It must have been. I can't think of any other reason why she'd want me, and she certainly never spent any of that money on me."

"So, I'm confused. How did you end up in the hospital all those years later then?"

"Well... I... I guess I developed a few issues after the murders, but what would you expect after everything I had been through? Aunt Julie never did anything to help me with them in all the years I was with her. All she did was taunt me, shout at me, and punish me. She never cared."

"What kind of issues?"

"Phobias, anxieties, you know. The wind especially, the sound of it, the sight of shaking trees, the feel of it upon my skin...It brought back memories from the storm, from the murders. It freaked me out, still does really. I...I used to wet the bed a lot, I couldn't help it. She used to scream at me for it, rub the wet sheets in my face, and call me a dirty little..." Matthew paused, unable to repeat the obscenity and deciding to spell it out instead. "... A dirty little c-u-n-t!' She was a nasty woman, I hated her."

"I'm not surprised. That's horrible!" Tammy mumbled with growing sympathy.

"Yeah, it was. I had no friends either, they all bullied me at school, thought I was a weirdo. There was a storm one December, not a massive one, but, you know, big enough for *me* to freak out, and I ended up wetting myself in class. They all called me 'Pissy-Pants Mason' ever since then. One day, this real horrible kid called Jason Selby was being especially nasty to me – he was the school bully and was horrible to everyone, but I was always his number one target, his 'special interest'. He followed me home from school, taunting me and throwing rocks at me, and I... I flipped out. I turned around and punched him so hard that I broke his nose. He was taken to hospital and I got suspended for two weeks. Julie didn't like that at all, and I spent that entire two weeks locked in my bedroom. I screamed and begged for her to let me out, but she just ignored me, occasionally sliding a little food under the door."

"And this went on for ten years?"

"Yeah, and it just got worse and worse. My phobias all got worse too. I got expelled from school and I ended up spending all my time in my bedroom, alone. Too scared to go out, too scared to do anything. Julie was supposed to home-school me but she never bothered, threw a few old school syllabus books in my room and pretended I didn't exist. Then, on the week before my eighteenth birthday, when my trust fund was due to mature, when Julie's allowance was due to stop, she had me committed to the hospital, probably in the hope that the money would then go to her, and that's where I've been ever since; locked up in the horrid place and left to rot!"

Matthew took a breath and composed himself, shaking off the angry memories and hoping that his prolonged rant of a story had not made Tammy feel too uncomfortable.

"So... Where's your aunt now?" she asked.

"In hell for all I care..."

"I...I don't really know what to say Matthew, it's a horrible story," Tammy told him with a sympathetic smile as she finished off her tea. She knew there must have been more to the story, as a mental institute would hardly lock someone up for a mere few phobias at the request of an uncaring aunt, but decided not to push him any further. –"Least now you can start afresh though. You can forget about the past and start a new chapter in your life," she continued.

"Yeah, you're right. Okay, your turn now."

"...My turn for what?"

"...For your story. I've just told you my horrible story, now it's your turn," he told her with a smile.

"Maybe another time."

"That's not fair, surely?" he replied playfully.

"Maybe not, but you're late for your pills," she told him, looking at the grandfather clock as it struck five-thirty-five.

"Do you need any Diazepam tonight?"

"No, it's fine. I don't really take much in the summertime."

She nodded and walked through to the kitchen. She filled a glass with water, emptied the contents from the evening section of the pill box into her palm, and then returned to the lounge again.

THE DAMAGED

"Here ya go Matthew, you know the drill," she said as she placed the water and pills down upon the side table again.

"Yep, I do indeed, Tammy," he replied, and swallowed the pills without hesitation.

"Okay, well take it easy and I'll see you again in the morning, alright?" she asked, aware that Matthew would probably prefer her to leave before the effects of the medication kicked in.

"Yeah okay, Darling. See you tomorrow," he replied with a warm smile and another gaze of his big blue eyes.

Tammy paused for a second, debating whether or not to comment on the 'Darling' part of Matthew's address. It was definitely inappropriate of him, and had it been another client, Mr Carlson for example, she would have made a stern objection; but in the case of Matthew she decided she didn't mind it, and just smiled back at him instead. She picked up her bag and made for the front door.

"See you soon," she called.

SIMON LAW

DEAD MAN'S SHOES

Fifteen years of finger painting, kid's cartoons and abuse from overzealous orderlies had left Matthew with a strange disconnection with the real world. His only memories of freedom had encompassed ten years of loveless neglect and abuse from his Aunt Julie, and a brief seven years of childhood happiness. It was unsurprising therefore, that his new freedom would take some getting used to.

From the bloody murders, to the abuse of his aunt and the abuse he later experienced in the mental hospital, a life of fear and violence was all that Matthew knew. A life of calm and peace now felt out of place and unusual to him, as if something was missing.

Being back in his family home again after so long away had now ignited something in his brain that dredged up those long-forgotten memories from the past, memories that he thought were gone forever. Memories of his parents' love for him, and for each other; the sound of his dad's Ford Capri as it pulled up outside the house each evening, and the smell of his mother's floral perfume as she leant in to kiss him on the forehead. The memories were good, and welcoming to Matthew. They reminded him that there was more to life than the atrocities he had endured. It reminded him what normality was really like, and inspired him to have that life again, to be like his father, an honourable man who cared for his family. But along with the memories of a life filled with love and security inevitably came the memories of how that life had ended. Reminders of the storm and his parents' death were still littered throughout the house, despite the twenty-five years that had passed since they occurred; the shattered window above his bed, the missing knife from the kitchen woodblock, and the eerie cold cellar where he had spent a day and a half paralysed with fear until the police had discovered him.

The boards that now covered the windows in the house were comforting to Matthew. He could sit inside his family home and pretend that the world outside was not there. He could pretend that it was still 1987 outside and that the past twenty-five years had just been a dream. It was a daunting thought to him that the world had changed so much in that time and he worried how he would adapt to it. The wooden boards that encased the house also had the added bonus that they completely masked any kind of weather outside, being wind, rain or snow. The Diazepam was a great help at calming his nerves in times of adverse weather, but he knew that popping pills at the mere sight of a blowing tree was not a sustainable future for him, it demasculinated him and made me feel weak and feeble, despite his physical strength and bulging biceps.

The men were coming today to remove them all, and although Matthew knew that he could very easily call and cancel the work, he knew that doing this would murmur doubts in the mind of his releasing doctor, and he had come too far now to be sent back to the hospital again. He would rather die.

Matthew rolled over in his single bed and looked over to his plastic blue alarm clock that sat on his bedside table. '6 a.m.' it read. Without the clock it would have been impossible to guess the time, as the absence of sunlight in the house made night indistinguishable from day. He pulled off his Transformers duvet and sat upright on the side of his bed, thinking to himself for a moment. Matthew's distant memories of his father George were his only point of reference to gauge how an upstanding person should act. His father was an early riser, getting up at 6am every morning, and therefore Matthew would too.

He stood, stretched his muscles, and made his way down the hallway to his parents' bedroom. Matthew had spent the previous days thoroughly cleaning the house and had been through his father's wardrobe to throw away the items which had become too frayed and moth-eaten to be of any use. Now, at the grand age of thirty-two, Matthew was exactly the same size as his father was at the time of his death, and his clothes fit him perfectly. By the same logic as getting up at 6am, Matthew decided that these were the clothes he should wear if he was to aspire to be like his father, and so he selected a clean shirt and trousers from the wardrobe, and dressed himself in them with pride. He washed and brushed his teeth before descending the stair to make himself some breakfast, porridge, just like his father had eaten.

SIMON LAW

The social worker who had escorted Matthew home and helped him to get settled had supplied him with some of the bare essentials for his cupboards: milk, bread, porridge, etcetera... but his supplies were quickly running out. She had explained to him that his bank accounts had all been reopened and that his debit card and pin were on their way, but had clearly forgotten to take into consideration Matthew's intense fear of going outside. The mere thought of going to the supermarket for supplies, all alone and surrounded by strangers, was a daunting idea to him to say the least. He hoped that his newfound freedom would allow him to gradually conquer some of these fears, but this goal was still a long way away. Until then, he would need some help.

Matthew's thoughts turned to Tammy, who he knew would be more than happy to help him. It had only been a few days now since they first met, but Matthew already considered her to be a friend. She was kind to him, friendly and caring. He knew that this was her job, and maybe she was just good at it, but he hoped that there was more to it. It had been a long time since there had been anyone in his life that he could consider a *friend*, and the thought excited him.

Tammy was attractive too, with her long sleek legs and silky black hair, and he found himself attracted to her almost immediately. Beneath her obvious beauty, it was clear to Matthew that she was troubled too, which was an extra quality that added to her allure. It intrigued him, and it was something that he could relate to. She would be the perfect girl for him, to share his new life and his new freedom with. A smile quickly appeared on his face as he considered the possibility of it, and he wondered if she could possibly feel the same for him. It then occurred to him that maybe he was getting ahead of himself. They had only just met and it was silly to be thinking such things already. Matthew had never had a girlfriend before and it occurred to him that maybe he was just being over excitable about his first interaction with a nice girl; a girl who more than likely felt nothing for him at all. Why would she? She probably thought nothing more of him than she did for her other clients. After all, he wasn't exactly a catch; he was a weirdo, a mental case with a psyche damaged beyond repair. What could she possibly find attractive about that? He didn't even know if she had a boyfriend or not. The elation of the possibility quickly became muddied with doubt, and so Matthew parked it at the back of his mind, and finished his porridge.

Matthew sat himself down in his father's Chesterfield and eagerly awaited Tammy's morning arrival. Calm and peaceful, he waited with a smile, eyes shut and fingers interlocked upon his chest as he listened to the distant noises of tweeting birds in the street, occasionally opening his eyes to glimpse a quick view of the time on the grandfather clock. As the clock struck 8am he heard the street begin to wake, as the sounds of laughing children passed his house and car engines began to ignite.

Matthew had noticed on Tammy's first arrival that her knocks upon the door had not coincided with the sound of a car engine, and by her second visit had already linked her arrivals within minutes of the sound of the local bus from the top of the road. It was then obvious to him that she did not drive, which came as somewhat of a mystery to him, as Maureen had already implied otherwise. He therefore knew that the sound of the 8.45 bus was his cue.

When the distinct sound of the bus finally appeared, Matthew immediately stood from the chair and made his way to the kitchen. He switched on the kettle, placed two teabags in two cups, and waited for the water to boil. A hot cup of tea on her arrival would hardly be the catalyst for her falling in love with him, he knew that, but it definitely wouldn't hurt either. At minimum it would show he was caring and attentive to her, if nothing else. Until his money came through there was very little he *could* do to impress her anyway, aside from just declaring his undying love to her, but that would be a little hasty, even in his own skewed opinion.

The expected knock came just as Matthew was throwing the used teabags into the bin. He picked up both mugs and carried them through to the lounge, brushed himself down, straightened his shirt, and opened the door.

"Morning Tammy!" he greeted her with a longing smile, as he looked down at her glowing in the morning sun.

"Morning!" she replied.

They stood and gazed at each other for a brief few moments, each completely ignorant of the other's growing attraction for them, whilst both pondering curiously if the other felt the same.

"Come in then," he told her, as he stepped aside and shut the door. – "How are you today?"

"Yeah, I'm good. Thank you. You?" she told him, though her eyes looked tired and unrested.

"Yeah, I'm good too. Have a seat, I made you a cup of tea, milk and two sugars, just like you like it," he told her.

"Oh, okay then. Thanks," she replied, sounding both surprised and pleased.

She took a seat in her usual position on the sofa and placed her bag down beside her.

"I had a call from Maureen last night," she began explaining, as Matthew returned to his position on the Chesterfield.

SIMON LAW

"Yeah? What about?"

"She was just asking how you were getting on and stuff. She wanted to know if you were looking after yourself okay, and if you were eating properly. I think she has to report back to the social worker on Friday and just wanted to make sure we were doing everything you need of us."

"Oh I see."

"I told her I thought you were doing well, but I said I would ask you this morning."

"Fair enough, yeah I'm alright. Thanks."

"..And you're eating properly and stuff?"

"Well, now you mention it, I am kind of running out of food now."

"Right, okay. Would you like me to arrange meals on wheels for you?" she asked ignorantly, though she knew what he really meant.

"What's that?" he replied with a slight frown.

"You know, when people bring your dinners round and cook them for you?" she explained.

"Oh right, no. I can cook fine, well, sort of anyway. I just need someone to do my shopping for me."

"Oh, okay. Can't you get down to the shops then?" she asked, continuing with her ignorant guise.

"No, I don't go outside, Tammy!"

"...Why not?"

"You know why not," he quickly told her with a smile, beginning to realise her angle.

"I know you have a few anxieties, yes, but there's no wind out there at the moment. It's a beautiful day outside today. Haven't you looked?" she replied, fully aware that she was starting to push at the boundaries.

Matthew smiled and nodded dismissively.

"I...I'm not ready yet, Tammy."

"I can come with you if you like? If that would make it easier," she continued to push.

"I know you're trying to help, Tammy, but it's just a bit too early at the moment. Let me get settled for a few days then maybe I'll give it a go."

"Okay. You can't blame me for trying," she confessed with a friendly smile. –"You wanna make me a list then and I'll pick it up for you this morning?"

"I don't have my money through yet."

"Oh, don't worry about that. You can owe it to me."

"Are you sure?"

"Yeah, its fine, Matthew."

THE DAMAGED

"Thank you. You're too good to me," he told her, while asking himself if that was something she would do for *all* of her clients, or whether maybe he was special to her in some way. *Maybe she did fancy me too after all?*

Tammy looked at him and nodded, before standing from the sofa and heading towards the kitchen. Matthew immediately turned to watch her leave, and couldn't help his eyes from running up and down the curves of her slim, toned body.

He continued watching her as she leant forward on the kitchen counter to remove his pills from their plastic box, and unwittingly arched her back and protruded her bottom slightly in the air. His eyes fixated upon her rump, as if he were a lion and she were a tasty rare cut of beef, juicy and irresistible. He started to wonder if she was aware that she was doing it, maybe even doing it on purpose to allure him. *My God, I want you!* he thought to himself, and became so lost in his own thoughts that he failed to notice her turning around again and catching a glimpse of him staring. He quickly looked away sheepishly, a guilty look apparent on his face, as she started walking back with the medication in her hands.

Was he checking me out? she asked herself, as she placed down the pills and looked at him curiously.

"Here ya go," she told him, as she sat back down for a slurp of her tea.

"Thank you," he replied, the look of guilt still lingering upon him.

Tammy smiled in return and quickly looked away before she started to blush. She reached into her handbag and removed a notepad and pen and placed them down on the table next to him.

"Here, you better make me your shopping list before you take your pills this morning."

He sighed and nodded in agreement, before picking up the pen and starting to write.

"You know, I used to take anti-depressants when I was a teenager. I know it's not quite the same, but they used to send me into a daze too, so I do understand why you don't like them," she confessed, offering him a smile of empathy.

"Really? Why was that?" he asked, as he stopped writing to look at her curiously.

"Teachers caught me in the toilet cutting myself and sent me to a 'shrink'; I didn't have a choice really."

"Cutting yourself?" he asked, finding the idea odd, but somewhat arousing.

"Yeah."

"Was it really that bad?"

"I thought it was, yeah. I don't know why though to be frank. I didn't have a bad childhood or anything like that, but when I became a teenager I just started to feel really lonely, disconnected with people. You know what I mean?"

"You didn't have any friends either then?"

"Nope, no one close anyway. My mum was always there for me, but it's not the same really, is it?"

"No, it's not. I didn't even have that...." he began, before stopping himself from hijacking the conversation. "So what changed then?" he continued.

"Well that was when I met Keith."

"Keith?"

"Yeah, that's Jessica's father."

"Oh I see."

"He made me feel special, he was good to me. I stopped taking the pills shortly after that."

"You still together now then?" he asked curiously, quietly hoping the answer would be no.

"No, not anymore," she replied.

"Oh, why's that?" Matthew asked, trying his best to sound sympathetic when really he was elated.

Tammy paused, debating with herself whether to tell Matthew the full story or not. She hadn't talked about her problems with anyone who she wasn't 'legally bound to' yet, but she somehow felt comfortable with Matthew, as if she knew he wouldn't judge her like she assumed others would.

"We split about seven months ago now..." she began, before pausing again to find the right words. –"You remember I told you that my mum died recently?"

"Yes..."

"Well, it was actually about a year ago now and...Well, I took it quite badly. I hadn't really been there for her much during her illness 'cos I was too consumed with all my own crap, silly things that really shouldn't have mattered. She died all alone in the hospice, all by herself. I felt so guilty...She deserved more from me, after everything she had done for me in my life, and...Well, I started drinking, heavily. I got through a bottle of vodka a day sometimes. I was drunk-driving, I was turning up to work drunk, and I was an awful mother to Jessica..."

Tammy paused again to calm herself and regroup her thoughts, wondering if maybe she was saying too much.

"...so Keith left you?" Matthew asked with a puzzled frown, confused as to how this could be true.

THE DAMAGED

"Yep! And he took Jessica with him," she told him, trying to shake off the growing look of sorrow upon her pale face.

Matthew nodded sympathetically and started to chew on the end of Tammy's pen.

"...and then what happened?" he prompted.

"What do you mean?" Tammy replied, confused as to why he would assume there was more.

"Well, I've noticed you don't drive anymore, and I've never smelt any alcohol on you, so I'm guessing something must have happened?"

She looked at him curiously and smiled.

"How do you know I don't drive?" she asked. "You can't even see out of the windows." She glanced over to the wooden boards.

"No, but I can hear, and I'd hear a car pulling up outside if you drove."

"You're quite astute, aren't you?" she told him as she studied his face for a moment, careful not to get too lost in his big blue eyes again as she felt them drawing her in.

"Sometimes," he replied dismissively. "...When I'm not drugged up, anyway."

"Well...I felt alone again, like I did when I was younger and my drinking got even worse. I got really drunk one evening and I decided to kidnap Jessica. It was a stupid thing to do." She paused again for a breath. "And I crashed the car into a tree..."

"Oh, God. Was she alright?"

Tammy smiled and nodded.

"She didn't have a scratch on her, but that's not really the point though. I could have killed her," Tammy replied, her voice sounding increasingly unsteady and close to tears.

Matthew could see her bottom lip starting to quiver and so reached out to take her hand.

"It's okay, we all make mistakes," he told her, holding her hand gently in his grip and stroking the top of it tenderly with his thumb. Her vulnerability was alluring to Matthew and the touch of her trembling skin was even more arousing.

Tammy closed her eyes and steadied her lip, determined that she wouldn't cry in front of him. She gave his hand a squeeze before then retracting it and picking up her cup of tea.

"I still have nightmares you know," she explained as she took a sip from the cup, her voice now starting to steady again.

"You had one last night, didn't you?"

"Yeah, is it obvious?" she asked with a frown.

"You look a little tired, that's all."

* * *

"You're not gonna tell anyone any of this, are you?" Tammy asked, suddenly sounding worried at the realisation that her secret was out.

"Who would I tell?" Matthew replied, mildly offended.

"I dunno...Maureen? The social worker? Anyone! I could lose my job. Promise you won't tell anyone, please?" she blurted in a panic as she stood from the sofa and began to pace the room.

"What...and lose my favourite carer? I don't think so!" he told her with a reassuring smile.

"You promise?"

"Of course I won't, Darling. Don't be silly!"

She smiled nervously back at him and began to chew upon her thumb nail.

"Do you mind if I have a cigarette?" she asked.

"Sure, not in the house though. My parents wouldn't have approved."

"Thank you."

Tammy picked up her bag and stepped out into the fresh air, closing the door gently behind her. She took in a long deep breath and then sparked up a cigarette. *Have I just made a massive mistake?* she asked herself.

Matthew's attraction for Tammy had grown stronger with the passing of each new revelation she made, and he was now certain of his feelings for her. The demons of her past may not have been comparable to his own, but their effect on her was clear. They had damaged her in a way that was all too familiar to him, and it was this similarity that had triggered such arousal in him. It had also occurred to him that her openness and willingness to share such demons with him must have only been indicative of a connection she felt with him too. There could be no other explanation.

Matthew pondered his thoughts of Tammy for a moment longer with a smile, before returning to the pen and pad in front of him and continuing with his list.

The door opened again and Tammy returned, a sheepish look of embarrassment upon her face that quickly dissipated as he offered a smile and a longing gaze.

"Finished?"

"Yep, all done," he replied, ripping out the sheet and passing it to her along with the pen and the rest of the pad.

"Thanks," she replied, casually passing her eyes over the list. "...Anything else you need while I'm out?"

"Err, maybe a catalogue, if you can get one?" he asked.

"A catalogue?"

"Yeah, you know, like a shopping catalogue. They still do shopping catalogues these days, don't they?"

"Yeah, sure," she replied with a grin. "...Anything else?"

"Could you get that photo print for me?"

"...Of your parents?"

"Yeah, I found the negative for it."

"Of course!"

Matthew smiled and reached underneath the coffee table, removing a small white envelope which he then passed to Tammy.

"Thank you."

"How big?"

"About so big?" he told her, gesturing the size with his hands.

"Okay. I'll shoot into town now; I'll probably be a couple of hours or so."

"Okay, Darling, thanks for doing this for me."

"No worries Matthew."

Tammy offered a final smile and made for the door, before suddenly remembering the purpose of her visit. She stopped and turned back to Matthew again, raising her eyebrows and looking down at the two blue capsules on Matthew's little side table.

"Pills?" she called.

Matthew looked back at her and returned a playful grin, as if he thought he had gotten away with it.

"Yes miss!" he replied light-heartedly, before throwing them into his mouth and swallowing them down with the water.

"Okay, see ya soon," she told him, and left the house for the last time.

Matthew closed his eyes and relaxed back into his father's Chesterfield, listening out as Tammy's footsteps slowly disappeared into the distance. He then stood from the chair, climbed the stairs to the top of the landing, and pushed open the bathroom door. He carefully unbuttoned his shirt, laid it gently across the rim of the bath and lowered himself down to his knees in front of the pea-green toilet. Pushing back the toilet seat and leaning in, Matthew inserted two fingers down his throat. After gagging and heaving for a few moments the contents of his stomach quickly came gushing from his mouth. A mixture of tea and porridge spluttered into the toilet with a splash and a putrid smell of bile, and along with it came the two blue capsules.

Matthew remained knelt for a few seconds longer, catching his breath and wiping the dripping vomit from his lower lip. He then peered into the toilet to verify the presence of the offending items, before pulling the flush and rising to his feet again.

This had been Matthew's routine for the past three days now, and he could already start to feel the drugs leaving his system. It felt good. He was feeling clear-headed again and free from the zombified mash of blurred emotions that the pills gave him. It was liberating, but he knew it was not something he could continue for long. His growing love for Tammy was real, but even so, he knew this was not a secret he could share with her. She would not approve, she would report back to the doctors that he was off his meds and they would lock him back up again. This was not something he could allow to happen.

He washed his hands and rinsed his mouth out with mouthwash before then descending the stairs again and returning to his father's chair to think about how he could overcome his predicament.

It was at this point that Matthew noticed something strange out the corner of his eye. In the middle of the room lay a single feather, black and shiny like a stone of Whitby jet. The feather was large, and Matthew quickly concluded it to have been from either a raven or a crow. It was possible that the mysterious feather had blown in the door when Tammy had arrived that morning, but unlikely, as Matthew would have noticed it earlier.

Matthew reached for the feather and was quickly met by an electric jolt as his fingers brushed upon it, followed by an unearthly sensation that his skin was on fire, singeing his hairs and boiling his blood inside of him. He released the feather and the strange sensation immediately disappeared again, leaving him with only the mildest of residual tingles. Gazing down with a look of disbelief, Matthew wondered what the hell had just happened to him. He reached for the ominous black plume once more before thinking better of it, and deciding to leave it where it lay. *Maybe it was just static or something,* he pondered, before deciding to dismiss it and returning his thoughts to his previous predicament.

Wandering through to the kitchen, Matthew looked down at his medication in contemplation. Unclipping one segment of the pill box, he removed a single blue capsule and placed it in his palm, toying with it in curiosity. He then gripped it with his fingers and gently pulled it apart, releasing a fine white powder that gracefully fluttered through the air and onto the floor. Carefully piecing the capsule back together again, he continued to toy with it for a while longer. The weight and appearance of the capsule was clearly different with the absence of its contents and Tammy would notice this difference straightaway. He therefore needed something to replace it with. Matthew peered at the bag of sugar that sat next to the teabags on the kitchen counter in contemplation. The sugar was definitely not a match in consistency to the powdered drug that the capsule once contained, but once inside the difference may not have been obvious. Pulling the empty capsule apart again, Matthew filled it with the sugar, before removing a second capsule from the pill box and comparing the two in his hand. The weight now seemed to match perfectly and the appearance was too

THE DAMAGED

similar to worry about. He grinned and nodded to himself reassuringly, before proceeding to replace the contents of all the remaining pills in the same manner, pouring the drugs of each capsule into the kitchen sink and washing it all down the drain.

Alerted by the metallic clanging climax of the rattling letterbox, Matthew dashed excitedly through the house, peering down at the doormat and to the mail that now lay waiting for him. He bent down and scooped up the letters with a smile, before carrying them through to the lounge for a closer look.

The mail contained two white envelopes, both addressed to 'Mr Matthew John Mason'. This was the first time in Matthew's life that any letter had been addressed directly to him, and the sight of his printed name was uplifting, it was symbolic of his new found freedom, and it reinforced his new identity as a free man. He quickly ripped them open and began reading.

'Dear Mr Mason,' the letter began. 'Please find enclosed your new debit card as requested....'

Matthew quickly skimmed through the rest of the wording before coming across his brand new debit card attached to the bottom. The card was smooth and shimmering and embossed with his name in bold silver letters across the bottom. Carefully peeling the card away from the adhesive strip, Matthew then gently caressed the embossed lettering with his thumb. A look of proud achievement soon grew upon his face, as he began to ponder what his first purchase would be. He placed the card back down again and opened the next letter.

'Dear Mr Mason, Please find enclosed your new pin number...' the second letter started, ending with a four digit number hidden underneath a grey rectangular flap. '7891'

Matthew closed his eyes and repeated the four digit number in his head a dozen times until he was sure the information was sufficiently stored. It wasn't until he had placed the envelopes down that he suddenly noticed the absence of the mysterious black feather. He looked underneath the coffee table and the chairs, but it was gone, vanished without a trace. *Did I just imagine it?* he quickly asked himself. He was a logical man and didn't believe in God or in magic, and so the only possible explanation was his own imagination. *But why? What possible significance would a black feather have for my mind to feel the need to manifest it?'* he continued to ponder. Confused, he began to search again, all around the living room, but still nothing. *Could this really be the result of not taking my meds already? Surely not!*

SIMON LAW

Matthew's desperate search for the ominous black plume was interrupted by a stern knocking upon the front door. Matthew paused and tried to clear his mind, but then the knocking came again, harder. He tutted and huffed, before discarding the search and starting to make his way to the door.

There was then an almighty crash from outside and the room immediately flooded with bright blinding sunlight. The shocking rays were almost overwhelming to Matthew; they invaded and assaulted him; scorching his dilated pupils and sending him into a fearful cower. The shock of the incident quickly faded and turned to vexation, as Matthew blinked away the sting in his eyes and continued to the door.

Before him stood a short stocky man with a scruffy beard and a shaven head. In the man's mouth burned a crudely-rolled cigarette. Its smoke immediately blew into Matthew's face. He was dressed in a pair of tatty jeans with a dark green T-shirt that bore the logo of the local council.

"Mr Mason? We're here from the council to do some work on your property today. Here's the worksheet for you," the man told him without pause or hesitation. He passed Matthew a white sheet of paper clipped upon a tatty clipboard with a black Biro attached to the top.

"Hi," Matthew replied bluntly as he snatched the clipboard from the man's hand, clearly unimpressed with his unkempt appearance.

Matthew scanned through the document and looked back up at the scruffy man, who stood impatiently for his approval. Matthew's vexation then grew in intensity, as the man removed the cigarette from his mouth to hock up a globule of phlegm from the back of his throat. The horrid, resonating sound cut through Matthew like nails on a chalk board. Matthew stared at the man with a grimace as he watched the man roll the phlegm around his tongue before projecting it onto the lawn beside him.

Vile peasant! Matthew thought to himself. *Was it really too much to expect a little civility and decorum from people? Surely even the blue-collared workers of the world grasped the concept of dignity? Or had manners simply become a thing of the past?'*

Matthew forced a smile through gritted teeth, as he pictured himself grabbing the man by the scruff of his collar and fiercely beating the life out of him with his bare hands, or maybe removing the Biro from the clipboard and jamming it deep into the man's eyeball with a satisfying squelch. Ridding the world of such vileness seemed like an honourable man's duty to Matthew, but he was also sure that the act would not be greeted with the gratitude that it deserved. It would be frowned upon, police would be called, and Matthew would be right back where he started. This was not a happy thought, and so he took a deep breath instead and tried to suppress his anger.

"Okay, thanks," Matthew finally replied, though the tone of his voice did not convey gratitude at all.

Matthew then peered around the corner of the door to catch sight of a second man, slimmer and taller than the first, but just as scruffy and unkempt. The man was perched upon a small step ladder in front of the house, crowbar in hand while prising away at the wooden boards.

"We also have a window pane to replace..." the short man then told him. " Which one would that be?"

"Bedroom, top floor, back of the house," Matthew replied blandly.

"Right... and how do we get around the back, mate?

Matthew slowly exhaled through gritted teeth. *I'm not your 'mate'!* he thought to himself, his hatred of the man growing by the second.

"Walk around the side of the house, and there's a gate!"

"Right, well we'll give you a knock when we're done then," the man declared. He turned and re-joined his partner with the boards.

Matthew glared around at them with discontent before then closing the door again. He paced back through to the lounge and placed the clipboard down upon the side table before turning to stare out the window at his newly-revealed surroundings. He looked at the houses, the grass and the trees, and then to the clear blue sky and blazing sunshine above him. He suddenly felt exposed and vulnerable to the world and felt his hands starting to shake.

Another enormous crash resonated through the ground as a second board collapsed to the ground, flooding the house with even more blisteringly relentless light. Matthew clenched his fists to try and subdue his growing anxiety, and took a step closer to the lounge windows. Looking down and tilting his head, Matthew read the obscene graffiti upon the two wooden boards that now lay flat upon the grass. 'Pissy-Pants!' 'Freak!' 'Weirdo'.

Matthew looked away with disgust, and it was then that he noticed all the neighbours that were gathering by the roadside for a view. They pointed at him and whispered to each other with snarls, and although Matthew could not hear what they were saying, he knew it could not have been complimentary.

Matthew returned a bitter snarl of his own. He stepped back and furiously wrenching the curtains shut with such force that they almost ripped away. The room quickly became dark again as the sun was banished from sight, and Matthew slowly began to calm himself. His view of the crowd had been far too brief to distinguish any of the faces with any certainty, but by the glimpse of aging grey hairs Matthew was certain they knew who he was, and what had happened to him. *Surely*

SIMON LAW

if they knew, then they would understand my nerves and the need to let me be. Why couldn't they show me a little respect? Instead of just gawking at me like some kind of freak show from the circus?

Matthew took a seat in his father's Chesterfield, closed his eyes, and gently began to rock back and forth, occasionally opening them to glance at the time on the grandfather clock, and hoping that Tammy's return would be soon. Her presence was comforting and reassuring to him and this was something he now felt in urgent need of. The bringing down of the boards should have felt liberating, like the demolition of the Berlin wall, but it didn't. It felt like an invasive violation that exposed him to the world and shone a bright spotlight upon him.

The sound of crashing boards continued all around Matthew and he could ignore the distressing sound no longer. He stood from the armchair and walked over to the CD player that lay next to the TV upon a mahogany cabinet. He opened the doors to the cabinet and grabbed the first CD that his hands brushed upon, quickly sliding it into the CD player and pressing play. Vivaldi's 'Four Seasons' quickly began emanating from the CD player's speakers, successfully blocking out the noise of the workmen's crude actions outside.

As Vivaldi's bright uplifting strings made their way into Matthew's ears he found himself immediately transported back in time to 1987, to the last dinner he had shared with his parents.

"Chicken nuggets and chips with spaghetti letters," he muttered aloud with a nostalgic smile.

Although the sound of the crashing boards had been muffled underneath the sound of the music, the intense burst of sunlight that blazed through from the back of the house could not be ignored. Matthew groaned with discontent before standing once again and making his way through to the kitchen. He reached over and grabbed the kitchen curtain and was ready to wrench it closed when he caught a glimpse of the rear garden for the first time since his return, and paused for a moment to take it in.

He stared out into the green wilderness with nostalgic awe, unable to stop a grin from spreading across his face. His eyes passed over the soaring luscious conifer trees that bordered the left and right of the garden, unable to believe how tall they had grown over the years. His sights then passed over the six-foot wooden fence that bordered the rear of the garden, still standing strong and proud, yet faded and flaked from twenty-five years of sun exposure. He then noticed the old rusted swing in the middle of the garden, now almost hidden beneath the overgrown grasses of the lawn. Memories quickly flooded back to him of his father, pushing him higher and higher on the swing with the hot summer sun upon his face. He remembered his mother delicately caring to the roses and flowers. He remembered home-made ice-lollies and barbecues. He remembered smiles and laughter and the feeling that his idyllic life could never end.

A workman then carried a ladder past the window and the images quickly faded from Matthew's mind. His smile slumped, as he reaffirmed his grip upon the curtains and continued to pull them shut.

Matthew sat back down in his chair, and by the time Vivaldi had reached his climax, the workmen were done. Matthew signed the work sheet, debating again whether or not to impale the scruffy man with the pen, before then sending them on their way again.

Tammy returned to the house as expected a few minutes after that, but to Matthew's disappointment her visit was brief; too brief to share his joy about his debit card arriving, too brief for her to persuade him to open the curtains and let the glorious sunshine into the house, and too brief for Matthew to properly thank her for all her kindness. She offloaded the bags full of groceries along with the requested shopping catalogue and a bag from the photo shop, before then explaining she was late for her midday visit to Mr Carlson, and leaving.

Matthew unpacked the groceries and put the items away in the cupboards and the fridge before then coming across the bag from the photo shop. He took it through to the lounge with excitement. He sat back down upon his father's chair, carefully pulled open the orange plastic envelope and gingerly removed the photograph from within it. His parents' faces beamed at him with joy from the photo, and Matthew smiled back. His mother's pearl necklace glimmered and twinkled in the hot sun while her beautiful white dress hugged her figure delicately. His youthful father, impeccably groomed and dressed in a pristine tailored black suit, held her hand tenderly with the golden wedding band glowing from his finger. Matthew's smile quickly turned mournful, as he reached down and tenderly ran his fingers over the image, wishing that he could somehow turn back the time and bring them back.

Reaching back into the carrier bag, Matthew removed the large glass frame that Tammy had also purchased for him, removing the back piece and mounting the cherished photograph inside. He stood and carried the frame to the mantelpiece where he proudly put it in place before returning to his seat and admiring it for a moment longer. *Life could be so unfair,* he thought as he continued to gaze at the image nostalgically. *What did they ever do to deserve that? Where's the justice? Where's the karma when their killer still roams free?*

Matthew's mournful thoughts then turned hopeful again, as he remembered Tammy's kind gesture. He picked up the shopping catalogue from the coffee table and flicked to the jewellery section in search of the perfect 'thank you' gift for her. He perused through the pages of sparkling rings and the earrings until finally coming to the pages of necklaces, where one in particular caught his attention: an elegant eighteen karat white gold chain interlaced with white shiny pearls. *That's the one!* he thought with a smile, immediately flicking to the back of the book for the order form.

THE DAMAGED

THE BURDEN OF LIBERTY

The Great British weather was world renowned for its dreary prolonged winters and miserable rainy summers, but yet, to the joy of the Olympians and to the great British public, the rain clouds had not been seen over the south of England for over a week now. Tammy was sure that it must have been some kind of record, as she stared from her bedroom window at the blazing morning sun and the azure blue skies.

Her first week caring for Matthew was now drawing to a close and any feelings of anxiety or trepidation she had once felt had completely disappeared, leaving her with a new sense of ease and endearment for him. There were many things that Matthew was still clearly keeping from her; where his aunt was and what exactly had happened to his parents to name a couple, but she figured he was entitled to a few secrets.

Matthew's troubles and her own actually seemed quite similar to Tammy. Their troubles had left them both feeling ostracised and abandoned by the world, socially awkward, lonely and isolated. To feel a close kinship with Matthew was therefore inevitable, as was her desire to help him overcome some of his issues. Her desire to 'fix' him was also a sign of her growing feelings, fuelled by the nurturing void that was left behind when her daughter was taken.

Matthew's big blue eyes and bulging muscles had only added to Tammy's growing attraction to him, and she found herself pondering inappropriately many times. She had caught him checking her out more than a few times now too, and so it was obvious to her that the attraction was mutual. It wasn't the first time that Tammy had been ogled by one of her clients, as Mr Carlson had been inappropriate on many occasions, but Matthew was the first that couldn't be dismissed. He was the first to make her feel good about herself, sexy and confident.

SIMON LAW

Getting involved with a client was unprofessional to say the least, not to mention the morality of it. Tammy knew that if even a rumour of involvement made its way back to Maureen that she would be sacked, and so she was left torn as to what to do. She hadn't had feelings like this for anyone in a long time, and they were strong and hard to ignore.

Arriving on Oak Street that morning, Tammy was pleasantly surprised by the distinct lack of gawking neighbours, as if the novelty of the freak show was now starting to wear off. She was greeted by Matthew's usual joyous smile and big blue eyes, and sat down for a cup of tea with him. They had begun exchanging the usual pleasantries when her attention was drawn to the curtains still firmly shut across each and every window. She frowned at him disappointedly before walking over to the lounge window and pulling them wide open and letting the glorious sunshine spill throughout the house. Matthew scowled and tutted in return before letting out a sigh of resignation.

"Oh come on Matthew, don't be like that!" she told him with a grin. "What was the point of the boards coming down if you're not even gonna open the curtains!"

"Well I didn't want the boards down in the first place really!"

"Come here..." she beckoned, as she stood by the window.

"What for?"

"Just come here," she repeated.

The scowl quickly returned to Matthew's face as he stood and begrudgingly started to edge his way over to the window, his gaze fixed firmly upon Tammy's face and his hands beginning to shake.

"Look!" she told him, gesturing towards the window.

Matthew turned his head towards the window, squinting at first as the light bounced around inside his eyes.

"It's a beautiful day out there, don't you agree?" she asked.

Matthew looked out into the quiet street ahead, up to the peaks of the roof tops to the overlooking trees behind, and then to the clear blue sky above him. He took a quivering breath and took in the views, his anxiety starting to fade and a sensation of calm beginning to flood through him.

"Yeah, it looks nice out there today," he finally replied, turning to her with a little smile.

"It's beautiful; it's not likely to get much better than this."

"No, you're probably right."

Tammy paused for a second, watching Matthew with intrigue, before then posing him a question.

"Would you like to go for a walk?" she asked, raising her eyebrows with anticipation.

THE DAMAGED

"No, it's okay thank you!" he vehemently declined, shaking his head with another scowl.

"Why not?" she asked, undeterred.

"Well, because, I...I just don't want to, that's all," he replied in a flustered stutter, the anxiety of the suggestion starting to kick in again.

"Come on Matthew, you've got to face your fears at some point and you're not likely to get a better day for it," she persisted defiantly.

"Ah yes, but what about my pills? I can't go anywhere after taking them!" he told her, satisfied that he had found a suitable excuse.

"That's okay; you can just take them when we get back. We don't have to be out for long."

"Yeah, but what if I...I..." he blurted.

Matthew quickly ran out of excuses and began to panic. He felt his heart racing and his skin starting to tingle. He closed his eyes and inhaled deeply to try and calm his nerves, and it was at this point that he felt the touch of Tammy's soft skin upon his, as she reached out and gently took hold of his hand.

"It'll be fine Matthew, trust me," she told him reassuringly.

Matthew looked back at her and tried to search his mind for another possible excuse, but he found nothing. He quickly began to realise that she was right, he did have to face his fears at some point, and he would hardly be on the road to recovery if he couldn't even leave his own house. It also occurred to him that if he was ever to gain Tammy's affection and admiration then he needed to do something to show he was a 'real man', as opposed to the cowardly recluse he was in fear of becoming.

Matthew turned back to the window again and stared back out into the distance, focusing in on the leaves and branches of the trees and watching out for any movement.

"What's the weather report for today?" he asked hesitantly.

"Dry and sunny all day," she quickly replied, her voice sounding hopeful of her persuasion.

"No wind?"

"Not much, no. There might be a little breeze I guess, but nothing to write home about. Besides, a little breeze in this hot weather is nice."

"You sure?"

"I'm sure, yes. What's the worst that could happen if there was anyway?" she quizzed.

"The trees could fall and crush us to death!" he told her sternly, his face filled with genuine fear of the possibility.

"And how likely do you think that is to happen?" she asked as she looked him in the eyes.

SIMON LAW

Matthew's own suggestion of the possibility quickly flooded his susceptible mind with memories and images of roaring winds and crashing trees that thumped and echoed through the ground, each vibration fiercer than the last and every one resonating with the fear that the end was nigh. He stared back out at the trees again and tried to subdue the growing fears and images with logic and rationality. He was an intelligent man and knew that the plausibility of such an event occurring was negligible, and therefore to fear it was irrational. He repeated these thoughts over and over through his mind until eventually the images started to fade, and the anxiety retreated back to his subconscious once again.

Matthew gently released the breath that he had been holding and his thoughts turned to the Diazepam tablets inside Tammy's handbag. He could easily pop a few and would feel perfectly fine to go outside, he would feel mellow and calm and the wind wouldn't bother him at all. He opened his mouth to speak and make the suggestion when he stopped again. He was a grown man and shouldn't need a security blanket. Popping pills that completely subdued all anxieties would not be 'facing his fears' at all; it would be nothing more than a cop-out.

"Yes?" Tammy asked with anticipation.

"Where did you want to go?"

"Wherever you like. There's a park just a few streets away, that might be nice today." she replied enthusiastically. "Is that a 'yes' then?"

"Yes, fine," he replied with half a smile.

Matthew rubbed the back of Tammy's hand with his thumb before giving it a little squeeze and releasing it. He then turned away and made his way to the hall where he slipped on his father's shoes and tweed jacket before standing and waiting expectantly.

"You got your house keys?" she asked, as she slipped her handbag over her shoulder.

"Good thinking!" he said with a smile. "I've never needed them before!" he continued, as he stepped past her through to the kitchen.

He returned a few moments later, jingling the keys at her comically.

Tammy opened the front door and the bright sunlight immediately covered them both. Matthew felt the hot sun against his skin and took a step closer to the open doorway, reaching out to take hold of Tammy's soft hand again before then taking his first step onto the garden path. He closed his eyes for a moment and breathed in the fresh summer air, the scent of flowers and freshly mown lawn filling his lungs. A mild breeze then fluttered gently over his skin, sending a tingle down his spine and goose bumps across his arms.

"Alright?" Tammy asked, squeezing his hand reassuringly.

"Yep!" he replied unconvincingly.

THE DAMAGED

Tammy closed the front door shut again and began to lead Matthew slowly down the garden path. He followed sheepishly, his anxiety and anticipation precariously balancing upon the scales with her safe assuring grip preventing them from toppling.

Curious faces quickly turned to watch them, both from the street and from the windows of the houses that surrounded them, but Matthew remained oblivious to them as he focused his concentration straight ahead and continued to walk, his confidence growing with each and every step.

They reached the end of the street, turned into the next and continued walking towards the park. Tammy gave Matthew's hand another squeeze of reassurance before letting go and reaching into her handbag for her cigarettes. She removed one from the packet and sparked it up.

"You shouldn't smoke, you know that?" Matthew told her, trying his best not to look too disgusted with her.

"Yeah, I know," she replied with a shrug as she blew a stream of smoke into the air. "No one's perfect though," she continued, reaching out to take his hand again.

Matthew took her hand again with a smile, resisting the urge to continue his anti-smoking lecture with her.

They continued down the street, passed the houses and the shops until finally reaching the park. Matthew paused at the entrance, pulling Tammy back from walking any further. He looked around, staring nervously at all the people that were gathered around; children threw balls and chased each other while their parents watched on, teenagers laughed and smoked cigarettes with earphone cables dangling from their ears, and various couples strolled casually hand in hand. Matthew suddenly felt extreme panic flooding through him as if everybody was watching him, judging him, laughing at him. He started to feel his heart rate increase, his hands become sweaty and his skin begin to tingle. He quickly became dizzy and short of breath, as his head started to spin and his throat seemed to swell.

The sound of the crowd echoed and circled around him in a muffled incomprehensible cyclone of noise. He closed his eyes tightly shut and cupped his hands over his face, desperately trying to settle the crashing waves of disorientation that sloshed from side to side within his brain. He felt his knees become weak and unsteady, and just as he felt the horrid sensations start to peak he suddenly heard Tammy's sweet voice piercing through the cacophony.

"You're okay, Matthew. Just try to relax," she told him as she noticed him starting to freak out. "Try taking a deep breath, hold it in and count to ten," she continued. "Then breathe out and count to fifteen."

SIMON LAW

Matthew nodded and obeyed her instructions, slowly breathing in, and then out. He repeated the actions again and slowly the sensations that had consumed him started to subside again. A cold flooding sensation then slowly passed through him, followed by calm and complete exhaustion. He looked around at the crowd with a frown and then turned to Tammy.

"You alright now?" she asked him.

Matthew hesitated, confused and lost for words.

"Matthew?"

"What the hell was that?" he whispered to her breathlessly.

"Looked like a panic attack to me, you not had one before?"

"No, well, not like that anyway. That was horrible."

"They're not nice, I know. I have them all the time."

Matthew turned back to the crowd again and took a deep inhale of fresh air. He looked out at the sea of happy faces around him and was shocked at the complete lack of attention he had aroused.

"Do you want to go back home?" Tammy asked.

"No, it's okay, Tammy. I'm fine now," he replied, turning to her with a smile.

"Come on then!" she told him as she started to walk on, her hand still firmly grasping onto his and a reassuring smile upon her face.

They walked further into the park, past the initial crowd of people and through into an area of picnic tables and benches. Tammy sat herself down upon one of the benches and Matthew sat down beside her. She released his hand briefly to check her phone for messages while Matthew continued to stare out at his surroundings. He looked out at the different shades of greens and browns in the trees and plants around him, the deep blue of the sky above and the speckles of bright colours of the distant flowers. It had been a very long time since Matthew had been able to appreciate the beauty that now surrounded him, and it was almost like he was now experiencing it for the first time. He felt calm and peaceful and happy, and even more so for the fact that Tammy was there with him too.

It was during this period of calm and tranquillity that Matthew was startled by a large bird that swooped past his head at tremendous speed, its wings so close that he could feel the back draught of air against his skin. He followed the bird with his eyes as it then soared back up into the sky above, its silky black plumes glimmering underneath the sun. He continued to gaze upon it as it glided effortlessly through the sky, gracious and majestic, before then swooping to the ground once more and disappearing off towards the horizon.

It was at this point that Matthew noticed a man in the distance, approaching from where the bird had vanished, the sun blazing from behind him and blurring his figure to a murky silhouette. Matthew watched as the man got closer and could start to make out his features more. It was an old man with scruffy greying hair, and a dog that led enthusiastically ahead. Matthew raised his hand to his brow to shield the blazing sunshine from his eyes and continued to watch as the man walked closer and closer to them. Matthew could now start to make out the scruffy ripped clothes that the man wore, the woolly gloves upon his hands and the hair and dirt that covered his face. It was a tramp, and it was this sudden realisation that caused Matthew's anxieties to flare once again.

Tammy looked up from her phone and caught sight of the man too, but instead of sharing Matthew's fear, she smiled at him instead.

"James!" she called out as she started to wave at him.

Matthew turned to her with a look of disgust, as if acknowledging the man's existence would somehow infect them both with his putrid stench.

"I'm just going to say hello to my friend," she told him, as she rubbed his knee and stood, completely obviously to Matthew's revolted expression.

"*Friend*? How on earth could she call that *thing* a friend?" he muttered to himself as his anxieties slowly turned to anger and rage, as he watched her walking over to him. He studied the man's dirty face and although not similar, he immediately saw the face of his parents' killer in his mind.

"Hey James, how are you today?" she asked with a friendly smile.

"I'm very good, thank you my dear. It's another beautiful day today."

"And how's Bronco today?" she asked as she bent down to pat the dog upon the head. "New collar?" she continued, noticing the new black leathered studded collar around his neck.

"Yes, Bronco and I found it in the bins outside the back of the pet shop. It looked perfectly good to me."

"Looks very fetching!" she told them both.

Matthew looked on at the conversation with daggers growing in each eye. The man was so close now that Matthew could start to smell the putrid stench that emanated from him, and could feel his stomach starting to churn. His hands quickly began to shake with a mixture of anxiety and adrenaline and so he clenched them together tightly, his biceps bulging to bursting point.

Matthew's eyes quickly fixated upon the tramp's beard-covered throat, as his mind became ablaze with contemplations. *You stay the hell away from me!* Matthew growled inside his mind. *One step closer and I'm getting my keys from my pocket, grabbing a firm hold of the jagged Yale key, and jamming it deep into your Adam's apple. I'll twist it around, wrenching it back and forth until you drown in your own blood! Don't you tempt me!*

"Come and say hello to my friend," Tammy said to James and started to lead him over.

Matthew watched them approach, gritting his teeth so hard that his jaw muscles tensed and began to pulsate. He looked away and took a deep breath, hoping that when he looked back the man would be gone, but he wasn't.

"Matthew, this is my friend James," she told him before noticing the angry grimace upon his face.

"Nice to meet you, Sir," James told him, offering out his gloved hand to him.

"Get your filthy hand away from me! You revolting peasant!" Matthew raged at him as he leapt up from the wooden bench, pumping out his chest and tensing his biceps. "You vermin make me sick!" he continued to rage, before turning his back and walking away.

Bronco immediately leapt up from the ground and burst into a tirade of vicious barks and growls as if he had understood every word that Matthew had said.

Tammy watched in horror as Matthew walked into the distance, dumbfounded and lost for words, before then turning to James with an apologetic frown upon her face.

"Well, he's not very friendly, is he!" James told her with a bemused grin, seemingly unaffected by Matthew outburst. He reached down to Bronco and affectionately scratched him behind the ear. "Shhh, it's okay boy," he told him.

"I...I..." Tammy began, unable to find the words to express her remorse.

"It's alright, my dear, I'm used to that kind of reaction to be honest," he told her with a smile and a shrug. "Can't let silly things like that get to me!"

"I'm really sorry James, I didn't know he would react like that!" she explained with exasperation.

Matthew paced furiously through the park, enraged and charged with adrenaline. He quickly reached the entrance and paused to catch his breath, turning back to face the crowd and watching as Tammy appeared in the distance. He immediately regretted exposing his bad side to her, knowing that it would almost certainly affect her opinion of him, but felt no remorse at all for his treatment of James. In his mind, the world didn't need people like 'him'; they were an embarrassment and a blight on the community. Had it not been for vermin like him roaming the streets, his parents would still be alive today, and had

THE DAMAGED

Tammy not been there, his actions towards the tramp would have been far worse.

Matthew watched as Tammy started to catch up, trying to think of an apology that would not be insincere, but he couldn't. He studied her face as she got closer, trying to analyse her expression. She smiled at him empathetically, looking confused and somewhat guilty with herself. *Maybe an apology wasn't even necessary,* he thought. *After all, it was her that dragged me outside in the first place!*

As Tammy slowly made her way through the crowds, Matthew noticed two teenage boys, pointing and jeering at her from where they lay upon the fields. He watched as Tammy scowled at them and continued walking, increasing her speed to avoid interaction. He continued to watch as the two boys then leapt to their feet and began to follow her, continuing to jeer and call out to her provocatively. One of the boys then reached forward and pinched Tammy's bottom, laughing and high-fiving the other with glee.

With adrenaline and anger still pulsating through his body, Matthew could stand back and watch the harassment no longer. He charged forwards, grabbed the boy by the scruff of his black hoodie, and ploughed his clenched fist across the bridge of the boy's nose, visualising the face of school bully Jason Selby as he then took another thump. A squelching crunch resonated in the air as the boy then plummeted to the ground below, clutching at his face, writhing in agony, and wondering what the hell had happened to him. Matthew glared down at the boy with a scowl and then to the crimson blood splatters across his knuckles. The outburst felt exhilarating and calming at the same time, and Matthew liked it. He turned to look at the second boy, crouching down to help his wounded friend, and stared at him menacingly.

"Look, we're sorry...Please..." the boy blubbered, as he helped his friend back to his feet and scurried off back into the crowd.

"Come on, Matthew, let's go!" Tammy told him with a sense of urgency to her voice, grabbing his bloodied hand and dragging him away. "You can't just hit people like that, you'll get arrested!" she yelled damningly, looking over her shoulder to check that they weren't being followed.

They hurried away from the park and down the street towards the house, eyes straight ahead and not saying a word to each other. She looked around to him curiously, analysing his expression and secretly feeling a little chuffed. The boys had been a nuisance to her for weeks now and the fact that Matthew felt obliged to protect her from them was a warming feeling. Despite this feeling, she hoped that this would not be a sign of things to come, remembering the words 'violent outbursts' in Matthew's medical report.

They reached the house again and sat themselves down in the lounge, still nervously avoiding eye contact and struggling for a way to break the awkward silence.

Matthew looked down at his hands, seemingly fascinated by the blood splatters across his knuckles. He watched with interest as the dry blood began to flake away from his skin like dust. Inside, he felt completely exhilarated by the experience, so much so that he almost forgot the anger of his encounter with James just moments prior. He wondered to himself whether the feeling was normal, whether 'normal' people also felt such elation over inflicting pain on another. He soon decided that this was probably not something he should admit to, that it may ring certain 'alarm bells' and get him sent straight back to the hospital again, and so tried his best to hide the smile that was forcing itself upon his face.

Tammy stood from the sofa a few moments later, gave Matthew a brief smile, and made her way through to the kitchen. She returned a few moments later with Matthew's two blue 'sugar' pills and a glass of water. She placed them down upon the little side table, sat herself down, and looked across at him in contemplation.

"Do you wanna talk about it?" she asked, finally breaking the awkward silence.

"...About the kid? Don't you think he deserved it?" Matthew replied defensively, unsure why she would protest.

"Well, I guess that's debatable really," she told him, trying hard to resist the urge to gratify him for it. "...I meant with James?"

"Oh, I see," he answered, the very mention of the tramp causing his growing smile to immediately subside and slump. Remnants of the elated feeling were quickly replaced with images of the disgusting tramp again, and the rancid smell that he emanated. Feelings of anger and anxiety began to rise, bringing memories of the cold musty damp of the cellar, the icy wind which had whistled against his skin, and the sight of his parents' blood-soaked corpses that lay lifeless upon the kitchen's lino floor.

"Is it my fault? Should I have not dragged you out?" Tammy asked with a frown, a mixture of confusion and guilt upon her face.

"No, it was good to get out. I'm grateful," he told her, trying to shake off the unwelcoming images that were now flooding his mind.

"So what was it then?" she persisted.

"He's just a tramp, what does it matter?" Matthew replied bitterly.

"Because he's still a person, he still deserves respect!" Tammy snapped back abruptly.

THE DAMAGED

"Respect? What for? What's he done to deserve my respect? These people are homeless for a reason you know, they're all druggies, or alkies, or gamblers! They all deserve to be homeless!" Matthew spurted with conviction, confused to why Tammy didn't share his views.

"Well that's not true at all!" Tammy quickly defended, "James is none of those things. He became homeless when his wife divorced him!"

"...and why did she divorce him? Did he cheat on her? Was he abusive?"

"I don't know," she replied hesitantly.

"See!"

"Okay, well what about Mr Carlson, who I care for? He became homeless in the eighties when all the coal mines closed. That wasn't his fault, was it?"

Matthew scowled, exasperated with the conversation but unable to answer. He breathed out heavily and shook his head.

"I just don't like tramps, they disgust me!" he finally told her frustratedly.

"Well I think that's a bit ignorant, Matthew. What have they ever done to you?"

Matthew scowled at her again, trying not to let the insult anger him. He looked down to the floor and took a deep breath, the ghastly images of his murdered parents still circulating through his mind with anger and sadness. He remembered their desperate dying faces, the last breath that expelled from their lungs, and the empty loneliness that then filled him up.

He looked back up at Tammy with a half-mast smile of resignation, as a single tear then emerged from one eye, trickling down his cheek and leaping from his jaw to the floor below him. Tammy looked over at the growing sadness upon his face and the expression soon spread to her own as she realised she had touched a nerve.

"My..." Matthew began before stopping to swallow the lump in his throat. "...My parents were murdered by a tramp," he told her solemnly, his eyes then reverting back to the ground again.

Tammy was left stunned and silenced in an instant. The comment had immediately justified his unrepentant opinion and left her overflowing with feelings of guilt and churlish misjudgement. She looked to the floor herself, ashamed of her interrogation and wishing again that she had thought before speaking.

"...He forced his way into the house during the storm, and he stabbed them both to death." Matthew continued, wiping away the track of his solitary tear.

SIMON LAW

"I... I'm sorry, Matthew," Tammy finally replied, struggling for the right words.

"I watched the whole thing from the cellar stairs, peering through the gaps in the slats. I was paralysed with fear during the whole thing. I couldn't move. I couldn't stop it."

"Did they ever catch him?" she asked hesitantly.

"No, they never did. I gave them a description and everything, but no, they never found him."

"I'm sorry Matthew," she repeated again, unable to find anything else appropriate to say to him.

"Yeah, me too," he replied, looking over at the wedding photo that sat proudly on the mantelpiece. "They were good people, my parents. I miss them," he continued, fighting back another tear.

Lost for words, Tammy wanted to maintain her position by explaining that not all homeless people were the same, that they were all individuals like the rest of society, but she stopped herself. She looked over at the melancholic exhaustion upon Matthew's face and sighed quietly. She knew that her argument was not going to help the situation now, and any continued attempt to reinstate Matthew's faith in people would only exacerbate his feelings further.

Matthew peered down at the side table and to the two blue pills that awaited him. He picked them up and stared at them in the palm of his hand, wishing that on this occasion they actually did contain the doctor's potent concoction that would save him from the growing sadness consuming him. He threw them to the back of his throat and swallowed them with the water, knowing that this would be Tammy's cue to leave, and that the conversation would be over. She watched on as he swallowed the pills and nodded as if to acknowledge his unspoken request. She leant towards him with a look of empathy and placed her hand tenderly upon his knee. He placed his hand on top of hers forgivingly, and smiled.

"I'll be off then Matthew," she told him.

"Yeah, okay then Darling," he replied, squeezing her hand and beginning to act out the effects of the pills. "I'll see you at five."

She smiled and stood, watching as Matthew appeared to act distant and foggy-headed, slumping deep into his father's red leather Chesterfield and staring aimlessly at the walls in front of him. He clasped his hands together, closed his eyes and listened to the gentle rhythmic ticking of the grandfather clock until the sound of the closing front door sounded from behind him. He continued to listen, rocking gently and reassuringly in the chair until the sound of Tammy's footsteps slowly faded away into the distance.

THE DAMAGED

Matthew remained quiet and solemn, listening to the clock and rocking gently for a while longer as he pushed away the horrid images in his mind and tried to replace them with happier ones. He pictured his parents' happy faces, laughing and joking, pushing him on the swings and playing in the park. He remembered the welcoming sound of his father's Capri as it pulled up on the drive each day. He remembered his mother's beautiful curly brown hair and the smell of her perfume as she reached around to hug him.

The feeling of emptiness then locked Matthew in its clutches, rumbling in his gut like the hunger of a starving man. Pulling himself lethargically to his feet, Matthew slowly made his way up to his bedroom and removed a black rucksack from underneath his bed. He unzipped the top of the bag, gently removed a tattered black sketchbook from within it, and sat down with it upon the bed.

Opening up the book, Matthew looked down at a series of charcoal sketches that he had done during his time at the hospital, each one depicting the same image of his parents' killer derived from his fleeting memory. He gazed deep into the images, fighting to maintain composure as he studied the features of the vile face before him. From his depictions, and from the remnants of his memory, Matthew estimated the man to have been late thirties, early forties at the time, and so would now be in his mid-sixties. Continuing to stare at the picture, Matthew visualised how the passing of twenty-five years would have changed his appearance, adding wrinkles and grey hairs before then scorching the newly-imagined face deep into his mind so that he would never forget it again. *I'm going to find you!* he thought, *and when I do, you're going to pay for what you've done to me!*

MUMMY'S LITTLE GIRL

Tammy awoke Saturday morning to the gentle sound of birdsong from outside her bedroom window. Pulling herself to a sitting position, Tammy groaned and reached for her cigarettes. Her nightmares had visited her again that night and the blood-stained sheets of her bed were evident of her 3am rush for the trusted razorblades.

Saturday's schedule was much the same for Tammy as the rest of the week, but with one main addition: today she got to see her beautiful daughter at the contact centre. The thought of seeing Jessica after a long week apart should have filled her with excitement and joy but instead it filled her with fear and anxiety, like it did every week.

Rising to her feet, Tammy drew the bedroom curtains and stared out at the glorious morning sun to try to calm her nerves. She looked down at the streets below and gazed aimlessly as the morning dog walkers strolled to the shops for the morning papers, her mind firmly fixated upon Jessica. She imagined Jessica getting dressed and ready for the day, then Keith and his mother taking her to play in the park, or taking her down to the pond to feed the ducks, wishing longingly that it was her instead.

Tammy hadn't taken a single day's holiday since Jessica had been taken away; with nobody to share it with, it just seemed too bleak and depressing. Had things been different then she would have gladly booked off the whole summer for the sake of quality time with her. She would have taken her on picnics, or to the fairground, or to the zoo; wherever she wanted to go, just to make her happy and to see her innocent little smile again.

Tammy sighed and walked over to her wardrobe. She nervously sifted through her clothes for something smart to wear for the day, not for Jessica's benefit, but for the benefit of the supervisor who would sit

THE DAMAGED

watching her from the corner of the room, scribbling notes on her little clipboard and reporting back to the judge on her progress. She chose herself a smart purple blouse and a black knee-length skirt from the wardrobe and took them to the bathroom to dress. Slurping on a strong black coffee and forcing another fruit yoghurt into her aching stomach, she sat down with the bus timetable and planned the best route to get to the centre for 10am.

Upon Tammy's arrival on Oak Street, Matthew could tell straight away that she was distracted. She paid no attention to his warm smile or big blues eyes and made little effort to engage him in conversation. She had declined a cup of tea and made her way straight to the kitchen for his morning pills. Matthew looked at her curiously, wondering if she was still upset about their encounter with James the day before, or if he had done something else to upset her. He noticed the smart blouse and the look of anxiety upon her face and decided not to quiz her. He remembered her conversation with him about her troubles and quickly realised that her strange mood was unlikely to relate to him. Instead, Matthew kept quiet and maintained his smile. After taking his little blue pills as requested, he put on his usual drowsy performance and watched her leave from the lounge window, silently wishing her good luck in whatever it was that she was doing.

Arriving at the centre with ten minutes to spare, Tammy nervously drained two cigarettes on the trot, her hands starting to shake with anticipation. She threw some chewing gum into her mouth to mask the smell, took a long deep breath, and stepped into the building through the glass double doors.

"Hi, I'm here to see my daughter at ten," she told the receptionist, trying to force a smile upon her face.

The woman smiled back at her and looked across to her computer screen.

"Name?"

"Tammy Atkins."

"Okay Tammy, you're in room B this morning, down the corridor on the left."

"Thank you."

Tammy turned and walked down the cold sterile corridor ahead of her, pinching her nails fiercely into the flesh of her thigh as she went. She reached the room and opened the door.

The room was brightly painted in various shades of prime colours, with a big comfy sofa in the middle of the room and boxes of various toys around it. In the corner of the room sat a small wooden desk with a single chair and a telephone. At first glance the room may have seemed friendly and happy, but to Tammy it just seemed faked. It was like a movie set where each item was nothing more than a prop, specifically designed and selected to give an illusion. In reality, it wasn't a friendly room at all. It was a room for broken families, for druggies and alkies like her. It was a room for abusive husbands and love cheats and for sexual predators who couldn't be trusted alone with children. It was a horrible room. Horrid or not, Tammy knew that this was the way it had to be, for now. It was either this horrid 'pretend' room with video cameras and security systems, or nothing at all.

She placed her bag on the floor and sat herself down upon the sofa, interlocking her fingers and anxiously twiddling her thumbs. The door opened again a few moments later and a woman entered the room. She was dressed in a cheap grey suit with a white blouse and held the despised black clipboard loosely in one hand. She looked at Tammy through her square, green-tinted glasses and offered her a staged smile.

"Hello, Miss Atkins, I'm Alice, I'll be your supervisor today," she told Tammy in a dubiously pleasant tone, offering out her hand.

"Hi," Tammy replied, standing from the sofa and shaking her hand.

"You've been here before I understand?" the woman asked.

"Yeah, I come every week," Tammy replied, slightly annoyed by the stupid question.

"Good, then I'll assume you're au fait with all the rules," Alice replied with a mild smugness to her voice.

Alice took a seat at the desk, unclipping a pen from the top of the clipboard and beginning to fill out the start of the form. Tammy let out a nervous breath as discreetly as she could, before returning to her sitting position, interlocking her fingers again and returning to her anxious twiddling.

A few minutes then passed, and just as Tammy was starting to get restless and impatient, the phone upon the desk began to ring. Alice answered it and replied to a voice in a series of affirmative hums, before replacing the receiver and standing from the chair.

"Okay, Jessica's just arrived, Miss Atkins, so if you can please wait here, we'll be back shortly."

Tammy nodded and smiled in return, the smile being genuine this time at the excitement of seeing her daughter. Alice left the room and Tammy started nervously straightening out her blouse and skirt, and checking the smell of her breath. She stood in anticipation, anxiously shifting her body weight from one foot to the next and staring intently at the handle of the door, waiting for it to turn.

A few more minutes passed, then after what seemed like a lifetime to Tammy, the door handle finally started to turn. The door opened and Alice stepped back into the room, Jessica nervously holding her hand and staring sheepishly at the floor below. Her long golden blonde hair and soft pale skin seemed to glimmer in the light from the window that illuminated her like an angel. Jessica was dressed in a canary-yellow pleated skirt and a pink strappy top, and in her spare hand she clung tightly onto a brown fluffy teddy bear.

"Hey Jessica!" Tammy called across to her in a welcoming happy tone, as she bent down on her knees and opened out her arms to her.

Jessica slowly shifted her eyes from their gaze upon the floor and looked over to her mother timidly. She looked at her mother's smile, her open arms, and quickly looked away again, squeezing Alice's hand tightly.

The look of rejection was heart-breaking to Tammy, but she refused to let it show. The estrangement between them was her own fault and not Jessica's, and any expression of upset upon her own face would only hurt her daughter further, even though it was killing her inside.

Alice squeezed the girl's hand in return before bending down to her level and whispering gently in her ear.

"It's okay Jessica, say hello to your mummy," she told the girl reassuringly.

Jessica frowned discontentedly, before then gingerly shifting her eyes back up again.

"Come on sweetie, it's only me!" Tammy told her, maintaining her smile and open arms to her.

Jessica slowly eased her grip on Alice's hand before tightly wrapping both hands across the teddy. She returned her gaze to the ground and began nervously shuffling towards Tammy, gently chewing upon her bottom lip as she went.

Tammy wrapped her arms around the girl tenderly, kissing her cheek and feeling her soft skin upon her own.

"How you been? You alright?" Tammy asked, releasing the girl from her grip.

Jessica nodded solemnly in return, her eyes still fixed upon the ground. Tammy took another deep breath and released it gently, using all her might to withhold the tears that she could feel brewing inside. Alice looked down at them both curiously, before returning to the desk and continuing to scribble notes. *What the hell are you writing? You judgemental little bitch!* Tammy thought to herself, before quickly turning back to her daughter again.

"Have you been enjoying the summer holidays then sweetie?" she asked.

Jessica nodded in return, still yet to open her mouth.

"...Yeah? And what have you been up to?" Tammy continued.

Jessica shrugged her shoulders, still clinging tightly to the teddy bear.

"You don't know?" Tammy asked in a playfully disbelieving tone. "Well, have you been down to the duck pond? To feed the ducks?" she continued.

Jessica nodded.

"Yeah? And what sound do ducks make? Huh? Do they go quack-quack?!" Tammy continued jokingly, making the sound of a duck in an awkward attempt to try and connect with the girl.

Jessica nodded solemnly again, still yet to speak or even break a smile. She looked up from the floor and peered around to Alice in the corner, as if to check she was still there, and that she was still safe.

Tammy frowned, confused as to why Jessica was acting so distant and frightened. She knew it would be a long road to fully rebuilding her bridges with Jessica, but she seemed to be more despondent than ever.

"Jessica? What's wrong sweetie?" Tammy asked, reaching out to hold the girl. "Has daddy been saying bad things about me?"

Alice cleared her throat loudly in the background, looking over at Tammy with a piercing stare.

"Jessica?" Tammy persisted, ignoring Alice's clear warning. "Tell me what he's been saying to you..."

"Tammy!" Alice interrupted sternly.

"What?!" Tammy replied sharply, turning to her to return the angry stare. "He's clearly been badmouthing me to her again, hasn't he? It's obvious!" she continued furiously.

Alice stood from the chair and started to make her way over to them. It was at this point that Tammy could hear her daughter starting to weep.

"I want to go! I want my daddy!" the girl cried out, finally breaking her silence.

"It's alright Jessica, I'll take you to your daddy now," Alice replied delicately, taking the girl's hand and leading her towards the door.

"Mummy loves you Jessica!" Tammy called out desperately as she stood, panting with exasperation. The door then slammed shut and Tammy was alone again.

"For fuck sake!" Tammy screamed in frustration before bursting into tears. She slapped her face with both hands and began pacing up and down the room, crying into her palms and immediately regretting her behaviour.

"Stupid, stupid, stupid!" she muttered to herself between weeps of tears.

Tammy then walked to the window and peered around for a view of the main entrance, watching with daggers in her eyes as Keith led their daughter back towards the car.

THE DAMAGED

"You bastard!" she growled.

Tammy burst out of the room and paced furiously down the corridor, barging past Alice on the way and almost sending her flying. She ran out into the street just in time to catch sight of Keith's car disappearing into the distance. She stared out; gritting her teeth as her heart rate began to soar, thumping away in her chest like a drum.

"Tammy, you need to come back so we can talk," Alice called from behind her.

Tammy turned and aimed a piercing scowl back at her, visualising herself breaking those stupid green glasses upon her face, before taking off down the street, placing her headphones into her ears and blasting her music up to full volume.

Tammy dashed frantically through the streets, desperately trying to keep hold of her composure. She passed a line of council offices, library and town hall, and reached a small metal-walled public toilet where she darted into one of the cubicles. The sound of sparking electricity crackled and hissed from the florescent tube above her as it flickered and strobed erratically. The pulsating light flashed ghastly images of filthy faecal-covered walls and pools of urine that streamed past her on the floor, but Tammy was too consumed to notice.

Sitting down upon one of the grimy toilet seats with her head in her hands, Tammy shook from head to toe, her drumming heart lodged in her throat. An intrusion of cockroaches sailed casually into her cubical upon the river of foul reeking urine, before creeping and scurrying around by her feet, but again, Tammy was oblivious, her thoughts too sternly fixated upon Jessica amidst fears that her daughter would never love her again.

Tammy bit into her bottom lip to subside the quivering and slowly removed her shaking hands from her face. Her eyes still closed, she could sense the flashing light through the thin skin of her eyelids. Streams of tears forced their way to freedom from within her fastened eyes and ran down her skin, leaping into the puddles of urine below. The pungent stench of rancid faeces then finally penetrated through her mental block, invading her nose and her throat and causing her to start to heave. Repulsed, she opened her eyes to her revolting surrounding and her hopeless mental state of despair was then joined by disgust. She heaved and convulsed, jerking forward violently, but her aching stomach had nothing to expel. She continued to heave, tears streaming down her face and barely able to breath, until finally gushing bile onto the floor below.

Tammy panted for air, but every inhale was tainted in the rancid stench of the room. She reached to her handbag and removed a tissue, quickly thrusting it against her face in an attempt to somehow filter the offending stench from her senses. Biting deeper into her lip, she hoped the pain would help her to regain control of herself, but it didn't.

She turned her eyes back to her handbag, and holding the tissue to her face with one hand, Tammy started rummaging, desperate to try and find a handy razorblade. She rummaged through notebooks and lipsticks, cigarettes and sleeping pills, but found nothing. She pushed aside her rubber gloves, mobile phone, some loose change and a lighter, before then finally setting her eyes upon her goal.

Releasing a careful sigh of relief, Tammy let go of the tissue for use of both hands and slid out a blade from its plastic container. Looking down at the blade she then scowled in frustration, seeing that it was blunt and rusted up with a dark orange crust around the edge. She threw the blade to the floor and immediately slid out the next blade, the last one, merely to find it in the same state as the previous. She exhaled in an exasperated groan as she threw down the plastic box and returned her scowling eyes back to the last remaining blade.

Swallowing the awkward lump in her throat, Tammy reached down and hesitantly pulled her skirt up to her waist, before rolling her tights down to her knees and gently pushing the white blood-stained bandage to one side. She ran her shaking fingertips along the collection of wounds and gently placed the orange-crusted blade at the very end of them.

Taking another look at the crumbling orange edge of the blade, she paused, her trembling hand unable to keep the razor still. She gritted her teeth and looked away in self loathing, gripping the blade firmer, pushing it hard against the flesh of her thigh, and slashing the ragged edge against herself.

Tammy cried out in whimpering agony, immediately dropping the blade and returning her eyes to her thigh. She watched as the wound gaped open and gushed with blood, the jagged ridges of the wound infested with the orange crumbling rust of the corroded blade.

She quickly grabbed another tissue from her bag and plunged it deep into the gushing wound in an attempt to wipe away the infective rust, but it merely pushed it deeper into the gash, leaving behind small segments of paper in the wound too.

The infliction hurt in a way it never had before, it stung and pulsated and immediately started to itch, and Tammy regretted her actions straight away. She breathed deeply and could feel her heart begin to slow, leaving her calmer and composed, but completely repulsed with herself for what she had resorted to.

The florescent light above Tammy's head then fizzed and flickered for the last time, as it finally short circuited and plunged the putrid room into darkness. Tammy closed her eyes again, completely

THE DAMAGED

exhausted by her emotions and her frantic actions. She put her head back into her hands and listened to the sounds of the scurrying cockroaches around her, paddling in the growing pool of blood below as the gaping wound continued to dribble and drip from her thigh.

SIMON LAW

VII

THE OEDIPUS COMPLEX

Matthew watched as Tammy boarded the bus in her smart purple blouse, curiously contemplating her possible destination. Barely ten minutes had passed since her arrival that morning, making it her briefest visit to date. The anxiety and preoccupation upon her face made it clear that her destination was important and worrisome, almost certainly involving the courts or her daughter. Tammy had been the most genuine and caring person that Matthew had met in a long time, and despite her past mistakes he was certain she must have made a good mother too, and somewhat undeserving of her harsh situation. He wished that he could somehow shield her from any further heartbreak, to wrap her up tightly in bubble wrap and protect her from the horrors of the world; after all, wasn't that the duty of a loved one to do? But while he wished that this was a plausible task, he knew that there were far too many horrors in the world to hide from. *The horrors find you,* he thought. *Wherever you go, wherever you try to hide; even in a padded cell, secluded and isolated from the world outside, the horrors still find a way to infiltrate, to gently seep inside your mind to haunt you.*

Matthew sat himself down upon his father's Chesterfield and reached over for Tammy's untouched cup of tea. He took a slurp and looked up at his parents' wedding photo again, smiling with nostalgia and awe at their unblemished happiness. He wondered to himself whether Tammy and *he* could ever be as happy as them – if he were ever to confess his feelings, that was. He wondered if they would ever live together, get married and have a child. He wondered if true happiness could ever come to him at all, or whether the concept was nothing more than a mere fairy tale. He would certainly treat her like a princess, that much was for sure.

Matthew smiled at the thought of their potential relationship for a while longer, drinking the rest of Tammy's tea and listening to the soothing ticking of the old grandfather clock in the background.

"What do you think of her, Mother? Do you like her?" Matthew asked, gazing up at his mother's gleaming smile expectantly. "She's nice. I like her," he continued.

He looked up at his mother for a while longer with bitter-sweet sadness in his eyes, remembering the smell of her floral perfume, the touch of her skin and the comfort of her loving embrace. He closed his eyes and pictured the image in his head with a smile, but before he realised where his train of thought was heading he quickly found himself picturing his mother naked, and began lusting over the curves of her body. The image was arousing to him, evident by the engorged throbbing within the tightness of his underwear.

Matthew opened his eyes abruptly and frowned, confused as to where the twisted thoughts had come from, and disgusted with himself for having them. He shook his head and squeezed the bridge of his nose, trying to shake the creepy feeling and quickly banishing the sordid image to the back of his mind.

When the last dregs of the tea were gone, Matthew stood and took the empty mug to the sink, before commencing with his daily household routines. He started by loading his laundry into the washing machine and then carefully combing the house with the vacuum cleaner. When that was done he meticulously polished all the furniture and then began his ironing, and it was at this point that a knocking came upon the door.

He answered the door to find a young man in a parcel force uniform, two large boxes beside him and a smaller one on top, all bearing the logo of the catalogue company. The man was refreshingly well-groomed and smart, and wore his uniform with pride. He offered Matthew a pleasant smile and Matthew smiled back, pleased to finally meet someone with pride in themselves and in what they did. The man offered Matthew a sheet to sign, then went on his way again.

Matthew stood at the doorstep of the house looking out into the street, and to another day of glorious bright sunshine. He was almost certain that the neighbours were watching him: peering sneakily from behind the net curtains of their lounges, but Matthew didn't care. He breathed in the sweet summer breeze and stretched out the muscles in his neck before then turning his eyes down to the array of brown cardboard boxes that awaited him.

SIMON LAW

After carefully hauling each of the boxes inside the house, Matthew ripped them open in eager anticipation, showering the clean carpet in flakes of card and balls of polystyrene in the process. He laid out his shiny new television on the floor and without hesitation began excitedly ripping out the cords from the back of his old and decrepit set. He then lugged the cumbersome old box to the back door and lifted his smooth lightweight television upon the old stand, eagerly plunging all the cords instinctively into the right holes and switching it on.

The television gently faded from black to blue with a gentle friendly hum and automatically entered into set up mode, quickly scanning through the channels with a brief fleeting glimpse of each one. Matthew inserted the enclosed batteries into the new remote control and eagerly ran his fingers over all the smooth rubbery buttons, smiling with excitement and anticipation. The television quickly finished tuning itself and after displaying a quick 'Set up Complete' message, reverted to 'BBC One' just as the lunchtime news started playing. The first news item was a report of a house fire in the next town over where a family had been burnt alive. Matthew focused in with morbid curiosity, wondering if they were going to show the charred corpses of the family members being removed from the house, but they didn't.

Turning his eyes back down to the remote again, Matthew pressed upon the friendly blue 'TV Guide' button in the middle. The screen immediately filled with a vast array of different channels, and Matthew quickly scrolled through them all. He scrolled past the entertainment, home and news channels, heading straight for the kid's cartoons. The screen filled with an explosion of bright colours and friendly voices which instantly made Matthew feel calm. Contented and happy, he smiled with mesmerized glee, releasing a long and satisfying exhale.

With the cartoons playing reassuringly in the background, Matthew then proceeded to open the rest of his packages; a new vacuum to replace his tired old machine, and the glimmering pearl necklace for Tammy. He gently held the necklace up with both hands, admiring it as the array of freshwater pearls and white golden links glistened and twinkled in the sunlight. *They look beautiful,* he thought to himself with a smile – *just like Tammy is*. Matthew hoped that she would like them too, and that his gesture would make his gratitude and his feelings clear to her. He carefully laid them back into their velvet-cushioned box and placed it down underneath the coffee table, ready to present to her upon her return.

Matthew plugged in his new vacuum cleaner and began meticulously re-cleaning the house again, bagging up the empty boxes in black bin liners and dumping the old vacuum next to the back door. *Tidy house-*

THE DAMAGED

Tidy mind! he thought to himself, remembering his mother once saying the same words to him as a child.

After the cleaning session, Matthew turned to inspect the garden. The unsightly overgrowth was a clear blemish upon him, and almost made the pristine state of the house pointless. He was sure that if he continued to ignore it that people would look poorly upon him, Tammy in particular, who he desperately wanted to impress. He looked up and down at the soaring conifers on either side of the garden and quickly assured himself that the garden was secluded, private, and completely out of view from any of the neighbours' prying eyes. He then remembered his father's old petrol-powered mower and decided that the task at hand was far from beyond him, even if it did involve descending down into the depths of the dank and dusty cellar to retrieve the mower. After all, the cellar was just a room, nothing for a grown man to be afraid of.

Matthew turned to the cellar door and tentatively reached out for the handle, pulling it open and staring down into the black abyss with uneasy trepidation. He began his descent on the staircase, spiralling and twisting underneath the kitchen and dining rooms of the house, the light diminishing with each and every creaking step until plunging into total darkness at the bottom. The dank musky smell of the cellar rose up from the concert base and flooded him with tingles and shivers, and memories of that fateful night back in '87. Dust dislodged from the forgotten tools and wine bottles around him, causing him to violently sneeze the particles from his nostrils. His eyes slowly adjusted to the darkness as he squinted and fumbled for the hanging light switch. His hands passed over dusty wooden beams and cold concrete walls until finally fingering upon the cord and pulling it. The light flickered and hummed ominously, teasing him with flashing snapshots of the room, before finally bursting into life and fully illuminating it.

Resting upon the concrete steps, Matthew covered his nose while he waited for the dust to re-settle, staring out in awe and soothing recollection at his father's vast collection of vintage ports and wines. Bottles of all shapes, sizes and colours, all sat upon the wooden shelves on either side of him, all smothered in thick layers of dust that muted any shine from the bright fluorescent light above. Matthew then cast his sights towards the end of the cellar, where the wine collection ceased and tool collection began. His eyes passed over the array of power and hand tools that hung from rusty hooks upon the walls before finally resting upon the green tarpaulin-covered machine at the end. He rose to his feet and began to walk over, ignoring the swarm of creeping spiders and bugs that scurried and shuffled around by his feet. He grasped hold of the tarpaulin and carefully pulled it away, revealing his father's grand Suffolk Colt lawnmower with its bold red and green paintwork and its razor-sharp coiling cylinder blades.

Reaching across and sliding over the bolt, Matthew pushed open the external cellar doors, dislodging the moss and grasses that had grown between the gaps in the slats and flooding the cellar with fresh air and sunlight from the garden. Grasping the hefty lawnmower with both hands, he lifted it up off of the ground, carrying it up the rear concrete steps where he laid it down upon the wild weed-infested lawn.

Matthew stopped again for a second and double-checked that all viewpoints were definitely blocked, which they were. Turning back to the machine again, Matthew grabbed the engine's pull cord and wrenched it back, bringing the brutal machine roaring back to life with a deafening growl from the engine. The cylinder blades span around below him with such power and speed that he could feel the vibrations through the ground. The grasses below were thick and coarse and infested with dandelions, nettles and various other garden weeds, but the razor-sharp blades of the brutal machine seemed to plough through them all with ease, filling the air with the perfumed scent of freshly-severed grass.

The blazing heat from the sun that beat down upon Matthew was almost too much to bear. He could feel the back of his neck burning up as sweat poured from his brow and dripped into the blades of the roaring machine below, but 'a real man wasn't afraid of hard work' as his father used to tell him, and so he continued to mow. Tammy would surely be impressed too, not just by the hard work, but by the fact he had forced himself outside, alone.

After mowing a crisp, thick strip down the right hand side of the lawn Matthew stopped and prepared for the return, when suddenly he became aware of a rustling from within the dense grasses. He watched as the rustling dissipated and then carried on mowing, but moments later found the blades of the mower become snarled into an object below. The blades jarred and fought to cut through the object, and after a few seconds turned red and engulfed in blood, which spat out into the air and splattered across the crisp mowed strip beside him.

Matthew quickly cut the engine and pulled the mower back to reveal two large twitching rats, mangled and ripped apart by the powerful blades of the machine. Matthew squatted and watched with strange fascination as the two rats convulsed and shook below him, gushing with blood and desperately clinging onto their fleeting lives. They panted and struggled for breath, Matthew's strange fixation growing deeper by the second, when suddenly his attention was diverted to the deep sound of a croaking bird from above him.

THE DAMAGED

He gazed upwards, using his hand to protect his eyes from the blazing sun, and gradually focused in. A large raven perched itself upon a branch three quarters of the way up the towering conifer trees, staring down at Matthew and cocking its head to him curiously. The bird then croaked again, the sound bouncing and echoing down to him between the trees. Matthew watched as the raven then launched itself into the air and glided down to the ground with graceful majesty, landing with a gentle flutter upon the lawn in front of him. It looked across to the bleeding carcasses and then back up to Matthew again, as if it were somehow asking for his permission. Matthew looked back at the strange bird in contemplation, wondering whether he was just imagining the peculiar series of events. He then nodded to the bird and stepped aside, curious if the bird could understand, and it could.

Matthew was captivated in morbid fascination as he watched the bird towering over the twitching corpses of the bloodied rodents, pecking and rummaging inside their carcasses and wrenching out the remains of their bloody entrails. The raven then threw the entrails into the air with a backward flick of its neck before catching them again in its open beak and swallowing them whole. Turning back to Matthew with blood dripping from the sides of its shiny black beak, it nodded in appreciation. Matthew frowned, finding this sight difficult to believe, as the bird then took off into the air again and returned to its nest within the trees. Matthew stood, hoping for another glance of the mysterious bird or its nest, but he could see nothing.

Matthew paused for a second longer, gathering his thoughts and wiping the sweat from his brow, before deciding to dismiss the strange events and continue with the mowing.

Within an hour Matthew had completed the lawn, raked the loose grass together into black refuse sacks, and had disposed of the remnants of the rat carcasses. He stood by the back door of the house looking out at his achievement with a smile. The garden was a far cry from its glory days when his mother had meticulously maintained it, but it was certainly an improvement.

Matthew took one final lungful of fresh air and returned to the house, shedding his sweaty clothes and taking a shower. He towelled himself dry and looked at his reflection in the bathroom mirror, noticing the bristly 24-hour stubble that had appeared on his face. He looked back at the sight with disgust, ashamed of himself for allowing it to get too long. To anyone else, the tiny bristles would have gone unnoticed, but to Matthew only perfection would do.

"How could Tammy ever fancy me looking like this!" he muttered with insecurity.

SIMON LAW

He quickly lathered up his face and began to shave it off with careful and precise upward strokes. It was at that point that he suddenly caught sight of something frightening in the mirrored space behind him, the blurry sight of a man with a ghastly face – the face from his charcoal sketches, creeping up slowly from behind him and brandishing a bloody knife. The face was rabid and feral, foaming at the mouth, smothered in filth, and infested with weeping bloody pustules that oozed and streamed with pus. His long greasy hair was drenched in sticky congealed blood and his scraggy brown beard was riddled with wriggling ants and spiders.

"Come and get me!" the foul man taunted.

Matthew dropped the razor and turned to face the vile intruder, fist clenched and ready to protect himself, but to Matthew's amazement, the phantom apparition had vanished.

Matthew creased his brow and quickly stepped out into the corridor, both hands shaking with adrenaline. He stared out desperately in both directions, frowning deeper in bewilderment and carving a deep red ridge into his brow. The man had completely vanished without a trace, with the exception of a single black spider that silently crept along the carpet of the landing.

Matthew took a deep breath and rubbed his eyes, absolutely convinced of what he had seen in the mirror. He peered down at the small black spider on the carpet and watched as it tried to scurry away from him, before lifting his bare foot and viciously squashing it dead into the fibres of the carpet. Matthew shook his head and exhaled again, baffled and panicked and starting to worry that he might be losing his mind. He leant over the handrail of the landing and peered down to the descending stairs below, before then checking the bedrooms and his father's study in one final attempt to find the rancid-looking man, but he found nothing.

"Maybe I'm just tired," he told himself, trying to dismiss the clear fragility of his mental state.

He paused for a moment to compose himself before then returning to the bathroom. Looking back to his half-shaven reflection, he then noticed the stream of blood that was slowly trickling down his face and onto the lino below. He leaned in for a closer inspection and then peered down to the bloodied razorblade in the sink below, realising he must have caught himself in the haste. He huffed and tutted in exasperation as he reached down for the toilet roll, gently wiping away the crimson streak from his face and blotting a small sliver against the cut.

"Well that's just great!" he muttered to himself angrily.

THE DAMAGED

It had been the first time that Matthew had cut himself shaving since he first taught himself how to shave when living at his aunt's house, and the inevitable scab that would soon appear on his face would be a conspicuous blotch upon his otherwise perfect complexion. *Tammy would hardly find **that** attractive now, would she?*

He picked the razor back up and continued to shave, watching the mirrored space behind him intently in case the phantom returned, but it didn't. He dabbed his face dry, being careful not to dislodge the bloodied tissue, and dressed himself in a fresh crisp set of his father's clothes.

Making his way back downstairs, the sound of the chirpy cartoons beckoned him from his new television set, and he immediately found himself drawn into them. The bright friendly colours and soothing cartoon voices were a refreshing distraction from the harrowing grisly face that was still etched into his mind. He took a seat down in his father's reassuringly comfortable Chesterfield armchair, and slowly tried to forget all about the events.

The day drew on as the glorious sun continued to blaze down at record temperatures. Matthew had remained mesmerised by the back-to-back cartoons until eventually falling asleep in the chair, waking later on with a refreshed mind and finding himself replaying the bizarre events of the day. Strangely, he found himself thinking not of the grisly man who had appeared in his bathroom mirror, but of the curious bird who had asked his permission to eat the entrails of the dying rat. *Did that really happen? Did I really share that moment of acknowledgement with a bird?* Matthew pondered, before also remembering the electric black plume that he had found previously, and the large black bird which had swooped past his head in the park. With the contemplations still digesting in his mind, Matthew retrieved his charcoal and sketchpad from his bedroom and set himself at the dining table to draw the mysterious bird.

At a few minutes to five, Matthew put down his charcoal and boiled the kettle, pouring out two cups of hot sweet tea in preparation for Tammy's arrival. The expected knock upon the door soon arrived and Matthew greeted her with enthusiasm, eager to show off his hard work and his new television to her, but he could tell straight away that her day had not been a good one. Her clothes looked messy and dishevelled, a far cry from her pristine appearance earlier that morning. Her eyes were red and puffy and it was clear to Matthew that she had spent most of the day in tears.

"You alright, Darling?" he asked with concern and an empathetic smile.

"No, not really, Matthew," she replied with a false smile, trying her best to sound indifferent about it but unable to hide the clear torment in her eyes.

Matthew held out his arms to her and Tammy was quick to accept the embrace. He wrapped his arms around her tightly, smelling her perfume and the conditioner in her hair while feeling her breasts pressed tightly against his chest. He could feel her tears rolling from her face and trickling down the back of his neck and so continued to hold her, gently rubbing her back reassuringly.

He broke free of his grip a few moments later and gave her a gentle kiss on the cheek, leading her over to the sofa with a tender smile.

"I made you a cup of tea," he told her.

"Thank you," she replied, her exhaustion clear in her croaky voice.

Tammy sat herself down upon the sofa and removed her shoes, tucking her feet up underneath her bottom and clutching onto her warm cup of tea with both hands for comfort. She wiped her tears away on the sleeve of her blouse, took a long slurp of her tea, and snuggled herself deep into the fabric of the sofa in a foetal-esque position.

Matthew watched her with sympathy but remained quiet for a few moments longer, allowing her a little time to try to relax. He sat himself down and began to sip his tea, intermittently peering over to the loop of children's cartoons that continued to play upon the television set.

Tammy peered over to the television too, the friendly cartoons calming and soothing her torment, but it wasn't for a good few minutes until the change dawned on her.

"You bought a new TV?" she asked, peering around to him with sudden realisation.

"Yep!" he replied with an enthusiastic smile and a nod. "...New television and a new vacuum cleaner!

"Cool!" she replied with a nod, smiling back through her puffy eyes. "...You get to watch your cartoons now then!" she continued with a mild chuckle.

Matthew nodded and smiled back with child-like contentment.

"I mowed the back lawn today as well, it looks quite nice now," he told her, the pride of his achievement clear in his tone.

"Really? Outside, on your own?"

"Yep. The garden's so secluded that you can't really count it as 'outside', but it's a start. 'baby steps', as they say..."

Tammy smiled in a moment of genuine happiness, before returning her attention to her cup of tea, taking another slurp and watching the spinning brown vortex as she swished around the last dregs in the bottom of the cup. She then began to think about Jessica again, and the solemn look of dejection quickly returned to her face.

"Do you want to talk about your day?" Matthew asked as he watched her expression morph.

"Not much to talk about, Matthew, she hates me," Tammy replied sadly, her eyes slowly starting to well up again.

"Who? Jessica?"

"Yeah, it was my visitation day with her this morning and... well she hates me! That much is clear!"

"I'm sure that's not true, Darling, what makes you think that?"

"She couldn't even look me in the eye, Matthew. It's obvious. She hates me, and she's never going to forgive me for what I did to her, not if that *bastard* Keith has got anything to do with it anyway. I know he's badmouthing me to her, I know it! I'm gonna cut his fucking balls off if I see him!" she blurted, briefly losing the grip on her composure.

She placed her empty cup down onto the coffee table with a loud thud and placed her head in her hands, trying to subdue her volatile temper. Matthew paused and looked at her with sadness, wishing that there was something that he could do to help her. Her expletives grated upon him with an irksome cringe, but he couldn't blame her for the outburst.

"You're a good person, Tammy, and I've no doubt that you're a good mother too. I wouldn't like you otherwise," he told her, offering a smile of condolence.

Tammy chuckled into her hands with mild hysteria, before removing them and smiling back at him through her fresh tears.

"Thank you, I appreciate that," she told him, her voice shaky and vulnerable. "...It's not true though, is it? A good mother wouldn't have done what I did, would she?"

"You made a mistake, Tammy, we all make mistakes sometimes. She'll come around eventually; you've just got to give her time."

"You think so?"

"Definitely."

Tammy nodded reluctantly and stood from the sofa, picking up both empty tea cups and taking them through to the kitchen where she looked from the window and briefly admired the freshly-mown lawn. She filled a clean glass with water and then returned to the lounge again with Matthew's two blue pills in her hand. She placed them down upon Matthew's small side table and suddenly noticed the blistering red scorch marks upon the back of his neck.

"Christ, Matthew! Have you seen the back of your neck?" she told him with horror.

"No, it does feel pretty sore though. Is it burnt?"

"It looks awful! Didn't you put any sun cream on when you were outside?"

"No, I didn't think to."

"You need to be careful, Matthew. Pale skin like yours is gonna burn up straight away!" she informed him with motherly concern.

She reached across for her handbag and began to rummage around within it, shortly removing a small bottle of lotion and shaking it up and down.

"This might be a little cold," she warned him, as she unclipped the top of the bottle and squeezed a few drops onto the back of his angry burning neck.

She spread out the cream with her fingertip and began to gently rub it in. The touch of her soft skin upon his neck was sensual and arousing and Matthew could feel himself getting an erection straight away; he was just glad that he was sitting down and that it might go unnoticed.

"You can... you can stick around for a bit, if you wanted to? You know... if you didn't want to be home by yourself that is?" Matthew asked her with hesitation.

Tammy paused and pondered the question. She knew how unprofessional it would be to accept his offer, but Matthew was right, she didn't want to be alone at all. There was a brand new pack of Wilkinson razorblades waiting for her at home, and she couldn't be certain how deep they would cut.

"Actually, Matthew... that would be quite nice, if you don't mind having me that is?" she replied, her ponderous frown quickly morphing to a grateful smile.

"No, of course I don't mind, Darling. It's not as if I've got any plans, have I?" he replied with an ironic chuckle.

"You're a good guy, Matthew," she told him as she rubbed the last of the cream into his shoulders and neck. "...If there were more people like you in the world then it wouldn't be quite so bad."

"I wouldn't go that far..." he protested, enjoying the last few rubs of her soft fingertips.

Tammy sat herself down upon the sofa again with the release of an exhausted sigh, and gestured down to his little blue pills.

"Yeah, I know!" he told her, throwing them into his mouth and swallowing them down.

She watched with empathy as Matthew commenced another rendition of his well-rehearsed performance, glazing his eyes and staring numbly into the middle space. She turned her attention briefly back to the cartoons again before deciding to show Matthew the respect of leaving him alone while the initial effects of the pills wore out. She slipped her shoes back onto her feet, grabbed her bag, and made her way back

THE DAMAGED

through to the kitchen, pulling open the back door and stepping out onto the freshly-mown lawn.

Matthew sat with his eyes closed and listened as Tammy departed, wondering to himself how long he would have to keep the act up for, or how long he could possibly keep her convinced of it. He remained sat in his father's Chesterfield and listened to the cartoons playing in the background, allowing an appropriate amount of time to pass and waiting for his erection to die back down again. He kept his eyes closed until he started to hear the end credits on the television and opened them to peer over to the clock. Ten minutes had now passed since taking the pills, and this seemed more than sufficient to convince her of their effects.

Rising to his feet, Matthew peered around the room, over to the window and out into the garden where he spotted Tammy upon the swing, peacefully swinging back and forth with a cigarette in her hand. He began to walk closer to the window, staring out at her with awe and longing and fighting hard to prevent his erection from returning. She looked beautiful, like a flower blowing in a gentle breeze, her fragile and vulnerable state of mind only adding to her allure.

Matthew opened the door without arousing her attention and slowly walked up behind her, enjoying the sight of her for a few moments longer. The early evening sun was still bright and blazing above them and its heat had only just started to dissipate, with shades of orange and red slowly melting into the azure blue around them. The street was peaceful and calm and the only sounds were the distant chirping of birds and the rhythmic squeaking of the rusty links of the swing's chain.

"Hey," Matthew said to her, finally announcing his presence.

"Hey!" she replied, turning to him with a smile as she scuffed her feet upon the ground to slow her momentum to a halt. "...I didn't see you there."

"I used to love this swing as a child," he told her with a nostalgic grin. "...You don't really worry about anything as a child, do you?"

"Not normally, no," she replied thoughtfully. "...Not about the small things anyway."

"I loved being a kid," he told her, as he placed his hands down gently upon her shoulders. "I'd been rehearsing for the school play the day that it happened. Guess what the play was?"

Tammy shook her head, enjoying the touch of his hands upon her.

"Noah's Ark! Quite ironic really isn't it? You know, with the storm and everything that night... I never did get to play the part."

Tammy grinned contentedly as she cocked her head over to rest upon Matthew's hand, nestling against it tenderly.

"I was never good at anything like that," she told him. "...Jessica sang in the preschool choir apparently. I wasn't allowed to go and see it."

"Well I'm sure you'll get to watch her next time, Darling."

Tammy nodded glumly, before reaching into her bag beside her and removing her iPhone from it. She brought up her photo gallery and flicked through to a copy of her favourite picture, the one with her mother and daughter together, smiling euphorically into the camera.

"That's Jessica," she said as she passed her phone to him.

"She looks beautiful," he replied, gazing down and passing the phone back to her.

"Yeah, she is."

Tammy smiled mournfully and placed the phone back into her bag. Her attention was suddenly drawn to the rattle of the rear fence. She looked up with curiosity to see a cat strolling inquisitively through the garden.

"Aww, hello little one!" she cooed, clicking her fingers together and luring the cat over with a smile.

Matthew then noticed the cat too, but his face was not filled with the same pleasant smile. He scowled with bitterness as his eyes turned to daggers.

"Hey, get out of here!" he quickly raged, startling both Tammy and the cat in the process.

The cat quickly turned and dashed back over the fence as Tammy sighed and shook her head in bemusement.

"You... You don't like cats then?" she asked nervously.

"No... I... I'm sorry, I shouldn't have done that," he told her with remorse. "They just remind me too much of... of my aunt. She cared more for those damn cats than she did for me... It's silly I know. I need to get over the past and move on. I'm trying to, but it's hard to forget things...."

"I understand, Matthew. Don't be so hard on yourself," she told him with empathy. She understood all too well how something seemingly innocuous could trigger off a bad memory.

They returned to the house together a few minutes later, Tammy taking a seat at the dining table as Matthew boiled the kettle for a fresh cup of tea. She tapped her fingers nervously upon the table, listening to the kettle as it started to boil and cut through the awkward silence that had fallen upon them. Tammy then noticed the sketchpad and sticks of charcoal upon the table that had previously gone unnoticed. She leant forward and stole a curious glance at Matthew's drawing, her smile widening as her curiosity and intrigue grew. She turned and gave Matthew a quick glance for permission, before then reaching forward and turning the drawing to face her. She looked down and began to nod, making agreeable humming noises as she followed the artistic lines and shading around the page.

"This is quite good, Matthew. I didn't know you could draw..." she told him, her voice sounding genuinely surprised and impressed.

"Thank you. I've always like drawing, even from before everything happened. It probably comes from my father, he was an architect."

"Oh yeah? That's pretty cool. Did he design any of the buildings around here?"

"A few, yes. I'm not sure which ones are still standing though. That was a very long time ago now. The company mostly did designs for overseas projects, as I remember anyway. He was a clever man, my dad. I always wanted to be an architect too, to work with him at the company, to travel the world and see my creations come to life."

"You still can, can't you? ...Become an architect, that is, if that's what you want to do with your life. You still got plenty of time."

"Maybe... I didn't even finish school though. I don't have a single qualification to my name."

"You could enrol in a course. You're certainly smart enough to," she told him with a slightly flirtatious smile.

Matthew smiled back and shrugged his shoulders, turning back to pour out the tea. "And what about your father? What did he do?" Matthew asked.

"No idea, never knew him," she said dismissively.

"Oh, I'm sorry..." Matthew replied, now feeling awkward for having asked the question. "...I didn't realise," he added, placing down the two cups of tea and taking a seat next to her.

"It's fine, I'm over it. My mum said that she would tell me all about him when I was older, and then, when I got older, I realised that I didn't care, I didn't want to know. He was a local man, I know that much. I think he was probably married with a family or something; it was some kind of scandal anyway. My mum was the only parent I'd ever known, and she was all I needed. So..." Tammy paused for a sip of tea, knowing that it would still be far too hot to drink, but despite her claim that she was 'over it', was actually quite eager to change the subject. "So... what is it?" she asked, soothing her burnt lips with her tongue and gesturing down to the drawing. "A blackbird? A crow?"

"I... I think it's a raven actually."

"You 'think'? You drew it!"

"It was a bird that landed in the garden earlier. I 'think' it was a raven because it was massive. I've seen crows before and I don't remember them being that big."

"Oh right, okay. I didn't think we got them here."

"I've no idea."

"I've got a fun fact about ravens....!" Tammy announced with a sense of childish glee in her voice.

"Yeah? What's that?" he replied, acknowledging her excitement with a little grin.

"A group of ravens can have three different names depending on what they're doing: a constable, an unkindness, or a conspiracy!" She punctuated her statement with a nod and another flirtatious grin, as if it were a bow or an exclamation of 'ta dah!'

"A conspiracy of ravens, hey? I like that!" he replied, returning back the flirtatious grin. "Where did you hear that?"

"Pub quiz. Me and Keith used to go all the time before Jessica was born. He was the smart one, I just went for the company," she told him, though 'for the drink' would have been more accurate.

Matthew took a sip of his tea, then suddenly recalled the velvet-lined jewellery box underneath the coffee table. He had almost forgotten about his gift to her, but now seemed the perfect moment to present it.

"I've got a present for you!" he announced seemingly out of the blue, rising from his seat with his cup of tea and gesturing her over to the lounge.

Tammy frowned with a look of disbelief, but stood regardless, picking up her cup from the dinner table and gingerly following him through to the sofa.

"Just a little something to say 'thank you' for everything you've done for me," Matthew continued, taking a seat and reaching down underneath the coffee table.

"A present? You don't have to buy me presents, Matthew!" she told him with confusion, taking the box from him hesitantly. She looked down at the velvet box and gently stroked it with the tip of her thumb, expecting straight away for it to be expensive.

"I know I don't, but you've been really nice to me and I just wanted you to know that I appreciated it. Please, open it up," he told her eagerly, certain that the gift was going to win him her heart.

Tammy smiled uncertainly, and looked back down at the box again. Had the gift been from one of her other clients it probably would have freaked her out and made her nervous that an unhealthy obsession had begun to unmask itself, but with Matthew the thought never entered her mind.

Tammy turned the box so that the opening faced her and slowly began to pull the lid up on its hinges. The light glimmered and sparkled from each pearl and white golden nugget as she exposed them, and she was left completely lost for words. The necklace was absolutely

THE DAMAGED

beautiful and she loved it straight away, but her conscience immediately started to niggle away at her.

"It's beautiful, Matthew, but I...I can't accept this from you! It's too much!" she told him, the frown across her brow clearly indicative of her sorrow not to keep it.

"Of course you can, Tammy, It's yours."

"No, I'm serious, Matthew. I'll lose my job if I accept this."

"Oh, rubbish. I won't tell anyone if you don't. Do you have any idea how much money I've got just sitting in my bank?"

Tammy took a breath and chewed upon her bottom lip, unable to respond.

"Too much!" Matthew continued, "...and no one to spend it on either. Please accept it."

Tammy exhaled and looked back down at the beautiful necklace again, frustrated in her indecision. Matthew stood and smiled at her reassuringly, gesturing for her to stand too. She rose to her feet with the necklace carefully in her grip, her face still showing signs of doubt but starting to succumb. Matthew took the necklace from her and unclipped the clasp. Tammy smiled at him with appreciation and longing in her eyes, as she cocked her head and held her hair to one side. Matthew placed the necklace delicately around her soft supple neck and fastened the clasp, stepping back and gazing at her in awe.

"You look amazing," he told her.

Tammy gazed back into his deep blue eyes and could no longer resist. She wrapped her arms around him and held him tightly, beginning to cry once again.

"Thank you, Matthew," she whispered gently into his ear.

They continued to embrace, and soon found themselves kissing with uncontrollable passion and lust. Matthew ran his hands eagerly over the curves of her slim and supple body, from her bum to her waist to her breasts. He moved his lips to the side of her neck and kissed her down to her collar bone as she began to grasp and fondle the toned muscles of his chest and his arms.

"Upstairs?" he asked, briefly breaking free.

Tammy nodded back with a flushed alluring grin. Matthew took her gently by the hand, eagerly leading her up the stair as his excitement and anticipation began to soar. They kissed again as they reached the top before Matthew led her along the hall and into his parents' bedroom to avoid the child-like embarrassment of his own.

Tammy unbuttoned her purple blouse and threw it carelessly down upon the bedroom floor as Matthew placed his hands gently upon her bare sides. He bent down to his knees to kiss her belly before unbuttoning and unzipping the top of her skirt and pulling it down to her ankles. He then reached up to grab the rim of her tights with both hands, pulling them down to expose her pale legs, black knickers, and the blood-stained bandage upon her thigh.

He gently kissed her ankle, her shin, and then her knee, before curiously unravelling the bandage upon her thigh. Gingerly fingering over the array of scabs and scars with his fingertips, the feel of each rough and smooth texture aroused him even more. Matthew's morbid fascination with the wounds was strange and slightly disconcerting to Tammy, but yet she didn't stop him. It was at that point that she suddenly yelped out in discomfort after Matthew dislodged a scab and caused a trickle of blood to run down her leg.

Tammy grabbed him by the shirt and pulled him back to his feet again, kissing him and reaching down to fondle his crotch. He pulled off his trousers and shirt and threw them to the floor before pushing Tammy gently onto the bed and climbing on top of her.

She ran her hands over his hard abs and pecs, before then unclipping her bra and discarding it, exposing her pale and perky breasts to him. Matthew cupped her breasts in each hand excitedly, rubbing each nipple with the tip of each thumb and planting kisses down the side of her neck. She wrapped her arms around his lower back, digging her nails into his flesh.

Matthew kissed her breasts and her nipples and then her gaunt ribcage and stomach, before grasping hold of the rim of her knickers and pulling them down her legs. Tammy pulled down his boxers, and lay back upon the bed expectantly. He caressed her thighs again, spreading her legs wide and smudging the trickling blood down her scarred thigh to her knee below.

Matthew's history of sexual experiences comprised of nothing more than sordid teenage masturbation and an awkward blowjob he once received from Leila – a promiscuous manic-depressive from the mental institute who liked to char holes in her flesh with the smouldering tip of her Marlboro Lights. His awkward inexperience was obvious to Tammy, but somehow alluring to her as well. After a few minutes she decided to take control of the situation, rolling Matthew over and climbing on top of him.

The evening sun glistened against her skin from the bedroom window, illuminating her in a faint orange hue as she began to find her rhythm, slow and steady to start, her long black hair and string of white pearls bouncing with each and every thrust. Matthew looked up at her with an exhilarated smile as she arched her back and began to speed up. He watched the blood on her thigh as it continued to meander down her leg, the crimson flow beginning to increase and starting to splatter out onto his stomach.

THE DAMAGED

Matthew then watched as Tammy's face and skin began to slowly ripple and flow like the waves of the ocean, morphing and reforming like a sculpture of plasticine. Her silky black hair started to kink and to twist around on itself, forming into bold ridged curls of mousey brown and chocolate. Her exhales and whimpers of pleasure and ecstasy echoed and bounced around the room, erratically modulating in tone and in pitch. The smell of her perfume then started to change too, morphing from the scent of sweet fresh summer nectar to the smell of old talcum and flowers. Matthew watched the transformation with intrigue and confusion, but before his mind had the chance to question it, he realised he was now looking up at his mother.

"You okay, sweetheart?" his mother asked him as she continued to ride upon him.

Instead of the shock and disgust that Matthew had felt that morning when thoughts of his mother had turned sexual, Matthew now accepted his hallucination with a loving smile, looking deep into his mother's eyes and curly brown hair that bounced back and forth with every movement. He then reached out and placed his hands firmly upon her hips, aiding her thrusts and building their momentum upon him.

ALL THAT WE SEE OR SEEM
IS BUT A DREAM WITHIN A DREAM

The amber scorch of the setting sun slowly faded into black speckled darkness as Matthew and Tammy slumbered in his parents' bed. The moon and the stars that twinkled above them were crisp and clear in the night sky, picturesque and magical like a scene from a movie. The clunky 80's bedside clock that sat upon the dressing table beside them slowly ticked over to 3am, and suddenly Matthew was awake.

Matthew opened his eyes and stared motionlessly into the swirling patterns of the white artexed ceiling above him, remembering his previous night's conquest with a grin. He turned his eyes to the side to double check that he hadn't simply imagined the whole experience, and there she was; silent, still, and gleaming like an angel, her sweet breath gently cascading over the side of his face. Tammy's appearance had now reverted to its former shape and Matthew felt seemingly lucid once again, calm and peaceful.

He looked over to the clock and then back to the ceiling again, feeling his heavy eyelids pulling themselves shut and deciding not to resist. He listened to the sound of Tammy's gentle breathing, subconsciously aligning it to his own, and felt himself slowly falling unconscious again.

Somewhere between reality and the dream world, Matthew started to hear the faint sound of what seemed like coarse sandpaper rubbing against wood. The sound grew louder and louder, echoing through his ears as if his own eardrums were being sanded down themselves. He then felt the movement of tiny footsteps at the end of the bed, gently pressing and brushing against his feet. Opening his eyes again, unsure if he was actually awake or merely imagining consciousness within his dream, he tipped his head forward and peered towards the end of the bed, seeing two small figures silhouetted in the faint blue hue of the moonlight. His sleepy eyes slowly began to adjust, and as the murky blurs came into focus he could make out two white Persian cats, their sandpaper tongues licking upon something held within their paws.

Reaching his arms back and hoisting himself up to a sitting position, Matthew rubbed his eyes and refocused in on the two unfamiliar prowlers. The two cats seemed blasé and arrogant to Matthew's stares, continuing to lick their paws with apparent delight. They turned to face him, their piercing green eyes glimmering with the light of the moon. The blue moonlight then bathed against their white motionless faces, revealing the blood that dripped from their mouths and the bloodied ripped flesh within their paws. Matthew flinched with a look of horror as the cats hissed and spat at him. They then leapt from the edge of the bed and dashed out the bedroom door.

Matthew threw open the covers and leapt to his feet, ready to chase the intruders down, when suddenly an enormous crackle of thunder shook the house. He froze in his tracks as an eerie shiver ran down his spine. He looked out of the window and saw bolts of lightning striking the ground outside and lighting up the night sky like an atomic bomb. The sounds of shattering glass and plummeting trees then echoed all around him as the wind began to blow, howling and bellowing through the angry sky and rattling the window panes with deafening force.

Matthew took a deep breath and tried to calm himself, but there was no way to slow his racing heart. He felt his hands and feet begin to violently shake as he urinated himself in fear, clenching his eyes shut as tightly as he could and praying that he would wake from the dream.

"George? What's wrong?" Tammy asked, waking from her slumber and taking on his mother's image once again.

Matthew looked back with a frightened grimace, breaking free of his paralysis before then dashing out into the hallway.

The two bloodied cats greeted him with another hiss, before running down the stairs and into the front room. The violent atmosphere grew louder and louder as Matthew began to cry, feeling increasingly disoriented and certain that his head would explode at any moment. He stumbled along the landing and slumped to a sitting position upon the top step, placing his head in his hands and digging his fingernails deep into the flesh of his forehead as if thinking the pain would centre his spinning mind.

The deafening noise around Matthew was then accompanied by the purr of an engine. The noise perked his attention and he removed his head from his hands, tears streaming down his pale quivering face. The noise of the engine grew louder as the vehicle pulled up and parked in the driveway of the front yard. Matthew's tears then began to subside, as the undeniable sound became clear to him; it was the sound of his father's Ford Capri.

He rose to his feet and dashed down the stairs, the overwhelming joy at the thought of seeing his father completely overpowering his state of fear. He flung open the front door and stepped out onto the front porch, the wind swirling around him and gushing through his blonde hair.

"Daddy!" he cried out at the top of his joyous lungs, but the car had vanished. His smile sunk as he stared in desperation at the driveway, but tyre marks and scrapes of rust were all that remained. Matthew fell to his knees and wept, loathing his own pathetic desperation.

The angry clouds above crackled and exploded, erupting with droplets of blood that plummeted through the sky and rained down upon him, soaking him to the bone in crimson red.

Matthew fell forwards onto his hands and screamed, clenching his fist and punching it violently and repeatedly into the concrete driveway below him. His knuckles ripped open and the bones below began to break, but still he continued, screaming with every ounce of energy that remained. Exhausted, he fell flat to the wet ground, rolling onto his back and staring aimlessly into the angry sky above him, hopeless and drained. Raindrops of blood pelted down relentlessly upon him, bouncing against his face and running down into his eyes and his mouth.

The two Persian cats strolled from the front door of the house in single file, swinging their hips back and forth in a silky fluid motion, cocky and confident and unafraid of the deafening torrential blood-storm around them. The blood rain pelted down upon them, but their perfect white coats of fur remained completely unblemished. They strolled up to Matthew and began to pace around him in a circle, sniffing him and watching him. The lead cat then stopped in his tracks beside Matthew's head, lapped at his lips, and sunk its piercing feline teeth deep into his earlobe, perforating through the skin and wrenching away a segment of flesh.

Matthew screamed and clutched at his ear before jumping back to his feet again. He looked down and watched in horror as the cat began to lick at the bloodied flesh, the sound of its sandpaper tongue resonated in his gushing ear. The second cat looked up at him with a hopeful expression, as if begging for some flesh for himself, purring and jumping up at his legs.

In a burst of anger and adrenaline, Matthew reached down and grabbed the begging pest by the scruff of his neck. He lifted the cat up and held him at eye level, staring deep into its menacing green eyes, before throwing it with all his might against the side of the house. The cat hit the wall with a bone-cracking thud, before then falling to the

THE DAMAGED

ground dead. The first cat hissed and swiped its claws at Matthew's legs, before dropping the remnants of Matthew's ear and running off into the darkness again.

The rain became increasingly ferocious by the minute, pelting down stronger and stronger, hitting against Matthew like solid ball bearings. The road became engulfed, as the crimson fluid flowed down it like a river of blood, swirling like rapids and crashing down the drain holes like waterfalls. The force of the wind grew stronger too, howling and bellowing and gusting upon Matthew at gale force speeds, but as its strength grew stronger, his resistance to the fear grew stronger too.

Matthew's sights were then drawn to the distance, to the silhouette of a man glowing orange underneath the hue of the street lights. It was the man from the mirror, the face from the charcoal sketches; it was his parents' killer. This he somehow knew with certainty, despite being unable to decipher his features clearly through the rain. Matthew stared and scowled with bitterness in his eyes, as his mind became flooded with thoughts of wrath and retribution. His sights remained locked without falter or flinch, as he watched the figure begin to approach.

"Come and get me, if you dare!" Matthew heard taunting in his head.

Matthew turned and ran for the house, not in fear, but in search of a knife to finally take his revenge. He dashed through the door and into the lounge, but as he reached the kitchen he was met by a ghastly sight that stopped him in his tracks. He grimaced and looked away, feeling his heart skip a beat and the oxygen vanishing from his lungs. Matthew gulped and tentatively cast his eyes back, finding his mother and father upon the kitchen floor below, gasping for air and staring up at him in hopeless desperation. They writhed around amongst the pool of their combined blood, clutching at their wounds and twitching frantically.

Confused between the vague boundaries of reality and delusion, Matthew still knew that his parents could not be helped. Their fates were sealed, and all he could do was look away. He took a deep breath and tried not to panic, humming in his head and trying to blank out the gargling sound of the blood bubbling from the gaping hole in his mother's throat. He clenched his fists and his eyes as tightly as he could, and as soon as the gargling seemed to cease, he suddenly felt the piercing agony of a phantom blade plunge into him, slipping deep between two ribs and collapsing his right lung.

Matthew's eyes pinged open in shock, as the pain pulsated through his body and the taste of blood flooded through his mouth. He motioned to scream but his lungs would not allow it. He looked down to the kitchen knife embedded within his chest and reached down to grasp hold of it, gritting his teeth and slowly pulling it free with a gloopy squelching splutter. His chest immediately gushed with blood that surged from him like a tap until he stopped the flow with the palm of his hand, creating a vacuum that sucked and secured his hand in place.

Disorientated and weak, but still determined, Matthew strengthened his grip on the bloodied kitchen knife and ran back out of the front door with it, crazed with irrepressible fury.

Lunging frantically into the street, Matthew was instantly hit by a cold wall of silence. The storm had passed, the river of blood had dried up, and his prey had completely vanished. He felt the air rushing back into his lungs and could now breathe again with ease. He looked down to his wound, but it had gone. Exhaling with exhaustion, he slumped his tense muscles to a loose hang of resignation. The gentle night breeze whistled over his skin as he looked to the ground in shame, confused and tormented.

Turning to make his shameful return to the house, Matthew noticed Edgar Brown's lounge light flickering on. A figure then appeared from behind the white netted curtain of the window, staring out at Matthew in disbelief. Matthew stood and stared back in return, the kitchen knife still firmly in his grip. He watched the figure scowling at him in discontent, looking down at the knife and then disappearing from view again. Matthew snarled and grimaced, damning him for daring to pass judgement on him, before then returning to the house again and closing the front door firmly shut.

The ghastly images of his parents had now vanished from sight too, and the only sound to be heard was the gentle rhythmic ticking of the clock. He slowly walked through to the kitchen again, where he gently slid the knife back inside its wooden block holder, before reaching into Tammy's handbag on the kitchen side and removing his pot of Diazepam. He wrenched open the lid and threw three little pills to the back of his throat, washing them down with water that he guzzled straight from the running tap. He then skulked his way back to the lounge where he slumped himself down into his father's welcoming Chesterfield, stroking its soft leather arms for comfort. Gazing up to his parents' wedding photograph with an apologetic smile and a sombre shake of the head, Matthew placed his thumb inside his mouth and sucked upon it like a whimpering child. His parents looked back at him from within the photograph, but their euphoric smiles had gone. Instead their foreheads had crinkled into a displeasing frown and their eyes stared through him with disappointment.

THE DAMAGED

IN THE COLD LIGHT OF DAY

The shiny brass pendulum of the grandfather clock swung rhythmically back and forth within its polished wooden body throughout the remainder of the night; standing tall and proud in the corner of the room where it had stood for the past thirty-five years.

The inanimate machine looked down upon Matthew as he slept peacefully below it. Its glimmering brass hour-hand then slowly ticked over to eight o'clock and Matthew gradually started to stir. The morning sun had been beaming down upon his face through the gap in the lounge curtains since the break of dawn, and a small pool of sweat had now started to form in the creases of the chair. The side of Matthew's face had glued itself to the tacky leather of his father's Chesterfield and his neck had begun to ache from the awkward position in which it had spent the night. He yawned and grumbled at the ache, before opening his eyes and slowly peeling his skin away from the leather. He checked the time on the faithful clock and started to look around the room, recalling the events of the night and struggling to differentiate reality from delusion.

Pulling himself to his feet, Matthew rolled his neck in an attempt to loosen the tight muscles that had clamped shut awkwardly to the side. Rubbing his face briskly, he continued to try and piece the events back together again; he remembered the blood storm, the two Persian cats and the figure of his parents' killer. In the cold light of day he was certain that these were nothing more than figments of his own imagination, but the fact that he had awoken downstairs in his father's chair was a disconcerting anomaly.

Running through the events again, he then remembered his conquest with Tammy and immediately dashed up the stairs to check she was still there, but found nothing more than an empty messy bed.

SIMON LAW

He exhaled in frustration, briefly doubting that his conquest had even occurred, before the pungent smell of sex in the air quickly put his doubts to rest. *Where did she go?* he asked himself. *She doesn't seem like the type of person that would simply up and vanish in the middle of the night, especially when she was due to give me my pills in less than an hour's time...*

Matthew hoped that her reasoning for leaving would be as innocent and inane as needing a shower or changing her clothes, and not through regret or through witnessing his psychotic actions during the night. Tammy's rejection at this stage would be heart-breaking to him, and would leave him with an empty void. He hoped that the previous night's 'conquest' would be interpreted in the manner it was intended; not just a physical act, but a display of his growing love for her. He also hoped that her participation indicated that she felt the same.

Matthew tried to push his uncertainties to one side, fully aware that their rumination would undoubtedly start to brew an anxiety attack within him. He proceeded to make his parents' bed before then washing and dressing himself and making his way downstairs to the kitchen, an insatiable hunger for meat growing strangely stronger inside of him. He opened the fridge and squatted down to take a look inside, rummaging through the contents until he came upon a fresh beef steak. He removed it from the packaging, splashed a little oil into the frying pan, and cooked the steak for a mere 15 seconds on each side. Removing a fork and a sharp steak knife from the kitchen drawer, he cut into the steak, watching the blood seep out of the barely-cooked meat and swim around on the plate. He stared down at the blood in fascination, before removing a segment of juicy meat and placing it inside his mouth. Sliding the meat carefully between his back molars he began to chew, feeling the juicy blood oozing around his mouth and trickling down the back of his throat.

Swallowing the meat down, Matthew then cut himself another segment, savouring the juicy taste in his mouth as he stared into the rear garden from the kitchen window. He watched the gentle morning breeze as it fluttered through the needles of the conifer trees, and noticed his friend the raven once again, poking his head through a break in the branches. He watched the bird curiously, as the bird seemed to watch him back, tipping its head to one side and edging towards the end of the branch. Matthew looked down at the bloody steak below him and then to the bird again, curious if the bird was hungry. Pushing the window wide open, he watched as the raven spread its wings and gently glided down to the lawn, before then hopping toward the open window in curious anticipation. Matthew smiled at the bird in strange delight, before throwing a segment of the steak to him. The bird croaked as if to show its appreciation, before grasping the bloody meat within its black shiny beak and transporting it back to his nest once again and disappearing from sight.

Matthew looked back to the grandfather clock, watching the minute hand as it slowly ticked over to 8:50. Still hopeful that Tammy would return, he flipped the switch on the kettle and began to make his usual two cups of tea. One for him, and one for her.

The doorbell rang a few minutes later and Matthew was immediately filled with relief, his anxieties of abandonment all pushed aside. He smiled and exhaled, before approaching the door and pulling it open.

"Hey!" he called, before realising that the figure at the door was not Tammy at all, but a policeman bearing a stern expression upon his face. The oversized brown handlebar moustache upon the man's face made him look like a member of the Village People, or a redneck from the deep south of America. Under any other circumstance, the sight would have been comical to Matthew, but the stern unforgiving look upon the officer's face vehemently eradicated any humour from the situation.

Matthew frowned disconcertedly, briefly debating slamming the door shut once again and running off to hide.

"Good morning sir. My name's PC Lang. May I please come inside?" the policeman asked as he quickly flashed Matthew his badge, his expression remaining stiff and unwavering.

Matthew looked at the badge and then back up to the policeman nervously, uncertain of what was happening, or what he should do. He felt his anxieties starting to rise as his view became fixated upon the pepper spray and the telescopic baton upon the officer's sturdy black utility belt.

"Sir?" the policemen repeated impatiently, which broke Matthew from his gaze with a nervous jolt.

"Err, yeah okay," Matthew finally replied, slowly stepping to one side so that the officer could enter.

"Okay, can I take your name please, sir?" the officer asked, removing a pen and a small notepad from his inside pocket.

"It's Matthew, Matthew Mason," he replied warily, closely watching the officer's every action.

The officer looked at him and nodded sternly, writing Matthew's name down upon the notepad before leaning into his radio and pressing upon the button on the side.

"Two-zero-six to dispatch, do you copy?"

"Dispatch, go ahead Two-zero-six."

"I need a ten-twenty-nine on a Matthew Mason of number eight Oak Street.

"Ten-four."

"Okay, sir, please take a seat," the officer then asked him, releasing his radio and returning his attention to Matthew.

"Err, okay," Matthew responded hesitantly. "Have I done something?" he continued, gingerly walking past the man and taking a seat in his father's Chesterfield.

"I'm responding to a report of an incident in the early hours of this morning. Do you know anything about that, sir?" Officer Lang asked him, looking down at Matthew from his towering position, poised and ready with his pen.

"Incident? What kind of incident?" Matthew replied elusively.

"A man was seen running down the street brandishing a knife, sir. Do you know anything about that?" the officer continued, his gaze fixed sternly upon Matthew.

Matthew looked away and fidgeted nervously in the chair, hesitating to reply.

"Err, no. I... I never heard anything last night, Officer," he replied.

"Oh, well that *is* strange, sir, because your neighbour said that it was you, that they saw you coming back to your house afterwards," Officer Lang then revealed, raising his eyebrows and continuing to stare accusingly.

"Oh, I see," Matthew replied, continuing to cower away in the chair.

"It's a criminal offence to lie to a police officer, sir, so I suggest you start talking," he told Matthew with a disgruntled huff. –"So was that yourself or not, sir?"

Matthew sighed and rubbed his face, looking up at the officer and then down again, debating the best way to proceed. He knew that he risked being arrested regardless of what he said and that an arrest under such circumstance would certainly affect the state of his new freedom. His mind then turned to the knife in question, as he debated his ability to dash to the kitchen to get it, plunge it deep into the officer's chest, and somehow get rid of the body, all without drawing further attention from the prying neighbours and before the officer could call the station for back up. Matthew sighed again; placing his head in his hands and realising these ideas were ridiculous.

"Yeah, okay. It was me," Matthew finally admitted.

"Okay, Mr Mason, would you like to explain to me *why* you were seen running down the street with a knife?" Officer Lang proceeded to ask, continuing to write everything down upon his little note book.

"I... I don't know," Matthew replied remorsefully, thinking again of the nights events and searching his mind for an intelligible answer to give.

THE DAMAGED

"I'm afraid you're gonna have to do better than that, sir?" the officer persisted, tapping his pen upon the notepad agitatedly.

"I…I thought I heard an intruder downstairs…" Matthew told him, his voice sounding embarrassed and ashamed.

"Okay, and *what* exactly did you plan to do with the knife, Mr Mason?"

"I don't know…Just scare him off I suppose," Matthew replied, starting to sound frustrated.

It was at that point that their conversation was interrupted as the officer's radio crackled into life again.

"Two-zero-six, do you copy?"

"This is two-zero-six."

"Ten-twenty-nine on Matthew Mason. No outstanding warrants."

"Ten-four."

"Okay, Sir, carry on please. Did you find an intruder?"

"No, no I didn't," Matthew replied solemnly.

"Okay, sir. I'm gonna let you off with a warning this time, but if I get another report like this then you will be arrested for possession of a dangerous weapon. Understood?" he told him, finished off his notes and returning his pad and pen to his inside pocket again.

Matthew released a sigh of relief and nodded, feeling his racing heart finally starting to slow.

"Okay. Thank you," Matthew replied with a smile.

"Okay. Have a good day then sir, I'll let myself out," the officer concluded, turning his back to Matthew and exiting through the door.

Tammy stood in the shower, leaning against the white-tiled wall as the water cascaded down upon her, the voices in the back of her head damning her for her sordid promiscuous behaviour the night before. They spoke to her with loathing and disgust, demanding her to feel shame for her actions, as she fought to overpower them. They were the same voices that had awoken her at 7 o'clock that morning and had panicked her into fleeing from the house.

If she had thought that the events of the night were nothing more than a mere act of lust then the situation wouldn't have been quite so bad, but as she looked across to the beautiful white golden pearl necklace that lay carefully upon the side of the white porcelain sink she knew that it meant far more than that for both of them.

She couldn't deny Matthew's clear instabilities and failings, as they had manifested themselves in her presence many times, but were they really good enough reason for her to deny her feelings for him? After all, she hardly had the best mental state herself.

The consequences of her actions then slowly started to dawn on her. Regardless of whether she decided to continue her sordid affair with Matthew or not, she would certainly be reprimanded if her actions became known, probably even dismissed from the company. She could be banned from working as a carer ever again, put on some kind of register for 'Misuse of trust', and maybe even prevented from seeing her daughter again.

Tammy's thoughts then fluttered to Jessica, as she began to relive the events in the contact centre in her head. She remembered the fearful look of rejection upon her daughter's beautiful face, the way she cowered away from her, and the way she sobbed for her father to return. Tammy immediately became overwhelmed with feelings of self-loathing again, as her head span with damning thoughts. *At least Matthew made me feel good about myself!* she thought. Tammy soon began contemplating the idea that maybe Jessica was actually better off without her. Although her intentions had always been good, it was undeniable that she had been an awful mother to her, and since the accident they had only drifted further and further apart. Despite her differences with Keith, she knew he was a good father to her. He was patient and caring, generous and loving, and would do a good job of raising Jessica without her.

Tammy felt the rising panic from within her, but as her thoughts inevitably turned to her trusted razorblade she found herself repulsed with the memories of the grim public toilet, the filthy rusted blade, and the insects that scurried around below her.

She reached for her shower puff and lathered her body in soap, scrubbing gently at the blood which had dripped from her thigh and dried upon her leg during the night. She then moved the puff to the wound itself, dabbing at it tentatively through gritted teeth as she felt the infected wound begin to throb.

Tammy sighed with exasperation and leaned back against the wall again, flustered and tormented with self-doubt and indecision.

Her thoughts then returned to Matthew as she imagined the devastated look upon his face if she were to break the bad news to him. Despite his clear failings, Matthew was a good man trying to make the best of a bad situation, and after all he had been through in his life he certainly didn't deserve further heartbreak, especially not from the very person tasked with caring for him and aiding in his rehabilitation. Tammy was immediately consumed with feelings of guilt and shame, realising the betrayal and hurt that she was destined to cause him, and wondering how the news would affect his mental state. *Could it tip him over the edge?* she contemplated. *Could it cause an incident? – A breakdown? What if he ended up hurting himself or getting readmitted into the hospital again? How could I live with myself if I was the cause of that?*

Tammy desperately searched her mind for other options, and possible outcomes, but none of them ended well, for either of them.

She slumped down into a sitting position in the shower, crinkling her face in a frustrated tormented frown. She buried her head in her hands and began to cry, her salty tears seemingly invisible behind the spray of the shower.

Tammy's anxiety and desperation began to steadily rise again, quickly peaking and sending her head into a spin. Her heartbeat raced, her skin began to tingle, and she started to find it hard to breathe. Her thoughts quickly returned to the packet of razorblades in the cupboard next to her, and this time she was unable to fight them off. She quickly stood, almost slipping on the wet porcelain floor, and reached out for the cupboard.

The blade slipped into her skin like a knife through butter, without hesitation or resistance, oozing with blood that immediately diluted into the stream of the shower, riding the current of the water and swirling in a gentle vortex down the plughole. She dropped the blade and closed her eyes in anticipation, but the expected euphoric rush failed to come, like an addict's resistance preventing the high.

Tammy exhaled in disappointment and tried to pull herself together, stepping out from the shower and patting herself dry, her body still shaking from her lingering anxieties. She wrapped a clean bandage around her wounds and dressed herself before then combing her silky black hair and brushing her teeth. Looking down at the time upon her iPhone, she suddenly realised that she was already an hour late for Matthew's appointment. Tammy shook her head in frustration, deciding that Matthew would just have to fend for himself for now. After all, missing one dose of pills would hardly be the end of the world, and after the events of last night Matthew was hardly going to call Maureen to complain about her.

Gathering her things together, along with the beautiful pearl necklace which she slipped gently into her bag, Tammy slowly made her way to the door. She slowly meandered towards the local shops, scuffing her feet and scowling at the ground as she went, her head continuing to ruminate over the outcome of her pending decision. Entering the chemists, she offloaded her handbag full of repeat prescriptions for her clients' week ahead, and piled them all down upon the counter.

The chemist's young assistant looked down at the large pile with discontent before peering back up at Tammy again with a raised eyebrow.

"Will you be waiting for these?" he asked, tapping his fingers agitatedly against the counter.

"Yes," Tammy replied lethargically, barely moving her eyes from their distant gaze upon the floor.

"Okay. It'll be about twenty minutes, or so," the assistant replied reluctantly, scooping the prescriptions together and taking them out into the back area.

Tammy turned her back and walked out of the shop again, before then stepping inside the newsagents next door.

"Twenty Bensons, please," she asked the shop assistant. As he turned to grab the cigarettes from the counter, Tammy found herself staring longingly at the rows of beckoning spirits upon the shelves before her, calling to her, luring her, silently making promises of taking away her pain. She closed her eyes and steadied herself, trying to find the strength inside of her to resist.

"Would you like anything else, Miss?" the assistant asked, looking at Tammy strangely as she continued to stare hypnotically at the bottles.

"Yeah...Can I...Can I have a..." she began hesitantly. Frowning and pinching the bridge of her nose with her index finger and thumb, imagining the sharp crisp taste of the vodka as it flowed gently down her throat.

"Miss?" the assistant repeated.

She pulled her eyes away from the bottles and turn to face the assistant, still looking at her with strange bewilderment.

"No... No that's all, thank you," she finally replied, forcing a smile upon her face and sliding a ten pound note onto the counter.

Tammy collected the medication and proceeded with her daily rounds; dishing out the medication, changing a few soiled pads, and trying her best to blank out Mr Carlson's sexual and verbal abuse. Before she knew it, it was then time to face Matthew again, and time for her to make a decision.

Approaching the house nervously, and still undecided as to what she would do, Tammy knocked gingerly upon the door. The door quickly flung open and Matthew stood in the doorway, looking down at her with a wide smile and a look of relief upon his face.

"Hey!" he greeted her enthusiastically. —"Where have you been? I've been worried about you!" he continued, starting to frown at the sight of Tammy's tormented expression.

"Hey, Matthew. I'm sorry I never made it this morning, I lost track of time and then I needed to get some prescriptions and get to the next clients and I... I'm sorry..." she rambled at him, obviously trying her best to avoid eye contact.

THE DAMAGED

"It's okay, Darling, don't worry about it!" he replied, returning the warm smile to his face. –"You coming in then?" he continued.

Tammy stepped inside the house with a forced smile and made her way straight to the kitchen, unloading the following week's worth of pills from her bag and beginning to count them into the appropriate sections of Matthew's plastic pill box.

"Did you take your pills this morning?" she called out as she noticed them missing from the morning section of the box.

"I did, yes," he replied, stepping up behind her with the hot cup of tea that she had completely ignored.

Resting the cup down upon the kitchen counter, Matthew placed his hand upon the small of her back and rubbed it tenderly.

"What's wrong, Tammy?" he asked, looking down at her with a frown, but already knowing what the answer would be. The expression upon her face was not that of a person who shared his feelings of love and joyousness, the feelings of excitement at what the future may hold, or the feeling of wholeness. Her expression was of torment, of awkward anticipation, and he knew with certainty that his heart was about to be broken.

Tammy stopped fiddling with the pills and took a deep breath, looking around to the cup of tea and then up to Matthew, looking deep into his big blue eyes and wishing that life wasn't so damn complicated for her. She contracted her facial muscles, which dragged the corners her mouth up to form a curve, but to call it a 'smile' would be a fallacy, as it lacked the sentiment of the gesture. She then motioned to speak before hesitating, looking back down at the counter again, the torment upon her face clearly growing by the second.

The room filled with an awkward silence. Matthew continued to gently rub the small of her back, hoping that it would somehow ease her torment. He searched his mind for the courage to finally tell her how he felt, in one last ditch attempt to try and change what he knew she wanted to say, but the words never came.

"I think last night was a mistake, Matthew," Tammy finally uttered, her quiet timid voice only just audible.

"Oh, I see," he replied dejectedly, his face slumping down with limp sadness. –"Did I do something wrong?" he asked, raising his eyebrows and removing his hand from her back.

"No, no. It's not you, Matthew, it's me!" she told him, embarrassed by the cliché line as soon as she had spoken it. –"I just can't get involved with a client, especially at the moment with all the problems with my daughter," she explained further, anguish flustering upon her face.

Matthew nodded and smiled before looking away and gazing deep into the secluded rear garden, searching for the composure to accept his rejection with dignity.

"It's okay, Darling. I understand," he replied in a surprisingly calm tone. –"You love your daughter; I can't hate you for that, can I? Maybe in the future when things are different? Yeah?" Matthew continued, but his composed response was nothing more than a façade designed specifically to save her from her guilt. Tammy remained silent, nodding, her eyes resting upon the floor with sombre relief that Matthew had taken it so well.

Matthew maintained his smile and gave Tammy a gentle peck on the cheek, whilst inside he felt his world slowly crumbling away. All his dreams and aspirations of a normal, happy life now seemed like nothing more than an unreachable pipe dream once again. His newfound freedom now seemed meaningless and purposeless and, as the thoughts of loneliness and emptiness began to swirl around his head, he felt a longing ache within his stomach start to groan.

They both stood in awkward silence for a few moments longer, before Tammy nervously returned to the pills, removing the last two 'sugar pills' from the evening section of the plastic container and placing them down in front of him.

"Don't forget these," she told him, her quiet voice remaining weak and vulnerable.

Matthew looked down to the pills and then back up to Tammy with an ironic chuckle, reaching forward to fill a glass with water.

"How could I forget?" he replied, throwing them to the back of his throat and swallowing them down with the water.

Tammy nodded and gathered her things, slowly making her way to the door with uneasy footsteps.

"I'll see you in the morning then, yeah?" she asked, trying her best to sound cheerful but unable to mask the quivering wave in her tone.

"Sure," he replied with another forced smile, fighting to prevent his tear ducts from erupting right in front of her.

Tammy turned her back one last time and made her way out the front door, carefully pulling it shut behind her.

Matthew released a long, anxious breath before pacing over to the lounge window and watching as Tammy slowly made her way back up to the bus stop, staring at her longingly and accidentally letting a tear escape from his eye.

"I love you, Tammy," he whispered gently.

THE DAMAGED

QUOTH THE RAVEN, THE DEMON AMON

Matthew sat bolt upright in bed, confused as to what exactly had caused the awakening. The room was silent and still, blanketed in complete darkness. He rubbed the sleep sediment from his eyes, stretched the muscles in his back, and turned to switch on his bedside lamp. It was then that he noticed it, lying at the foot of the bed like a ghostly calling card: the ominous black silky plume again.

He gingerly picked up the large feather by the stem and twirled it around between his thumb and index finger, perplexed and intrigued. The feather sparked again like it had before but the sensation was different, less intense and somehow welcoming, like a warm feeling of contentment. Matthew considered the possibility that it belonged to his friend the raven, that maybe the bird had gotten inside the house somehow and shed it, but yet, the long silky plume seemed far too large.

The deathly silence was then interrupted by a faint tapping sound that travelled through the house and summoned his attention. He stood from the bed and hastily dressed himself in yesterday's clothes which had spent the night sprawled upon the floor, before stepping out into the hallway to find another large black feather upon the edge of the top step. The tapping then repeated from underneath him, from the kitchen or from the cellar maybe.

Matthew took his first step upon his descent down the stairs and it was then that a cackle of thunder cracked from the dark clouds above him, followed by the gentle splatter of rain that echoed upon the drainpipes of the house. The wind started to gather force as it whistled down through the treetops and blew against the walls of the house. Matthew could feel his anxieties starting to grow within him, but he refused to let them take control.

He reached the bottom of the stairs and reached for the light switch.

SIMON LAW

The bulb lit and flooded the room with light before sparking and exploding. The glowing sparkles of the filament gently floated down through the air and soon enough the room was dark again. Then came the tapping again, tap-tap tapping upon the cellar door. Matthew considered the thought that maybe it was just the wind, blowing in through the garden entrance of the cellar and rattling upon the inner door, but he dismissed it just as quickly.

He gingerly stepped though the lounge and into the kitchen, just in time to catch a glimpse of two wrinkled spindly fingers before they disappeared through the gaps of the cellar's slatted wooden doors. Intrigued, but strangely unafraid, Matthew quickly paced through the kitchen, slid out a kitchen knife from its wooden block, pulled open the creaking cellar door, and descended down into the depths.

There before him, in the dark shadows of the musty dank room, lurked a strange creature with a red translucent glow. Matthew squinted to make out its figure as it shifted agitatedly from side to side between the wine racks in a fuzzy murky blur. Matthew's eyes slowly adapted to the dark, and as his night vision kicked in, the creature's fuzzy outline became crisp and defined. The strange creature had the body of a man, muscular and pale and charred from the flames of hell from whence it came. Its head and wings were that of a raven – black and silky, and between its legs slithered the long scaly tail of a serpent.

The winged beast tipped its neck and it croaked into the air, sending out an incomprehensible noise that echoed and bounced against the wooden beams of the cellar. The noise travelled through the air and as it reached Matthew and resonated against the hammers of his ears, he understood what the beast was yearning. The beast was hungry, but the void that ached within his stomach was not for food, but for blood, for murder, for vengeance.

The beast vanished in an instant before then re-materializing again behind him, its putrid rotten breath raising goose bumps across the back of Matthew's neck while its slithering serpent tongue lathered it in viscous dripping slime.

It croaked again, louder and stronger than before, and by the time the sound had dissipated into obscurity, Matthew felt the beast's void within himself. It grew and rumbled within him like an addict craving a hit, and soon the desire grew stronger than his will to deny it.

The beast cocked its head and gazed at him expectantly, its piercing black eyes shimmering with speckles of crimson red. It ruffled its feathered wings and flapped them angrily with frustration and discontent, before then slowly vanishing once more into the darkness.

A strong gust of wind blew into the cellar from between the gaps in the rear cellar door, engulfing and embracing Matthew within it. He felt the air all around him, tingling over his skin with its icy and unforgiving touch, but yet, somehow, he finally felt no fear of it.

Matthew held out his arms, opening his palms and welcoming the sensation in. Another gust of wind suddenly ripped the rear cellar doors wide open and exposed the rear garden to Matthew's view, the blades of grass glimmering before him under the light of the moon above, beckoning and luring him out.

Matthew slid the kitchen knife between his belt and his trousers and pulled a pair of his father's old work boots upon his feet, his eyes mesmerized and transfixed upon the stormy night sky and the gleaming blue moon.

He stepped out into the garden, pulling the cellar doors shut behind him and edging his way towards the rear gate. His friend the raven watched intently from its branch within the conifer tree. Matthew slowly slid across the rusty orange bolt of the gate with a grating screech, pulled the gate open, and disappeared out into the night.

Creeping eagerly though the dense wooded area behind the house, listening to the rustle and crunch of branches and leaves below his feet, Matthew finally reached the main road. It was empty, deserted and silent. The concrete path sloped down to a damp cold subway underneath the road, where the pungent stench of urine and faeces filled the dense air.

As he emerged from the other side, the angry night sky started to settle; the dark clouds had dissipated and the wind had diminished to a mere gentle breeze. Matthew felt calm and peaceful, as if the weather and his mind were somehow connected.

He continued to walk down the road, his gentle pace slowly accelerating with each footstep. The only sounds to break through the silence were the mild distant hum of the night bus and the rhythmic tapping of Matthew's own shoes upon the cold concrete ground below. The air felt cool and refreshing upon his skin and the gentle blue hue of the full moon was soothing.

As Matthew continued to venture further into the dark night, his sense of purpose and urgency began to grow with hungry yearning within his gut. With every further step that he took, he felt his hands and fingers began to tingle and twitch, not through anxiety which he was accustomed to, but through excitement and anticipation at the thought of the fulfilment that the night may provide.

Matthew's pace increased, the urge within him becoming more overwhelming by the minute. He reached a main street where the hue of the night quickly faded from blue to orange, but this area was just as deserted as the rest. Clenching his fists in an attempt to subside the pulsating through his body, his eagle eyes searched through the night for prey.

The local train station slowly came into sight. Matthew quickly approached, and made his way to the dusty alleyway around the side of the building. He slowed his pace back down again, silencing the tapping of his footsteps upon the echoic concrete ground and returning to a state of inconspicuous stealth, as he approached the fly-ridden bins and spotted a stray leg protruding from between them.

Matthew stopped in his tracks and stared down at the leg in contemplation, pondering his first move with excitement and anticipation. It was at that point that he felt the flutter of air upon the back of his neck, as his feathered friend glided past his head and soared up into the night sky above him, landing with grace and poise upon the roof of the building and croaking loudly into the air. To Matthew, this was all the sign he needed that the time was right, and that his search for prey was now over.

He carefully gripped the handle of the kitchen knife and slowly slipped it out from between his trousers and belt, gingerly pacing forwards towards the stray leg. The overpowering stench of stale urine bombarded the receptors in his nose and he was immediately taken back to that night in eighty-seven. He remembered his crippling terror as he watched the events from within the cellar, he remembered the sight of his parents' blood as it flowed across the kitchen lino and dripped down between the gaps in the cellar's wooden doors as he stood paralysed and powerless.

Matthew clenched his teeth and edged closer to the stray leg between the bins, giving it a gentle tap with his father's steel-toed work boot. A figure slowly shifted and wriggled from underneath a pile of old newspapers, before releasing a quiet disgruntled groan and then becoming motionless once more. Matthew kicked the leg again, more forceful than before, and watched as the pile of inanimate newspapers suddenly sprung into life.

"Uh? What?!" the man groaned in a husky delirious grunt, pulling the paper away from his face and staring up at Matthew from the ground. "What the fuck do you want?" the man demanded.

Matthew looked back at the figure and studied the contours of his dirty, bearded face. The man was clearly too young to have been his parents' killer. His face was the wrong shape and his nose didn't bend off to the right like it should have; but to Matthew, it almost didn't matter. He was still a filthy tramp, almost certainly a raging alcoholic by the smell. Who knew what else he was guilty of too. He was vermin, a disease of society, no better than the filthy rat that the raven had devoured before. No one would miss him, and Matthew's burning urges were far greater than his pity to spare the man.

THE DAMAGED

"I said, what the fuck do you want? You little prick!" the man repeated in an angry slur.

Matthew rolled his eyes and increased his grip on the kitchen knife, the man's expletives grinding upon him and infuriating him further. Matthew took another step closer to the man, towering over him with dominance and omnipotent superiority. The orange hue of the street light bounced upon the edge of the kitchen knife as it sparkled and glared, finally bringing the blade to the dishevelled inebriate's attention. His eyes widened and fixated upon it, the disgruntled anger in his face quickly slumping down and filling instead with profound dread.

"There's no need to swear, is there?" Matthew asked, his voice remaining calm and centred. "I don't understand people's need to swear all the time, it just highlights your incompetence of using the Queen's English."

"Look, I'm... I'm sorry, fella. Okay?" the man replied abruptly, his voice beginning to quiver with uncertainty as his eyes remained fixed on the shimmering blade. "What do you want from me? I have nothing!"

Matthew increased his grip on the blade further, turning the tips of his fingers white under the pressure. He extended his arm, pointing the knife directly at the pleading man's throat and staring down at him in disgust.

"What's your name?" Matthew asked.

"Mark. My name's Mark," the man replied nervously, raising his hands in surrender and backing himself into the brick wall behind him. "...and what's *your* name?"

"You can call me King-Kong for all I care!" Matthew replied, grinning to himself in twisted angry reminiscence, his heart starting to beat faster and sweat starting to drip from the side of his head.

"What do you want from me?" the man repeated again. He started to sob and shake with increasing fear and frustration.

"Nothing. I don't want anything from you," Matthew told him, his tone becoming agitated as he stared deep into the throbbing vein upon the man's throat. "I just want you to die."

Matthew retracted the blade and swiped it fiercely against the man's throat, through his vocal chords, and through the pulsating vein that had teased him. The man's throat spurted up in the air in seeming slow motion, allowing Matthew the time to admire each individual crimson rippling droplet as they glistened and sparkled with light and lit up the sky like a macabre bloody firework.

Adrenaline and ecstasy immediately flooded through Matthew's body, tingling and pulsating through him in intense waves more pleasurable than he could ever have imagined, leaving him feeling breathless and warm inside. He felt fulfilled, whole again, as if the void in his stomach and the missing segment in his life had now been filled, if only temporarily.

The man clutched frantically at his throat as blood poured and splattered all over the brick wall and against the bins either side of him, his skin becoming paler by the second and his eyes filling with hopeless desperation.

Matthew watched in awe as the man continued to thrash about, violently crashing into the bin and convulsing, a twisted, tormented look upon his face as his jaw locked open in a silent breathless scream.

The bloodied spectacle was a visual amazement to Matthew, who soon found himself aroused by the sight of it. He took a deep intake of air and released it slowly, watching as the man became increasingly limp and lifeless, his entire attire drenched in his own blood. Matthew then approached again, raising the knife back up and plunging it deep between the man's ribs, twisting it around in the wound and scraping it along the bone.

"That's for my parents!" he whispered gently into the man's ear, twisting the blade further before wrenching it back out again.

Matthew took another long satisfying breath and watched as the last ounce of life departed from the man's limp body, before it slid down the brick wall and slumped into the pile of blood-soaked newspapers and garbage.

Matthew took a step back and checked the area to see if the events had aroused any attention, but the streets were still deserted like before. Lifting the lid of one of the large bins and propping it open against the brick wall, Matthew then grasped the body by the scruff of the neck and the buckle of the belt and lifted it up into the air. Projecting the rancid corpse with all his might, Matthew watched it fly through the air and plummet down with an echoic crash into the filthy, fly-ridden bin where it belonged.

THE DAMAGED

PERFECTION BY DESIGN

Monday morning slowly broke upon the sleepy town, but whilst most were still slumbering within their soft comfy beds, the local train station was ablaze with deafening screams of horror.

The police arrived in droves within minutes of the chilling morning phone call, and listened to the young Portuguese cleaner as she sat sobbing hysterically in the station staff room, explaining her grisly find that morning while taking out the trash.

The alleyway was quickly cordoned off with yellow police tape before the forensics team then got to work, analysing the various blood splatters upon the cold brick walls and combing the surrounding area for evidence.

PC Lang was among the first on scene to catch a glimpse of the ghastly mutilated body, but was soon pushed aside upon the arrival of his superiors and tasked with standing guard along the yellow cordoned line. The local press soon arrived after that, eager with their cameras and desperate to catch sight of the bloody crime scene. The town was far from a place of utopia, it had its faults and its bad eggs like any other, but an actual murder was rare, and to be the first to get the scoop was morbidly exciting to all of them.

Within an hour the station had become a bustling circus of curious bystanders and news crews, all desperate for a piece of the action, as PC Lang fought hard to try and keep them all at bay.

The London Olympics and its closing ceremony were the key talking points of the national news that morning, but as the newsreaders passed over to the local news, the murder was the first thing on the agenda.

Matthew stared deep into the TV screen with glee and contentment in his face, as his moonlit exploits were deconstructed and discussed. His excitement then grew further, as the reporter cut to a fuzzy CCTV recording of the incident. Matthew had not been aware of the camera at the time, but was pleased that it had captured the moment, allowing him the pleasure of reliving the entire act again from the comfort of his lounge.

Matthew was aware that his newfound pastime was far from consistent with his desire for an amiable life that would have made his parents proud; but despite the contradiction, he felt satisfied, more so than he ever could have imagined possible.

The feeling that had pulsated through his body had been amazing, and even now, over four hours after the event, he could still feel the residual tingles from it. He knew for certain that he wanted to do it again, to feel that buzz pulsating through him, but whilst the thought of release excited him, the fear of getting caught and sent back to the hospital was starting to creep into the shadows of his mind.

Matthew prised his eyes away from the glorious images upon the TV screen and looked up to his parents' photo, silently asking them for understanding and approval. It was then that he noticed the absence of the frown lines that had once consumed their brows, and stood from the chair to take a closer look. The smiles upon their faces seemed wider than before, and their eyes seemed kind and accepting. A voice within his head then spoke to him, blessing him and exonerating him from regret or guilt for his actions. Matthew smiled back at the image, tenderly running his fingers upon the frame and gently nodding back in appreciation. *I'll find who did this to you,* he thought, *and anyone else who fits the bill, well, they're all fair game too. The world will be a better place for it!*

Returning his eyes to the TV screen, Matthew analysed the CCTV footage closer, noticing his mistakes and his countless carelessnesses throughout. If he were to commit the act again then he needed to perfect the art, reduce the evidence, eliminate any chance of getting caught and sent back to that hell-hole of a hospital again.

His first mistake was the fingerprints that he had undoubtedly left across the lid of the rubbish bin, although luckily his prints were not on file. His second mistake was not noticing the CCTV that had captured the entire event, and it was nothing but pure luck that the camera had not seen his face.

He began to make a mental note of things he needed to address during his next outing, when it suddenly occurred to him that the biggest piece of evident of all was the body itself. If there was no body at all, then there would be no evidence that a crime had even taken place. After all, no one would file a missing persons report for a tramp, would they? But how could he dispose of a body?

Matthew continued mulling over his killing process as he turned to the fridge in search of his breakfast. He removed his last steak of beef from the fridge and cut it free of its plastic wrap with the same knife he had used to murder the tramp. He placed it down upon a clean white plate, completely raw, and stared down with awe and lust at the trickling blood oozing from the meat. Taking a seat at the dining table, Matthew devoured the entire steak with insatiable hunger, splattering the cow's blood carelessly around the twenty-four hour stubble on his chin. The taste of the blood within his mouth was a glorious sensory wonderment, and was almost as arousing to him as the act of spilling the blood himself.

Tammy arrived at the house late that morning, but Matthew had expected this, as her morning bus route needed to pass through the chaotic crime scene at the station. She finally arrived at nine-twenty, apologising for her tardiness and citing the aforementioned commotion as the reason. Her morning cup of tea was cold by this point and so Matthew quickly made her another.

Tammy looked gaunt and exhausted to Matthew that morning, more so than usual, and the smell of cigarettes upon her breath was pungent, as if she had spent the entire morning chain-smoking. Her appearance and persona were worrying to Matthew, who, despite her rejection of him, still wanted her to find happiness in her life. Despite her apparent slovenliness, Matthew still looked upon her with attraction and longing. He had hoped that his new moonlit hobby might have distracted him from his feelings for her, but as he stared upon her gleaming figure he knew that this was not the case.

Tammy's visit was brief and sterile that morning, as she awkwardly tried to avoid eye contact or any prolonged conversation with him. She watched him take his morning 'sugar pills' with a vacant look in her eyes and a forced smile upon her face, before leaving him deceptively comatose in his father's Chesterfield and making her way off to her laborious AA meeting.

With his parents' killer still in mind, Matthew retrieved his charcoal sketches from the bag below his bed. He took them into the dining room and laid them all out upon the table, studying each one and re-imagining how the passing of twenty-five years would have changed the man's appearance. Removing a clean sheet of artist paper from the bag, along with a fresh piece of charcoal, Matthew began to create the new face he had imagined, paying close attention to the bulbous curve of the man's brow and the right-sided crook in his large Roman nose. He then added the expected wrinkles around the brow, the eye, and the mouth, along with the expected slump of the muscles around the cheeks and the chin. Placing down the charcoal he then gazed upon his creation, studying the image intensely until it was scorched firmly into his mind.

A series of discouraging thoughts started to flutter across Matthew's mind – *what if he was dead already?' What if he was no longer homeless? How on earth would I ever find him?*

Matthew's ruminations were broken by a strange throbbing sensation in his right shoulder blade. The pain had been present since he had awoken that morning, but he had dismissed its origin as simply sleeping upon it awkwardly. The pain had faded away with the excitement of the morning news report, but now it beckoned his attention again, as the tingles and throbs began to intensify.

Reaching around with his left arm, Matthew ran his fingers over the skin curiously, searching for the cause of the pain and stumbling upon a strange lump, tender and sharp to the touch. He fingered it gingerly with one finger, causing the throb to morph to a sharp stabbing pain that shot through his body. He released a mild yelp and began to frown in confusion and discomfort, before proceeding to gently squeeze the small lump with two fingers. The lump began to weep and ooze with fluid that he felt trickling down his back, as the sharp point of the lump ejected further from his skin. Matthew pulled off his shirt and tried to gaze around at the strange infliction, but his neck would not bend enough for him to see it, and so he made his way to the bathroom instead.

Standing in the bathroom, shoulder blade facing the mirror, he peered around curiously at his reflection. The lump itself was red and puffy and dripping with a mixture of blood and pus. In the centre of the lump, protruding a good inch from the puffy skin, was a long black twig-like object.

Matthew fingered the object curiously again, before gripping upon it with his index finger and thumb, and slowly starting to pull. The object was tough and resistant to move at first, but with a little stern persuasion it suddenly started to budge. Matthew grit his teeth as the pain increased, as he continued to pull at the object with determination and felt the strange object moving around between his muscles and layers of skin. The smooth black twig-like stem of the object was then joined by a bulky soft black body, as more and more of the object became exposed. The more that Matthew pulled, the more of the bloodied black object appeared from his sore and weeping back. The object seemed never-ending, but just as Matthew began to lose the will to carry on, he finally reached the end and pulled it clean from the gaping hole in his back. He released a deep sigh of relief.

Matthew regained his breath and his composure, before looking down in ghastly disbelief at the bloodied object he had removed. It was

THE DAMAGED

a feather, a black silky plume that belonged to the raven – not the one that lived within the firs, but to the beast from the cellar that now seemed to breathe within him.

Fear and repugnance suddenly tried to flood Matthew's fragile mind, but as quickly as the feelings appeared they were superseded by feelings of calm and reassurance. The beast was his friend, his ally, his tour guide on his mission of vengeance. He meant Matthew no harm, only guidance and comfort.

He smiled down at the bloodied black plume in understanding of its message to him, before gently placing it down upon the sink and washing the blood and pus from his hands. He proceeded to shave and shower before returning again to his charcoal sketches in the dining room and re-examining them once again.

The pictures needed to be on display as a reminder, as a point of reference, but somewhere out of sight from Tammy and everyone else. After gathering them all together neatly, Matthew looked around in consideration. His eyes then rested upon the door to the cellar; dark, secluded, and out of view. It was perfect. Descending down into the dark, dank depths, Matthew switched on the flickering light and began to search through his father's tools, retrieving an old rusty hammer and a selection of old crooked nails. He placed the sketches down and one by one he began to hammer them into the top rung of wooden beams around the room, his newest creation taking pride of place at the beginning of the home-made gallery.

Placing down the hammer again, Matthew stared up at all the faces surrounding him, watching them all as they watched him back, taunting him, laughing at him. He gritted his teeth and breathed deeply, feeling his anxiety starting to rise. His heart started to race away, but just as the feeling began to peak, it vanished, replaced immediately with the strange sense of calm he had experienced previously. He looked around the cellar curiously, examining the shadows and the gaps between the wine racks. He was alone, that was for sure, but he could feel the presence of the beast, helping him, soothing him, filling him with confidence. He released his breath and smiled calmly, looking back up at the images again with a new sense of self-assurance.

"I *will* find you!" he gently whispered with certainty.

Matthew vacuumed and polished the house, washed and ironed his father's clothes, and spent the rest of the day exercising. He performed fifty press-ups followed by fifty sit-ups, and then repeated them again, all the while continuing to reminisce upon his gruesome crime and further contemplating his dilemma of 'the body', and how he would dispose of it.

SIMON LAW

At 3pm he ended his routine, took another shower, and made himself a cup of tea. He switched the television over to the cartoons and enjoyed them from the comfort of his father's chair, where he remained until Tammy's return at 5pm.

Tammy's visit that evening was as brief and clinical as it had been that morning, and her shifting eyes continued to avoid any contact with his. Just before leaving again, Tammy made a quick visit to the toilet, and it was then that Matthew saw an opportunity. He quickly grabbed her unattended handbag from where it sat upon the coffee table and proceeded to sift through it for any item of use.

The oversized bag was heavy and filled to the brim with various different items, which he rummaged through at speed. He pushed aside the paperwork and binder of clients' addresses that lay at the top of the bag, and began to examine the items below; a set of keys, a mobile phone, a hairbrush. He then came across the small box of disposable latex gloves which he had expected to find and immediately removed a pair, sliding them discreetly into the back pocket of his trousers. At the bottom of the bag, Matthew came across a pot of pills; the prescription label had Tammy's name in bold letters, and below it read 'Zolpidem 10mg', followed by 'To be taken once-daily before bed'. Matthew recognised the name immediately, as it was one of the drugs used frequently in the hospital where he had once resided. They were sleeping pills.

Matthew heard the flush of the toilet upstairs and started to panic. He hurried to empty a few of the pills into his hand, deciding that they might come in handy at some point. He frantically screwed the lid back on as he heard the footsteps approaching, rearranged the bag to how he had found it, and quickly returned it back to the coffee table. Tammy reappeared in the room mere seconds later, but was completely oblivious to Matthew's intrusive actions. She smiled at him numbly, presented him with his usual blue pills, and then she was gone again, back to the bus, back to her lonely two-bedroomed flat.

Matthew made himself some dinner, made a new shopping list for Tammy in the morning, and went to bed early, ensuring to set his bedside alarm for 3am. He tossed and turned in his bed for a long time, the excitement and anticipation of the night ahead swirling around his mind like that of an excited child on Christmas Eve and preventing him from turning off, but eventually his fatigue became too strong to fight, and he finally nodded off at around 10pm.

The alarm clock sprang into life at 3am as expected, but Matthew was fully awake long before then, staring at the blue-hued twinkling night stars from his bedroom window as if hypnotised by them. The

THE DAMAGED

very thought of the night had already caused an erection to throb within his pants, and the adrenaline already running through him was immense. He took a breath and tried to curb his enthusiasm, knowing full well that he needed to remain calm and focused to ensure that everything would go to plan.

He switched off the alarm and dressed himself in a fresh clean set of his father's clothes – a crisp ironed white shirt, a pin-striped jacket and trouser set, and a silky black tie. Standing at the bathroom mirror, Matthew admired his appearance with an arrogant smile.

He strolled to the kitchen and removed the customary knife from the wooden block, inspected the sharpness of the blade, and slid it carefully between his trousers and belt where it hid behind the long pin-striped jacket. He slipped the stolen pair of latex gloves upon his hands, slid on his father's smart polished black shoes, and grabbed his black leather wallet from the side.

Matthew departed the house through the cellar, went out the back gate, through the dense wooded area, and crossed under the road via the faecal-stinking subway. The throbbing bulge in the front of his pants had yet to dissipate, and as he strolled further and further into the night his excitement only increased.

He meandered his way through the dusty deserted streets, hiding inconspicuously in the shadows with his eyes wide and vigilant, until reaching a small convenience store. The store had long since closed for the day and sat silently in the dark, its shop-front windows now securely hidden behind sturdy metal shutters. To the side of the store, illuminated under a dull fluorescent light, was an ATM machine that gently glowed out through the darkness.

Matthew slowly approached the machine, carefully checking he still had no unwanted attention, and slipped his debit card gently into the slot. He typed his pin number (7-8-9-1) into the glowing keypad of the machine, and proceeded to withdraw two hundred pounds in crisp fresh twenty-pound notes. Sliding the cash carefully into the breast pocket of his jacket, he removed his card from the machine and quickly continued on his journey into the night.

Ensuring that his footsteps upon the cold concrete were dull and quiet, he carefully carried on up the road. He soon reached the rear entrance to the local park and entered. The orange hue of the street lights slowly started to fade behind him, as the natural blue twinkle of the night stars became more visible. The pavement turned to dirt, and then to grass, as he continued further into the park, listening to the distant cooing of nocturnal birds in the surrounding trees and the mild rustling of his feet against the blades.

He stopped, motionless and silent, focusing his eyes upon a park bench he had spotted in the distance. He stepped closer, his eyes fixated upon the bench as his heart began to speed and his adrenaline started to rise. The night was dark and his sight was murky, but the figure lying down upon the bench was undeniable.

Edging his way closer and closer to the bench, Matthew stretched out his fingers and rolled his shoulders in anticipation. He looked up to the sky, to the gleaming moon and stars above him, looking for confirmation from the raven. The raven didn't disappoint, and responded on cue, croaking loudly into the quiet night sky and gliding gracefully above Matthew's head.

Matthew smiled and edged closer still, close enough now to look down upon the figure's features and begin to compare them in his head to the charcoal sketches that hung within the cellar.

The figure's hair and beard were long and greasy, and the flickers of grey throughout them were evident of his growing age. His skin was dirty and dry, with patches of cuts and scabs, but the light was too dim to compare any further. The dishevelled tramp released an awkward phlegmy snore and rolled over on the bench, completely concealing his face from view.

Matthew calmed and centred himself, before clearing his throat loudly to gain the man's attention. The tramp immediately woke, turning to gaze upon Matthew with a confused disgruntled frown upon his withered and wrinkled face. Matthew smiled welcomingly in return, continuing to size him up in contemplation.

"Hi there, I'm sorry to wake you," Matthew began, his soft pleasant tone becoming reassuring and comforting to the startled man. –"I just wondered if you wouldn't mind helping me with something," he continued.

"Help you? H-Help you with what?" the man replied hesitantly in a timid husky voice, backing away from Matthew cautiously.

"I just need someone to help me carry something to my house, it's quite heavy you see," Matthew replied, offering the man a smile and reaching into his breast pocket for the cash. "I'll make it worth your while?" he continued, flashing the cash into the man's sights.

The tramp's eyes immediately fixed upon the money, and his frown slowly faded. The elated thought of being able to buy food and alcohol again was overwhelming to him, and the offer was impossible to refuse. He smiled back at Matthew, exposing his black and rotting teeth, and nodded his head in agreement.

"Excellent, thank you very much indeed," Matthew told him, placing the wad of cash into the man's grimy eager hands and watching his face continue to light with glee.

"It's just this way, please," Matthew told him with another smile, gesturing his hand toward the opening from where he had come.

The man obeyed with trepidation, following the dirt path down to the entrance as Matthew followed closely behind.

"What's your name?" Matthew asked as they continued down the street.

"Elliot, my name's Elliot," the tramp replied, looking back at Matthew over his shoulder.

"And how old are you, Elliot? –If you don't mind me asking?" Matthew continued.

"I'm...I'm 58," the man replied hesitantly, suspicious of Matthew's questioning but answering regardless, the excitement over the wad of cash in his pocket still overwhelming him.

"Tell me, Elliot, have you been on the streets for long?" Matthew continued further, pondering the man's responses in his head and comparing them to that of the killer.

"About ten years or so, I can't really remember to be honest," the man replied, again looking back at Matthew over his shoulder with suspicion.

Matthew quickly realised that the man's answers were not entirely consistent with that of the killer, but it was also possible that he was lying. Matthew needed to get him back to the house, to compare his face more closely to that of the charcoal sketch before he would know for sure.

They continued down the road, past the convenience store and down through the meandering streets, Matthew's excitement and anticipation now rising so high that his hands had begun to shake.

Matthew reached back and gently fingered the handle of the knife with his trembling hand, ensuring it was still there, still in easy reach, still ready for its imminent use, and it was.

They then reached the subway and Matthew gestured for them to enter.

"It's just this way, not long now. Thanks again for your help!" Matthew told him.

They descended the stairs of the subway. Matthew reached his hand around to the knife again, feeling his heart pounding away within his chest and his fingers starting to tingle.

Matthew gripped upon the blade tightly and discreetly removed it from his belt, edging himself closer and closer to the tramp. He took one final gasp of air and grabbed him fiercely by the throat, pushing him hard against the wall of the subway, gripping his throat so tightly that no sound or breath could escape.

The same look of terror that Matthew had seen the night before then immediately consumed the man's face. His eyes became startled and wide and the veins along the side of his head began to bulge and throb. He tried to scream, but as Matthew compressed his throat tighter the scream became nothing more than a phlegmy gargle that Matthew felt vibrating underneath his palm. The man struggled and threw his arms at Matthew, but as he felt the piercing blade slipping gently between his ribs he knew that his struggle was futile.

The euphoric surge of adrenaline that pulsated through Matthew's body was immense, and equally as glorious as it had been before. He stared deep into the man's eyes with a smile, maintaining his stern pressure upon the man's throat and upon the knife that penetrated through his beating heart.

Frantic desperation froze upon the man's face as his struggles then slowly started to dissipate into random involuntary twitches, and then stillness once again.

Matthew kept the blade firmly within the man's chest, careful not to let too much blood escape onto the subway floor. He released his hand from the man's throat and slipped behind him to support the weight of his limp and lifeless corpse, wrapping his arm around the man's chest and dragging the body to the end of the subway.

Gripping the body tightly, Matthew dragged it to the top of the subway stairs, through the wooden area behind his house, through the rusted back gate, and down through the door of the cellar.

Matthew released a heavy sigh of exhaustion as he sat the body down upon the floor and leant it against the wall of the cellar. The last few euphoric surges were now fading away and his throbbing erection now started to finally subside.

Looking down at the limp body before him, Matthew smiled at his achievement, as he rolled his neck and stretched out his tiring muscles. He pulled the slatted exterior doors closed again, slipped on the cellar light, and made his way up to the kitchen to make a cup of tea.

Sipping from the cup, Matthew turned to his parent's CD player and slipped in his father's Vivaldi disc. The bright uplifting sound of harmonious strings began to fill the room, as Matthew pretended to conduct the music with his spare hand. Adjusting the volume as to not wake the neighbours, he then left the room again, continuing to drink his tea as he took a roll of black refuse sacks from below the kitchen sink and returned to the cellar once more.

He placed his tea down upon one of the tool shelves before pulling out an old wallpaper-pasting table. He erected the table in the middle of the room, all the while humming contentedly to the calming strings of Vivaldi in the background.

Turning to the body in contemplation, Matthew mulled over how best to proceed with the gruelling task at hand. He began by wrenching the

THE DAMAGED

kitchen knife out from the man's chest, placing it down upon the floor next to him. The removal of the knife caused a sudden eruption of blood from the wound. It gushed down the front of the man's ragged clothes, but the pressure of the flow was minor and soon receded to nothing more than a slight trickle. After retrieving the blood-speckled wad of cash from the man's pocket, Matthew removed the man's clothes, holding his breath in disgust of the rancid stench that emanated from the rags. Once removed, he stuffed them all inside one of the black sacks and placed it in the corner of the room. Grasping upon the man's naked and bloodied body, he lifted it and placed it face-up on the pasting table for inspection.

Matthew looked down at the man again, studying his face carefully underneath the cellar light and then looking up to his charcoal sketches. The ages of the men were very similar, and the general shape of his head was about right too, but as he compared them closer he could see that the corpse did not share the same bend of the nose, nor did it share the prominent bulge of the brow. Elliot was not the killer, Matthew knew that for sure. The revelation was unfortunate, but not as disappointing as Matthew had feared. With the killer still on the loose, Matthew still had reason to continue to kill, and it would have been a shame to have to stop now.

Matthew took another gulp of his tea and started to look through his father's tool collection, searching for something appropriate for the job at hand. After a while of deliberation, he then removed a handsaw and a Stanley knife from the selection, and placed them down upon the dead man's abdomen.

With the Stanley knife in hand, Matthew began to cut into the man's right arm, half way between his wrist and his elbow. The blood flow was minimal. It did not spurt or gush as Matthew had expected, but simply dribbled from the flesh like juice from a piece of rotting fruit. Matthew continued to cut, but it was soon apparent that the blade was too blunt for the job at hand. Instead of cutting smoothly through the flesh, it ripped it open jaggedly, and took a lot of Matthew's strength.

Matthew stopped and reassessed. He returned the blunt blade back to the tool box and searched for a replacement. With nothing suitable to be found, Matthew returned to the faithful kitchen knife once more, and continued with the job.

Resuming the slicing, Matthew cut through the thin layer of subcutaneous fat, and into the red oozing muscle below. He was surprised at how similar the muscle looked to the tender rare steaks of beef that he had recently gained such a love for. It looked alluring, appetising, and for a brief few seconds Matthew contemplated ripping out the flesh to consume it, but he resisted, unconvinced that the meat was not diseased.

He continued to cut all around the arm until the radius and ulna bones of the arm were fully exposed. Placing down the kitchen knife, Matthew then picked up the handsaw, holding the arm as still as he could with his left hand as he began sawing his way through the two brittle bones with his right.

Bone dust sprayed upon the wet crimson flesh as Matthew continued to saw. He soon reached the end of the bone. With a pleasing crack, it completely detached from the lower arm. Matthew released a grunt of manly satisfaction, as he released the saw and picked up the dismembered segment of arm. He looked at it with a smile of intrigue, as he shook it playfully and watched as the fingers started to jiggle.

Opening a new black sack, Matthew placed the bloody body part inside, before turning his attention to the other arm. He made his way through the left arm in the same manner as he had the right, before placing it inside the black bag and turning to the top two sections of each arm, cutting through each of the humerus bones between the elbow and the shoulder. He placed these two sections in the black bag as well, and tied the top of the bag in a knot.

As Matthew made a start on the legs, it was clear that rigor mortis had already started to set in, making the muscles stiff and removing the playful wiggle of the flesh that had previously kept Matthew so amused.

By the time the legs were successfully dismembered and placed in a bag, Matthew was starting to tire. The task was far more arduous than he had first expected, but he knew he now had no option left but to complete it. His sights continuously glanced longingly over to his father's array of power tools that would make light work of the task, but he knew that the noise would undoubtedly disturb his nosey neighbours who would jump at the chance of reporting him again, and it would certainly be inconvenient to have PC Lang knocking upon his front door right now.

After a short tea break to recuperate, Matthew returned to the cellar once more, reinvigorated and determined to get the job finished with time enough left to grab a few hours' sleep before Tammy's arrival at 9am.

He clenched the kitchen knife sternly and sliced it deep across the abdomen of the man, inadvertently slicing through the intestine and immediately filling the cellar with the rancid stench of vomit and bile. Matthew turned away with a repugnant grimace, holding his nose to shield himself from the overwhelming smell. But it was too late, the odour had bonded to the cilia of his nose and he could do nothing to escape from it.

THE DAMAGED

He felt himself starting to heave, and his attempts to relax the convulsing muscles were unsuccessful. He threw the knife down hastily upon the body and dashed up to the kitchen, finally releasing the pressure and gushing putrid vomit into the kitchen sink and upon the pieces of unwashed crockery within it.

"Oh, ruddy hell!" Matthew growled, regaining control of himself just in time to prevent any further obscenity from leaving his lips.

"I'm sorry, Mother. I didn't mean to swear," he whispered gently in the direction of the photograph, wiping away the vomit chunks from his lips with the sleeve of his father's shirt.

Regaining composure, Matthew descended the cellar stairs once more, gritting his teeth and more determined than ever. He moved the knife to one side and reached his hands deep into the gaping incision in the man's abdomen, gripping firmly upon the intestines and ripping them fiercely from the hole. They pulled from the wound with very little resistance, snaking out of the hole like a putrid stinking reel of sausages. He continued pulling with determination until finally reaching the end and ripping them away from the inner rectum.

Discarding the vile organ into another black bag, Matthew dived straight back into the wound again, rummaging around for the other organs and ripping the incision wider and wider each time. After piling the stomach, liver, kidneys and bladder all into the black bag, he tied the top in a tight knot, before placing the bag inside another bag and tying it tightly again, hoping that that would somehow confine the God-awful smell inside.

After briefly composing himself again, Matthew continued with the butchery. He picked up a sturdy-looking hammer and struck it aggressively into the rib cage, cracking his way through the cage two ribs at a time. He ended by cracking through the collarbone of the man, and then with his bare hands he ripped the chest open, throwing the bloody front section of the cage onto the floor and diving straight back in for the heart and lungs.

Matthew continued to chop, cut, and saw his way through the rest of the body until there was nothing recognisable left, placing all the bits in black plastic bags that he stacked up at the back of the room. By the time he had finished, his anger and frustration were all gone, and he was left in a state of exhaustion and relief that the job was finally completed.

Taking one final deep breath and releasing it euphorically, Matthew stared down at his work with a smile of unadulterated pride and achievement. *I must remember to put black bags on the shopping list for tomorrow*, he thought.

XII

ON THE BRINK OF THE ABYSS

By the following Saturday the long British summer was showing its first signs of fading away. The nights were now drawing in and the mornings were becoming increasingly bitter and fresh. With the Olympic Games now done and dusted with for another four years, Tammy felt it safe to turn on the television without fear of bombardment of irrelevant self-indulgent rubbish. She sat glued to the news that morning with a cigarette and Redbull in hand, trying to distract her mind from obsessing over her pending visit with Jessica later that day. To add to this anxiety, it was also her mother's birthday, her first birthday since her death, and Tammy needed all the distractions she could get to stop herself from falling apart.

Her last visit with Jessica had been an unmitigated disaster, and she desperately needed today's to be better, not just for the sake of the court's perception of her as a mother, but for the sake of Jessica and the future of their relationship.

It was just over a week now until Jessica was due to start primary school, and Tammy could imagine her excitement and anticipation. It should have been a time that filled Tammy with the same emotions too, but her lack of involvement had left her feeling disconnected and frustrated. She didn't even know where Keith had decided to send her, and the current court order prevented Tammy from even asking.

During the preceding week, Tammy's relationship with Matthew had become increasing cold and frosty too, with neither of them sharing more than a brief few words of conversation. Despite the lack of conversation, and Tammy's deliberate distantness, it was clear that Matthew's infatuation for her had not faded as she had hoped. He still looked upon her with longing and still ogled her with lust when her back was turned, but the desire and longing in Matthew's gaze now seemed bitter-sweet, tainted with the essence of sadness and hopelessness.

Aside from the subtle change in Matthew's smile, Tammy had noticed other changes in him as well. He seemed tired and preoccupied, and the bags below his eyes were becoming a permanent feature. Tammy had attributed the change in Matthew to the heartbreak she had caused him with her rejection, but through her dismissal she had completely missed the more serious warning signs on display. She had failed to notice the smell of vomit in the house on Tuesday and she had failed to notice the padlock that now fastened the cellar door firmly shut.

Tammy stubbed out her cigarette before immediately sparking up another, continuing to gaze numbly at the television screen as the national news then passed over to the locals. The reporter cut to an interview with the local police as they explained their progress into the investigation of the murder of Mark Burgess, the homeless man who was stabbed to death on Monday. Tammy's attention was aroused to see her own town on the news, and so leant forward to pay it closer attention. She watched as they showed the CCTV footage again before then appealing for witnesses to come forward, both indications to the audience that the police had made no progress into the case at all.

A bizarre thought suddenly occurred to Tammy, as the report triggered her memory of how Matthew had reacted to James the week before – *it couldn't have been Matthew, could it?* She dismissed the outlandish thought just as quickly, laughing it off as an absurd and fanciful suggestion. After all, Matthew couldn't even leave his house on his own.

Tammy finished off her can of Redbull and threw it directly onto the lounge floor. The coffee table itself was now completely overflowing with empty cans and rubbish by this point, so trying to confine it at this stage seemed to be a futile exercise. She switched off the television and stood, stretching her arms and making her way to the bathroom to wash and dress.

After another brief and awkward visit with Matthew, Tammy found herself in the familiar sterile setting of the contact centre. She booked herself in at the front desk and made her way down the corridor to her usual room, sitting nervously upon the chair and awaiting Jessica's pending arrival.

Tammy breathed in and out with steady, deliberate breaths, trying to hold back her rising panic and reminding herself once again of the importance of keeping calm, relaxed, and welcoming to her beautiful daughter. She clenched her teeth and tried to steady her shaking leg, fixing her gaze firmly upon the floor and trying to ignore the piercing looks from Alice, who studied her intently from her desk in the corner.

Chewing nervously upon her bottom lip in anticipation, Tammy was unable to control her twitching leg from thumping rhythmically upon the floor. Alice raised her eyebrows at Tammy in condescending judgement, before returning to her clipboard and jotting down the nervous behaviour under the 'Observations' section of her session form.

A further few minutes passed and Tammy's nerves were becoming unbearable. She reached into her handbag and removed her mobile, checked the time on the display, and returned it to her bag again. Jessica was now five minutes late arriving and the tardiness was doing nothing to appease her peaking anxiety. She slowly lifted her eyes from the floor and gazed around the room in an attempt to distract herself.

Maybe there's just a lot of traffic, Tammy contemplated. *Or maybe Jessica was late getting out of bed,* she considered further. *She'll be here soon, that's for sure. Keith would never miss an appointment. He wouldn't dare. Would he?*

Tammy bit harder upon her bottom lip, hoping that the pain would focus and align her spinning head, but it did not.

The clock reached ten past, then quarter past, and Jessica had still not arrived. Tammy's heart was now thumping in her chest like a drum on speed and she could feel her rising blood pressure pulsating fiercely through her head. She stood from the sofa and began to pace up and down the room, staring desperately from the window in the hope of catching a glimpse of Keith's car, but there was nothing. Alice was starting to stare at her watch too by this point, but continued to wait patiently, continuing to note all of Tammy's behaviour upon the form.

"Oh come on, Keith, for God's sake!" Tammy growled under her breath, continuing to pace the room with growing agitation, tensing her hands into fists and curling her toes inside her smart shoes.

She clenched her eyes and tried to reassure herself that everything would be okay, but her mind was overflowing with images of her daughter's timid, rejecting face. 'I want my daddy!' the image cried out, turning her back on Tammy and running for the door.

Tammy felt herself start to hyperventilate and her spinning head reach the brink of eruption when suddenly the phone began to ring on Alice's desk. Tammy opened her eyes and released a long satisfying sigh of relief, as Alice picked up the receiver.

"Is that her? Is she here?" Tammy asked excitedly, a smile of joy spreading across her tormented face.

"Please wait here, Miss Atkins, I'll be back in a few minutes." Alice replied dismissively, carefully avoiding the question and making her way to the door.

THE DAMAGED

Alice returned to the room a few minutes later with a sterile look of attempted sympathy upon her face.

"Please take a seat, Miss Atkins," she said, maintaining the strange look upon her face.

"No, I want to stand. What's going on? Where's my daughter?" Tammy replied sharply with a stern, piercing gaze.

"She's not coming, Miss Atkins. The father no longer feels that these meetings are beneficial for her," Alice replied bluntly.

Tammy nodded and smiled solemnly, turning back to the window and trying to stiffen the growing quiver in her lip.

"He can't do that," she muttered breathlessly to herself as she began to well up. "No, no, he can't do that!" she muttered again with a frown of disbelief, feeling herself becoming weak and consumed with cold hopelessness.

"As the custodial parent, this is the choice of the father. However, in the situation that this contradicts a court order then you have the right to contact the courts and advise them of a breach of the order...." Alice continued, but the words never registered in Tammy's mind, floating past her like nothing more than muffled background noise.

"He can't do that!" Tammy repeated once again, sitting herself gently back down upon the sofa and beginning to sob into her hands.

"Would you like a tissue, Miss Atkins?" Alice asked, but again her words did not register.

"He can't fucking do that!" Tammy repeated, as if her thoughts were stuck in a groove, unable to process, unable to accept. She repeated the line again, louder, her voice becoming crazed and hysterical as her tears escaped through the gaps in her fingers and dripped down onto the carpet below.

"HE CAN'T FUCKING DO THAT!" she screeched at the top of her voice, standing again from the sofa and kicking a box of toys as hard as she could, scattering the random assortment all across the room.

"You need to calm down, Miss Atkins. There are other children in the building!" Alice told her with a stern, unsympathetic grimace.

"Fuck you! Why don't you make me fucking calm down? Huh? You fucking bitch!" Tammy screamed in response, her face enraged and flustered as she stared at Alice with irrepressible daggers.

"This really isn't helping your case, Tammy." Alice replied hesitantly, her voice invaded with apprehension as she gingerly backed away from Tammy's aggressive stance.

"Like you even give a shit!" Tammy raged further, ripping the telephone from its wall socket and hurling it at Alice's head. Alice flinched and covered her face as the telephone flew past her head, missing her by a mere few millimetres and smashing to pieces upon the wall behind her.

Tammy grabbed her bag and stormed from the room, down the corridor and out through the main entrance. Adrenaline pulsated through her shaking body as she continued down the street, sparking up a cigarette and turning her thoughts to her trusted razorblades.

Tammy did not cut herself, nor had she since her underwhelming experience in the bathtub, but in its absence her craving for alcohol had steadily increased. Within the hour Tammy had found herself strolling through the local cemetery, tears still steadily dripping from her sore eyes as she clutched tightly upon an unopened litre bottle of vodka.

She slowly meandered her way through the graves with a heavy head, emotionally exhausted and despondent, her body quivering like a leaf. She reached a headstone and stopped, gazing down upon it with a desolate melancholic smile. Placing down her bag and the bottle of vodka, she gently knelt herself down before the grave. She reached out with her trembling hand and tenderly brushed her fingertips upon the headstone's engraving; 'Abigail Rosemary Atkins'.

"Happy Birthday, Mum," she said in a weak, fragile voice, staring longingly at the grave with sadness and shame while her red and puffy eyes continued to stream tears down her face.

"I'm sorry..." Tammy whimpered, as she shook her head dejectedly. She turned her eyes to the ground and imagined how disappointed her mother would have been in her.

Tammy reached for the bottle and grasped it in her hand, looking down at the fluid with surrender and disgust, imagining its forbidden touch upon her lips. She released a long quivering sigh before then turning her eyes to the sky and weeping with desperation, as if praying for divine intervention, for the strength to carry on.

It was at that moment that she noticed the ominous black clouds that had consumed the skies above her, looming and brewing, personifying her mood with eerie perfection. She exhaled with dismal defeat and shook her head despondently.

Turning to the grave once more, Tammy pictured her mother's face so clearly that she could almost reach out and touch it. She pictured her smile, the sound of her voice, her laugh. Closing her eyes, Tammy trawled desperately through her mind for a memory of her mother's loving embrace; a memory long before her cancer had ravaged her body, back when hugs were more than careful, bitter-sweet clutches of haggard skin and bone, a memory from when life was good. Finally arriving upon one, Tammy smile sadly, gripping tightly onto the memory and refusing to let it slide.

THE DAMAGED

"Please help me. I can't do this on my own anymore," Tammy gently whimpered in a desperate breathy exhale. "I miss you, Mum. I'm so lonely! You're gone, Keith left me and now my own daughter can't stand the sight of me!"

Tammy gently wiped away the tears from her puffy eyes with the sleeve of her purple blouse, before reaching lethargically into her handbag for her phone. She read the time on the phone's display and grunted resentfully. She was due to be with her next client in twenty minutes, which would have been impossible to make, even if she wanted to.

She paused for a moment longer, contemplating her options, before then finding Maureen's number in her phone and dialling it with dread, thinking up an excuse whilst listening to the dial tone and preparing herself for the oncoming onslaught.

"Yes, hello?" Maureen answered in her characteristically emotionless tone.

"Hi, Maureen? It's Tammy," she spoke weakly.

"Hi, Tammy. What can I do for you?"

"I...I'm not really feeling too great this afternoon, Maureen. I don't think I'll be making my afternoon slots," Tammy told her anxiously.

"What? Why? What's wrong with you?" Maureen growled back abruptly, punctuating her sentence with an unsympathetic tut.

Tammy paused for composure, the temptation to tell Maureen to 'shove the job where the sun didn't shine' growing strong within her. She moved the phone away from her face to release an anxious breath and wipe away the tears that had begun to reform in her puffy eyes before continuing.

"I'm just feeling run down, Maureen," she explained. "Could you get Aggy or one of the other girls to see to my clients for me, please?"

"For God's sake, Tammy..." Maureen continued to growl at her, before starting to rummage through some papers. "Fine, yes. I'll get the slots covered for you. Will you be alright by tomorrow? Or do I need to redo *all* of the rotas again?"

"No, no. I should be okay by the morning, thank you."

"Fine. Well, I guess you'd better go home and rest then!" Maureen growled with apathy.

"Okay. Thank you," Tammy replied through gritted teeth, before then hanging up the phone and throwing it back into her bag again.

"Fuck you!" she uttered with a snarl.

Tammy slumped back down again, placing her head back into her hands and rocking gently back and forth on the spot. She felt a gentle breeze upon her, followed by a few raindrops that gently bounced against the back of her head and neck.

Tammy laughed to herself despairingly, noting how even the heavens above found it funny to mock her. The raindrops increased, soaking her silky black hair through to the scalp, but Tammy remained still, letting the water cascade down upon her as if she deserved every last drop of it.

She turned her eyes back down to the bottle and held it up in front of her, watching the raindrops crashing into the glass and trickling steadily down along its sides. She reached for the lid and broke the metallic seal with a gentle twist, before bringing the bottle to her face and breathing in the fumes that tingled her senses and reminded her brain of what she had been depriving it of.

Lowering her head in shame, Tammy raised the bottle up to the grave as if to toast the occasion. She thrust the cold glass upon her lips, tilted back her neck, and guzzled the forbidden liquid down. She felt the cold liquid over her tongue, down her throat, and into her stomach, before feeling its warming comfort radiating back up through her again. Continuing to cry in shame and self-loathing, Tammy glugged from the bottle again, and again.

Within a mere few minutes Tammy could feel the effects of the forbidden liquid upon her, swirling through her head, destabilising her balance and numbing her growing torment. Standing from the grave, she turned her head to the sky, feeling the rain upon her face as it continued to drench her. She blew a kiss to the grave with a sorrowful smile, gathered her things together, and began to slowly stumble away.

"See you later, Mum. I love you," she slurred.

Tammy wandered aimlessly through the town, stumbling drunkenly and scuffing her feet through puddles as the rain continued to drench her. Cold and shivering, she eventually made her way back home, but instead of ascending the stairs to her dark and lonely flat, she made her way to the rear, through an alleyway, and into the courtyard of communal garages.

She fumbled clumsily through her bag as she swayed back and forth on the spot, focusing all her concentration on not falling over. Eventually fingering upon her keys, she removed them and attempted to insert the garage key into the hole. The key bounced upon the metal, scratching and scuffing it, before finally slipping its way inside. Gripping upon the handle, Tammy wrenched the garage door up, and then stared down with sobering recall at the sight of the crumpled wreckage of her silver Renault Clio.

THE DAMAGED

Tammy focussed her blurry vision upon the vehicle, following the crinkled scars of the impact with a hesitant grimace on her wet and flustered face. Reaching down, she ran her quivering fingers gently over the array of jagged dents, stroking and caressing them as if they were throbbing wounds that needed her love to heal.

It was the first time that Tammy had set her eyes upon the car since the accident, and the sight of it immediately flooded her with images and memories that overwhelmed her with further guilt and bitter self-loathing.

She walked around the car, continuing to caress the buckled metal with her hand. Suddenly a rusted shard thrust itself into her finger. Tammy felt the pain pulsating through her, but in her intoxicated state the pain seemed to have little impact. She glanced down at her finger, to the blood now dripping from it, but merely disregarded the incident as if it had never happened. Continuing to stumble around the car, Tammy smeared the blood from her finger across the remainder of the bonnet, over the remnants of the wing mirror, and across the driver's door.

Opening the car door, she slid herself onto the driver's seat, placing her handbag down upon the seat next to her and sparking up a cigarette. Leaning her dizzy head back against the headrest of the seat, she removed the cigarette from her lips and released a dense white puff of smoke into the air.

Drunken thoughts of hopelessness and despair circled their way around her inebriated mind, reminding her of her failings and germinating the concept that maybe her broken life was beyond repair. Maybe it was about time she stopped fighting back and just admitted defeat. Jessica would never forgive her for what she did, and would never love her. Tammy would be forever alone, disassociated from society, and would never find peace.

The remnants of the vodka bottle peeked out from the top of her handbag and stared over to her with allure and promise. Tammy stared back with longing and immediately accepted its offer, deluded into thinking that *this* time its promises would be kept.

The voice inside continued to whisper words of loathing and revulsion to her, words of debilitating demoralization and disparagement, showing her images and memories of her failings, her weaknesses, her ugliness, and the inevitable desolation the future held for her.

Tammy felt her heavy eyelids gain weight as her blurry vision became fixated upon the pulsating vein on her wrist. *One little cut and it would all be over*, she thought. *The pain, the torment, it could all be eradicated in a single carefully-aimed slash.*

SIMON LAW

She allowed her eyelids to fall gently closed, resting them while she tried to recoup the energy to move, to get up and make her way to the flat where her razorblades were waiting for her. She listened to her breathing, feeling the gentle rise and fall of air in her lungs, but as she tried to shake off the drowsiness from consuming her, it merely got worse. Her eyelids would not reopen, her body would not move, and she could feel herself falling deeper and deeper. Visions of her mother soon appeared to her, beckoning to her with open arms and promises of forgiveness. Reality and delusion soon began to merge, overcoming Tammy's ability to grasp onto lucidity and carrying her away into cold, numbing paralysis.

The wind and rain continued until the sun slowly dipped down below the distant horizon. Silence then consumed the evening and night, until the morning birds began to chirp out at the rising morning sun. Tammy slowly felt reality forcing itself back into focus again, and although she lacked the inclination to prise her eyes open, the pain throbbing through her head could have only indicated consciousness.

Tammy groaned and twitched in discontent as her other senses started to awaken. She felt the ache in her neck, the wheeze in her smoke-filled lungs, and an unexpected piercing pain in her right leg and fingers. She groaned again and rolled her head over on the headrest, feeling it slap upon a wet and sticky substance that glooped onto her face. The vile smell then started to register, as the putrid stench of vomit invaded her nostrils. She grimaced in disgust and rolled back over again, forcing her sticky eyelids to open and gaze down upon the pool of wretched filth in which she had spent the night.

Whining out in pain and torment, Tammy hoped to somehow undo her actions with her mind, but she couldn't. She then felt a churn within her stomach, followed immediately by uncontrollable heaving, causing bile to regurgitate from her stomach and burn unforgivingly against her sore oesophagus.

Tammy held her breath, forcing the spasms to dissipate, before mustering all of her energy together to reach forward for the steering wheel and gripping upon it tightly with both hands. She pulled with all her might, wrenching her aching body upright and ripping her hair free of the congealed vomit upon the headrest.

Rolling down the car window she quickly snatched a breath of fresh air, trying her best to focus her head, which continued to spin and thump mercilessly. The pain in Tammy's fingers returned, throbbing and stinging, and so she gazed down to examine them. Frowning in confusion, she set her eyes upon two sore blisters that had inexplicably appeared between her index and middle fingers. She then looked down

THE DAMAGED

to her leg where she had felt a similar pain, finding a similar blister, exposed by a large burn hole in the fabric of her trousers. Fingering the blister curiously, Tammy then noticed the ash upon her trousers and the inflicting cigarette butt upon the floor.

Tammy moaned aloud in despair, starting to remember her thoughts of suicide the night before and wishing that she had gone through with it whilst she still had the courage to do so. She sighed disappointedly, as a bird outside started chirping again. The sound echoed through Tammy's sore head like an exploding steel drum. She took a long breath and dragged herself lethargically out the car, grabbed her handbag, and stumbled her way wearily back towards the flat.

Matthew sat upon his father's Chesterfield watching the morning cartoons. Two hot cups of tea sat steaming upon the coffee table while he anxiously awaited Tammy's arrival. The arrival of Agnieszka the day before had been disconcerting to him to say the least, and his fears for her well-being were growing.

Her knock upon the door finally came, and with it welcomed relief, but her dishevelled and drained appearance did not go unnoticed. Matthew smiled down at her welcomingly, wanting to hug her and tell her that 'everything would be okay', but his smile was not returned. She entered the house with a numb, zombified look upon her face, making her way straight to the kitchen and removing Matthew's two blue pills from the plastic pot.

After placing the pills down upon Matthew's side table, she took a seat upon the sofa, laying her head back and resting her tired eyes. Matthew frowned, trying to think of something to say to her, something he could do to make things better, to help her, to end her obvious suffering. He smiled sympathetically and sighed.

"Tea?" he asked, trying to sound upbeat.

Tammy opened her eyes and forced a weak smile upon her face, looking down to the steaming cup in front of her and nodding.

"Thanks," she whispered, reaching for the cup and grasping it tightly in both hands before slumping back into the sofa again.

"Tammy?"

"Yes, Matthew?"

"What can I do to help?"

Tammy glanced up at him inquisitively, catching sight of his big friendly blue eyes and finding herself gazing into them longingly.

"Nothing. There's nothing you can do, Matthew," she replied dismissively, sighing and turning her eyes down to the tea again.

"But I'm worried about you, Darling."

SIMON LAW

"Don't be, Matthew. I deserve to feel like this. I deserve everything I get," she told him numbly.

"No. No you don't, Tammy. You deserve much more than this," he insisted, leaning forward to place his hand upon her knee.

"Don't! Please! I can't!" she snapped, quickly brushing his hand away with a frustrated frown.

Matthew nodded and looked away sheepishly.

"I'm sorry," he whispered in return.

"Look, I should go," she announced as she stood from the sofa, shaking her head and placing her cup back down upon the table with a twitching hand.

"No, stay. Please?" Matthew protested, but it was clear that Tammy would not. "You don't need to be alone, Tammy."

Ignoring Matthew's plea, she continued to the door, shaking her head despondently.

"Don't forget your pills," she muttered quietly. She pulled open the door and departed without hesitation.

It was clear to Matthew at that point that Tammy's torment would not dissipate of its own accord; it would merely eat away at her piece by piece until it had completely destroyed her. Matthew couldn't let that happen. He owed her more than that for the care she had shown him; he owed her the chance to be at peace.

It was also clear to Matthew that the source of Tammy's pain was Keith. He could kill him easily, but simply killing him would not eradicate her problems. It would not guarantee Jessica's return to her. Even with Keith out of the picture, the world would still never accept their love for each other; it would never allow them to be together, especially not now with all the blood on Matthew's hands.

The future seemed hopeless for them both – bleak, futile. Even Matthew's murderous pastime would have to end at some point, and where would he be then? Captured and returned to the mental home? Successful in finding his parents' killer, but then left with an empty and meaningless existence again?

Matthew sighed and sank into the soft reassuring red leather of his father's Chesterfield. He turned his eyes numbly back to the brightly-coloured cartoons, and reached for his cup of tea.

"Why can't life just be simple?" he asked, turning his eyes to his parents' photograph and staring upon their happy smiles with admiration and a touch of envy.

It was then that Matthew had an epiphany, a strange realisation that entered his head like the missing piece of a puzzle. Maybe the only way that they could be together, the only way that either of them could find the peace they both desired, was in death; the only place where they could both finally escape the pain and judgemental eyes of the world around them.

Matthew mulled upon the idea with the growing certainty that it was the only logical option for them both, thinking of it as both 'tragic' and 'beautiful', like the story of Romeo and Juliet. He would make it completely painless for Tammy of course, drugging her somehow and sliding his favourite kitchen knife into her while she slept, before then turning the knife on himself. Their spirits and energies would intertwine, spiralling upwards together towards the heavens where they could spend eternity in the warmth of each others' love.

The idea seemed perfect to Matthew, but he knew that before he could even contemplate such a thing that he needed to finish what he had started. He needed to appease the beast inside and find his parents' killer. He needed to make him suffer.

THE FEELING

Nine days had now passed since Tammy had first fallen off the wagon in the graveyard, and she was now drinking again full-time. With Iron Maiden blaring mercilessly into her ears, she snuggled herself into the back seat of the bus, tucking her feet underneath her bottom and resting her sleepy head against the glass of the smeared window. She stared out blankly, watching the world blur past while she ruminated anxiously over her journey ahead. It was Monday, and Mondays were 'AA' days, but not today. Not for Tammy. The group were presumably sat waiting for her expectantly, but Tammy had no intentions of joining them. With Keith now denying Tammy her weekly visit with Jessica, the 'AA' sessions now seemed superfluous, and with the clear stench of alcohol on her breath it would do more harm than good. Tammy had a different journey to make.

The bus left the busy town centre and began to meander through the suburbs, twisting and turning through the quiet residential streets. Tammy's eyes then began to focus as she searched the distance eagerly. She chewed nervously upon her bottom lip while tapping her foot rhythmically upon the floor of the bus, her nerves growing by the second. Eyes wide, she finally spotted her destination approaching and pressed her fingers upon the bus's bell. At the same time, she stood and rushed towards the exit.

Trying to calm her excitement and anticipation, Tammy removed her deafening earphones and sparked up a cigarette. Looking out ahead at the large red-bricked building that she had spotted, she began to pace forwards. As she got closer she noticed the bright multi-coloured window ledges, the six-foot metal fence that completely surrounded the building, and the large sign upon the front entrance – 'South Green Primary School'.

THE DAMAGED

The court order against Tammy had strictly prohibited her from making any contact with Jessica outside of their agreed visitation times, but with Keith already breaking their agreement Tammy didn't think twice about breaking it herself.

Prior to their split, Tammy and Keith had discussed sending little Jessica to South Green because of their outstanding Ofsted reports. The school also ran an after-school choir, which Jessica showed great enthusiasm for. Tammy had no idea if Keith had kept to their original plans or not, but with no other information to go on it seemed like an obvious place to start.

Tammy continued to pace around the perimeter, nervously shifting her gaze back and forth from the grounds to the windows of the classrooms, eager to glimpse a view of Jessica. She soon reached the rear of the school, where she was met by a large colourful playground, with hopscotch and friendly animals painted all across the cold concrete. She stopped and stubbed out her cigarette, checked the time on her phone, and waited anxiously, chewing upon her fingernails and pacing up and down.

The school-bell echoed out from the building, and the playground was immediately flooded by a sea of blue jumpers and tiny faces. Tammy peered out eagerly, frantically scanning through the faces for her little girl. Taking a step closer, she pressed her face against the cold metallic lattice of the fence and clutched it firmly with her fingers.

Tammy continued to scan the bustling crowd of children with desperation, feeling her heart beating in her throat and her fingers shaking nervously upon the metal fence.

The children screamed and shouted excitedly, chasing each other around and playing together with innocent joyous smiles, but as Tammy squinted and scanned through the crowd there was no sign of her daughter among them. She clenched the fence tighter, frowning and gritting her teeth with frustration, but just as she was about to lose hope, the flash of long blonde hair suddenly caught her eye. Tammy squinted further and focused her sights in on the girl. Her frown lines slowly started to melt away and a fragile smile appeared upon her face.

A strange sensation of calm flooded through her as she gazed out at her beautiful daughter with bittersweet pride in her eyes. Jessica looked so grown up in her uniform, and Tammy wondered where the five years since her birth had all gone to. The world was now the little girl's oyster; she could achieve anything, be anyone she wanted. It was all down to her.

The contemplation of snatching the girl again had occurred to Tammy throughout the morning, and with the girl now in her sights the thought had returned. She mulled over the idea with angst, but as she mused over her options she realised how futile and churlish they would be. They were selfish desires, born from her own need to feel wanted, and held no benefit to the girl's well-being.

Tammy continued to stare at Jessica with longing, watching as she played with her new friends in her smart new uniform. A tear slowly rolled down her cheek as she sighed and closed her eyes, wishing again that things were different.

Reaching back into her bag, pushing aside the small half-drunk bottle of vodka, she removed her phone. She switched on the phone's camera and placed it against the fence, zooming in onto Jessica and snapping close the shutter. Another tear then joined the first, as she gazed down upon the fuzzy, pixelated photo with a smile.

Tammy gazed back up to the playground again, and that was when she noticed the disgruntled-looking teacher pacing towards her with a stern, disapproving glare. Tammy rubbed her face and sighed in defeat, returning her phone to her bag and quickly walking away, down the street and out of sight.

Tammy continued with her day in a strange trance, daydreaming about the future of her beautiful little girl and continuously gazing down at the stolen fuzzy snapshot on her phone. After finishing her rounds and enduring another awkward encounter with Matthew, she returned to the bus and made her way back home again.

Alighting from the bus at her flat, Tammy noticed James and Bronco at their usual spot – but something was different. James's usual carefree expression was absent, and replacing it was an eerie look of sunken dread and grief. It was the downbeat, broken look that would usually seem befitting of someone in his situation, but for James to display the expression was strange and worrying.

"You alright, James?" Tammy asked, the broken expression upon his face piercing clean through the dreamy thoughts of her daughter.

"Oh, I... Yes, I'm fine thank you, my dear," James replied in a disjointed, downbeat variation of his usual American twang. He quickly lifted his head and shook the haunting expression from his face as if it was never there to start with.

"You sure?" Tammy persisted, removing her headphones and taking a seat down upon the bench next to him.

James looked to the ground and then back up to Tammy again, taking a moment and accepting the fact that his morbid expression had not gone unnoticed.

"I...I was supposed to be meeting a friend today, and... well, he didn't turn up," James told her hesitantly.

"Oh, I see," Tammy replied, slightly perplexed and underwhelmed by his explanation. "I'm sure there was a good reason," she continued.

THE DAMAGED

"No... I don't think you understand, Tammy," James replied, shaking his head with a nervous smile. –"He always turns up. He's got nowhere else to be. I...I think he might be dead!"

"Dead? What makes you think that?" Tammy asked, her eyes widening at the mention of the idea.

"I... I just have a bad *feeling* about it," he explained, putting strange emphasis on the word 'feeling', as if it was actually much more than just a paranoid conclusion.

"A feeling?" Tammy pried curiously. –"What do you mean?"

James sighed and ran his fingers through his grey bristly beard in contemplation, before looking down to Bronco beside him for some kind of assurance. Bronco, who appeared to have been asleep until that point, immediately opened his eyes and turned his head up to James with a look of forlorn. He whimpered gently with a sense of unease before then nestling his head affectionately against James's leg and returning to his previous position. James smiled down at Bronco, briefly musing over the dog's strange ability to sense his discontent, and to seemingly empathise. He sighed again before then returning his eyes to Tammy, who was still gazing at him expectantly.

"It's a difficult feeling to explain, my dear," James began hesitantly. "...It's like an icy breeze fluttering through the back of my mind, grinding all my thoughts to a halt, and then I know, I just know that something is terribly wrong," he continued, briefly looking around to Tammy again to gauge her reaction to the claim.

"Carry on..." she replied, seemingly intrigued and a tiny bit spooked.

"It's not the first time I've had this feeling either, so I know it's not just a coincidence. I've had this feeling many times, and it's always been right before," James explained further, before stopping again to formulate his next words coherently. "You remember me telling you about my wife Jodie? ...and how I caught her cheating on me?"

"Yeah, sure. You said that you came home early from work one day and... and you found her in bed with another man..."

"That's right, my dear. What I probably didn't tell you, was that I knew something was wrong before I even got home, before I opened the door and caught them at it like animals. I didn't know the bitch was screwing around as such, but I definitely knew something was wrong. I had the 'feeling', the same feeling I had back in '98 when my father passed away on the day the Denver Broncos won the Super Bowl."

Tammy's forehead creased up in contemplation as she tried to digest and make sense of what James was telling her. She was normally very sceptical over people's supposed 'sixth senses', but from James – a man she had always considered wise, the idea seemed to carry far more creditability.

SIMON LAW

"Oh...I see," she finally replied, beginning to chew upon her bottom lip.

"I'm sure you think I'm just a silly old man, but my friend is dead, that much I'm sure of."

"No, I don't think you're silly at all," Tammy replied reassuringly. Then she suddenly remembered the news report she had seen previously. "Wait, you don't think your friend was murdered, do you?"

"I... I think so, yes."

"A homeless guy was murdered last week as well; do you think it's linked?"

"I'm sure of it, yes," James confirmed with a solemn nod.

"But they haven't mentioned any murders since then..."

"No, well, maybe they haven't found the body yet, my dear."

Tammy frowned again, continuing to chew upon her lip.

"Well, you're not safe on the streets then, James. Do you wanna stay with me?" she offered, surprising herself that she would make such an offer.

James's smile quickly returned to his face as he began to chuckle to himself dismissively.

"You're a kind girl, Tammy, but I couldn't possibly accept. You don't want a smelly old man like me in your house!" he replied, the suggestion still fuelling his smile with elation.

"Don't be silly, James. It's fine. I'd hate for anything to happen to you!" she immediately protested, but it was obvious that James could not be persuaded.

"The world is blessed to have kind souls like yourself, my dear. If only there were more like you!" he told her, his smile still radiating from his face. "You can run from your fate, but you can't hide from it forever," he continued in a more serious tone. "That much I know, and I've been running for a very long time now."

"There must be something I can do for you," she insisted, becoming slightly frustrated by this point.

"Well, there is something. If you insist, that is?"

"Yes? What is it?"

"I'd love a hot drink, my dear."

Tammy smiled and shook her head with resignation, disappointed and bemused at the simple, mundane request.

"Coffee?"

"I'd prefer tea, if you have some?"

"Tea? Really?"

"What? You think that because I'm American I only ever drink coffee? That's a little bit racist, my dear," he continued with a playful grin.

THE DAMAGED

XIV

THE DAY THE SERPENT COMETH

Matthew smiled and twitched in his sleep as the ominous raven glided effortlessly through his subconscious mind, casting its distorted black shadow wherever it flew. Blood-splattered thoughts of murder and vengeance fluttered through him like the wings of the beast through the night sky, conjuring feelings of warmth and comfort that soothed his angry longing for atonement.

The intricate brass hands of the humble grandfather clock ticked quietly and rhythmically from down the stairs, as they slowly ticked over to the killing hour once again. Matthew's bedside clock then erupted as well; dragging him viciously through the wormhole of reality, away from the blood-drenched nirvana of his personalised dream world, and hurtling him back into the waking world once more.

Matthew slowly prised his sticky eyelids apart and sluggishly reached over to silence the infernal alarm clock that was raging in his ears. He moaned resentfully as he felt the aches and fatigue pulsating through his tired and unrested muscles, and allowed his heavy eyelids to gently drop once more.

Just a few more minutes, he thought, as he nestled back into the pillows again.

Lying motionlessly in the darkness, he began to formulate his plan of action for the night ahead while simultaneously pondering the peculiar tingling sensation that was now developing within his mouth. He rolled his tongue around in his mouth curiously, rubbing the tip of it against the backs of his teeth and then up against the roof of his mouth, analysing the change in sensation and trying to formulate a logical explanation for it.

The sensation quickly began to magnify, morphing from a curious tingle to a throb, a painful throb which then seemed to erupt, filling his mouth with thick sweet-tasting fluid that began to trickle down the back of his throat. The fluid gushed and gargled, so much so that Matthew was overcome with anxious feelings of drowning. He projected it out onto the pillow beside him. Spent, he panted and gasped for air, panicked and confused. As the air re-entered his lungs and his panic began to subside, he became aware of the curious taste once more. It was blood; that much he knew for sure. Matthew had tasted blood many times and the taste was undeniable, but the taste this time was intense and overwhelming, like nothing he had ever experienced. Even with the fluid now expelled from his mouth and the remainder of it swallowed down, he could still taste it, as if he could somehow smell the bloodied pillow beside him with the receptors in his tongue.

Matthew reached for the lamp and flooded the bedroom with light, looking down at the crimson wet stain upon the pillow beside him and racking his brain for an explanation. *Did I bite my tongue in my sleep?* he pondered, but it seemed unlikely as the pain would have surely woken him, and it didn't explain the intense taste sensation either. Still perplexed by the situation, Matthew stuck out his tongue and reached up to finger it. As his fingertips brushed gently upon it he was met by further surprise. It seemed as if the tip of his tongue had somehow split in half along the centre seam, with each 'fork' seemingly able to move independently from the other. His tongue now also seemed thinner and longer than before; able to lap at his own nose and chin like it never had before, tasting or 'smelling' each surface that it lapped upon with intensity and defined distinction.

Matthew threw down the covers and dashed through to the bathroom. He pulled frantically upon the light cord and stared in disbelief as his reflection flickered into focus on the bathroom mirror. His confusion and panic then began to rise again, bubbling up from inside him and shaking his entire body as he released his lips and let the silky serpent tongue slither out from between them. Matthew's attention was then drawn to his peculiar eyes, to his black vacuous pupils that narrowed and stretched into thin elongated ovals before him. He gulped and tensed his eyelids closed once more, breathing deeply. Just as he thought the rising panic would overcome him, the beast began to squawk from within, calming him, reassuring him, informing him that this was merely the next stage of his ongoing transcendence. He exhaled nervously, gingerly opening his eyes in the hope that his transformation was merely an illusion, but it wasn't. It was real.

Staring at himself for a while longer, he studied his long and slender reptilian pupils in the reflection and curiously manipulated the slim prongs of his new forked tongue. He wiggled them into the air, familiarising himself to their dexterity and to the sensation of his new acute sense of smell. Before long he found himself completely accustomed to it, and was able to detect and identify the most minute smells that surrounded him. The scent of the tiny splodge of toothpaste upon the sink below him, the smell of the dirty laundry in his bedroom, and the stench of the rotting dismembered body parts of James' friend in the big black bags by the rear cellar door were all now registering clearly and distinctly in his mouth and nose.

Matthew grinned smugly, now more welcoming of his newfound ability and fully calm once again. He quickly washed and dressed himself in another one of his father's smart suits and made his way downstairs, his thoughts now reverting back to his nightly task with more energy and enthusiasm. He blew a kiss towards his parents' photograph and slapped on his latex gloves, before grabbing his faithful kitchen knife and descending his way down into the dark, damp cellar below.

His serpent tongue tingled and slithered inside his mouth, alive with the scent of the rotting body parts as he moved through the darkness towards the bags. He reached down, hoisting the fully laden bags over his shoulder and gently pushing open the rear doors of the cellar. The crisp air of the night-time embraced him welcomingly, as the picturesque stars twinkled peacefully above.

Lugging the heavy bags through the garden and out the rusted back gate, Matthew eagerly entered the woods. He continued through the dense trees, his tongue tingling the entire way from the vast assortment of smells that bombarded him. Eventually he reached the clearing, placed the heavy bags down upon the ground, and sat himself down upon the trunk of a large oak tree that had fallen during the storm of '87.

Sitting calmly, staring out at the thick muddy swamp in front of him, Matthew listened to the subtle rustlings of the night-time creatures around him. Again, he let his slippery tongue slither out from between his lips and protrude into the air. He closed his eyes and concentrated on the smells with curiosity, using the prongs of his tongue to see if he could identify and locate each smell separately. Concentrating further, blocking out the overpowering stench of the decomposing body parts beside him, he magnified the subtle underlying smells that surrounded him. He quickly detected the musty smell of a rodent in the distance, the two-day old faeces of a dog to his right, and to his immediate left something slimy, slightly fishy. He opened his reptilian eyes once more and peered down at the ground to the left of him. He could see nothing – nothing obvious anyway. Peering closer and honing in on the smell with his tongue, he slowly reached out his hand to a small mound of wet leaves. He reached closer, and closer, the smell magnifying with every passing second, when suddenly the mound erupted and a frog leaped out from inside it. Matthew laughed jubilantly as he watched the little creature hopping away, pleased with himself for seemingly mastering his new ability.

It was at that point that he heard a croak from above him, and turned in time to glimpse the shadow of the raven, gliding through the tree tops above him, anxious for Matthew to desist and to focus on his task. Matthew huffed and nodded in return. He agreed; now was not the time to waste with such procrastination.

He stood from the trunk, flexed his muscles, and returned his attention back to the heavy black bags. He lifted the first, swung it back, and projected it out into the swamp, where it sank with a wet, gloopy splash. Then he disposed of the second, and then the third, watching as the three heavy bags sank below the surface of the murky swamp water.

The news reports of Matthew's first kill had slowly disappeared from the television in recent days. There had been no reports at all of the three vagrants that he had since murdered, dismembered, bagged, and dumped in the very same swamp; proof in itself to Matthew of the effectiveness of his refined killing process.

Smiling as the final bag bubbled and sank below the muddy surface, Matthew turned and retraced his steps through the woods, taking the subway underneath the road and making his way quietly through the dark streets of the sleepy and unsuspecting town.

James awoke with a sudden shudder as his strange and ominous feeling returned, blowing frostily across his mind and tingling against the backs of his eyes insistently. He felt himself sinking, falling, and he knew immediately that something was amiss.

He reached his hand out below the park bench until it brushed reassuringly upon the coarse hair of Bronco's back, and stroked upon it comfortingly. The dog murmured in return, whimpered, and became motionless once more. James stroked the dog again, resting his hand gently against the dog's ribcage and feeling his heart beating softly and rhythmically within him.

Gazing thoughtfully at the stars above, James sighed downheartedly. The end was nigh, that much he was certain of. His fate was all but inevitable, the 'feeling' was never wrong. He listened out carefully into the cold dark silence for any sign of movement, but there was none, despite his eerie certainty that he was far from alone in the park.

Pulling himself to a sitting position on the bench, James squinted into the distance of the murky park, looking deep into the trees and the

THE DAMAGED

bushes around him, but still there was nothing to be seen. *Maybe I was wrong,* he pondered hopefully. *There's a first for everything, after all.*

James's ears then suddenly tuned in to the sound of rustling leaves and the crunch of a twig below a shoe, and his enlightened hopes immediately plummeted back down into obscurity. He looked up and quickly scanned the tree-line again, left to right then right to left. He squinted harder, slowly focusing in through the ominous darkness, until his eyes settled upon the distant moonlit silhouette of a man.

James's heart skipped a beat as his 'feeling' quickly returned, stronger, flowing through him like icy water. Staring deep into the black and motionless silhouette, he could feel the figure watching him back, studying him, and contemplating its next move. James reached down and grabbed Bronco by his new black leather, studded collar, shaking him awake, before then standing from the bench with his eyes glued to the figure anxiously. Bronco jumped to attention too, standing loyally by his master's side, eyeing up the dark figure and snarling with discontent.

"Yea, though I walk through the valley of the shadow of death, I will fear no evil," James muttered to himself nervously, clenching both his fists and his teeth while he watched the figure slowly starting to step towards him.

James watched as the figure then turned its head skyward, watching something in the treetops that remained unseen to him, before croaking into the air like an angry bird. The sound echoed through the trees as the figure continued to pace towards him, but James remained still, unflinching, ready to face the man who was destined to take his life, overriding the desperate urges pulsating through him to just run, run for his life and to not look back.

The figure took another step, out of the shadows of the trees now and into the open grass, finally illuminating his face in the faint blue hue of the moon. James frowned in confusion, recognising the face before him and scanning his memory to place it.

"Hey, I know you!" James called across the park. –"Matthew? Isn't it?"

Matthew stopped in his tracks, recognising James too, but denying a response. James was not his parents' killer, Matthew knew that with certainty, but yet the raven inside of him didn't seem to care anymore. The raven wanted him dead, he had already demanded as much, and who was Matthew to argue?

Matthew stared back at James from behind his sleek reptilian pupils and continued walking towards him. He knew that his usual allure of money would neither tempt nor trick James into playing his game, and so decided to simply forgo formalities. He reached back and removed the kitchen knife from between his trousers and belt and teased the blade to James in the moonlight, continuing to pace towards him with a twisted sadistic grin until finally stopping a mere few feet away.

"You don't scare me, Matthew," James told him calmly, as Bronco continued to snarl and growl by his side. –"You're a fucking psycho and they're going to lock you up for good after this!"

"Watch your mouth!" Matthew told him, finally breaking his silence. –"There's no need to swear about it. Let's just be civilised, shall we?"

"Civilised?" James echoed back at him in bewilderment. "There's nothing civilised about you, Buddy! Your parents installed some real fucked up values in you! That's for sure!"

Matthew scowled in resentment and lunged at James with the knife, cutting through the crisp air in a single motion and plunging it towards James's chest. Bronco exploded with rage, immediately pouncing upon Matthew's straying arm and locking his jaw tightly around it. Matthew roared in pain as Bronco's teeth pierced clean through his father's jacket and embedding themselves deep into his flesh. He dropped the knife and fell to the grass below, thrashing his arm in the air in a frantic attempt to shake the dog loose.

James stepped back and took a breath, relieved and surprised that the blade had not reached him. He patted down his chest, just to make sure, before then turning his eyes back to Bronco again.

"Bronco! Off!" he called, edging back further, seeing his opportunity to escape and finally giving in to his urges to run for his life. If not for his own sake, then for the sake of warning Tammy of Matthew's murderous impulses.

Bronco clamped his jaws around the arm tighter, and as Matthew continued to thrash about he could feel his flesh starting to tear and blood begin to run down his arm.

"Bronco! Come on!" James called again, desperate and frustrated, briefly debating abandoning the faithful dog who had just saved his life, but he knew he couldn't.

Matthew rolled on the grass as he continued to tussle with the dog, gritting his teeth through the throbbing agony of the bite. Turning his head to the side, Matthew's reptilian pupils set their sight upon the fallen blade beside him. He stretched out with his left arm, his fingers crawling closer and closer towards the handle of the knife. One final stretch and he clasped onto the knife once more. He tightened his grip and plunged the blade deep into the side of Bronco's neck.

The dog yelped with a deafening echoic screech, before finally releasing his bloodied grip upon Matthew's arm. Matthew pulled it free, grimacing through the pain as he stretched and tensed his throbbing fingers.

THE DAMAGED

"Bronco!" James cried as he froze on the spot, traumatised by the horrific sight of his beloved dog being ruthlessly murdered.

Matthew continued to twist the knife through the dog's bloodied throat, carving it forcefully through the dog's flesh until the animal's whimpers finally desisted. Matthew rose to his feet, holding up the dog by its collar as he continued to slice, eventually severing through the dog's spine and sending its lifeless body hurtling to the grass with a dull thud.

Matthew gripped the dog's head by the ruff of its hair, scowling at the animal's face with revulsion, before removing the studded collar from its gushing neck stump and throwing the bloody head at James's feet. He slid the collar into his father's jacket pocket as a grim souvenir, before then reverting his reptilian pupils back to James again.

James mumbled, his lips quivering but unable to formulate words. Matthew stepped towards him, smiling at him like a child eyeing up an ice-cream truck on a hot summer's day. James turned and ran as fast as his frail body would allow, into the trees and the bushes, zigzagging and meandering erratically between the obstructions. Matthew immediately gave chase, following James into the dark dense woodland and following his scent with his slithering serpent tongue. He dodged and side-stepped through the trees, hot on James's tail, slicing through bushes and branches with the kitchen knife and gaining on James with every passing second.

James panted in anguish as he pushed himself onwards, dashing between the trees, through the woodland, until street lights started to come into sight. *Just a little further!* he told himself, adrenaline pulsating through his body as he forced his aching legs to keep going. Onwards he continued, his mind so consumed with getting away that he was oblivious to how close Matthew was behind him, but aware he had no time to stop and check.

The street lights got brighter and the houses got closer, so close now that James could almost reach out and touch them. He pelted towards them with every ounce of energy he could muster, breathless and desperate. Suddenly he felt the kitchen knife slicing deep into his back.

James tumbled face-first into the mud, groaning in despairing anguish for getting so close. He felt the air gushing from his punctured lung and the blood pumping from his back as he began struggling to breathe. He heard the footsteps approaching from behind, crunching down upon the twigs and fallen leaves until finally feeling a foot press down against his back, as Matthew reached down and retracted the bloody knife from the wound.

"You're a monster!" James uttered in a bloody gargle as he struggled to maintain consciousness.

Matthew did not respond. Instead, he rolled James onto his back and stood back to watch the life slowly escaping from his dishevelled, bearded face. He listened to the raven croaking with delight from within him, enjoying the exhilaration that pulsated through his veins. Slithering his long serpent tongue in the air, he felt it tingle with the perfumed scent of fresh blood, and he sighed with contentment.

"Yes, maybe I am," Matthew finally replied in a patronising tone, crouching down into James's dwindling sights. −"Or maybe *you're* the monster, and *I'm* the hero in this situation."

THE DAMAGED

THE CONSEQUENCES OF A LACK OF CONVICTION

She knocked again, louder and harder, starting to worry now that something might be wrong. Tammy had been waiting at the doorstep for a good few minutes now, and she could feel the prying eyes of the neighbours burning holes into her back as they twitched behind their net curtains.

"Matthew?" she called, propping open the letterbox with her fingers. "Is everything alright?"

Tammy's alcohol-induced headache drummed mercilessly inside her skull and her hypersensitive eyes flinched sheepishly away from the unforgiving morning light. After checking the time again on the display of her iPhone, she started to chew upon her bottom lip agitatedly, anxious as to what she should do next.

She banged upon the door one last time before finally hearing the reassuring sound of frantic footsteps upon the stairs. The door burst open moments later, revealing a dishevelled-looking Matthew wearing nothing but his boxer shorts. Tammy looked at him with a frown of confusion, his scruffy appearance almost overlooked by her attraction to his bulging abdominal muscles and pecs.

"I'm sorry. I... I slept through the alarm I guess. Come... come in, please, we don't want to give the neighbours anything more to gossip about, do we?" Matthew spluttered, wiping away the sleep sediment and rubbing his tired face.

Tammy nodded and entered the house, offering a crooked smile as she continued to battle the throb within her head. Matthew reached to close the door, and Tammy immediately noticed the bandage upon his arm. It had been crudely wrapped in a hurry, with the bloody impressions of Bronco's teeth marks gently seeping through the white cottoned wrap.

"My god, what happened to your arm, Matthew?" she asked, staring at the series of blood stains in concern.

"Oh this, it's nothing. I...err, I fell, that's all," he replied, hesitant and unconvincing.

"Looks pretty bad. Shall I take a look at it? – I do have first aid training," Tammy offered, stepping towards him slowly.

"No! No, it's fine, I promise!" Matthew insisted abruptly.

"Okay then, if you're sure?"

"I am."

"Okay, Matthew. Look, why don't you go and put some clothes on, and I'll make some tea, yeah?" Tammy suggested, her eyes flickering back and forth between Matthew's muscles and the bloodied bandage wrapped around his arm.

"Yeah, okay. Sounds like a good idea," he replied, still half asleep and somewhat flustered. "You know where everything is, right?"

"Yeah."

Matthew nodded and wiped his face again, before then turning back to the stairs and beginning his ascent.

Tammy took a steadying breath, trying to concentrate as the drums inside her skull threatened to unbalance her. She stumbled through to the kitchen and switched on the kettle as promised, before leaning upon the counter with her head slumped lifelessly in her hands. A craving for another cigarette hit her. She had smoked a good ten that morning already, but they had completely failed to quench her, as they often did on mornings with a hangover. Lifting her heavy head, she peered over to the back door in contemplation. *Matthew wouldn't mind,* she thought, *not if I went outside anyway.* She pulled open the door and stepped out into the garden, removing her cigarettes from her bag and sparking one up with a satisfying exhale.

Matthew stood listening from the top of the stairs, silent and motionless, peering out from the landing window that looked down upon the rear garden. He watched as Tammy leant herself against the house, cigarette in hand, while she gazed up at the tall fir trees that surrounded her. *You are so beautiful!* he thought to himself with a bitter-sweet smile. *You have no idea how much I love you, Tammy. Your pain will all be over soon, Darling. I promise you that.*

Matthew continued to stare, watching her every movement intently, obsessively. He pressed his face against the window, while his breath steamed up the glass. He felt his boxer shorts begin to tighten as thoughts of sex and murder began swirling around his head. The thoughts excited him, aroused him. He continued to look Tammy up and down from the window, remembering her hot naked body on top of his. The racy images then morphed to that of his mother again, naked and steamy, riding upon him furiously, her curly hair bouncing up and down as she panted and whimpered. Matthew reached into his pants and gripped himself, thrusting his hand at the glorious images in his head.

Suddenly, Tammy was startled by a rattle at the window above, but as she turned to look Matthew had already disappeared. As she looked back down and took another drag of her cigarette she noticed the strange tracks upon the lawn, long scuff marks starting from the rear gate and continuing across the garden as if something heavy had been dragged through the grass. She studied them a while longer, a perplexed frown growing upon her face as she pondered what Matthew could have possibly been dragging. Her confusion deepened as she realised that, whatever it was that Matthew had been dragging though the garden, must have originated from somewhere outside of it entirely.

Did Matthew actually leave the safe confines of the garden on his own? Tammy pondered. *Could he really have taken that leap and neglected to mention it to me? Surely not! Surely he'd be brimming with pride for such an achievement!*

Tammy traced the track lines with her eyes, following them from the gate to where they sloped down and stopped at the rear entrance to the cellar. Her intrigue grew and would not relent; she just had to know what Matthew had been up to.

Tammy edged her way towards the cellar door and tentatively reached her hand out for the handle. A cold eerie chill rushed through her body as her fingertips brushed upon it. At the same time, a faint rotten scent fluttered through her nose. Undeterred, she affirmed her grip upon the rusted handle and slowly started to pull it open.

The door released an ominous whining creak, as she gently opened it wide enough to spot three large black sacks upon the inside of the door, each one bulging at the seams and seemingly ready to burst. On top of one of the bags, almost completely camouflaged, was a studded black strap, a choker or a collar maybe, possibly even a dog's collar.

Isn't that Bronco's collar? she considered with a bewildered frown, her thoughts then fluttering back to the blood-stained bandage upon Matthew's arm. *Were they teeth marks? Bronco's teeth marks?*

"Tammy?" Matthew called sharply from behind her, now dressed and standing by the back door of the house. He frowned in her direction with a look of worry and anger.

Tammy quickly released the handle and the door immediately slammed itself shut. She turned to Matthew with a startled, frightened expression.

"What are you doing?" he asked accusingly, his frown lines deepening with increasing suspicion as he gradually paced towards her.

Tammy stared back at him, unable to speak, her expression mixing disbelief with mortal fear as her mind quickly flooded with horrible possibilities.

"Tammy? What's wrong?" Matthew persisted, studying her frozen expression and continuing to edge closer towards her.

"Nothing, I... I..." she mumbled sheepishly, the look of fear growing more apparent upon her face with every step closer that Matthew took. "I've got to go!" she blurted, quickly running past Matthew and into the house.

"Are you alright?" he called after her.

"Yeah, I'm fine," she called back, trying her best to sound calm. "I'm just not feeling well, that's all. I'll see you later," she added, rushing through the house and slamming the front door behind her.

Matthew turned as if give chase, but knew that he would never catch her without causing a scene, and so relented. He gritted his teeth and shook his head in frustration, glaring at the cellar door and knowing with certainty that the game was up. She had discovered his secret, she must have; there could be no other explanation for her extreme reaction.

He opened the cellar doors and scanned the room to establish exactly what he had left on display. The room was spotless of blood, the knives and tools were all out of sight, and James's body was all packed and sealed neatly in the bags. Scowling in confused anguish, Matthew finally noticed the black dog's collar and sighed.

Surely she wouldn't go to the cops over that? he thought in disbelief. *She couldn't know for sure what I had done over that? I could have got the collar anywhere. Maybe I used to have a dog myself, she didn't know! Surely!*

Matthew paced up and down frantically, desperately trying to convince himself that he had no cause to panic, no need to act imprudently. His thoughts quickly turned to his capture, to his incarceration, to the mental hospital that was destined to be his home once again. He thought about Otis, the overzealous orderly who got his thrills from roughing Matthew up, forcing needles full of sedatives into him and locking him in a padded cell in a straitjacket.

He continued to pace, faster and faster, scratching nervously at the blood-stained bandage upon his arm as his anxiety grew stronger and stronger with no sign of the raven to help him. His panic continued to rise, bubbling up from the pit of his stomach before travelling up through his chest and lingering in the back of his swollen throat. The panic flooded into his head, causing his vision to blur and spin in a frantic vortex. The skies above became angry, filling with dense black clouds that blocked out the morning sun. The wind grew, whistling and

THE DAMAGED

howling as it blew against him relentlessly, tingling against every goose-bumped pore of his body.

Matthew dashed inside the house as the ominous clouds quickly erupted, grabbing the knife from where it lay upon the kitchen draining board and sitting himself down in his father's Chesterfield. He turned the chair to face the front door, grasped the knife with such force that it turned his knuckles white, and stared towards the door intently.

If she calls the police then they'll be here very soon, he thought. *They wouldn't hesitate, not for something like that, especially not if PC Lang caught wind of it! But it's okay. I'll be ready for them; I won't go without a fight!*

Matthew waited, gritting his teeth and listening to the wind and rain that raged outside as his beady eyes fixated upon the door, waiting for the impending knock.

He continued to wait, scratching angrily at the throbbing wound on his arm, but the impending knock upon the door never came. Eventually, after over an hour of waiting for the police to storm his door, Matthew's grip upon the knife finally began to loosen, allowing the blood to flow back into his knuckles once more. His adrenaline drained away and his fatigue then returned, overpowering his anxiety and leaving him feeling numb and detached. It was during this state of surrender that Matthew started to hear a faint whisper from behind him, only just audible above the wind and the rain, calling to him in a sweet, familiar voice.

"Matthew? Sweetheart?" the voice softly cooed.

Matthew turned his weary head in the direction of the voice and smiled, comforted by the welcoming sight of his mother looking down at him from within the wedding photo.

"Hello, Mother," he replied, his euphoric delirious smile growing as he admired her radiant beauty.

"Sweetheart, that girl has to die. She's a liability to you," his mother told him softly, ending the sentence with another reassuring smile.

"I know, Mother," he mumbled with an exasperated exhale, the frustration and torment returning to his face. "But I can't, not yet, I'm not ready yet! I need to find who did this to you first. I don't want to be on my own again."

"But you must, Matthew. It's only a matter of time before she spoils it all for you."

"Mother, please!"

Matthew stood, shaking his head in frustration and continuing to scratch at the irritating wound upon his arm. He scratched harder and fiercer, but the more he did the stronger the itch grew. He wrenched up his sleeve and quickly unwrapped the bloodied cloth from his arm, looking down at the swollen wound and gently squeezing the pus from the gaping perforations.

Grimacing and growling in pain, Matthew turned his back on his mother's gaze and paced through to the kitchen. He placed his arm in the sink and turned on the tap, washing the blood and pus from the ripped and ragged skin and watching the mixture swirl away down the plughole.

Tammy's finger hovered nervously above the illuminated green 'call' button as she looked down at the three looming nines that she had typed into her phone's display. The previous certainties in her mind were now disappearing quickly as doubt and indecision began creeping in. Tammy knew that the consequences of her actions would be devastating, to Matthew and to her, and even more so if her accusations turned out to be nothing more than mere fantasy. Having armed police bursting into the house would surely traumatise Matthew even further than he already was, and if she was wrong about the whole thing then he would never trust her again. Right or wrong, her sexual indiscretions with him would almost certainly come to light too, and how would that look on her? She would lose her job for sure.

A bead of sweat dripped down from her brow and splashed upon the screen of the phone, blurring the numbers on the display as she continued to search her mind for the conviction to act. She sighed angrily in torment, throwing down her phone upon the bus seat beside her and reaching into her handbag for the miniature bottle of vodka that resided among the clutter. She unscrewed the lid and gulped, downing the entire bottle in a single motion and discarding the empty bottle back to her bag once again.

Releasing another angry sigh, she began chewing upon her thumb, her teeth burying into the knuckle so fiercely that it sent electric shudders through her body, a sensation that she welcomed and found some degree of comfort in. The bus had now completed two full circuits of its route since Tammy had boarded and she could feel the driver watching her with suspicion, raising his eyebrows to gaze upon her through his smeary rear view mirror, but Tammy didn't care.

She turned her mind back to the last morbid words that James had uttered to her the day before, as he talked about his 'feeling' and his certainty of his impending doom. She debated whether his words could be considered 'proof' of Matthew's actions upon him, or whether they were merely the fallacious seeds that had caused her mind to conjure the suspicion in the first place.

Maybe it wasn't Bronco's collar that she had seen at all. After all, she didn't really get a good look at it. In reality it could have been anything.

THE DAMAGED

She didn't even know for sure that James was even dead. It was more than possible that he would be waiting for her at the bus stop at the end of her shift like he did every day. How could she possibly know otherwise until that moment had passed?

Tammy picked her phone back up again and deleted the nines with uneasy duress, deciding that the doubt in her mind was simply too great to risk. Instead, she opened her picture gallery and flicked through to her prized picture of Jessica in her school uniform, the sight of it causing the frown lines on her forehead to slowly loosen and smooth. She smiled, thinking how proud she was of her beautiful daughter, admiring her long flowing blonde hair and her angelic innocent face, and feeling her anxiety slowly starting to settle.

After another full circuit of the bus route, Tammy finally departed the vehicle, shying her face sheepishly away from the perplexed frown of the baffled driver as she exited and scurried off to her next client.

Tammy tried to resume her daily duties as if nothing had happened that morning, travelling from one client to the next, making tea and administering the daily meds, but inside her cold, distant exterior her mind was still ablaze with dread. The all-consuming fears inside Tammy's mind circled and span incessantly, battling and refuelling themselves with the rise and fall of her doubts and her certainties, jolting and jarring her thoughts continuously with morbid images of James's mutilated body that forced their way into her mind.

The preoccupation in her mind was clear to all, as she crudely fumbled her way through the day in a befuddled manner, administering the wrong dosages and forgetting how her clients liked their teas.

By the time Tammy reached Craig Carlson's house, the battle in her mind had completely exhausted her. Even Aggy (who normally seemed to show nothing more than indifference towards Tammy) expressed concern at the sight of her pale tormented face, but Tammy paid no attention. Craig, however, was not a man of sympathy or patience, immediately snapping at Tammy's tardiness and at the repugnant aromas of alcohol and cigarettes that trailed behind her like the tail of a comet. He scowled and grunted at her, wriggling and resisting when she and Aggy tried to bathe him, but Tammy remained unfazed, too distracted to even care.

By the time she finally returned to Matthew's house, she had all but convinced herself of the lunacy of her accusing thoughts, her dread and uncertainties still alive and niggling away in her mind, but overshadowed by the growing embarrassment she now felt for her actions that morning.

She knocked upon the door with trepidation, certain that if Matthew was actually guilty of what she suspected, that he would be long gone by now – fleeing the house in a frantic attempt to escape persecution. If he answered, opening the door with a smile and a hot cup of tea awaiting her, then this would surely be evident of his innocence.

Tammy took a nervous breath and waited, her hands shaking as her anxieties continued to simmer inside of her. Her heart suddenly skipped a beat at the sound of the inside handle starting to rattle. The door slowly began to open.

Matthew stood before her, looking down at her with his deep azure blue eyes and wide welcoming smile, and Tammy immediately felt safe once more. She looked back up at him, returning the smile and temporarily losing herself in the deep blue oceans of his eyes like she had done so many times before.

"Hey, how are you feeling, Darling?" he asked calmly, gesturing her inside.

"Better, much better now, thank you," she replied, releasing a long sigh of relief and slowly stepping inside the house.

"What happened this morning? Did I do something wrong?" he posed, closing the door and following her into the lounge.

"No, I... I'm just a little stressed, I guess. I'm sorry about that," she explained with an awkward expression, sitting herself down upon the sofa in front of a fresh, steaming cup of tea.

"Is this about Jessica?" he asked, gesturing to the tea and sitting himself down into his father's Chesterfield.

"Yeah, that and a few other things," she told him reluctantly, reaching forward and taking a small sip of her tea. "I guess things are just getting a bit on top of me at the moment."

Matthew sighed and looked at her sympathetically. "I can see your pain, Tammy. It hurts me to see you like this," he told her with a gentle nod. "The world can be a horrible place, but you don't need to worry, everything will be fine now."

"I wish that was true," she replied with a lethargic sigh, turning her attention around to the cartoons that were playing on the TV.

She smiled as she relaxed further into the sofa, taking another sip of tea and watching as Winnie the Pooh dashed through The Hundred Acre Wood to evade a swarm of angry honey bees.

"That's right, this was your favourite, wasn't it? I remember you saying," Matthew commented with a light-hearted chuckle, his eyes flittering between the images upon the television screen and the white porcelain mug within Tammy's grip.

Tammy smiled again and nodded. "That feels like a lifetime ago now," she mumbled dismissively, unable to avert her eyes. She took another slurp from the white mug and swallowed, noticing a mild, bitter after-taste that lingered in the back of her throat. The bitterness was slight

THE DAMAGED

and barely detectable, and so she decided to ignore it, continuing to gaze nostalgically at the cartoon.

Tammy continued to sip at her tea, the strange bitterness getting stronger and stronger as she neared the bottom of the mug. The taste seemed familiar to her somehow, but she failed to place her finger upon its significance, brushing it off as stale milk or the remnants of a dirty mug. She began to feel the dizziness creeping into her head and her eyelids slowly starting to droop, but told herself that it was merely the effects of her broken sleep pattern, or maybe because of the lack of food she had consumed of late. *It'll pass*, she told herself, clearing her throat and forcing her eyelids back open again.

The swaying in Tammy's heavy head grew stronger, but it wasn't until she attempted to stand from the sofa that she finally realised that something was seriously wrong. That was when the taste in her throat finally registered in her memory; it was the taste of her sleeping pills. She had been drugged.

Tammy strained again to move but found herself paralysed on the sofa, able only to turn her head in Matthew's direction and gaze upon him in petrified terror. Her suspicions were true, all of them.

Matthew gazed back upon her intently, offering her back an eerie look of sympathy and comfort, but the comfort was not received.

Tammy felt the panic within her taking control of her entire body, but before her hopeless desperation could peak, her ability to maintain consciousness began to fail her. Her eyelids drooped further and further, unresponsive to her demands for them to open. Her swaying world slowly started to fade to black, leaving Matthew's smiling face etched deep upon the eye of her mind as she gently floated away.

XVI

A CAPTIVE AUDIENCE

At first there was silence, darkness, an abyss of pure nothingness that spread out to the far reaches of the visible distance. Weightless and numb, she drifted, floating aimlessly like a particle caught in a cosmic stream, unrestrained and free. Absent of thought or feeling, she drifted further, deeper and deeper into the void.

The passing of time now felt completely irrelevant to her, as if her consciousness somehow now existed outside the confines of its causality, expanding and contracting around her with seemingly inconsequential effect. What felt like a mere fleeting second to her could have easily been the passing of a hundred years – it was impossible to tell, and impossible to care, but still she continued floating, deeper and deeper into the black abyss.

Ever so slowly, like the mind of a foetus slowly developing in the safety of its mother's womb, she gradually began to regain her sense of self-awareness, feeling the faintest of tingles in her fingers and her toes. Her memories soon followed suit, slowly seeping back into her mind again like flickering images on a broken television screen viewed through the frosted glass of a shop window, but completely devoid of their attached emotion or significance to her.

As she drifted further she became aware of a faint light in the distance, glowing and twinkling to her like a star. The light got closer as she floated towards it, growing brighter and stronger. The light was beautiful and hypnotic, luring Tammy towards it and filling her with inexplicable feelings of love and elation, feelings so strong that she began to doubt that she had ever truly experienced them before that point.

From within the bright light emerged a face, a young and beautiful face with pure unblemished skin and golden flowing hair. The face glowed with angelic radiance as it gained definition, absorbing the bright light that had carried it and moulding it to form her limbs and her body.

The bright light then started to flicker and dim, as the angelic face slowly started to turn timid and sombre. It looked at Tammy nervously, shying its eyes away and beginning to chew upon its bottom lip.

"Mummy? the apparition called to her, its breath carrying an icy cold breeze that fluttered and tingled across Tammy's tender skin.

"Yes, Jessica?" she replied, looking over at the girl with a smile that quivered uneasily upon her face.

"Why don't you love me, Mummy?" the girl asked, looking deep into Tammy's eyes, the sombre words cutting deep into Tammy like a knife through her beating heart.

Tammy's feelings of love and elation soon started to dwindle, fading into obscurity as feelings of sadness and regret began to rise up and slowly devour them. She felt a shiver tingling down her spine as she swallowed an uncomfortable lump in her throat.

"But I do love you, Jessica; I love you with all my heart!" Tammy protested.

"No, no you don't, Mummy," the girl replied, shaking her head with sadness. "You hate me, don't you? Mummy?"

"No, I love you!" Tammy protested again, tears beginning to stream down her pale face. "I love you more than anything in the world!"

"You want to hurt me! Don't you, Mummy?" the girl continued, starting to gently whimper.

"No, Jessica, I would never hurt you!" Tammy told her, her voice becoming increasingly desperate and frustrated.

"You do! You want to hurt me!" the girl cried in frustration as a stream of blood began to trickle down from her blonde hair and run across the side of her face.

"Jessica? What's wrong?" Tammy cried in a grief-stricken panic, but as she gestured to move towards the girl she found herself completely paralysed in the void.

"You, Mummy! You're hurting me!" the girl screamed in anguish as the flow of blood increased, coating her entire face in shimmering crimson. The girl reached her arms out for help, crying uncontrollably and staring deep into Tammy's eyes. "Mummy! Please? Please stop hurting me!" she begged.

"Jessica!" Tammy cried in return, fear and anxiety consuming her like it never had before, inflating her brain inside her skull like a balloon at the point of bursting.

"Mummy, Stop! Please!" the girl screeched again at the top of her lungs, a sound so deafening that Tammy's ears began to ring with resonance and then slowly start to bleed.

SIMON LAW

Tammy watched as the girl's head cracked wide open before her, erupting with maggots and bugs that wriggled and scurried from the open wound and engulfed her entire body while she still continued to scream.

Tammy motioned to scream, but her breath was muted and muffled behind something in her mouth, something silky and smooth against her tongue. She clenched her eyes and wriggled, but still she couldn't move. Her arms were tied firmly behind her, and her feet felt glued to the floor. She opened her eyes again and the girl had vanished, though the ringing in her ears continued, the harrowing scream living on within her and bouncing around inside her swollen head like a squash ball.

Clenching her eyes shut again, Tammy breathed in and out through her nose, following the pattern that her shrink had taught her. 'Breathe in, count to five. Breathe out, count to ten', all the while feeling her racing heart beating away in her chest while the deafening ringing in her ears slowly started to dissipate.

Tammy opened her eyes again and kept them open, continuing her breathing techniques and watching as shapes slowly started to form in the darkness. First a table, then some shelves and a concrete stairway, all illuminated by a faint beam of dusty moonlight.

She wriggled and shook her body again, shaking the chair that she now realised she was sat upon. She then felt the tight plastic that was cutting into her wrists and ankles, gluing her to the chair and preventing her from moving. Tammy's panic refuelled and rose again, as she released another muted and muffled scream of desperation, continuing to shake and rattle the wooden chair upon the cold concrete floor below it.

As the ghastly images of her bloodied daughter gradually began to fade from her mind, she slowly started to remember what had happened to her. She remembered the black bags, she remembered her suspicions, and she remembered the strange taste in her tea. Her thoughts were interrupted by a rustling from the corner of the room, and she suddenly realised that she was not alone.

Tammy quickly turned her head, squinting her eyes to focus in through the darkness, and for a brief second she saw the eerie silhouette of a demon – a winged beast with the eyes and tail of a serpent, gazing at her from the shadows, its glowing eyes of amber piercing clean through the darkness.

She released another muffled scream of terror as the demon scurried to the light cord, but as it flooded the room with light she realised that

THE DAMAGED

it was no demon at all, it was Matthew. He looked down at her with an eerily calm smile, but the sight did nothing to calm her raging anxiety.

"Hey, Darling. How are you feeling?" he asked in a casual, nonchalant tone as he slowly stepped towards her.

Tammy muffled uneasily in return, pulling away from Matthew in fear and wrenching at the arm restraints – not in an attempt to escape, but to cause the thin plastic to cut into her flesh so that the pain would flood her body with the endorphins she needed to stop her heart from exploding within her chest, inadvertently tightening the ratchets with each sharp wrench of her arms.

"Shhh... It's okay, Tammy. Relax," he told her as he planted a gentle kiss upon her forehead and stroked his hands tenderly through her silky black hair. "Everything's going to be okay now, I promise," he continued as he squatted down beside her, staring lovingly into her eyes.

Tammy grimaced and flinched at his touch, continuing to pull at her restraints until she felt the blood begin to seep from the cuts and trickle down into her cold palms.

"These look good on you, you should keep them on," he told her as he brushed his fingers along the string of white pearls that he had placed around her neck while she slept.

Tammy pulled away from him again, desperate to try and avoid his touch upon her skin, before glimpsing down at the pearls that she only now realised she was wearing. She took a long breath through her nose and mumbled at him angrily, though her words could not be deciphered through the black silk tie knotted in her mouth.

Matthew's smile wavered as he sighed and nodded in return, seemingly understanding Tammy's mumbles.

"If I take this off, you can't scream, okay?" he told her sternly, raising his eyebrows and tilting his head forwards. "I'm serious, please. I don't want to hurt you." he continued, his voice sounding sincere and empathetic.

Tammy scowled in frustration before reluctantly nodding in agreement.

Matthew smiled and nodded again, before reaching forward, gently loosening the knot in the black silk tie, and removing it from her sore mouth.

"What the fuck is going on!" she yelled angrily at him, taking a large gulp of air to inflate her lungs.

"We don't use language like that in this house, Tammy!" Matthew immediately snapped back at her, rising to his feet and taking a step back. "...And keep your voice down too; the neighbours will hear you!"

Tammy shook her head and continued to scowl tormentedly, desperately trying to formulate her thoughts.

"What...What are you doing to me, Matthew? Let me go right now!" she demanded, lowering her tone as her exasperation sucked her energy.

"Come on, Tammy, don't play games with me. You know why I've had to do this. I didn't want to!" he replied, his voice sounding frustrated and remorseful. "You're a good girl, an honest girl, you would have gone to the police about me, I know you would! I'm not going back there, Tammy. I'm not going back to that hospital again, I'd rather die."

Tammy clenched her eyes and grit her teeth as she continued to shake her head despondently back and forth, breathing in and out deeply to keep her anxiety at bay. She slowly opened her eyes back up again to the sight of the bloodied bandage upon Matthew's arm, imagining Bronco's teeth sinking deep into Matthew's flesh as he desperately tried to protect his master.

"So it is true then? You killed James, didn't you? And all those other poor people too?" she asked, snarling at him bitterly.

"People? You could scarcely call them 'people', Tammy! They were low-life scum, evil diseased vermin, no better than rabid animals! I did the world a favour!" Matthew replied defensively.

"That's not true, Matthew! These people aren't evil just because they're homeless! Society needs to look after these people, not demonise them!"

"Society? There's no such thing as society, Tammy, it's just a made-up concept. There's only people. These people are responsible for their own problems, their own drug addictions, their own gambling and drink problems. Why does 'society' owe then anything?"

"You don't get it, Matthew. You were born into money. You have no idea what it's like to fall upon hard times."

"No, my family were honest, hard-working people. That's why we had money!"

"Well then you're a hypocrite, Matthew. You've never worked a day in your life!"

"That's hardly my fault, is it?!" he snapped defensively, the frown lines upon his brow deepening by the second. "I didn't want any of this! I wanted a normal life, a quiet life with a good job and a nice wife..." he continued with frustration, before then turning to the charcoal sketches nailed upon the cellar beams. "It's his fault!" he raged, pointing angrily at the most recent sketch. "He caused all of this! He murdered my parents! He ruined my whole life!"

THE DAMAGED

Tammy paused and gulped uncomfortably, realising that her antagonising was fuelling Matthew's anger and that if she didn't stop it could end very badly for her. She pulled at her restraints for comforting pain again before gingerly peering up to the sketches that Matthew had gestured to.

"You can't blame all these other people for the action of one man, Matthew," she told him as calmly as she could, feeling her bottom lip starting to quiver. "When is this gonna end?"

"It ends when I find him, and make him pay for what he's done to me."

"But it's been twenty-odd years now, Matthew. What makes you think you'll ever find him now? He could be anywhere now; he might even be dead already!"

"I'll find him, I know I will. The *raven* won't let me down."

"The raven? What raven? What on earth are you talking about, Matthew?" she shrieked in hopeless desperation.

"The beast. He wants to help me. He gives me the strength to carry on," Matthew explained with a smile.

Tammy paused again, trying to process Matthew's seemingly obscure statements while desperately trying to think of a way out of the situation.

"There's....There's no raven, Matthew. He's not real!" she finally told him with hesitation, her voice sounding genuinely sympathetic and understanding.

"He's real, Tammy. He lives inside me now. I can feel him in there, bubbling at the surface, guiding me."

"No, Matthew. Please, just listen to me. It's just your medication; it must not be working for some reason. You need to let me go so I can get you some help. Please?"

"My medication? I stopped taking those stupid blue pills weeks ago now. I don't need them. They... They just clouded my thoughts. I can think clearly now, better than I have in years."

"No, Matthew. You're not well; you need that medication, please?"

"No!" he snapped sternly at her, his face bubbling up with anger once more.

"Please, Matthew!" she pleaded in torment, feeling her sense of hopelessness begin to consume her. "Please let me go!" she begged again, tears now streaming down her face as her head slumped down despondently.

Matthew looked down and watched as Tammy sobbed despairingly, feeling her desperation pulsating through him like a crashing wave. The guilt and remorse he felt for what he had done to her was undeniable, but he knew he had had no other choice. He sighed as the anger melted from his face, now feeling his own eyes starting to well up but refusing to let them erupt in front of her. He composed himself and knelt down beside her, placing his hand gently upon her knee to offer comfort.

"I'm sorry, Darling. I know this can't be nice for you," he told her as she pulled away from him in disgust.

"Just let me go," she mumbled between her tears and shallow, counted breaths.

"As soon as this is over, you'll be free," he explained, though his definition of 'free' was almost certainly different from her own. "I never wanted to hurt you, Tammy. I...I love you..."

Tammy scoffed and shook her head dismissively.

"You don't love me, Matthew. You barely even know me," she replied quietly, keeping her solemn eyes upon the floor.

"I do. I love your hair, I love your smile, and I love how caring you are... I love everything about you!" he told her with a loving smile and a longing stare. "We're very similar, you and I, Tammy. We've both lost people that we love, we've both been shunned and ignored. We both..."

"I'm nothing like you!" Tammy quickly snapped through her tears, interrupting Matthew mid-sentence. "You're insane! I don't hurt people like you do!"

"No, you just hurt yourself instead," he retorted with judgemental discontent, running his hand over the scars on her inner thigh. "You cut yourself, you starve yourself, you fill your body with alcohol and tar...I've seen people locked up for a lot less than that in my time."

Tammy did not reply, starting to accept that her words would be futile against him, and that any response she gave would simple be returned with more tenuous justification. Instead, she simply remained still, silent, her mind running through various scenarios that might lead to her escape, but none of them seeming likely.

The awkward silence continued as Matthew stroked his hand through her silky black hair once more, each stroke sending shivers of disgust pulsating through her tired and achy body. He continued to stroke and caress her, the feeling of her soft skin under his fingers reminding him of their stolen night of passion together, the images in his mind arousing him to the point of wanting to take her again, right there and then.

Tammy concentrated her mind on steadying her trembles, blanking out the sensation of Matthew's murderous hands caressing her and detaching herself from the situation. She breathed in and out deeply, picturing herself leaving her body behind and travelling to her happy place in her mind. She pictured herself at the zoo, casually strolling

THE DAMAGED

past the enclosures with a smile on her face and her daughter's soft hand grasping tenderly onto her own. The sun above gently kissed their skin as they both sat down upon a bench, looking up in awe at the towering giraffes as the gentle, benevolent creatures ate leaves from a tree above them. A cloud of leaf debris gently fluttered down upon their faces as Tammy looked down and watched Jessica laugh and smile, amazed and captivated by the moment, hoping that this moment could last forever.

Tammy fought to stay inside the moment, clinging desperately to the serene and tranquil images that filled her with such calm and peace, but despite her determination they quickly faded with the sensation of a cockroach slowly creeping up her bare leg. Tammy immediately screamed in return, startled and confused by the sudden jolt back into reality.

The scream bellowed and bounced against the walls of the cellar, sending Matthew into an immediate state of panic that the scream would be heard, would be reported to the police, and that his reign of vengeance would be brought crashing to an abrupt end.

Suddenly, the cellar door burst open and fell from its rusted hinges, crashing down the stairs with a loud clatter and revealing a domineering silhouette in the doorway. The figure grunted to itself in a pleased manner, as it took a step forward, revealing itself to be Otis, the overzealous orderly from the hospital. He stared down at Matthew with a dirty grin, taunting him with a loaded syringe and laughing menacingly into the air.

Matthew quickly reacted, viciously striking Tammy across the face before savagely grabbing her throat with both hands, tipping the chair onto its back legs as he squeezed, and sending her head crashing into the bottles of wine behind her.

"I told you not to scream!" he growled angrily at her, squeezing mercilessly upon her throat so as to not let a single peep escape from it.

"I'm sorry!" she mouthed back in an inaudible whisper, her face streaming with tears and quickly turning beetroot red as she started to choke.

"I thought I could trust you, Tammy!" he muttered tormentedly as he scowled and shook his head in frustration, maintaining his fierce pressure upon her throat.

Matthew looked down at Tammy struggling for air and was suddenly bombarded with bloodied images of his mother, gargling blood from her sliced throat as she too struggled to breathe. He immediately let go and closed his eyes, shaking the grim images from his mind as he listening to Tammy coughing and gasping for breath.

"You made me do that, Tammy, You!" he told her in a tormented whine. "I didn't want to hurt you! I told you that already!" he continued, as he picked the black tie back up from the floor. "I'm sorry, Tammy, but if you can't be trusted then I have no choice!"

Matthew re-knotted the tie tightly around her mouth and made his way to the cellar door. Ignoring her muffled pleas, he pulled resentfully at the light cord, plummeting her into darkness once more and locking the cellar door angrily behind him.

Tammy's desperate muted pleas continued into the night as she wriggled and wrenched at her restraints, eventually ceasing a few hours later when she finally passed out through sheer exhaustion.

Tammy awoke again several hours later, to the sight of the morning sun forcing its way through the gaps in the rear cellar door and to the sound of the morning birds chirping from the tall branches of the conifer trees.

Tammy's entire body now ached and throbbed from her awkward unnatural position, her face throbbed from Matthew's strike upon it, her head pounded from its fierce impact with the wine bottles, and her mouth felt as dry and coarse as the Sahara Desert itself. On top of this, both of her wrists were now completely garrotted from the plastic cable ties, and her hands felt coated in a layer of dry and flaky blood that had gently drizzled from the wounds during the night.

She sobbed and moaned again, eager to alert Matthew's attention so she could once again plead with him for her release, but Matthew did not respond. The sound of her muffled groans and the rattle of her chair upon the concrete floor resonated up through the house to Matthew in the lounge, but he simply paid them no attention. *A crying baby needs to be weaned from its mother's attention, and Tammy's no different*, he thought, regardless of how much he adored her.

Sitting calmly upon his father's red leathered Chesterfield, Matthew absorbed his morning fix of children's cartoons while casually teasing a series of bloodied black silky plumes from each of the deep, purulent gouges that Bronco had left upon his arm, carefully placing each one down in a row upon the wooden side-table beside him. The appearance of the strange plumes no longer scared nor surprised Matthew, who now considered their extraction to be another normal laborious task that simply needed to be done, like cutting your fingernails or washing your hair. Once fully extracted, he discarded the bloodied plumes to the rubbish bin before re-dressing his arm in a fresh white bandage. Removing the vacuum cleaner from the cupboard underneath the stairs, Matthew began to casually clean and tidy the front room, using each of the various different nozzle attachments to get to the hard-to-reach

THE DAMAGED

places underneath the sofa and behind the television. *Tidy house-Tidy mind!* as his mother used to say.

Tammy sighed angrily in frustration, hearing the vacuum starting up above her and realising now that Matthew was almost certainly ignoring her cries for help. She gazed around the room despairingly, beyond the wooden pasting table in front of her to the shelving units along the far wall that mirrored the ones behind her. She followed the shelves along with her eyes, watching as the rows of wines and ports slowly morphed into the tools and machinery that were housed towards the end. Tammy then noticed the absence of the two black sacks that had previously sat by the door, and her mind immediately started to ruminate over the awful, morbid things that Matthew might have done to her dear friend James once more, picturing each possibility with vivid bloody detail.

Tammy's thoughts quickly turned to her own mortality, and what terrible things Matthew might do to *her*. She clung desperately onto the hope that Matthew had been sincere when he said that she would be 'free' at the end. *If he loves me like he says he does, then surely this was the truth?* she pondered optimistically.

The morning drew on as she continued to sit, too exhausted for her anxiety to grip her too fiercely and too disheartened to even bother to cry out to him anymore. She listened out to the rhythmic humming of the vacuum cleaner above her as it travelled its way throughout the house, relentlessly sucking upon every possible inch of carpet and upholstery that came before it.

The noise of the vacuum eventually faded away, to be replaced by the sound of the shower, and then nothing, silence again except for the sound of light feet creaking throughout the house.

Tammy continued to stare numbly around the room, her eyes often stopping and focusing in longingly upon the various different bottles of wine, any of which would taste amazing to her right now, cascading with a fruity glug across the receptors of her tongue and slipping down her throat with warm comforting reassurance. It seemed almost torture in itself that she was completely surrounded by the one thing that would comfort her right now, and that it was all just slightly out of her reach.

Matthew packed away the vacuum cleaner and returned the furniture polish to the cupboard under the sink as the hands of the grandfather clock slowly ticked over to nine-thirty-five. Opening his care-pack folder that lay upon the kitchen counter, he flicked through the pages to the list of contact numbers near the back, running his finger down the page until reaching the one he needed. He picked up the corded receiver of his cream Bakelite telephone and began to twirl the numbers around on the old-fashioned analogue dial, listening as the phone crackled in and out with each mechanical dial before eventually starting to ring.

"Yes, hello?" a voice answered in a lethargic monotone slur.

"Oh, hello. Is this Maureen?" Matthew asked with a tone of feigned concern.

"Oh...Yes. How can I help?" Maureen replied, quickly changing her miserable tone upon realising that it was not a familiar voice.

"Hi, Maureen, it's Matthew. Matthew Mason?"

"Hi, Matthew. Is everything okay?"

"I...I'm not sure to be honest, Maureen. It's Tammy, she hasn't turned up yet this morning and I was just a little worried, that's all."

"Oh, I see..."

"Yeah. She seemed a little upset when I saw her yesterday, something about her daughter I think, and I... I think she'd been drinking too."

"Drinking?"

"Yeah, I could smell it on her breath. I don't mean to get her in trouble or anything like that. I like Tammy, I'm just worried about her."

"Okay, Matthew. Well, thank you for letting me know. I'll give her a call straight away and see what's going on."

"Thank you."

"You're welcome. Do you need anything this morning? Have you remembered to take all your pills?"

"Yes, I have, and no, I don't need anything. Thank you."

"Okay, that's good then. I'll see if Tammy's okay to see you this afternoon, if not I'll send Aggy to you again. Is that okay?"

"Yeah, sure."

"Take care then, Matthew. Thanks again for calling."

"Bye."

Matthew cleared his throat and returned the receiver to the hook once again, before switching on the kettle and calmly proceeding to make two hot cups of tea.

Tammy listened out above her to the sound of the key clunking and twisting within the lock of the cellar door. She took a deep breath and braced herself for whatever was to come next.

The door gave out a whining creak as Matthew opened it. He began to descend the stairs, his deathly shadow stretching out before him from the light of the kitchen, cascading and twisting down the flight of stairs like the mangled distorted shadow of a demon. Tammy felt her heart start to race again as her mind span with thoughts of Matthew's possible intentions, but slowly started to settle again upon the sight of his warm, greeting smile and the two hot cups of tea within his grasp.

THE DAMAGED

"Good morning, Darling," he called pleasantly as he placed both cups down upon the pasting table.

Tammy scowled in return, her eyes filled with fear and disgust.

Matthew lowered his smile to a sad sympathetic frown and sat himself down upon the last step of the stairs.

"This will all be over as soon as possible, Darling. Please don't hate me for it," Matthew told her in a seemingly genuine tone.

Tammy lowered her scowl and turned her head away in disdain, breathing deeply through her nose and concentrating on keeping her anxieties at bay.

"I made you some tea! Just how you like it!" he told her, changing his tone to a feigned uplifting pitch in an attempt to somehow distract her from her dire situation.

Tammy turned back to him with another disapproving frown before shaking her head dismissively and mumbling a series of inaudible syllables.

"If I remove your gag, you have to promise not to scream this time, Darling. We don't want a repeat of yesterday now, do we?" he told her in the way a parent would talk to a small child, raising his eyebrows to her with condescending assertion.

Tammy deepened her frown further, gazing deep into his eyes for any signs of ulterior motives, before finally exhaling and reluctantly nodding her head. Matthew smiled in return. He reached forward and gingerly teased apart the knotted tie within her mouth.

Tammy gasped and panted gently, rolling her tongue in the hope of producing saliva to sooth the dry arid roof of her mouth. She cleared her throat and swallowed, turning her gaze up to Matthew once more and then to the steaming cup of tea that awaited her upon the pasting table.

"And how do I know that you haven't drugged it again?" Tammy asked hesitantly, croaking out her words through her dry, sore throat.

"To what end, Tammy? I have no need for that now, do I? You'll have to just trust me, I guess," he replied.

Tammy eyed up the cup once more, thinking how desperately she craved the fluid and slowly coming to terms with the fact that Matthew was right; she simply had to trust him, she had no other choice. She turned her gaze back to Matthew once more and pulled at her restraints with exaggerated, sarcastic motions.

"Well I need my hands, don't I?" she told him, growling in a gravelly, condescending tone, a tone overly brave for someone in such a dependent and fragile situation.

Matthew looked back at her blankly, gently chewing upon his bottom lip for a while as he contemplated the situation. He hadn't initially considered removing her restraints, his intentions being to hold the cup to her lips himself as she drank from it. He wanted to trust her though, just as much as he desired her trust of him, but after her clear display of defiance previously he wondered whether that was even possible. He continued to stare at her for a while longer, silent and motionless, his frozen countenance beginning to disturb Tammy even more than she was already.

Matthew finally relented and smiled, giving Tammy a gentle nod before stepping over to the toolbox along the far wall and slowly removing an old rusty Stanley knife from it. Tammy's eyes immediately widened and fixated upon the rusted blade, feeling herself unable to breathe as she watched the blade in his grasp travel towards her, concerned that it was no longer the restraints that Matthew intended to cut.

Tammy grit her teeth as Matthew towered above her with the blade, feeling tremors through her entire body until finally feeling her wrists liberated from the cable ties, after which she was finally able to take a breath.

Tammy forced a smile upon her face in feigned appreciation of Matthew's trust, before stretching out her newly-freed limbs in their aching sockets and tenderly examining the deep garrotte marks on each of her sore and bloody wrists. Matthew then noticed the bloodied gouges himself for the first time, and grimaced down at them in horror of what he had done to her. He offered her a half-mast smile of sympathy before quickly turning his head away in shame, realising his unjust treatment of the girl he loved and adored, but tormented by the certainty that he still had no other choice.

Tammy leaned forward on the chair and reached for the mug, cupping it in both hands for warmth and hesitantly starting to sip. She felt the warm fluid filling her mouth and soothing her arid throat like liquid gold, all the while tentatively trying to detect any remnants of the bitter grit of the sleeping tablets, but there was none. She released a long sigh as she swallowed the liquid down into her growling stomach and started to feel her racing heart begin to slow once more.

"People are gonna notice I'm missing, Matthew. You do realise that, don't you?" she told him, briefly casting her eyes over to him as he placed the Stanley knife down upon the pasting table and picked up his own cup of tea.

"Yeah, I know. But they won't look for you here. Why would they?" he replied dismissively, taking a sip from his cup and sitting himself down upon the bottom step of the concrete stairs.

"You should just let me go, Matthew, please. I won't tell anyone about you, I swear!" she pleaded again with a forlorn glance.

THE DAMAGED

"Oh come on, Tammy. We both know that's not true. I'm not an idiot. Am I?" he replied with a frown, clearly unimpressed with Tammy's continued deceit.

"I promise you! I could even try to help you find this man, if you like?"

"How could you possibly help me, Tammy?"

"One of my clients was homeless back in the eighties, remember? He might know something about it; he might have heard something from someone. It's worth a try, isn't it? You're searching for a needle in a haystack at the moment."

Matthew put down his tea and looked over to her in contemplation, remembering her mentioning the same thing before, but quickly dismissing it as another vague attempt to gain her freedom.

"Why would you even want to leave here anyway?" he then asked, tilting his head with a crooked frown. "What's waiting for you out there that you're so desperate to get back to? Your empty flat? The daughter you're not allowed to see? What? Why would you want to leave *me* for that? – Someone who loves and adores you?"

Tammy scowled and turned away, reeling from the audacity of Matthew's impertinent presumptions, triggering her mind to recall the harrowing image of her daughter's bloodied screaming face from her dream. *Fuck you!* she screamed at him in her head, but bit her tongue before the words managed to manifest themselves into audible sounds. The harsh comments felt like a knife in her side, not because of their inaccuracy, but because they were just a little bit too close to reality. It may have been true that her relationship with Jessica was strained and that her current situation seemed bleak, but even though her struggle often felt hopeless to her too, hearing Matthew's blunt conclusion that it was simply pointless made her realise just how brightly her desire for redemption still burned within her. Jessica was worth the pain.

Tammy tried to centre herself, and focused her sights back to her cup of tea once more, her hands shaking with such anger that the liquid inside the cup sloshed erratically back and forth and cascaded over the sides. She stared deep into the rising steam as it emanated upwards, watching as it waved hypnotically, flickering and soaring like fire as it gently dissipated up into the air. She began to contemplate the notion of sending the scalding liquid flying into Matthew's arrogant face, picturing the event in her head with smug satisfaction. She looked up at him curiously and then back down again, wondering if the blinding shock of the scalding tea would give her enough time to escape. She pondered upon the thought a few moments longer before quickly dismissing the idea as futile. How far could she possibly get with her ankles still tethered to the chair legs? How long would it take for Matthew to retaliate?

Tammy sighed in temporary defeat and continued sipping upon her tea, feeling her anxiety rising and falling inside her on a seemingly endless loop as her cravings for nicotine and alcohol both started to peak.

"So, what would you like for breakfast, Darling?" Matthew asked, returning back to his previous uplifting pitch as if the last conversation had never happened.

"Nothing," she replied bluntly, aiming a bitter glare in his direction.

"Well, you have to eat, Tammy," he persisted. "You're as thin as a rake already!"

"I don't want any breakfast!" she articulated more forcefully, her voice starting to growl with frustration. "I'd rather have a cigarette, please?"

"Well that's not an option. We don't smoke in this house, Tammy. My aunt filled my lungs with those horrible things for years. I hate them! Now, tell me what you want for breakfast? I'll force it down you if I have to. I'm not letting you make yourself ill by not eating," he told her, the irony of his comments completely eluding him. "I have bacon and eggs, or some cereal, or a yoghurt maybe? So what would you like?"

Tammy frowned in returned, completely perplexed by Matthew's seemingly odd set of priorities. "...Well, I'll have a yoghurt then," she finally told him with a flustered sigh, deciding that it would probably be less stressful to just go along with him.

She swallowed down the last few dregs from the cup and placed it back down upon the table, her eyes briefly straying over the unguarded Stanley knife that lay staring at her, mere inches from her grasp. She slumped back down on the chair and rubbed her face, her thoughts returning once again to the idea of escape.

Matthew collected the empty cups with a bland smile, turning back to the stairway and ascending up into the kitchen to fetch Tammy's yoghurt. Tammy saw her opportunity and immediately lunged forward, grabbing the rusted knife from off the table and quickly returning to her previous position. She stared down at the orange crust upon the blade as she nervously contemplated her next move, wondering if she actually had enough time to cut herself free and burst her way to freedom in the time it would take Matthew to return with her yoghurt, and wishing now that she had opted for the bacon and eggs instead. She continued staring at the blade in tormented indecision, feeling her heart beating away within her and anxious that her precious time to act was quickly fleeing.

THE DAMAGED

She turned her head to the cellar door, and then back to the knife again, convinced that if Matthew caught her even touching the knife that he would kill her there and then. Her anxiety quickly gained momentum, causing her hand to violently shake back and forth as she gripped tighter and tighter upon the handle of the rusted Stanley knife. Finally, she sighed in defeat and begrudgingly placed the blade back down upon the table again, immediately loathing herself for her complete lack of courage and conviction.

Matthew placed both of the empty cups into the sink before bending down to examine the sparse contents of the fridge, making a mental note to make a shopping list in time for Aggy's arrival that afternoon. He reached inside, pushing aside the half-empty tub of butter and removing a small pot of yoghurt from the back. He then grabbed a spoon from the cutlery draw and made his way back down to the cellar, finding Tammy cross-armed and solemnly awaiting his return.

"I need to use the toilet, Matthew," she told him in a quiet and tired voice, her eyes not leaving the floor.

"No! No way! I'm sorry, I can't allow that," he replied abruptly, thumping the yoghurt and spoon down in front of her.

Tammy pulled her eyes from the floor and aimed them at him with disdain and disgust.

"What? You expect me to just piss myself, do ya?" she retorted, her words laced with venom. "...This is how you treat someone you love, is it?"

Matthew scowled in frustration, deepening the tormented red creases in his forehead as he began looking around the room, his eyes finally settling upon an old brown bucket he spotted in the corner.

"No!" Tammy immediately growled, pre-empting Matthew's next suggestion. "...I'm not pissing in a bucket either! You're better than this, Matthew. You could treat me with a little dignity at least!"

Matthew gulped and shook his head dejectedly, immediately feeling the shame and disgrace that was intended by Tammy's comment.

"Okay, fine!" he snarled reluctantly as he grabbed the knife once more, oblivious to its subtle change of position from where he had left it. "...But if you try anything on, Tammy, I really won't be happy!" he continued.

Tammy stared back at him expectantly, but did not respond. Matthew then sighed again as he knelt down and hesitantly sliced through the plastic cable ties around both of her ankles before stepping back and looking down at her with dubious suspicion.

"Come on then," he told her, gripping securely upon the blade as a form of self-assurance as he offered the other hand out to her.

SIMON LAW

Matthew led her up the stairway to the kitchen, watching every move she made with intense scrutiny. He led her through the lounge, purposely ignoring the glaring scowls that emanated from his parents' photograph for not just killing her when he should have. They continued up the stairs to the landing, where Tammy slipped inside the bathroom and closed the door firmly shut behind her, leaving Matthew guarding the door with poised vigilance.

Tammy released a long breath as she sat down upon the toilet seat to relieve herself. Her eyes flitted across the room in search of anything she could possibly use as a weapon, but there was nothing.

She ran the hot tap and looked deep into her tired reflection in the mirror, searching inside herself for the courage to act, to fight back, to escape from Matthew's psychotic clutches and be free. The twinkle of the white gold in the pearl necklace caught her attention as it sparkled to her in the light. She snarled and grimaced at the sight of it, thinking of all the betrayal it now symbolised. She reached up behind her neck and immediately unclasped it, throwing it carelessly into the sink below with the disgust and repugnance it deserved.

Tammy gently washed her face and her bloodied hands in the sink as condensation from the hot water began quickly frosting up the mirror, revealing a faint four-lettered word smeared onto the glass with a fingertip. She stepped back and gazed upon it with confusion, the short word sending a cold chill down her spine as she then whispered it aloud.

"Amon."

Tammy considered its meaning with a bewildered look of concentration upon her face. Was it a name? Or a thing? She shook the tingling chill from her body and decided that the word made no difference, turning her mind once again back to the thought of escape.

With both her arms and legs now free of her shackles she knew that now was certainly the best (if not only) opportunity she would get to pull something out of the bag, But with every moment that she remained idle, Matthew's suspicions would surely be growing stronger. She needed to act, and act now.

She clenched her eyes and searched the depths of her soul once again for the courage to act. Her mind finally stumbled upon the memory of her daughter and the giraffe once more. She froze the image in her mind, magnifying it and concentrating deep upon Jessica's beautiful smile until the image was scorched into her mind with vivid, saturated clarity.

Tammy gulped one final breath to calm her nerves before grasping carefully onto the bathroom door handle as tight and firmly as she could, placing her other hand palm down upon the surface of the door.

THE DAMAGED

Feeling the adrenaline pulsating through her body and her heart beating in her throat, she slowly began counting down from three. Then, as swift and as fierce as she could possibly manage, she pulled down the handle and thrust open the door with every ounce of strength she could muster. The door flung around on its hinges with an almighty thud as it cracked unforgivingly into the side of Matthew's head, sending him flying into the banister in a daze.

Tammy immediately dashed past him as fast as she could, frantically bounding down the stairs three steps at a time. She reached the front door and grabbed upon the handle, desperately twisting and wrenching upon it, but the door was locked.

"Shit!" she cried in a flustered howl as she heard Matthew lolloping down the stairs behind her. She bolted frantically through the lounge and into the kitchen, clutching upon the handle of the back door in hopeless desperation and wrenching upon it with all her might. Locked as well.

"Kill her! Kill her now, Matthew!" cried his mother from within the photograph as he dashed through the lounge in hot pursuit. He stopped at the dining table as Tammy backed herself into the corner of the room, her face flushed with fear and torment. His mother screamed at him again, and while her insistent words bounced and reverberated throughout the sparking synapses of his brain, the beast that lived inside him suddenly sprung into life. It bubbled angrily from the pit of his stomach, clawing fiercely at his insides with its razor-sharp talons while nudging forcefully through his organs with its rigid black beak. It croaked aloud within him as it bubbled closer and closer to the surface, reinforcing his mother's stern demands and strengthening his grip upon the Stanley blade.

He looked over at Tammy, envisioning himself slashing the blade fiercely against her throat, blood gushing into the air and splattering against the kitchen walls behind her. He took a step towards her, his sleek reptilian pupils burning with an amber scorch as they locked in on her, tracking her movements with vigilance while the forks of his serpent tongue tingled with the pungent scent of fear that emanated from Tammy's every pore.

Thunder suddenly exploded above them, turning the sky from a peaceful azure blue to an angry ominous grey. Rain battered fiercely against the house, pelting against the kitchen windows and turning the garden into a mere opaque blur. Then, from within the smeary blur, emerged the face of Otis the orderly, gazing at Matthew through the window with a sly sadistic grin. He tapped upon the window and waved, removing a syringe of sedatives from his vast utility belt and widening his smile even further.

"No!" Matthew suddenly roared in belligerent defiance of his mother's demands, and of the overwhelming urges inside him, finally silencing the voices bouncing back and forth in his head. "Tammy! Please! I won't hurt you, I promise!" he pleaded with her earnestly, throwing the Stanley knife to the floor and baring his open palms to her. "Please don't make this worse!" he continued.

Tammy locked stares with him in return, but could not find the words to respond. Her lips quivered and her hands shook as the dread and adrenaline pulsating through her veins overloaded her capacity to formulate words.

Matthew edged slowly towards her with the tiniest of pigeon steps, and Tammy immediately sprang into life, grabbing a frying pan from off the kitchen side and spring-loading it over her shoulder.

"Get back!" she growled at him through gritted teeth, finally regaining her ability to speak.

Matthew frowned forlornly and held up his hands in apparent surrender, but took another step towards her regardless.

Tammy swung the pan in his direction, slicing the air with a cutting swoosh that missed Matthew's head by a mere few centimetres. Tammy quickly reloaded the pan again as Matthew gingerly retreated a few steps back, giving Tammy a brief nod in acknowledgement of her clear inclination.

"Get away from me, you bastard! I hate you!" she uttered venomously.

Tammy breathed deeply as she briefly broke the stare-lock for a glance of the cellar, remembering the flimsy padlock that kept the exterior cellar door closed and contemplating her ability to bust her way through it.

Quickly turning her sights back to Matthew, she discovered him another step closer, an advance clearly stolen during her brief lapse of concentration. Tammy intensified her piercing gaze as she slowly turned and edged towards the open cellar door, her grip firmly upon the handle of the pan and ready to attack in a millisecond's notice.

When Tammy broke the stare once again to line up her escape route, Matthew took a sudden lunge towards her. Tammy threw the pan at him with all her strength and ran, pelting with lightning speed through the kitchen towards the open cellar door. The pan hurtled towards Matthew, ricocheting off his forearms as he held them up in defence before then crashing to the floor below. Tammy hurried down the concrete steps into the darkness, the flimsy rear doors of the cellar now firmly in her sights. Suddenly she missed a step in haste, instantly losing her balance and toppling awkwardly down the stairs. Without time to break her fall, she twisted and tumbled to the ground, cracking

THE DAMAGED

her head against the concrete floor with a dull thud that rendered her immediately unconscious.

"Tammy!" Matthew cried anxiously, quickly dashing down the steps behind her. "Tammy? Darling? Are you okay?" he continued with a desperate frown, his heart thumping and his mind ablaze with the petrifying possibility of her mortal departure.

He slumped down beside her and nestled her head in his lap, stroking her ghostly-white face while he gingerly fingered the growing swell upon the back of her head. "Tammy? Tammy?" he muttered to her again, gently shaking her for some kind of response, but there was none.

A single tear trickled gently down his face as his panic started to rise further. Her death and his own were inevitable, and the time for that would soon come, but not now, not yet, not while he still had work to be done. She couldn't leave him now.

He gulped and steadied his nerves before leaning in and placing his ear to her mouth, trying to listen out for a breath or any sign of life, but there was none. He reached out for her wrist, trying to find her vein behind the bloodied gouge marks left by her restraints. He pressed two fingers down tightly and closed his eyes, holding his breath and praying to feel a pulse. He concentrated, trying to ignore the vigorous thumping of his own heart in his chest from distracting him, until finally releasing a long sigh of relief at the reassuring sensation of a faint pulse rippling steadily beneath his fingertips.

THE DEPTHS OF DESPAIR

Sitting numbly in his father's chair, Matthew stared at the rain through the lounge window, watching as it drizzled and smeared down the panes of glass, twisting and deforming the menacing faces of Otis and the nurses who continued to lock their gaze upon him, grinning and taunting him with the unspoken tease of the psychiatric hospital that eagerly awaited his impending and chronic incarceration.

Listening to the friendly voices of the kids' cartoons, Matthew tried to ignore the incessant clawing of the beast that continued within him. He stroked his hands gently along the red leather of the chair's arms, feeling the creases and cracks in the ageing leather and thinking about his parents, their warm loving smiles and the sense of security he always felt in their presence.

Slowly feeling his anxieties starting to fade, he watched as the dreary autumn rain started to gradually peter out, taking away the twisted faces along with it and giving further credence to Matthew's growing grand delusion that the weather was somehow in his control. He smiled, relaxing deeper into the soft leather as he closed his eyes, feeling the clawing inside him starting to dissipate as his thoughts drifted dreamily to his pre-formulated vision of the life that was never meant to be.

He dreamt that the house was full of laughter, smiles and uplifting joyous nuances, while the scent of freshly-baked bread drifted gently through the air. Tammy and Jessica were there too, greeting him with a warm loving smile as he returned from another day at the company helping his father with design plans for yet another architectural masterpiece.

The scent of the sweet bread then slowly turned sour, rotten, diffused with musty sweat and alcohol-concentrated-urine. The atmosphere turned cold and ominous, as an eerie sense of unease fell upon them. The deafening croak of the raven suddenly echoed through the room, quickly turning the blue sky into a melancholic grey as the harrowing face of the killer appeared, staring right through Matthew with soulless black eyes.

Matthew stirred and broke himself free from his day-dream musings, dismayed and dejected that even his own mind would deny him his brief flight of fancy. Defiant, Matthew settled back down into the soft folds of the red leather and continued to daydream, picturing himself in a church, standing proud in a smart black suit while he awaited his beautiful bride to join him at the altar. The church organ began to play the wedding march as the doors opened up and Tammy appeared before him, sparkling with elegant beauty and radiating joy from her brimming smile. She looked towards him with eyes of endearment as she delicately began to step to the music. Then, like before, the rancid smell drifted past them. Joy soon turned to dread as the cold winds blew into the church, tingling across their skin with an icy unforgiving shiver. The killer appeared again, standing in the church doorway, motionlessly staring at Matthew with those soulless black eyes while his mouth dripped with rabid white foam.

Matthew stirred again, releasing a long broken-hearted sigh of resignation as he looked out aimlessly into the empty mid-distance feeling the vast weight of depression starting to bear down upon him. He looked up to his parents' wedding photo for some kind of enlightened smile of encouragement, but their weary faces merely reflected the same dreary, melancholic expressions to match that of his own.

The wound on Matthew's arm suddenly started to itch, and so he scratched it, but no matter how hard or vigorous he scratched upon the bandage, the vexing itch could not be quenched. Matthew paused with a frown, concentrating on the sensation as he felt it morph, turning from a mere itch to an aggravated ripple below the skin. He unwound the bandage with curiosity, pondering to himself whether it was maybe just time again to further wrench the raven's bloodied feathers from his skin, but it was not.

Dropping the bandage to his lap, Matthew looked down, watching as the flesh on his arm now rippled and bulged before his very eyes as if something was scurrying just below the surface. Matthew watched with intrigue, as the bulge started to ripple towards the first of Bronco's savage tooth gouges. Suddenly, the gouge erupted with a putrid concoction of blood and fresh pus that drizzled down either side of Matthew's arm, revealing a small black spider in the wound that was eagerly pulling itself to freedom.

Neither shocked nor scared, Matthew gazed down upon the spider with blasé acceptance, as if arachnids crawling from one's skin was a mere everyday occurrence. He continued watching as the spider brushed itself off and began casually creeping down his arm, the brush of each furry leg sending tingles through his skin. Matthew lapped his lips with the tingling forks of his serpent tongue, before arching in further and capturing the spider in his mouth. Feeling the spider struggling frantically upon his tongue, he cracked open its brittle exoskeleton between his teeth, sending bitter juices drizzling down his throat and ending the spider's life with the same careless regard that he held for each of his worthless victims. The taste in his mouth was strange and unusual, but not entirely unpleasant, as if somehow satisfying a hunger he didn't know he had – maybe even that of the beast's.

While tonguing the remnants of the spider from between his teeth, Matthew's thoughts returned to Tammy once more. He reached into his pocket and removed the pearl necklace that he had retrieved from the bathroom sink, looking down at it with rejected sadness and thinking about the last words Tammy had spoken before her 'accident'. 'I hate you', she had told him, words that had cut him far deeper than any wound he could ever inflict with his favourite kitchen knife. *She didn't mean it,* he told himself, gently shaking his head in denial. *She couldn't. How could she? She was just angry, upset, confused. She'll realise that it's all for the best, sooner or later anyway.*

With Tammy's words weighing heavily upon him, Matthew got up from the chair and made his way to the cellar, carrying the necklace tenderly in his grip. He descended down the staircase into the partial darkness and sat quietly on the floor gazing up at Tammy sleeping in the chair, desperately clinging onto his fleeting images of happiness.

Tammy had yet to regain consciousness again since her fall that morning, but the increased strength of her breathing and her pulse were all good signs. He shuffled towards her on his knees and examined the fresh bandages that he had wrapped around her bloodied wrists, before gently fingering the tender swell that had grown upon her head. He grimaced at the touch of the throbbing bump, as if somehow feeling the pain himself, or at least the responsibility for it. Cupping her floppy head in his hands, he stroked each cheek tenderly with his thumbs, before leaning in and planting a gentle kiss upon her forehead.

"I love you, Tammy," he softly whispered, setting her head back down again upon the fluffy pillow he had taken from the bedroom.

He re-clasped the string of gold and pearls carefully around her neck once more and made his way to the door, giving her a solemn nod and padlocking the cellar door shut behind him.

THE DAMAGED

The bleak day slowly ground on, and Matthew's melancholic lethargy failed to improve. Aside from occasionally checking on Tammy's seemingly static condition, Matthew did nothing but simply wait for Aggy's arrival at five o'clock from the security of his father's soft chair, his ears filled with the numbing loop of repeating cartoons while his eyes fixated hypnotically upon the rhythmic swinging of the shiny brass pendulum within the grandfather clock.

Aggy's visit passed without incident or event, and was devoid of any suspicion of Tammy's captivity in the depths of the cellar below them. She arrived and left again within the space of a mere few minutes, leaving the house again during the latest rendition of Matthew's well-versed yet slightly tepid 'blue-pill' sedation routine. Matthew sighed at the welcoming sound of the front door closing again, relieved that the false smiles and sheer tedium of the event was over, at least for now anyway.

Returning back to the cellar for the countless time that day, Matthew noticed Tammy finally starting to stir. He sat down upon the floor in front of her and waited with anticipation, looking up at her with an anxious frown and a wavering smile. Tammy groaned, gently rolling her head as she cleared her throat, and slowly began to prise apart her eyes.

"Hey..." Matthew cooed with nervous trepidation, looking deep into her pale and weary face as he awaited her response.

Tammy did not reply. Instead, she frowned back with a dazed look of confusion, squinting her eyes as she tried to steady the queasy slosh of crashing waves in her head. She bit gently upon her bottom lip as she prised her heavy eyelids open further, aiming her dizzy gaze upon Matthew with an empty and vague expression.

"You okay? ....Darling?" Matthew asked gingerly.

Tammy sighed and dropped her jaw listlessly, letting her head fall back into the soft fluffy pillow behind it and again denying a response. As she rolled her head gently back and forth again, Matthew noticed her starting to grimace, the pain of her injuries now suddenly rising to her attention. Scrunching her face and wincing, she turned her head to the side and released a slow discordant groan, reeling and tensing herself to try and stifle the agony of the piercing throb.

"Shhh... It's okay, Darling," Matthew quickly told her reassuringly, propping himself up on his knees and embracing her tenderly. "You hit your head pretty hard when you fell. It's swollen up quite badly but you're going to be fine," he continued as Tammy began to quietly weep with despair.

Matthew broke free, feeling his guilt and sadness starting to overcome him again. He stood, taking a deep breath and denying his eyes their desire to well up themselves. He ascended the stairway and returned a moment later, a tall glass of water in one hand and Tammy's handbag in the other. He placed the glass down upon the blood-stained pasting table and rummaged through the bag, pushing aside the various clutter and finally removing the small box of paracetamol that he had noticed there previously.

"Here, take some of these for the pain," he told her, popping out two of the pills from their foil wrap.

Tammy subdued her sobs for a moment to turn to Matthew, looking over to the pills with a look of dubious suspicion and then back to Matthew with a frown.

"They're just paracetamol, Darling," he told her, unsurprised and understanding of her doubts. "Look, they're from your bag..." he continued, showing her the packet and the bag.

She sighed and slowly nodded in agreement, opening her mouth and watching carefully as Matthew placed the two pills upon her tongue. He then placed the glass of water to her lips, tilting it carefully as the water washed the pills down her throat. Tammy gulped and sighed again, turning her head back to the pillow and letting her heavy eyelids fall back down.

"I'm making some dinner now, Darling," he then told her, placing her handbag upon the top shelf out of her reach. "Anything specific you'd like?"

Tammy prised open her eyes once more and aimed them at him with desolate emptiness, but still declined any words.

"Okay, I'll be back soon," he told her softly, surprised she had not objected more.

Matthew made his way to the kitchen and returned again thirty minutes later, carrying two plates of his favourite childhood meal – chicken nuggets with spaghetti and chips. He placed one plate down onto the pasting table and placed the other upon Tammy's lap.

Tammy murmured and pulled her swollen head from the pillow, grimacing at the smell of the food as the scent forced its way up into her nose. She released a fluttering sigh of anxiety as she looked down at the plate with discontent, imagining the awkward feeling in her throat and stomach that was inevitably to come. She watched as Matthew knelt down beside her, cutting up the food upon her plate and loading a small stack of it onto the fork. Despite Tammy's deep sense of foreboding, still she remained silent and obliging, opening her mouth and allowing Matthew to shovel in the food with submissive compliance.

THE DAMAGED

The feeling that she had feared then arrived – the lumpy tickle as the food passed the back of her throat, the unnatural sensation of the food travelling down her oesophagus, and the awkward awareness of the food sitting in the pit of her stomach like a rock. She cleared her throat and grimaced again, reeling from the displeasure and starting to feel sick. She turned her head away from the next loaded fork and took a deep breath, waiting for the nauseous feeling to subside before returning for another swallow.

"See, it's easy. Right?" Matthew asked patronisingly as he continued to shovel the food into Tammy's mouth, but despite her clear vexation she still declined to respond.

Once Tammy's plate was empty, Matthew turned to his own, eating the now-tepid food with speed so to finish it before the temperature of it dropped to the point of unpleasantness. Slumping her throbbing head back down to the soft pillow with lethargy, Tammy watched as Matthew collected up the dirty crockery and cutlery and scurried back off to the kitchen again. Tammy closed her eyes in the assumption that their little dinner party was now over and started to drift, only to be stirred again a few minutes later by the sound of Matthew returning. She opened her eyes again with annoyance, wishing that Matthew would just leave her alone to rest and block out the painful gurgling of the digesting food in her stomach. She looked up at him with a pained scowl, a scowl which soon melted under the unexpected offering before her.

"A peace offering?" Matthew asked, offering her a cigarette from the box in her handbag.

The expression on Tammy's face gradually morphed through a strange cycle, from surprise to relief, then to suspicion, confusion, and then back to surprise again. She eagerly motioned to take the cigarette before Matthew could change his mind, forgetting that her wrists were both bound to the sides of the chair. The ratchets on the cable ties pulled and tightened like they had before, causing her wounded wrists to shoot with pain again despite the cushioning of the bandages upon them. She grimaced and sighed at her own absent-mindedness before nodding to Matthew with wide eyes and eagerly gesturing her open lips to the cigarette.

Matthew placed the cigarette in her mouth and lit it with a crooked smile, quickly turning his head away from the pungent smell of the smoke. Tammy exhaled euphorically as she blew a thick jet of smoke up into the air, feeling the endorphins zapping through her synapses like electricity. The plume of smoke glowed and shimmered in a faint beam of light as it hung in the air above them, twisting and curling and spiralling hypnotically.

SIMON LAW

The pungent smell of the cigarette grew stronger with every exhale. It forced its way up Matthew's nose and tingled against the forked receptors of his serpent tongue. As the smell slowly engulfed him, his mind became flooded with vivid images of his Aunt Julie, images of her gaunt and twisted face looking down at him as she blew foul smoke down into his young face and cackled hysterically at the sight of his disgust and humiliation.

Matthew clenched his eyes shut and endured the growing horrors with resolve, continuing to play attentive hand servant to the burning cigarette for the sake of his love for Tammy. Despite Matthew's resistance, the harrowing images grew stronger and darker, eating into his fragile mind like a ravenous cancer and filling him again with the feelings of hopelessness and hatred he once felt as a child.

'You filthy little cunt!' he heard cackling down at him, the words bouncing around in his head like a fly trapped in a jar, but still he persevered, thinking instead of the redemption he hoped to achieve from his sacrifice.

Numbing his mind to the images and memories that continued to flood him, Matthew's attention to the task at hand drifted away into the void, returning moments later when the cigarette began burning into the flesh at the top of his fingers.

Matthew gasped and reeled in pain as the cigarette scorched him back to reality again. He quickly threw the cigarette to the floor and began stamping upon it with barbarous relentless thuds, scowling and growling at the cigarette with fury. Tammy looked on with bewilderment and anxiety as Matthew persisted with the stomping long after the cigarette had completely disintegrated below his foot. After one final stomp, Matthew released a long pent-up breath from his lungs and placed his two blistered fingers into his mouth to soothe them. Releasing another long sigh, he shook his head in shame, turning to give Tammy a bitter look of blame before then ascending the cellar stairs in embarrassment, locking shut the door and retreating back to the comfort of his father's chair.

After five hours of broken sleep and dark tainted dreams, the killing hour came again. Matthew woke with a grimace and a groan, not from the raging beeps of the alarm clock, but from the tormented clawing from the beast inside of him – eager, insatiable, and angry. *Tonight needs to count,* he told himself as he dressed and got himself ready for the night's events. *Tonight needs to be the night that I find him and end this whole mess for good...*

He crept down the stairs and equipped himself with his favourite kitchen knife before continuing gingerly down into the cellar. Tammy

THE DAMAGED

was asleep, her head collapsed gently upon the pillow as she snoozed before him. *I need to end this,* he affirmed himself again, *for you, if for nothing else. You don't deserve to suffer like this.*

Matthew smiled down at her sleeping figure as he continued creeping past her towards the rear cellar door. His thoughts then turned to the issue of dismembering the corpse without causing her to wake, causing her to scream and wake the neighbours, but quickly decided to discard his worries until the situation occurred.

He unpadlocked the door and then relocked it again from the outside as the cool night air tenderly embraced him. He turned to face the night, breathing the air deep into his lungs as he pondered with himself why the thought of another kill wasn't filling him with the excitement and glee that it had before. The angry clawing returned from within him, gouging at his insides with its razor-sharp talons at retribution for his unenthusiastic thoughts, a clawing so fierce that he could almost taste the blood in the back of his throat.

Matthew calmed himself and stifled the sensation. As he was making his way through the garden he noticed a small set of glowing green eyes looking up at him from the grass, carefully watching his every move. He stopped and crouched down, staring back at the glowing eyes as his vision adjusted to the darkness and revealed the sleek feline body that surrounded the ominous green eyes.

Looking deep into the shimmering reflective eyes of the cat, Matthew saw the face of his Aunt Julie once more, looking down at him with repugnance and loathing. 'You filthy little cunt!' he heard cackling at him again.

Matthew smiled at the cat through gritted teeth as he cooed and lured it towards him with promises of strokes and petting. It was at that moment that the branches of the fir trees rustled from behind him and the raven croaked out into the silent night, filling Matthew with assurances and sparking his motivation. The cat meowed as it tentatively edged towards him, reaching out its neck and smelling him with curiosity. Matthew reached out his hand and stroked the cat from its head to its tail as he listened to it starting to purr with ease and contentment. With another echoic croak of the raven, Matthew's eyes turned sleek and amber as he grabbed the cat and pinned it forcefully to the ground. He lapped at the air with the tips of his tingling serpent tongue as he removed the kitchen knife from his belt with a malevolent scowl. The cat struggled and hissed as it clawed viciously at Matthew's hand, but Matthew barely flinched. He held the knife up high above the animal, the light of the moon gently shimmering from the blade, before slicing it through the air and burying it deep into the cat's ribcage.

SIMON LAW

The cat squealed and screeched as blood haemorrhaged from its mouth and its chest onto the grass beneath it. The cat continued to struggle and scratch desperately at Matthew's hand as he slowly dug the knife in deeper, twisting it in the wound and ripping the cat open as it twitched and convulsed helplessly before him. Looking down at the cat's desperate dying expression, Matthew smiled, imagining his aunt lying upon the grass in the cat's place, powerless and weak before him as she desperately clung to her fleeing life.

Another flutter of wind and the gentle drizzle of rain from above gave certainty to summer's firm departure. Matthew looked up to the sky to feel the cool rain spatter refreshingly upon his face, before looking down again to find the raven looking up at him from the grass inquisitively. The raven cocked its head to the side before hopping closer to the body of the twitching cat and re-engaging its inquisitive glance. Matthew nodded back at the raven in agreement, before retracting his blade from the chest of the cat and wiping off the blood on a clean patch of grass. The raven croaked in seeming delight as it mounted the lifeless body and buried its beak deep into the bloodied open chest cavity.

Matthew stood, peering down at the raven as it consumed the entrails of the cat, his serpent tongue tingling and twitching in the air as he began to wonder how the cat tasted. *Was it salty? Juicy? Bitter or sweet?* The curious smell of the blood and flesh was alluring against the tips of his tongue and he briefly gave thought to bending down and joining in the raven's feast, but resisted. He sheathed the blade back through his belt and exited the garden though the rusted back gate, leaving the voracious raven to devour the cat's juicy flesh at its own leisure.

He travelled through the woods, through the subway and up along the long deserted road that led to the park and the town, enjoying the refreshing feeling of the rain against his skin to begin with, but soon succumbing to the weight of the night's cold emptiness. He kept his eyes peeled, desperate and hopeful to finally catch his parent's killer and to bring his journey to its finale, but the streets were empty, deserted and barren as if stories and rumours of Matthew's bloody exploits had sent the homeless into hiding.

Anxious frustration started to eat at him as he lurked through the parks and the alleys, behind the shops and by the bins, only to find yet more desertion. As his torment grew within him, the beast began to bubble too, shaking and infecting him as it clawed at his insides again, demanding a kill, any kill at all. The beast suddenly burst through into his conscious mind and he was immediately reminded of the exhilaration of the first kill, the adrenaline that pumped through his veins, the euphoria. The seed of craving which seemed to have dwindled away was now replanted, and instantly germinated into an insatiable lust for blood.

With the lack of a clear thought, Matthew headed towards the train station, the scene of his first murder, hoping to visualise and relive those overwhelming feelings of uplifting joy once again. He increased his pace, the clench of his jaw and grip of the knife tightening with every step, until the gleaming train station came into his sights. He gingerly edged his way closer, his sight drawn to the dark alleyway where they kept the bins, the place where his glorious first murder had taken place. He continued edging closer, his eyes widening at the sight of a man-shaped mound by the side of the bin, a stray leg and a shoe confirming his hopes. *Is this it? Is this the end of my long journey?* he pondered hopefully, his heart pounding and his fingers twitching with excitement.

Matthew looked to the sky again, searching for a sighting of the raven for reassurance and confirmation of his target, but the bird was absent, presumably still busy consuming the innards of the cat, so Matthew proceeded alone.

He reached up and grabbed hold of the security camera which had once captured the back of his head, and twisted it around on its stiff pivot, facing it down along the ally where his impending actions would not be seen.

Edging closer to the mound of wriggling rags, he reached back to finger the handle of the kitchen knife as he envisioned the breathtaking firework of blood that had filled the sky there once before. The figure below him rolled upon its side, unveiling its face from behind a sheet of rag and revealing itself to be a young girl no older than seventeen. Her face was caked in a film of dirt and her hair was greasy and tangled, but below the mess the remnants of her glowing young innocence still shone through.

Matthew sighed in disappointment and his excitement quickly turned blue at the realisation that his futile search must continue. He looked down at the girl below him, his frown of disappointment slowly slumping to a strange look of contemplation as he loosened his grip on the blade and took a step back.

Maybe it was because she was a girl, or maybe because of her age, but the remnants of Matthew's conscience would not allow him to hurt her, despite the overwhelming cravings of the clawing beast within him. The young girl was clearly not a potential suspect and seemed somehow undeserving of the usual harsh judgement that befell those before him. Matthew suddenly experienced an unusual feeling of empathy and a growing desire to help the poor girl, to take her somewhere safe and protect her from the cruel unforgiving world, but yet, he knew that he couldn't.

About to turn and discreetly retreat, Matthew suddenly remembered the wad of cash in his wallet intended to lure his next victim to their doom. He then made the split-second decision to do something out of character, to help the poor girl lying before him. The cash meant nothing to Matthew, but to the young girl it could make all the difference, no strings attached, no gratitude required. He reached behind, gently brushing past the kitchen knife en route to the leather wallet in his rear trouser pocket. It was at that precise and unfortunate moment that the sleeping girl decided to wake. She caught sight of the shimmering blade and the towering man above her and screamed out into the night with a piercing howl of terror.

The harrowing scream bounced against the bricks of the alleyway and shot up into the night sky like a foghorn, alerting the whole world to the events in action. The bellowing scream soared and echoed in Matthew's head until morphing into the sadistic laughter of Otis the orderly. Fear of the mental hospital flooded Matthew's fragile mind once again, showing him images of padded cells covered in blood, and straitjackets so tight that they cut the circulation. Memories of casual abuse and drug-induced incapacitation crashed through his head, along with images of the dribbling, crazed lunatics who would be his only companions for the rest of his natural life.

The piercing scream halted abruptly, leaving only its echo to dissipate into obscurity. Shaking with fear and emotion, the panic-inducing images slowly dissolved from Matthew's mind's eye. He gulped and took a breath as he slowly cast his eyes back down to the strangely silent girl below him. The world froze, and so did Matthew, as his heart leapt into his mouth and his mind became numb and silent. The girl was dead.

Devoid of recollection but certain of his guilt, Matthew looked down in horror and shame at the young girl's blood dripping freely from his blade. His jaw began to quiver as the night's rain grew stronger, pelting down upon him with fury and soaking his clothes through to the skin. His numb and silent mind was filled by a single thought, a single instinct, to run. So run he did.

The mesmerizing sound of police sirens whirled in every direction and bounced against the wall of Matthew's skull as he dashed through the rain as fast as he could, unsure of whether the sirens he could hear were actually real or simply figments of his fragile imagination.

The beast inside of him croaked and squawked in a desperate attempt to assure him and to silence his throbbing conscience, but the growing

THE DAMAGED

feelings of guilt and remorse pulsated through his brain with such overwhelming vigour and strength that they reigned supreme. Overcome by his emotions, Matthew sobbed despairingly into the night as he continued to run, crying for the last remaining fragment of his shattered soul as it blackened and died from the guilt of his ghastly actions, the tracks of his streaming tears hidden only by the torrent of rain that battered his face with merciless persistence.

Dashing through the subway, the woods, and the garden, Matthew reached his house again in record time. He burst through the cellar door with careless indiscretion, dropping the bloodied kitchen knife to the floor and falling to a ball on the ground with a gagging howl of sorrow.

Waking suddenly from her drowsy paracetamol-induced sleep, Tammy pulled back in her chair, wide-eyed and startled. She looked down at Matthew with a bemused frown as her mind tried to make sense of his helpless sobbing, ignorant to the grisly act he had just committed. In an instant, Matthew's previous sins seemed to momentarily vanish from her mind as her mothering, empathic auto-response took over. She was filled with sadness and sorrow at the sight of his anguish and pain.

"Matthew? Matthew, what's wrong?" she called tenderly to him, the first words she had spoken out loud since her escape attempt the day before.

"I...I..." Matthew began to blubber between the tears, unable to formulate his words or bring himself to admit his abhorrent actions to her.

He slowly pulled himself to all fours and hung his head low to the ground, rain dripping down from his drenched hair and clothes.

"I...I..." Matthew attempted once more, but the words still didn't come. Panting and gulping for breath, he finally pulled himself together long enough to whisper two words – "I'm sorry!"

Looking down at the broken man before her, Tammy couldn't keep her misplaced empathy from growing. As her eyes slowly adjusted to the hue of the moonlight, she watched the rain gently drip from his golden blonde hair and began to remember how his sweet vulnerability had once become so alluring to her. She remembered the man who comforted her in her time of need, the man who defended her from the unruly teenagers, and the man who lavished her with love and gifts.

Matthew leant back and squatted upon his knees as he wiped away the rain and tears from his face, before taking another long, quivering breath and gazing upon Tammy with sore, red eyes of forlorn despair.

Tammy's frown deepened further as she looked back at him with a half-mast smile of sorrow and comfort. Finding herself staring deep into the azure blue oceans of his innocent child-like eyes once more, she almost forgot that she was a prisoner shackled to a chair in the bottom of his dark, dank cellar.

"Come here," she gently cooed, raising her smile up to an endearing three-quarter mast.

Matthew forced a smile upon his sorrow-stricken face and pulled himself to his feet. He stepped towards her, throwing his father's soaking wet jacket to the floor as he gently knelt down and embraced her lovingly.

"I love you, Tammy," he sniffled gently into her ear.

THE DAMAGED

XVIII

BEFSZTYK, RZADKO

By the morning light, the train station was flooded with police, reporters, and forensics teams for the second time in a fortnight, quickly making it the most infamous train station in Britain. The breakfast news team had erroneously declared the young girl as 'the second victim' of a potential serial killer, naming the girl as 'Samantha Jacobs', a young teenager who had run away from home a month earlier after a dispute with her stepfather. The media immediately burst into a front-page headline-grabbing frenzy, quickly making all manner of obscure comparisons to past serial killers from the area, including Jack the Ripper, and John George Haigh – the infamous 'Acid Bath Killer' from the 1940's.

Aiding in the investigation of such a high-profile murder case was good for the career of any aspiring officer, especially one with the ingenuity and fresh lucky hunches required to break such a case open. For PC Lang, an officer with a young family at home who currently earned less than a London bin man, the opportunity would have been greatly welcomed. Arriving at the police station that morning, PC Lang appeared to have pulled the short straw, having been assigned to another new case instead – a missing persons case. Unbeknownst to all, the two cases were intrinsically connected.

Slipping under the radar of the media frenzy that morning, was an unassuming call from Keith to report Tammy as a missing person. The call was made after visiting Tammy's empty flat following an irate phone call from Maureen the day before demanding to know why Tammy had not turned up for work. Keith had been too annoyed by the rude call to inform Maureen of their split, or of the fact that Tammy had clearly forgotten to update her next-of-kin information, and had stormed over to Tammy's flat with the intention of giving her a verbal ear bashing.

A brief background check quickly displayed Tammy's recent conviction for drunk-driving, and a little further digging showed her reported absence from her latest court-appointed 'AA' meeting. These two pieces of information led PC Lang to quickly conclude Tammy's disappearance to be the result of a 'bender' and presumed her to be merely sleeping off a hangover somewhere – a situation that was barely worth his time or attention. Luckily for Tammy, PC Lang's superiors were not as easily satisfied with the findings and insisted he investigate further.

Disillusioned and eager for reassignment to the murder case, PC Lang begrudgingly made a call to Maureen, a number listed by Keith in his original report, to request an address list for Tammy's clients for him to begin taking statements. Seemingly happy to help, Maureen faxed the list to the station straight away and PC Lang reluctantly made his way to the first address.

With the sound on low to conceal his despicable actions from Tammy, Matthew watched the morning news with a pained grimace upon his face, shuddering at the term 'serial killer' every time it was spoken. A photo of his young victim in her school uniform appeared on the screen to the narration of the news presenter reading a statement from the girl's parents. Matthew looked away and shook his head, his heart sinking with despair as the poignant heartfelt message was read. He felt the disappointed eyes of his mother and father bearing down upon him from behind, their heads hung low in disgrace- a feeling juxtaposed by the purring of smug and warm contentment from the beast that slumbered inside of him.

Descending the stairs with the morning cups of tea, Matthew hid his growing despair from Tammy behind a false smile and a blank expression.

"Morning, Darling," he greeted her with a forced upward inflection. It was then that he noticed the discomfort upon her pale face and arched his brow in concern. "What's wrong?" he asked, placing down the obligatory morning brew upon the pasting table.

Tammy groaned and prised apart her eyes in return, gazing up at him with a look of anguish before then groaning a little louder.

"I feel sick," she muttered out in a queasy uncertain voice before taking a careful long breath into her lungs.

Maybe it was the blow to the head, or maybe it was the strange sensation of food digesting in her aching shrunken stomach for the first time in a while, but *something* was definitely amiss. A third possibility briefly entered Tammy's mind too, a possibility with somewhat less credence than the others, and one that she could scarcely bear to consider, and so quickly flushed it from her mind.

Tammy groaned again as she pulled her head from the pillow and looked across to the steaming cup of tea in front of her. She motioned her arm towards it, forgetting her restraints once again and pulling the plastic even tighter around her sore bandaged wrists. Sighing with exasperation she leant back against the pillow again and cast her eyes to Matthew with an expectant gaze.

"Tea?" he asked, already grasping the cup as he spoke.

"Please," she replied lethargically, hoping that it might help to calm the rising nausea inside of her.

Matthew obliged, holding the steaming cup gently to her lips and watching as Tammy tentatively took her first sip. She slurped and nervously swallowed it down into her restless gut, immediately feeling her stomach start to gurgle and churn, the opposite reaction to what she had hoped. She heaved uncomfortably, feeling the acid from her stomach burning against her oesophagus as the tea travelled back up into her mouth again. She swallowed the tea back down for the second time with a repugnant grimace as she groaned and gently shook her head in frustration.

"Oh dear," Matthew declared sympathetically. "-Is there anything I can do?" he asked, deepening the arch of his brow.

Tammy released a long quivering breath and shook her head, closing her eyes again and resting her head back down upon the pillow. Matthew nodded solemnly in return and began sipping upon his own tea, his thoughts now reverting back to the haunting images of the young school girl whose life he'd extinguished in a flash so quick that he still could not recall it with any clarity, her eyes frozen open in a confused gaze as the rain pelted remorselessly against her unresponsive blood-splattered face. *Why, Matthew? Why me?* she gently asked without moving her lips.

Concentrating on her breathing to distract herself from the unsettling gurgle in her gut, Tammy gently drifted back off to sleep. Picking up the tepid unfinished tea, Matthew quietly sneaked back up the cellar stairs again, carefully relocking the padlock upon the door and returning once again to the safe comfort of his father's Chesterfield, waiting in anticipation of Agnieszka's morning house call.

"Good morning, Mr Mason. How are you today?" Aggy asked in her thick, deadpan Polish accent, as she stepped in through the door with Matthew's grocery shopping in hand.

"I'm fine, thank you," Matthew replied equally listlessly, taking the two bags from her and following her through to the kitchen. "Any news on Tammy yet?" he asked, feigning concern in his tone as he began to put away the shopping: cheese, bread, milk, and a big roll of black bin bags, among other things.

"No, I'm not hear anything yet, Mr Mason. I'm sure she is fine," Aggy told him with continued indifference, as she read through his care notes and began to remove his morning pills from the sectioned plastic box.

Matthew reached the end of the shopping and quickly realised that something was missing – his rump steaks.

"Did you forget the steak?" he asked, turning to her with a disappointed frown.

"Steak? No, you not ask me for steak, Mr Mason," she abruptly replied with a scowl and a look of imposition.

"I'm pretty sure I did, Aggy. I wanted to have steak tonight..."

"Nie mój cyrk, nie moje malpy!" she muttered under her breath.

Matthew didn't understand Polish, but by her tone it was clearly not complimentary.

"Excuse me?" he asked.

"No, no you not," she snapped back defensively, quickly reverting to English again as her scowl and look of disapproval grew. "...If you ask me for steak I would buy you steak, but you not. I buy all things on your list, Mr Mason!" she continued, the anger in her voice starting to peak.

Matthew looked back at her in contemplation, wondering where all the ferocity had suddenly appeared from. He sighed and conceded, deciding that the argument was fruitless.

"Okay, Aggy. My mistake."

Aggy scoffed and sneered in response, glaring at him with contempt as she reached into her handbag and removed the grocery receipt.

"Twenty-six-fifty please, Mr Mason," she told him, her voice still laced with condescension.

Matthew removed two twenties from his wallet and passed them to her with a solemn grin.

"I'm sorry; I have no change, Mr Mason."

"It's okay, just keep it!" he replied dismissively.

Aggy raised her eyebrows and nodded to herself smugly, before slipping the banknotes into her bag and returning to the pills on the kitchen counter once more.

"You take medication now please, Mr Mason," she told him sternly, thrusting the pills upon him as she filled a glass half-full with water.

"Yep!" he replied blandly, taking them from her and making his way back through to his father's chair.

THE DAMAGED

Matthew wriggled himself into a comfortable position in the chair and threw the two blue pills and the vitamin tablet to the back of his mouth, gulping them down with the water and commencing his usual 'spaced-out' performance – an act that wasn't too hard to perform that morning with the lethargy and self-loathing that weighed down heavily upon him.

Taking one final glance at Matthew's care plan, Agnieszka gathered her things and began making her way to the door. She made it half-way through the lounge when a strange sound suddenly caught her attention, a sound seemingly rising up through the floorboards below her, the sound of retching and vomiting.

Matthew sighed and rolled his eyes in annoyance as Aggy turned away from him and listened out carefully for the strange sound to return. Panic fluttered through him and vanished again in a fleeting moment, as the beast croaked with smug reassurance inside of him, safe in the knowledge that the situation had only one inevitable outcome.

The strange noise returned, and as Aggy crept slowly towards the cellar door, her ears perked and tuned into the noise. *Was it an animal of some description*? she wondered. *A stray cat maybe? Trapped in the cellar and coughing up a fur ball*?

So consumed in befuddled contemplation, Aggy failed to notice Matthew swiftly rising from the chair behind her and silently begin creeping towards her. With his eyes scorching amber and his serpent tongue lapping at the air with excitement, he felt the wings of the beast flapping within him as it croaked in anticipation and delight.

Aggy reached out her hand and stroked it curiously along the wood of the cellar door as the noise continued, looping around in a seemingly endless rotation of heaving, coughing, and vomiting. As she listened carefully, the idea of the noise emanating from a stray cat began to lose its credence for her, and the idea of it coming from a person slowly began to grow.

Suddenly finding a gap of air between the bouts of uncontrollable purging, and realising the imminent conclusion of her regrettable interruption, Tammy desperately yelled out Aggy's name through the slatted wooden cellar doors.

"Aggy! Run!" she yelled before quickly succumbing to her convulsions once again.

"Tammy?... Tammy is that you?" Aggy replied with a frown.

The cogs of Aggy's foggy brain then suddenly pieced the puzzle together with crude broad strokes, but for Aggy it was now too late. At the moment that the realisation finally dawned upon her, she suddenly felt the palm of Matthew's hand fiercely swaddling her mouth and a blade piercing deep into her back. Frozen solid as the pain shuddered through her like electricity, she felt Matthew breathing softly upon her neck and gently begin to whisper in her ear.

"Hush, it's okay..." he told her reassuringly as he lapped at the skin of her neck with the cold wet tips of his forked serpent tongue. "Just relax..."

Matthew continued applying pressure to Aggy's mouth and to the kitchen blade that he slid deeper into her back, slicing it through the rear of her deflating lung before impaling it into her beating heart. She convulsed and twitched within Matthew's tight embrace as blood expelled from her mouth and trickled out between the slight gaps of his long, taut fingers. The blood trickled gently down the back of his hand, almost reaching the cuff of his father's white shirt when his sleek reptilian pupils suddenly locked in on it, and he immediately lapped it up with one fluid brush of his extended serpent tongue. The taste of the blood was sweet and rich, tingling with bright alertness over the receptors of his slithering tongue as he savoured it and rolled it around in his mouth before finally swallowing it.

Aggy's twitches and struggles soon began to subside and her body quickly turned heavy and limp within his grip. He removed his bloodied hand from her face and allowed her body to slump down upon the linoed kitchen floor below, automatically unsheathing itself from the sturdy kitchen blade still firmly within Matthew's grip.

"Matthew! No! What have you done!" Tammy yelled at him, briefly finding another gasp of air in which to project her words.

"Me? What have *I* done?" he hollered back venomously towards the cellar. "This was your fault! I had no choice! Did I?"

Matthew shook his head and tutted as he turned to the sink and began washing the blood from the kitchen knife. Aggy's death was unfortunate, that much Matthew would agree. She wasn't a suspect, nor had she done him any particular wrongs – aside from her clear indifference, but her death was a necessity for self-preservation and that was enough justification to keep his fractured conscience at bay. She was certainly no 'Samantha Jacobs', but even if she *was*, a second mistake would never have had the same impact upon him.

As Sod's Law would have it, it was at that point that a loud, confident knock came tapping upon the door, a knock that echoed through the house and faded away into silence while Matthew stared sharply in the direction of the front door, frozen in a state of incomprehension and indecision.

"Oh shit!" he muttered under his breath, immediately feeling the disapproving scowls of his parents as he uttered the obscenity.

THE DAMAGED

Another loud knock upon the door broke him free from his perplexed daze and he immediately dragged Aggy's body into the cupboard underneath the stairs, the cupboard that usually only housed the vacuum cleaner.

"Just coming!" he yelled towards the door as he folded in Aggy's floppy limps, still unaware of who his visitor *was*.

He felt his heartbeat start to rise and pound against his chest as he grabbed a tea-towel from the side and desperately began scrubbing at the random splodges of blood upon the lino and the cellar door. His hands shook with adrenaline and his head spun as his anxieties began to reach new highs, but this time the beast could not subdue them quite so easily. It offered no advice, no words of encouragement at all.

He threw the bloodied cloth, along with Aggy's handbag, into the cupboard and closed the door, giving the room and himself a quick once-over before kneeling down to the cellar door and muttering down between the gaps in the wooden slats.

"You'd better cut that out now, Tammy!" he growled in a gravelly, threatening tone before running back to the front door.

One final deep breath and Matthew pulled open the door, revealing the overbearing figure of PC Lang standing sternly in the doorway and stroking upon his brown handlebar moustache in irksome consideration. The officer looked down at him, his eyes fixed and piercing as if looking directly into Matthew's soul to analyse his thoughts. Matthew gulped uncomfortably, feeling his heart sink and his skin turn cold with fear. He had expected that, through a predictable series of phone calls, that PC Lang or one of his colleagues would inevitably end up at his doorstep; he just never expected it to be at such an ironically inopportune moment. Matthew discreetly released a nervous exhale and forced a smile as he looked back at the officer with badly-feigned composure. *Just keep calm,* he told himself.

"Good morning, Mr Mason," he greeted, ignoring the intermittent voices that crackled from his collared radio. "I didn't expect to see you again so soon," he continued, his voice still clearly laced with the irritation of being assigned the lesser case that morning.

"No... Me neither," Matthew replied with a nervous scoff, his anxiety gaining more strength by the second as he began fixating on the assortment of accessories upon the officer's utility belt as he had done before.

"No more intruders, I hope?" PC Lang asked, his question laced with condescension and mockery in reference to his last visit.

"No, everything's been fine. Thank you," Matthew told him, deliberately ignoring the disrespect in the officer's tone as his nerves continued to soar, causing his jaw to shake as he spoke and for a bead of sweat to roll down from his brow, both clear signs of deceit, which PC Lang noticed immediately.

The officer looked at him suspiciously, arching his brow slightly in contemplation as he removed a pen and pad from his inner breast pocket and began casting his eyes casually around the visible sections of the living and dining rooms. He immediately noticed the strange absence of one of the dining chairs and logged it in his memory for later reference.

"May I come in for a moment please, Mr Mason?" he asked, raising his eyebrows back up again.

"Sure, can I ask what this is about?" Matthew asked, tentatively stepping aside and allowing PC Lang to enter.

"I'm just following up on a missing persons report for your carer, Tammy Atkins," he replied, stepping through to the lounge and taking an uninvited seat upon his father's Chesterfield.

Matthew looked down at the presumptuous officer in amazement, gritting his teeth in anger and trying his hardest to prevent a bitter scowl from spreading across his face. *How dare he sit there!*

"Oh, I see," Matthew replied, closing the door and taking a seat upon the sofa instead. "I thought she was just sick, I didn't realise it was more serious."

"Do you mind if I take a statement?"

"No, not at all."

"Right..." he began, clearing his throat and scribbling in the corner of the paper to get the pen to start working. "Could you tell me when you last saw Tammy, please?"

"It was the day before yesterday, I believe."

"Time?"

"It was the evening call, so she would have left at five-fifteen or so."

"And how did she seem to you?"

"A bit upset actually, I think she might have been drinking," Matthew told him, adding the extra nugget to try and steer the questioning in the right direction.

"Upset? Do you know what about?"

"About her daughter I guess. I think she was having custody problems."

"Oh, I see," the officer replied with an intrigued upward inflection, breaking from his questions for a moment to write up the conversation so far.

With the lack of background vomiting and with the questioning seemingly going in the right direction, Matthew's anxiety slowly started to settle.

THE DAMAGED

It was then that the faint tapping noise began. Tap, tap, tap, from the cupboard under the stairs, a tapping like that from the rigid black beak of the raven which came the night that the beast first appeared. Matthew curled his toes and squirmed in the sofa, hoping that the noise would disappear, but it didn't.

"You talked a lot then I take it, Mr Mason? Would you call yourselves 'friends'?"

"We talked a bit, yeah. She was my care-worker... *IS* my care-worker. We saw each other twice a day. I guess you could call us 'friends', yeah."

The tapping grew louder but the expression on the Officer's face strangely showed no acknowledgement of it, leading Matthew to believe that the noise was meant for him alone. He discreetly threw an eye to the cupboard door and back again without drawing the officer's attention, hoping to catch sight of the cause of the noise, but failing. He threw another, fixing it longer this time, and suddenly noticed a small pool of blood growing from underneath the door. Matthew's anxieties quickly shot straight back up to full throttle once again, as the beast started to croak and cackle and scratch at his insides with eagerness, reminding him of the kitchen knife that lay ready and waiting for him in the kitchen sink. He felt his bladder suddenly tense and relax, and for a moment he thought that he might actually wet himself with fear like he used to as a child, but managed to control it.

"Mr Mason, are you okay?" the officer asked, frowning at Matthew with a look of concern as he gazed up from his pad.

"I... I'm fine, sorry" Matthew finally replied, shaking the contemplations from his mind. "...I just need my medication, that's all," he continued, ignorant to how true the statement actually was.

PC Lang's look of concern and suspicion lingered a little longer as he stared at Matthew in deep contemplation. Matthew looked back with a blank innocent smile, gritting his teeth and praying that the Officer would not turn in the direction of the cupboard and notice the growing pool of crimson blood currently soaking deep into the carpet.

Matthew's wounded arm started to tickle as the stare-lock continued, bubbling and rippling with increasing irritation as if a cluster of newly-spawned spiders was now brimming to the surface of the skin in a desperate attempt for freedom. The officer's frown deepened as Matthew broke the stare and began scratching at his arm, dragging his nails deeply across his shirt and bandage in a vain attempt to quash the creeping cluster.

"And what medication are you on, sir?" PC Lang asked, tilting his head curiously to one side as he began tapping his pen rhythmically against the paper pad.

SIMON LAW

Rain began to drizzle gently down the lounge windows as the menacing smile of Otis appeared once again, grinning and waiving to Matthew through the smears as Matthew stumbled awkwardly upon his words.

"I'm... I'm on.... a-anti-psychotics," Matthew revealed with hesitation, watching past PC Lang's shoulder as Otis was joined at the window by the face of his childhood bully – Jason Selby, who stood smiling at the window while silently mouthing the words "Don't piss your pants now, Pissypants!"

"Right... I see," the officer replied with a self-assured groan.

PC Lang finally broke his piercing glare to return once again to his pad of paper, scribbling down a few additional notes and stabbing a loud exaggerated full stop upon the page.

"Well I think that's everything I need, Mr Mason.... For now, anyway," he declared, slipping his pen and notes back into his breast pocket and standing from his chair. "I don't want to keep you from your medication now, do I?" he added with a suspicious, crooked grin and a brief stroke of his handlebar moustache.

"No, well... I hope everything turns out okay. I'd hate for anything bad to have happened to Tammy."

The officer looked back at Matthew blankly, curiously following a bead of sweat with his eyes as it gently rolled down Matthew's temple. "I'm sure she's fine, Mr Mason. I wouldn't worry yourself over it."

PC Lang turned and left without further comment, but Matthew knew that it would not be his last visit. The look of suspicion in his eye was clear for all to see, it was just a matter of time before he assembled all the relevant pieces of the puzzle.

Matthew released a long sigh of relief, but his nerves continued to linger on, twitching through his fingers and buzzing through his head while Otis and Jason continued to taunt him from the lounge window. After listening to the police car slowly pulling away from the house, Matthew paced through the house in a post-adrenaline come down, pacing past the seeping puddle of blood and into the kitchen. He flung open the window and let the cool, wet breeze blow gently across his face, enjoying the fresh, bracing sensation and recalling with strange disbelief how the same sensation had once filled him with such dread. He breathed the fresh air down deep into his lungs before grabbing the pot of Diazepam that he had retrieved from Tammy's bag, and throwing a handful of them to the back of his throat.

Matthew stared calmingly into the garden, looking over to the grisly, emaciated corpse of the neighbourhood cat as his thoughts returned to Tammy, still silently obeying his orders in the cellar down below. Her silence was laudable and appreciated, as an unprepared altercation with the officer would have probably not gone well, but the continued absence of noise was worrying, especially as she had been so animated just moments prior.

"Tammy? Are you okay?" he called down through the gaps in the slatted door, but Tammy did not reply.

He took out the padlock key from his pocket and unlocked the door, pulling upon the light cord and beginning his descent down into the dank depths, the stench of vomit increasing with each step.

"Tammy?" he repeated, peering around the staircase to see her tensed up and shrivelled into her shoulder in shock, tears silently cascading down her pale, vomit-covered face while she rehearsed the breathing techniques that her therapist had taught her.

"I'm sorry, Tammy. You did well keeping quiet down here. Thank you," he told her, arching his brow in sympathy.

Tammy pulled apart her sticky lips and spat the remainder of the vomit into the puddle that lay upon the floor next to her. She took a shallow breath of air into her lungs and closed her eyes, shaking her head in disapproval and trying to stifle any further tears from flowing.

Matthew disappeared up the stairs and returned again a few minutes later, precariously carrying a glass of water, a wet flannel, and a set of his mother's clothes.

"Here you go," he declared solemnly, placing down the clothes and flannel upon the pasting table and placing the glass to Tammy's lips. "They're probably a little big for you, but they'll have to do for now." he continued, gingerly tilting up the glass as Tammy began to sip.

"H... How... How can you do that?" she asked in a quiet, quivering voice as she nervously swallowed down the water, carrying the remnants of the vomit back down into her gut again.

"Do what?" he asked obliviously, placing down the glass and beginning to wipe away some of the vomit from her face with the flannel.

"K...Kill... Just like that? Just... Just take someone's life away without a second thought?" she blubbered back, her own anxiety bubbling just below the point of eruption and taking away her breath.

Matthew paused and frowned in contemplation.

"...Some are easier than others," he finally divulged with trepidation, once again thinking about Samantha Jacobs, whose death he truly did regret.

He folded over the vomit-smeared section of the flannel, and using the clean section he gently wiped away her tears. "Most of them deserve it, Tammy. I didn't want to kill Aggy; you know that, don't you? I had no choice about it."

"Why am I alive, Matthew? Why don't you just kill me too?" Tammy asked daringly, her lips beginning to quiver even more.

"Because I love you, Tammy. I've told you that. I don't want to be alone in this world."

Tammy closed her eyes and leant back against the pillow again, contemplating what Matthew had told her and wondering how to pose him an awkward question.

"Matthew?" she asked, keeping her eyes closed.

"Yes, Darling?"

"Cut me."

"Excuse me?"

"You heard, I want you to cut me."

"But why?"

"Because I need it. I need to feel in control again."

Matthew threw down the flannel and rose to his feet, scowling at Tammy in frustration as he considered her request with resentment and anger.

"No!" he grunted with annoyance. "No, I'm not going to cut you, Tammy. I don't want to hurt you. I couldn't!" he protested.

"Please, Matthew! I need it to calm my nerves. I feel like I'm about to explode and pass out simultaneously. I can't think straight, I can't see straight. Please! Please do it for me!" she begged forlornly, pulling her head from the pillow again.

Matthew looked back at her with empathy, understanding the feeling she had described exactly. He grit his teeth and scowled even deeper, creasing up his forehead with torment and indecision until finally he growled and shook his head, climbing the stairs once again and returning with the kitchen knife. Tammy watched tentatively as Matthew slowly approached, bending down beside her with the knife firmly in his grip. He reached out, cutting through her arm restraints with a fluid slice before turning the knife around and offering it out to her.

"Here. You do what you need to, Tammy. I'm not going to cut you," he told her, sighing in defeat and offering her an uncomfortable smile.

Tammy reached out her trembling hand for the blade, but it wasn't until it was firmly in her grip that she realised the opportunity that had presented itself to her. She now had the knife and Matthew was unarmed. This could be her one chance to finally escape from her captivity. She could easily turn the blade away and impale it deep into Matthew's stomach, twisting it around in the bloody wound and ripping him apart. While he fell to the floor and writhed around in pain, clutching at his gushing wound, she could cut herself free from her remaining restraints and run – run for the daylight and be free. But yet,

THE DAMAGED

as she stared up into his caring deep azure blue eyes, she knew she didn't have it in her.

She looked down at the blade, twirling it around in her fingers until she glanced upon her own tattered reflection looking back at her. She thought about all the lives the blade had taken: James, Bronco, Aggy, and so many others too. She sighed and handed the blade back with a sorrowful shake of the head.

"I can't use that," she told him, as Matthew took back the knife with a confused look upon his face. "My bag, please. Hand me my razorblades."

Matthew nodded and obeyed, reaching up to the top shelf of the wines and retrieving her bag. He pulled apart the brass clipper and began rummaging around the cluttered contents, pushing aside her address book and mobile phone before coming across the small plastic box of blades. He handed them over to her and watched with morbid intrigue, feeling the Diazepam finally kicking into his system and smooth out his nerves to a numb and comfortable flat-line.

Tammy slid out a blade from the plastic case, dropping it to the floor and unwrapping the blade from its paper wrapping. She looked down at the glimmering blade with a warm familiar smile, feeling her excitement and anticipation beginning to rise. Taking a calming breath, she unbuckled her trousers, pulling down the zip awkwardly with one hand before realising that she needed help.

"Matthew?" she asked, casting him an expectant eye and a crooked smile.

Matthew smiled awkwardly in return, reaching forward and gently tugging at Tammy's trousers as she lifted up her bum from the chair. He pulled the trousers down past her thighs and knees and left them scrunched up by her ankles, looking back up at Tammy's bare flesh with arousal as she spread her legs wide to him and exposed her white cotton knickers.

Tammy looked over to Matthew with a numb expression as she stroked her fingers over the array of scars upon her thigh as if she wanted him to watch her, wanted him to lust over her skin and visualise her tight pussy concealed behind the white cotton panties. Maybe it was just his imagination running wild, but his arousal grew regardless, as he pictured himself taking her like he had before.

Tammy cast her eyes down to the criss-cross lattice scars upon her thigh and placed the twitching blade down upon her skin an inch below the scabby rust-infected gouge from her previous toilet slashing. She took another breath, her face remaining solemn and blank, and cut deep into her flesh with one smooth motion. Endorphins rushed through her tired body in flooding waves of orgasmic pleasure as she dropped the blade to the concrete floor below and blood began oozing from the severed flesh.

Matthew watched as Tammy released a slow, quivering exhale and groaned as she arched her back in pleasure, imagining that it was him that was causing her the intense euphoria and feeling his boxer-shorts grow tight with his engorged throbbing erection.

The thick red blood flowed down the inside of Tammy's thigh, staining upon her white cotton knickers before starting to create a small growing pool upon the dining chair. The pool grew larger as the blood flow continued, causing the pool to cascade from the edge of the chair and begin dripping gently onto the floor below, all the while Tammy continued to groan out in ecstasy.

Matthew watched on for a few minutes longer, debating whether he could slip his hand into his boxers and begin stroking his erection without Tammy noticing, but resisted. After a further few minutes, Tammy released a final long, pleasing exhale and leant forward upon the chair again, examining the cut as it started to congeal and gesturing to Matthew for her bag again.

"Tissue?"

Matthew nodded and began rummaging through the endless clutter in Tammy's bag once more, eventually finding the open packet of Kleenex near the bottom and handing one over to her. She gently blotted the wound before wiping away the trickle from her thigh and soaking up the pool from the chair. Dropping the blood-soaked tissue upon the puddle of vomit on the floor, she closed her legs and looked to Matthew in contemplation, but said nothing. Her eyes then cast over to the neat pile of women's clothes that awaited her upon the pasting table.

"Were they your mother's?" she asked.

"Yes," he replied with a solemn nod. "My Aunt Julie never bothered to pack the house up after their death, just boarded it up and ignored it, so all their old stuff is still here. Some of it is a little moth-eaten now, as you would expect, but I think these are okay."

"Where is she now, Matthew?" Tammy asked tentatively, mindful of his reaction the last time his aunt was mentioned in conversation. "You might as well just tell me now, after everything that has happened."

Matthew sighed and walked to the corner of the room, staring blankly at a selection of his father's white wines as he tried not to let the memory of Aunt Julie erupt into anger, the very thought of her having already completely dampened his previous arousal.

"She's dead, and *NO*... I didn't kill her, though my one regret is that I didn't," he told her, turning to face her once again and leaning lethargically against the far wall of the cellar.

THE DAMAGED

"So what *did* happen to her then?"

Matthew paused, looking at Tammy in contemplation as he slowly convinced himself to finally tell the story, agreeing that secrets between them were now pointless, especially as she had since learnt far worse things about him.

"She was taunting me, like she always did, because I'd wet the bed during a storm in the night..." Matthew began, his anger and indignity starting to stir the beast inside of him. "...Calling me the most horrid names with such venom that her words projected spit into my face," he continued, grimacing and gritting his teeth through the horrid repressed memory. "I cowered passively in fear, like I always did back then, as she thrust the soiled bed sheets into my face. I took it, like the scared little kid that I was, telling myself that it would soon be over, soon I would be eighteen, I would have access to my parents' estate, and I would be free of her for good. Then she started laughing at me, cackling down at me like a sadistic witch, telling me how she had made a call to the mental health services who were coming to see me on the Monday, coming to lock me up and throw away the key..." Matthew stopped and took a breath, rubbing his face and eyes and telling the clawing demon inside of him to *calm down* as it grew increasingly agitated.

"Then what?" Tammy eagerly prompted, hanging on Matthew's every word.

"...And then I snapped at her, the first time I had ever talked back, as if a switch had been flipped on in my brain. I told her I hated her, called her a f..." Matthew lowered his voice as to not arouse his parents' discontent, "...a *fucking bitch*, –language I would never normally use, and shoved the wet bed sheets back at her. She stepped back, startled and surprised that I was finally standing up for myself, unaware that her two precious Persian cats were huddled around her feet. She stepped on one of their tails and jumped in surprise, falling onto her back and cracking her head open on the wooden floor."

"Oh my... Did you call an ambulance?"

"No. I'm pretty sure that she died instantly, but even if there was a chance that she could have been saved, I still wouldn't have."

Tammy gazed at him with comforting sympathy, seeing the anger upon his face as he told the story and feeling her empathy and understanding for him growing deeper.

"So what *did* you do then?" she pried softly.

"Nothing, I did nothing. I looked at the door, wanting to run away and somehow start a new life for myself somewhere, somewhere where nobody knew me, nobody judged me, but I couldn't. My anxieties of the outside world were so strong that I couldn't even open the front door without feeling overwhelming dread come over me, though I tried several times. I sat upon the floor, curled into a ball and frozen stiff as I watched the two white cats circling my aunt, meowing and nudging her and licking upon her face to try to get a reaction. As the hours passed the cats began licking at the blood that drained from her gaping head as I just watched on..."

Tammy scowled and screwed up her face as her sympathy turned to horror, wishing that Matthew's story would now come to an end, but still he continued.

"...By the following morning the cats had begun pulling at her bloody flesh with their teeth and their claws, the white fur on their faces now completely stained red with blood. It was clear by this point that their interest was no longer concern for their owner, but now for their own hunger..."

"Matthew, stop. Please..."Tammy protested, but Matthew continued, oblivious to Tammy's revulsion.

"...By the Monday morning, when the doctors arrived from the clinic to assess me, the cats had ripped off and eaten the majority of the flesh down one side of her face. They knocked upon the door but I didn't answer. I knew who it was and what they were going to think about me, but I was paralysed. When they peered in through the window and saw my aunt mutilated upon the floor they called the police, returning minutes later to find me still curled up in the corner of the hallway, shaking and soaked to the skin in my own urine..."

"And that's when they took you away?" Tammy asked through her crinkled grimace.

"Yep, took me away and locked me up with a gang of dribbling lunatics and psychos for fifteen long, horrible years. And the orderlies... don't get me started on the orderlies. They were just as crazy as the inmates, brutal and overzealous, eager to shoot you up with god-knows what drugs whenever they felt bored enough..." Matthew pictured Otis in his head once again, grinning and laughing at him, as he taunted him with an ominous dripping syringe. "...and the rest is history, as they say," he concluded with a sigh, the daunting thought of Otis continuing to linger in his mind as the beast inside turned and wriggled uneasily.

Tammy nodded and looked to the floor solemnly. She felt overwhelmed with empathy for the things that had happened to Matthew, but kept her thoughts to herself, as she knew that any expression of empathy now would imply to pardon or justify his recent atrocities. Instead, she remained silent.

Matthew frowned in contemplation, fully expecting some sort of reaction from Tammy, but confused to receive nothing. He looked at her expectantly for a moment longer before shrugging it off and

THE DAMAGED

sighing. He grabbed an old rag and mopped up the blood and vomit from the floor and chair that surrounded her, before discarding the rag to an open black bag. Grabbing the kitchen knife from the table, Matthew cut Tammy free from her remaining restraints and stood guard by the foot of the cellar stairs.

"You can change your clothes now," he told her, gesturing over to the pile with a half smile.

Matthew watched on as Tammy removed her vomit-soiled clothes and began dressing herself in Matthew's mother's attire. She pulled up the long black skirt over her bottom and slipped her arms into the loose-fitting floral blouse. Matthew immediately saw his mother once again, blood gargling and bubbling from the gape in her severed throat as she gazed over to him in hopeless desperation.

Matthew turned and looked away as Tammy finished dressing, staring instead at the charcoal drawing of his parents' killer that hung from the wooden beam. The killer looked back at him, smirking through his scraggy, tobacco-stained beard as he winked and laughed. *Come and get me,* he silently whispered with a smug, self-assured tone. *Come and get me, if you can!*

Matthew stared back defiantly, watching as the animated sketch rippled and moved before him as if it were alive. *I will, I promise you that!* he thought back.

He continued staring, studying the curves and features of the man's rugged face as he began contemplating his 3am plan of action. It was then that his memory stumbled upon the harrowing image of Samantha Jacobs once again, lying bloody and lifeless in the rain and whimpering up to him through motionless lips, *why me, Matthew? Why me?*

It then started to dawn on Matthew that maybe he needed a change of tactics. The hunt so far, however satisfying it was to the beast inside, had produced little success in finding the killer, and now, with the fear of Matthew's spree spreading through the homeless community like a plague, it was hardly likely to. It was during this thought that Matthew suddenly remembered something that Tammy had suggested to him previously – a client who might know something about the murders. Maybe she was right; maybe he would have more success if he spoke to him. *Charlton? Coulson? Charleston*? He couldn't remember exactly what the name was, but it didn't matter, he could easily find it somewhere within Tammy's documents.

He turned to face Tammy once more, finding her fully dressed and sat back down upon the chair again, submissively and patiently waiting to be restrained once more. He gave her a crooked smile to acknowledge the strange obedience and re-tied her to the chair with the last four cable ties from his father's toolbox. He picked up the black necktie that he had discarded to the floor previously, and started to loosen the knot within in.

"What's that for?" Tammy asked with a disgruntled frown. "I'm not gonna scream any more, I promise."

"I know, Darling. It's not for your mouth..." he explained with an awkward expression. "I don't think you want to watch what I need to do now."

Tammy grimaced and screwed her face with revulsion as it dawned upon her what Matthew had implied. She grit her teeth and clenched her eyes as the thought of it began to visualise inside her mind. Matthew wrapped the tie gently around her face, ensuring that it fully covered her eyes before fastening it into a sturdy knot behind her head. He picked up her discarded clothes from the floor and carried them up the stairs to the kitchen, where he placed them inside the washing machine and turned to face the crimson pool of blood that seeped from the cupboard under the stairs.

Tammy scrunched her eyes even tighter, despite the blindfold already completely blanking her view, and gently hummed to herself to drown out the thump and thuds upon each of the concrete steps as Matthew dragged the corpse down the cellar stairs. She heard him heave and wrench the body upon the pasting table, all the while trying to find the happy place in her mind – the zoo, the feeding giraffe, her beautiful daughter Jessica. Matthew took out the kitchen knife and began to sharpen it against a long honing rod with swift fluid motions, the scrapes and screeches piercing sharply through Tammy's defiant mental detachment and cutting through her dreamy images with ease.

Matthew gazed down at the body in contemplation, to the baby-blue T-shirt that Aggy wore and to the care company's logo, which was embroidered upon the right breast. He thought about his new plan of action once again, the plan to see the man whose name he had forgotten.

Aggy was slim, not as slim as Tammy but still a good few sizes smaller than he was. The T-shirt would be tight on him, and he would need to wash out the blood stains to avoid undue suspicion, but maybe he could pull it off. After all, he wasn't trying to make a fashion statement.

He put the knife down upon Aggy's legs and reached for the rim of the T-shirt, pulling it slowly over her breasts, arms and head, to the sound of sloppy squelching from the blood that pooled from her gaping back wound. He twisted and scrunched up the T-shirt in his hands and wrung out the excess blood upon Aggy's pale, bare stomach before then taking the shirt up to the kitchen and placing it inside the washing

THE DAMAGED

machine with Tammy's vomit-soiled clothes. Searching through the cupboard under the sink, Matthew came across a dusty old bottle of stain remover and proceeded to empty the entire bottle into the plastic drawer of the washing machine. He closed the door and set the dial to a high cotton wash, watching in contemplation as the machine filled up and started to spin.

Matthew returned to the body and continued to remove Aggy's remaining clothes, placing them all inside the black plastic sack until Aggy's body was bare. He looked down at her pale blood-splattered breasts and began to feel his arousal start to flicker once again. He looked to Tammy, tensed and scrunched up in the chair, to check that she still couldn't see him, before then returning his gaze back down to the body. He reached down slowly and gingerly brushed the tips of his fingers along her cold lifeless breasts and nipples like a naughty child reaching for the cookie jar, feeling his boxers growing tight once more. He looked to Tammy again, his conscience starting to feel guilty and dirty for touching another woman, and briskly retracted his hands.

Lost defiantly inside her own head, Tammy looked down upon the warm, joyous smile of her daughter before following the long neck of the giraffe up to his head, watching with awe as it chewed upon the luscious leaves of the trees above them. Matthew then took his first slice into the flesh and the giraffe immediately gushed with blood, grunting and gasping as it fell crashing to the floor of the paddock with a ground-shaking thud while Jessica howled and wept with despair.

Matthew's serpent tongue started to tingle, its senses awakened and stimulated by the scent of Aggy's flesh as his mind became curiously aroused by the growing craving of hunger. He pushed the thought to the back of his mind as he tried to concentrate on the task at hand. He reached for his father's handsaw and began to grind through the bone of Aggy's arm. He continued steadily dismembering the body, packing the various body parts neatly inside the black sacks while taking extra care not to perforate through the gut, but the strange hunger only grew. It was unclear to Matthew whether the hunger was his own or that of the beast that lived within him – as the two were becoming increasingly intertwined. But the overwhelming craving was undeniable.

Left with just two bloody legs upon the sordid pasting table, Matthew could resist his urge no longer. The sight of the juicy pink meat beckoned him as it gently oozed fluids onto the table, the rich aromas tingling his senses and causing his mouth to salivate.

He looked once again to Tammy, verifying again that the blindfold was indeed obscuring her view, before increasing his grip upon the kitchen knife and gripping firmly onto one of the bloody legs. He sliced down through the flesh of the thigh, separating it from the bone and cutting the thick chunk of flesh free from the rest of the leg. He placed it down on the table, using the kitchen knife to cut away the skin and remove the layers of fat before then filleting out the prominent veins, leaving behind a thick prime cut of juicy pink meat. He carefully cut the meat in half, creating two steak-like cuts of meat, each about an inch thick. He put down the knife and picked up the meat in each hand, holding it close to his face as he breathed in and felt the sweet rich aromas of the flesh engulfing his primal serpent senses.

Matthew felt his heart begin to race with excitement and anticipation, but resisted the soaring urge of the beast inside of him to consume the meat there and then. Instead, he walked up to the kitchen and wrapped both steaks in cling film, placing them inside the fridge for later.

Returning to the cellar, Matthew packed the remaining parts of the legs into the black bags and knotted them all up tightly, placing them neatly by the rear door of the cellar and beginning to mop up the pools of blood upon the table and the cellar floor.

Tammy breathed deeply, her grimace still dominating her tormented face as she followed her breathing exercises and willed the ailing giraffe back to health in her mind. Jessica's weeps gradually started to subside and a small smile returned to her face as Tammy realised the sounds of slices and saws had finally concluded. She relaxed the aching, tense muscles of her face as she drifted away from her 'happy place' and returned to reality once more, listening out carefully for Matthew's movements and becoming aware of the faint sizzle of the frying pan.

 Matthew lightly peppered and salted both sides of the first steak as he waited for the frying pan to get up to temperature. It was then that he noticed the raven, emerging from its home within the branches of the fir tree and gliding down through the rain. It fluttered down gracefully upon the lawn and began hopping its way towards the house, before taking to the air once more and landing gently upon the kitchen windowsill.

Matthew nodded and smiled at the bird in acknowledgement, as it poked its dense black beak through the open window and croaked loudly into the room. Matthew frowned and looked down at the bird curiously as it croaked again and stared down at the juicy pink peppered steak. Matthew nodded again in understanding, as he picked up the meat and placed it carefully into the sizzling pan, searing it gently on both sides for a mere few seconds before transferring it to a plate. The bird croaked again impatiently as Matthew reached into the cutlery drawer and removed a fork and a steak knife.

THE DAMAGED

"Okay, okay. Calm down!" Matthew muttered to the bird as he sliced into the meat and presented a small cube of it upon the windowsill.

Matthew sliced into the meat again, cutting himself a larger slice as he watched the bird ripping apart the meat with its beak and throwing it to the back of its throat with satisfied glee. Stabbing the slice with his fork, Matthew brought the meat tentatively to his mouth and pulled it free with his teeth. He rolled the meat around in his mouth, feeling the juicy blood oozing from it and drizzling around his serpent tongue with an explosion of sensory overload. The meat tasted divine, a taste like nothing he had encountered before. It was soft and succulent in his mouth like a tender cut of veal, but with a slightly bitter undertone and hints of fine Italian prosciutto. The beast inside of him fluttered and flapped its wings in excitement and delight as Matthew chewed upon the juicy meat, revelling in its soothing and satisfying taste for a few moments longer before finally swallowing it down into his gut and eagerly moving in to cut himself another juicy slice.

GROUND ZERO

After scrubbing Aggy's blood from the carpet and hanging the laundry up to dry, Matthew found himself back in his father's chair once again. The chirpy voices of cartoon characters spoke in his ears as he watched the rain gently drizzling down the lounge windows, his thoughts focused upon his plan to see the man whose name he could not recall.

The rhythmic ticking of the grandfather clock slowly broke Matthew's attention, and so he turned to calmly watch it for a while. Following the sturdy brass pendulum as it steadily swayed from side to side, Matthew's impending doom came to the forefront of his mind, as if the clock itself was now counting him down to his final exit. His time of impunity was nearly at an end, it would be churlish to think otherwise. His near-miss with PC Lang was too close for comfort and Matthew knew he would soon return, especially when the disappearance of Agnieszka appeared on his radar.

He boiled the kettle and made two fresh cups of tea, peering briefly from the kitchen window for a hopeful glimpse of his friendly raven, but there was no sight of him. He shrugged and turned to the cellar.

"Hey, I made tea," Matthew announced as he descended down into the cellar.

Placing both cups down upon the blood-soiled pasting table, he reached for the blindfold and carefully pulled it free, revealing Tammy's trauma-stricken face behind. She cast her eyes to him and solemnly shook her head in disgust, unable to formulate the words to fully describe her bone-chilling repugnance of his abhorrent actions. Matthew rolled his eyes dismissively as he reached up for the top shelf, grasping hold of Tammy's handbag and carrying it down. Sitting upon the cellar stairs with the bag upon his lap, he began rummaging through it. The look of disgust upon Tammy's face was now joined with that of violation.

THE DAMAGED

"What are you looking for?" she asked him in a disapproving tone, a tone that really shouted 'get the hell out of my bag!'

"I'll know when I find it...." he replied ominously, continuing to rummage through the clutter with complete disregard.

Matthew eventually pulled a folded piece of scruffy white paper from the bag and unravelled it, reading the title: 'Visitation schedule' at the top. He grunted to himself, pleased, as he scrolled through the names and times, noticing his own name at nine and five each day.

"Carlson! It was Carlson!" he announced with delight, finding the name on the sheet and finally remembering it from their previous conversation.

"What was? What are you doing?" Tammy snapped, her brow scrunched up in red and white creases.

"I'm taking your advice, Tammy. I'm going to speak with this Mr Carlson like you suggested."

"I... No, I said that *I* would speak to him for you. *You* can't go and speak to him!" she quickly replied, recalling the conversation but remembering how she had only said it to him as a means of escape. "...You can't just turn up on an old man's doorstep and start interrogating him about *some* murder twenty-five years ago!" she continued.

"It wasn't just *some* murder, Tammy! That was my parents!" he snapped back angrily.

"Okay, I'm sorry, Matthew. I didn't mean it like that. Just let me go instead, he'll know something's off if some random man just turns up at his door."

"He'll think something is 'off' if *you* turn up at his door! You're a 'Missing Persons'! He's expecting a care-worker to turn up at four o'clock, so I'll go then. It'll be fine."

"Matthew, please! Leave him alone!" she protested loudly.

"You keep your voice down or I'm putting the gag back on you!"

Tammy sighed and recoiled with a tormented frown, wishing that she had never mentioned him before and immediately feeling responsible for anything Matthew might do.

Matthew put the paper to one side and delved back into Tammy's handbag once again, removing her bottle of sleeping pills, her latex gloves, and her pink soft-back address book. He flicked through to the Cs, found the entry for 'Craig Carlson', and studied the address closely. It was a street that Matthew knew, a street close to where his aunt used to live, which was lucky, as he really didn't want to have to stop to ask directions.

SIMON LAW

Standing at the lounge window again, wearing an old pair of trainers and Aggy's semi-damp baby-blue T-shirt, the daunting realisation dawned upon Matthew that he would need to leave the safe confines of his house, alone, in the daytime – something he had still yet to do since his release from the hospital. The thought had not occurred to him before, but now that it had, it immediately filled him with anxiety.

He stared at the rain a little longer, building up the courage to leave the house while the beast inside fought against his anxiety for supremacy of his mind. He picked up his rucksack and reached his twitching hand tentatively for the door handle. His anxiety soared higher and almost tipped the balance as his fingers brushed over it. Suddenly a soft reassuring voice cooed in his ear.

"Matthew? Sweetheart? It's okay. Everything will be fine," his mother called from the wedding photograph.

Matthew turned and smiled, watching his parents waving to him comfortingly.

"Go get 'em, Sport. Make your father proud!" his father chipped in, placing his arm around his wife and gesturing Matthew towards the door.

Matthew took a steadying breath and nodded to them, turning back to the door and opening it wide with confidence. The bright September sun immediately embraced him with unforgiving sobriety and the rain gently fell upon his head, causing his confidence to flicker and dip. He felt the eyes of his prying neighbours bearing down upon him from behind their twitching net curtains, and he felt his head begin to spin. He heard the screams of laughing children, running and chasing and playing, and his head began to spin even more, spiralling and sloshing out of control in a queasy, nauseating blur.

Closing his eyes, he wished them all away, counting a long intake of air, holding it and releasing it again slowly, just like how Tammy had told him to when the same thing had happened to him at the park. He scrunched his eyes tighter still and repeated the process, feeling the beast inside of him croaking loudly in disappointment of his laughable insecurity and causing a fresh black plume to immediately sprout from his weeping bite wound.

Gritting his teeth tightly together, Matthew prised apart his eyes with defiance, pleasantly surprised to find the spinning had now ceased. He took another breath, closed the door behind him, and slowly walked to the end of his path. Stepping onto the street, he looked over towards the laughing children with their mother, before then scoping out the rest of the street for reassurance. He flexed his neck and shoulders, eyeing up the bus stop at the top of the street and beginning to make his way towards it.

THE DAMAGED

He continued his pace steadily up the street, his eyes shying nervously to the floor as he saw the mother and laughing children getting closer through his peripheral vision.

"Hi, excuse me?" the woman called to him, eagerly trying to make eye contact whilst Matthew did his best to ignore her.

"Excuse me? Sir?" she called again, now too close for Matthew to pretend he didn't hear.

"Hello?" Matthew replied tentatively, slowing his pace and lifting his head slightly from the ground.

"Hi. Sorry, I don't mean to disturb you, but you haven't seen my cat, have you?" she asked, raising her eyebrow and giving him a smile.

The laughter of the children stopped in an instant, the mention of their missing moggy causing them to halt in their tracks and gaze up at him expectantly. Matthew looked back at them, but hesitated to respond, thinking of the rancid cat carcass in his back garden that the raven had devoured. He looked to the mother and then back at the children again, feeling his head beginning to spin again as the sun shone down upon him like an interrogation spotlight. His hands began to shake and the rain started gaining strength, but still he could not respond, his blank creepy stares at the family causing worry to grow upon the mother's face.

The woman frowned at him in confusion, as a loud crackle of thunder rumbled in the sky above them. Her frown then turned to disgust, as she quickly placed her arm around her children protectively and began to usher them away.

"Just forget about it!" she called, walking away from him with speed while checking him dubiously over her shoulder.

Matthew released a long sigh and turned his head to the sky, feeling the rain pelting down upon him refreshingly whilst telling himself; *it was just a damn cat!*

The bus soon arrived and Matthew swiftly boarded, passing the weary cantankerous-looking driver a blood-splattered twenty pound note and telling him to keep the change. The end-of-school-bus-rush was now petering off, leaving the bus mostly empty, with the exception of a few late stragglers sparsely occupying a few of the seats, but none of them paid him any attention. The bus pulled away, the deep growl of the throbbing engine resonating through the metal struts of the scruffy seats and vibrating the smeary glass of the windows. Matthew watched through the greasy glass as the thundering town passed him by, pondering how different his childhood town now looked in the daylight; vibrant and bustling, even in the September rain.

SIMON LAW

It was then that Matthew's wandering eyes locked in and focused on a small bungalow in the distance, watching it draw closer with a cold scowl of bitter recollection. He reached out and pressed the bell as his eyes continued locking in, his mind filling with feelings of foreboding and hatred as he heard a voice whispering in his ear; *You filthy little cunt! You should be ashamed!*

Matthew leaned into the window, steaming up the window with his warm breath as he watched the ominous building pass him by. He then reached up with his hand, placing his index finger upon the frosty condensation and writing upon it a four-lettered word that had been ruminating through his mind. *Amon.*

The bus ground to a halt at the next available stop and Matthew alighted. He set off down the street, eagerly reading the numbers upon the passing doors and pondering how he was going to pose the question. *Hi, Mr Carlson, Could you tell me who killed my parents, please?* Tammy was right, it sounded absurd, but how else could he phrase it?

Matthew reached the house and approached, raising his hand to knock when he noticed a small combination key-safe secured to the door. He then remembered the four-digit code he had seen pencilled next to Mr Carlson's name in Tammy's address book, and so retrieved it from his bag to double-check it. 7189. He typed the code into the display to release a small opening, reaching his hand inside and removing the single brass door key from within it.

He took a breath, slid the key into the lock and let himself into the house.

"Hello? Mr Carlson?" he called as he stepped into the hallway, his senses immediately filled with the stench of musty old men.

He walked further into the house, brushing past the folded wheelchair in the hall and entering the lounge where he discovered Mr Carlson with his back turned away. The old man's eyes were glued to the daily politics show on the television while he grumbled out his discontent at Prime Minister Cameron's comments on the benefit system. Between grunts, Craig turned to Matthew with a disgruntled scowl.

"Who the fuck are *you*?" he spouted unrepentantly.

Matthew did not respond, finding himself breathless and paralysed as he gazed back at Craig Carlson in the chair. His heart sunk and a cold shiver tingled down his spine as he locked his sights upon the old man with instant recognition. It was a one-in-a-million chance, and Matthew could scarcely believe it was possible, but the crook of his nose and the bulge of his brow were unmistakable. It was him; the man who had plagued his dreams for all these years, the man whose face he had sketched a hundred times; it was the tramp who had murdered his parents.

Matthew's reptilian pupils immediately exploded to amber like the glowing embers of the fires of hell. The beast inside him sprang to life, croaking and flapping with eager ferocity, projecting a deafening croak so powerful that it sent shock-waves of pain shooting from the depths of his gut up through to his chest. The shock-waves then exploded between his shoulder blades, immediately sprouting a series of thick, black silky plumes that burst through his skin and dripped with blood. Tiny spiders then erupted through the perforations and scurried down along the crevice of his back.

Lightning flashed in the sky and thunder rumbled through the ominous clouds as the sky became engulfed in a vast conspiracy of swarming ravens, their black malevolent shadows darting and dancing about the sky with excitement and glee as if somehow summoned by the croaking of the beast that lived within.

The urge to slaughter the old man there and then was great, but the beast inside of him roared with echoic croaks of protest. *No! Make him suffer for all the pain he has caused. Make him suffer more than any man has suffered before!*

"Are you a fucking retard, boy? Answer me!" Craig Carlson prompted him angrily, dribbling from the side of his slumped, twisted face.

"I... I'm Matthew, from the company..." he replied, tightly clenching his fists to maintain his drifting composure.

"Oh, for God's sake! Why does that useless company keep sending me new people? You're the third one this week already! And every time they do, I have to explain how I like my fucking coffee all over again!"

The repeated cursing grated upon Matthew like a knife twisting in his side, but he remained calm, biding his time for when the moment was right.

"My apologies for that, Mr Carlson."

"Well?"

"Well, what, Mr Carlson?"

"Are you gonna ask me how I like my fucking coffee, or are you just gonna fuck it up like everyone else does? You damn retard!"

"How do you like your coffee, Mr Carlson?"

"Strong, with two sugars, and when I say strong I don't mean just pour less fucking milk in it, I mean *STRONG*, as in *more* coffee granules! You got that?"

"Yes, Mr Carlson, I understand."

SIMON LAW

"Good! And for dinner I want shepherd's pie. None of that foreign curry shit that they've been feeding me all week!"

Matthew looked down at the pitiful, belligerent old man as he spouted his abuse, spotting the signs of a previous stroke that glared out with clear prominence. From the fallen dribbling half of his face, to his twisted crippled-claw of a hand; life had clearly already taken its own revenge upon him, but to Matthew this was not enough.

Matthew nodded to Craig and turned to the kitchen, his hands and legs trembling with anger and anticipation. He took his bag off of his shoulder and placed it down upon the kitchen counter before reaching for the familiar-looking care plan folder that he had spotted on the side.

Matthew briefly scanned through the notes in the folder before then turning to the various pots of pills stacked tall upon the counter. He picked up the first and examined it, his hands still shaking with adrenaline as cracks of thunder and squawks of circling birds bounced around inside his fragile head. He unscrewed the lid and poured a few pills into his hand, tilting his palm from side to side as he watched the pills roll and studied their size and shape. Reaching his hand inside his bag, he then removed the pot of Tammy's sleeping pills that he had brought along on the off chance, and took out a few for comparison. The two were not the same, they differed in multiple subtle ways from colour to shape, but he doubted that Mr Carlson would pay that much attention.

He poured out a small glass of water to accompany the pills and turned on the kettle, waiting for the sound of bubbling to become clearly audible to the old man before returning to the lounge again.

"Here's your medication, Mr Carlson," Matthew told him, forcing out a pleasant tone and a smile as he dropped a heap of the switched sleeping pills into the old man's 'good' hand. The old man snatched them away, immediately throwing them into his mouth and gulping them down with the water.

"And where's my coffee? Huh?" he snarled.

"The kettle's just boiling now, Mr Carlson," Matthew replied, his feigned smile starting to curl at the ends with sadistic joy as he cast his eyes to the clock and began counting down the minutes to Craig Carlson's impending unconsciousness.

Matthew returned to the kitchen, stepping discreetly out of Craig's view and sitting himself down gently upon the tiled floor. He breathed deeply, leaning his head back against the kitchen wall and closing his eyes as he tried to calm the frustrated, anxious croaking of the restless beast inside of him. He rubbed his face and eyes to force composure, feeling his thumping heart's attempts to escape from his chest as his mind became flooded with bloody, vivid images of his mother and father once more. *Make him pay, Matthew! Make him pay for what he did to us!* his mother demanded as she gurgled bloody bubbles from the flapping gape in her throat while his father lay bleeding to death by her side.

Matthew kept his eyes closed and gently rocked on the spot, feeling the creeping clusters of spiders crawling all over his bloody back as he listened to the old man continue to spout furiously at the television set, pausing every so often only to yell to Matthew – *Hey, retard, where's my fucking coffee!*

The beast within him continued to claw mercilessly at his gut, each rip and slash of his insides sending more shock-waves through his body, each one sprouting a fresh, new silky plume from his bloody spider-infested back.

Eventually, the bitter old man's angry words slowly started to quieten and slur before finally turning to silence. Matthew opened his eyes and exhaled, listening out for the sound of Craig's complaints but hearing only the voice of the Prime Minister and the roar of tempestuous commotion from the angry, malevolent skies.

Matthew stood, tentatively peering around the kitchen doorway and looking down at Craig as he slumbered wide-mouthed in his chair and drooled down his shirt. Matthew walked towards him, his eyes fixed upon his bulbous brow and crooked nose as he grit his teeth and clenched his fists. He raised them into the air, watching as his white knuckles continued to shake with adrenaline, and imagined the rush of delight he would derive from thrashing the pitiful old man to death in his chair, breaking every bone in his wrinkled old face until his knuckles started to bleed, but he resisted it. Instead, he leaned in closer, his eyes fixed on the man with a look of pure disgust as he released his fists from their tight clenches.

"I told you I would get you! Didn't I?" he gently whispered.

Matthew pulled himself together and gathered his things from the kitchen before then retrieving the folded wheelchair from the hall. He pulled it open and locked it into place before wrenching the old man's limp body from the chair and carelessly throwing him into it. He switched off the television and all the lights and wheeled the old man down the hall, through the front door, and out into the street where the rain and thunder greeted them both into its harsh embrace.

Matthew boarded the arriving next bus with his sleeping companion unchallenged, the unfazed driver barely even glancing down at the old man in his drug-induced slumber. Matthew parked the wheelchair in the disabled bay and calmly sat himself down as the bus pulled away. He gazed from the window, watching as the vast flock of ravens followed the route of the bus, weaving in and out of the dark angry clouds and circling the bus like buzzards around a corpse.

Tammy spent the duration of Matthew's venture frantically wriggling and wrenching at her restraints, stretching and contorting the stern plastic around her wrists and ankles until eventually tipping over the chair and crashing down onto the hard concrete floor. She yelped with pain as her shoulder and arm were crushed under her own weight, but no one came to her aid, her muffled screams for help shadowed by the ferocious rain and thunder that grew in strength with each passing moment.

Matthew alighted from the bus one stop early, taking the wooded back route behind the houses instead to avoid suspicion of his neighbours. The wind and rain pelted mercilessly against him as he wheeled Craig Carlson down the muddy, uneven dirt track, the force of the wind so powerful that it threatened to tip the wheelchair over with every sudden gust. Matthew ploughed onwards through the weather, quickly reaching the rear of his house and pushing open the rusted back gate. He pushed the wheelchair through the garden, past the swing and the decimated pile of cat bones, and down the slope to the rear cellar doors. He unlocked the padlock and pulled open the doors to the sound of crackling thunder above and quickly wheeled his companion inside, parking him neatly in the corner of the room next to the bags of Aggy's dismembered body parts.

He exhaled and shook the excess rain from his drenched blonde hair before suddenly noticing Tammy upon the floor, gently weeping as she struggled to try and right herself.

"Darling? Are you alright?" he gasped with worry, quickly rushing over to her and lifting the chair upright again.

Tammy declined a response, seemingly too flustered and pained to explain herself. She panted and groaned, rolling her twisted shoulder in the socket to try and free the strain. She suddenly became aware of Craig sat unconscious in the corner of the room. Her eyes widened and fixated upon him as her brow creased up with confusion and rising panic.

"What the hell are you doing, Matthew? What did you do to him?" You said you just wanted to talk to him!" she wailed despairingly, starting to fidget anxiously in the chair.

"He's just asleep, but you just wait until he wakes up! He's going to suffer then!"

"But why, Matthew? What has he done? You can't just keep hurting innocent people like this!"

THE DAMAGED

"Innocent? INNOCENT!?" he raged, stomping over to his sleeping guest and spinning around the chair so that the old man was facing them. "-It's him! It's who I've been looking for all this time! He's the killer!"

"Matthew, no! That's ridiculous! He's just some random old man to you!"

"I know it's him, Tammy. I'm certain of it!"

"No, you're not, Matthew. You want it to be him, I know you do, but you want it so badly that you're convincing yourself of things that just aren't true! It's too easy! It's too convenient for it to be him! Can't you see that?"

"No, I... I... " Matthew groaned in frustration and turned to stare down at the old man, the slightest of doubts starting to niggle at his mind as he momentarily contemplated Tammy's perspective. "- I just know, Tammy. I hear the ravens croaking to me and they tell me that it's true."

"There are no ravens, Matthew! Please, let him go, let him go before this goes too far!" she yelled with impatience, her volume starting to reach Matthew's breaking point – despite the storm almost completely drowning it.

"Settle down, please. I love you Tammy, but you have to calm yourself! Or else I'll have to put you to sleep like Mr Carlson over there!"

Tammy grit her teeth and shook her head in anxious frustration, pulling once again at her arm and leg restraints and stretching the taut plastic even more.

Matthew took a few more deep breaths and tried to calm his own nerves, before pulling the rear cellar doors shut to shield them from the wind and the rain. He removed his dripping wet coat.

"Would you like a cup of tea?" he asked, turning to her with half a smile.

"No, I don't want a fucking cup of tea, Matthew!" she growled.

"You watch your language!" he snarled back, stepping past her and ascending to the kitchen.

She listened out as the kettle started to boil, and released a long sigh of exasperation. She then cast her eyes over to Craig in the corner, watching as the old man gently snored and grunted in his sleep, thinking of all the times he had insulted her and slapped her arse like it was a piece of meat. An offbeat contemplation then fluttered through her mind as she remembered the promise that Matthew had made to her before, a promise that she would be set free when everything was over – still naively believing 'free' to mean what she thought it did. *Was this the end? Would I really be set 'free' at long last if I just sit back and let Matthew kill him?* she pondered, thinking again of Jessica's angelic face and longing for the chance to embrace her and make amends for all her mistakes.

Craig Carlson was not the killer, Tammy knew that with certainty. The possibility of it being him was too farfetched and unbelievable to even contemplate, but that didn't necessarily mean that he was a nice person. He was a miserable, twisted old man whose only joy in life seemed derived from the misery of others. He had no hobbies, no family that ever wanted to see him, nothing. Maybe he didn't deserve to die for his sins, but if he had to die in exchange for her freedom, then was that a fair trade-off? Or was that just selfish?

Matthew sat down in his father's chair, gazing upon the growing storm whilst sipping on his hot cup of tea. He pulled off the soaking-wet carer's T-shirt that he had been masquerading in and dropped it to the floor next to him. He rubbed his sticky back with his hand and felt some of the remaining spiders squash beneath his palm. Reaching up, he gingerly fingered the series of black plumes that now protruded from between his shoulder blades. They felt thicker, sturdier than any of the feathers that had preceded them, and when he tried to tug at them they resisted. He readjusted his grip and pulled again, but still they did not budge, as if somehow attached to the bones of his shoulder blades. He gave them one last tug and finally relented, feeling his back starting to throb with pain at his attempts to extract them.

He looked up at his parents' photo, noticing the wide smiles and raised eyebrows now present upon both their faces. They looked down at him with pride and eagerness before turning to each other and embracing. He smiled back and felt their warmth running through him, thinking how close he now was to the end, how close he was to seeing them again in his perfectly-imagined eternity with Tammy at his side.

"Almost there now, Sweetheart," his mother told him.

"We're proud of you, Sport!" his father chipped in with a grin.

Matthew took another sip of his tea and debated what now to do with Mr Carlson, how best to make him suffer for all the years of pain and anguish. He leant back in the chair, snuggling deep into the comfy red leather whilst listening out at the glorious crackles and roars of the thundering storm. Darkly delicious contemplations circled through his mind to the purring glee of the beast, leaving Matthew strangely aroused once again.

The sun soon began to set in the angry sky, its final red and orange rays slowly disappearing behind the horizon, as the storm raged on with the fury reminiscent to Matthew of that of '87. The almighty winds fiercely shook the window panes throughout the house while

THE DAMAGED

powerful gusts contorted the branches of the battered trees, sending leaves and twig debris whirling through the air.

Filled with dark and sadistic ideas, Matthew grabbed his favourite knife from the kitchen and returned to the cellar, pulling upon the light cord and watching the room flicker into intermittent strobing illumination. He place down the knife and turned to Tammy with a solemn smile.

"It's time," he told her, picking up the discarded tie from the floor and strapping it carefully around her eyes.

Tammy remained quiet and compliant, scrunching her eyes closed and reminding herself of her impending freedom, as she felt Matthew plant a gentle kiss upon her forehead.

Matthew hoisted Craig's limp body up onto the pasting table before tying him firmly in place with a length of rope. He glared down at the old man as his face flickered in the light, his eyes ablaze with burning amber while the beast wriggled and flapped with rising excitement. He walked to the side, breaking his stare as he rummaged inside his father's toolbox. He removed a range of various rusted tools which he laid down in a line upon the shelf.

"Time to wake up, Mr Carlson!" Matthew told him sternly, striking him around the face with the back of his hand.

The old man grumbled and groaned, but failed to wake, turning his head to the side and continuing to snore.

"I said it's time to wake up now!" Matthew repeated, louder this time, before striking him once again.

Tammy scrunched her face further and turned away, resisting her conscience's screaming demands for her to protest. She clenched her teeth and buried her head into her shoulders and attempted to count her breaths in order to stay calm.

The old man stirred again, briefly flicking his eyes and grumbling out a string of incomprehensible syllables, before settling back down into his daze. Matthew snarled and turned away, grabbing a chisel and an iron mallet from his tool selection before returning once more. He opened up the old man's 'good' hand, positioning it flat, palm-up against the wood of the pasting table, before holding the chisel point down and perpendicular to the wrinkly palm. He tightened his grip upon the hefty mallet, positioning it just above the rusted chisel, before then lifting it up in preparation to strike.

"Wakey-Wakey!"

Matthew brought the mallet crashing down through the air, connecting it so perfectly with the chisel that it sparked with a bright orange flash of light. The blunt, rusted chisel plunged straight through the old man's wrinkled palm with ease, continuing into the wooden table below where it halted and secured the hand firmly in place.

The old man immediately awoke in a blaze of shrieking agony – a scream so loud and harrowing that it almost seemed to dwarf the almighty rumbling thunder from outside. Tammy wrenched at her arm restraints once more, stifling her rising anxiety with the shoots of pain in her wrists as the agonised scream echoed inside her head.

Wide-eyed and traumatised, Craig continued to scream until his lungs ran out of air. He pulled at his impaled hand and desperately wrenched forward to sit, but his feeble muscles quickly surrendered against the tension of the rope across his chest. He fell back to the table in a flustered slump as he gazed up at Matthew's omnipotent silhouette in the light. Tears streamed from his terrified face as he desperately panted for air, his eyes locked upon Matthew's demonic figure as his mind frantically whirled to make sense of the situation.

"What the fuck is this! What are you doing to me?!" he slurred from one side of his mouth as he dribbled from the other.

Matthew stepped aside and walked around to where his face was illuminated, looking down sternly at the trembling wreck of a man as he dropped the mallet to the floor.

"It's called karma, Mr Carlson. It's penance for all your sins," Matthew told him in a low tone as he paced around the table.

"What the hell are you talking about?" the old man cried in a fluster, grimacing down in horror at his bloody, impaled hand.

"Come come, Mr Carlson. You know exactly what I'm talking about! You've been in my house before, haven't you? Eight Oak Street? Is this ringing any bells yet?"

"You're off your fucking rocker! You damn retard! Let me go right now!" he whined.

"We don't swear in this house, Mr Carlson. My parents do not approve!" Matthew snapped, increasing his pace as he continued to circle the table.

"Who are you? What the hell do you think I've done?"

"You might not know me, but I certainly know you, Mr Carlson! Or should I call you 'King Kong'? After all, that's what you told us to call you, isn't it?"

The old man's expression flickered as he exhaled in frustration, pulling at his bloody hand once again before then whimpering in pain.

"Fine, well maybe you'll remember this!" Matthew declared as he grabbed the kitchen knife and thrust it in front of Craig's face, stopping mere millimetres from the old man's eye. "-You see this knife? It used to be part of a set, a 'family' if you will. That set's now incomplete. Do you know why?"

THE DAMAGED

"No, why?" the old man asked with pained trepidation.

"Because one of the knives is now in an evidence bag at the police station, after you MURDERED MY PARENTS WITH IT!" Matthew raged, fiercely stabbing the knife beside the old man's head and burying it deep into the pasting table.

Craig flinched with shock. His heart missed a beat and leapt into his mouth. He sighed with relief when he realised that the blade had missed him.

"What? No! I never did that!" he protested with a desperate, wrinkled frown.

"Oh, yes you did! You slit my mother's throat and stabbed my father in the chest while I watched from the cellar! Didn't know I was down here, did you?"

"You have the wrong man! I swear!"

"No, I don't! Don't play games with me, 'Kong'; you'll only make it worse for yourself."

"No, I swear! I've no idea what the fuck you're talking about!"

"I've told you about that language, haven't I? I won't warn you again. Now, admit what you've done and I'll let you go," Matthew told him, despite having no such intentions.

"I haven't done a damn thing, you freak! For God's sake! Just let me go! Let me go right now, damn it!"

"Fine. We'll do things the hard way then."

Matthew huffed and reached over to his selection of tools once again, picking up a set of old pliers this time and returning to the old man with a twisted smile.

"Anything to tell me yet? 'Kong'?" he asked.

The old man looked over at the pliers in Matthew's hand and grimaced in terror, squirming and pulling away as he stuttered in a desperate attempt to string a coherent sentence.

Matthew nodded and shrugged his shoulders. He then gripped the pliers around one of the old man's fingers and began slowly increasing the pressure upon it.

"Please! Please just stop this!" he protested in despair, but Matthew did not stop.

He increased the pressure upon the pliers further as the old man began to screech in agony. Matthew continued, listening to the sound of the bone beginning to snap within the finger as he clenched the pliers even tighter. The old man's screams echoed throughout the cellar, bouncing sickeningly inside Tammy's head as her conscience once again demanded she take action. Tammy ignored the demands for a moment longer, reeling and grimacing and praying that Matthew would stop, but he didn't.

SIMON LAW

"Matthew, stop!" she yelled in frustration, tears streaming down her face as her jaw shook with adrenaline.

Matthew stopped and turned to her with a frown of surprise, having almost forgotten she was even there.

Craig gasped and tried to catch his breath, before turning his head to try and catch sight of where the woman's voice had come from.

"Tammy? Tammy is that you?" he cried out in a wounded and angry voice. "-You get me the fuck out of here, you little bitch! Or I swear to god I'll make you pay!"

Matthew removed the pliers from around the old man's broken finger and turned to face him once more, looking down upon him with a disappointed and expectant gaze.

"I warned you about that language, Mr Carlson. Didn't I?" Matthew told him in an eerily calm voice.

"You make this stop right now, Tammy!" Craig continued, ignoring Matthew's calm reminder.

"Matthew, please. Stop it now! You don't have to do this!" she pleaded, but Matthew paid no attention.

He laid down the pliers upon the table next to where the kitchen knife still stood embedded, and reached down for a small wooden dowel he had noticed upon the bottom shelve. Placing his hands upon the old man's face, Matthew forced his fingers into Craig's mouth and prised it open. Craig tried to resist, tensing his jaw in an attempt to bite viciously into Matthew's fingers, but the power of his jaw was no match for Matthew's strength. With his mouth prised open, Matthew jammed the wooden dowel between his teeth, forcing the joint of the jaw to open and lock past its usual limit.

Craig shook his head in futile desperation, tears streaming down his flushed, tormented face as he tried to dislodge the wooden dowel from his jaw. He thrashed and tensed and groaned with anguish as Matthew quietly chuckled, but his attempts to remove the dowel were hopeless. Matthew picked up the pliers once more and gazed deep into the old man's open mouth. He scowled and held his breath as his eyes followed along the rows of intermittent black and rotten teeth before inserting the pliers inside.

"Matthew, please?" Tammy repeated in a breathless whine, but again, Matthew paid no attention.

The old man scrunched his eyes and face as he continued to weep and groan, feeling Matthew continue to rummage around inside his mouth with the pliers until finally clasping them around a molar near the back. Matthew gripped the pliers tightly, and Craig could feel the tooth begin to wiggle inside his gum, sending waves of intense pain flooding and pulsating through his skull. Matthew increased the

THE DAMAGED

pressure, causing a stress crack to run far down into the root where it began to splinter into the nerve ending. Craig howled and shook with shock, pulling so hard at his impaled hand that it ripped and tore the hand open further. Matthew abruptly twisted the pliers, sending shards of broken tooth deep into the old man's bleeding gums, before wrenching back and ripping the tooth free, knocking away the wooden dowel with the force of his retracting hand.

The battered gum gushed with blood that flooded Craig's mouth, causing the old man's screams to cease as he swallowed and spat out the blood in a frantic attempt not to drown in it.

Tammy continued to whimper in traumatised frustration, listening to the harrowing screams and gargles and imagining what Matthew might be doing.

"Please! Please, Matthew!" she desperately wailed between her tears, pulling fiercely at her restraints and stretching the stressed plastic so much that she could almost free her hand.

With a sadistic grin, Matthew tipped his head back and croaked out maniacally in the voice of the beast, lapping at the dusty air with his slithering serpent tongue while a fresh cluster of spiders spilled from his open mouth. The beast purred from his gut with euphoria as the spiders trickled down his bare chest and scurried to the floor.

A huge rumble of thunder suddenly crashed outside the house, joining the vast ensemble of groaning and whimpering noises that filled Matthew's ears. His sadistic smile slowly started to fade, as he gradually became aware of Tammy's distress. He had become so caught up in the moment that he had failed to consider the effect that his actions would have upon the woman he loved. He looked down as she whimpered and sobbed in the chair, trembling with anxiety and shaking her head with despair.

His face turned sombre as guilt took hold of him. He gave the gargling old man one final look of disgust before turning to Tammy and kneeling by her side.

"Hey, Darling?" he cooed softly at her. "-I'm sorry. I didn't mean to put you through all this. I was ignorant; I just got carried away with myself."

"Matthew, please stop!" she gently begged in a breathy exhale, snuffling away her tears and wiping her face against her shoulder.

Looking at the torment upon her flustered, tortured face, it was clear to him that thinking the blindfold would be sufficient to shield her from the distress was foolish. Guilt-stricken and ashamed, Matthew swallowed the frog in his throat and sighed.

"I can't stop, Tammy. He has to pay for what he did to me, for what he did to my parents. Can't you see that?

"It's not him, Matthew. Just let him go, please, before it's too late!"

Matthew disregarded her pleas, reaching down for his bag and removing the pot of her sleeping pills.

"What's that? What are you doing?" Tammy asked with a flutter of panic as her ears tuned in to the sound of the rattling pills.

"I'm just giving you something to help, Darling. It's for the best."

"No! Matthew, No! I don't want them!"

"Just relax, Tammy. Everything's going to be alright now, I promise you. Just take these and it all goes away."

"No! Please! Don't! Just stop this Matthew, please!"

Tammy turned her head and clamped her lips together as tight as she could as Matthew poured out a heap of pills into his palm.

"Tammy, please. It's only because I love you! We don't have to do this the hard way."

Tammy groaned in anger and frustration but refused to open her mouth, turning her head further into her shoulder and gritting her teeth like her life depended on it. Matthew frowned with regret, as he leant in and planted a tender kiss upon her forehead.

"It's all for the best, Darling. Soon this will all be over and we'll both be free of all this."

Matthew brushed his fingers tenderly across her trembling face. He carefully pressed her nostrils closed between his thumb and index finger, holding them in place with a firm but gentle grip. Tammy struggled and panicked, shaking her head frantically to try and shake Matthew free, pulling at her wrist restraints and moaning desperately. Her deprived lungs quickly began screaming out for oxygen while her anxiety soared and pulsated through her body like electricity.

Tammy continued to resist, thrashing about in the chair in the hope that Matthew would see her distress and relent, but he didn't. Her pale face turned to red, and then to purple, as tears flooded down her face from behind the blindfold. At the point of exploding, Tammy could defy him and the cravings of her lungs no longer. She released the grip of her lips and teeth and gasped out for air. It was at that opportune moment that Matthew poured the mound of sleeping pills into Tammy's mouth, hitting them directly against the back of her throat and causing her swallow reflex to immediately gulp the majority of them down.

Matthew released Tammy from his grip and stepped away solemnly, watching as Tammy coughed and spat a few of the unswallowed pills onto the floor. It was impossible for Tammy to tell how many she had actually swallowed, but she feared that it was probably enough. She whimpered and wept and groaned in frustration as she hocked up phlegm and swallowed the bitter dusty taste in her mouth.

THE DAMAGED

"Please, Matthew, just stop! It's not him... it's not," she begged listlessly between weeps.

Matthew scowled and sighed before turning back to face Craig once again.

"It *is* him, Tammy, I know it!" Matthew replied in a low voice, keeping his gaze sternly upon the face of the worthless old man.

It was then that Matthew noticed the lack of screams, the lack of whimpers, and the lack of movement from the wretched old man lying before him. Disappointment and frustration briefly fluttered through his mind as he feared Craig Carlson had died prematurely, before quickly noticing the steady bubbles of blood and realising that he had merely passed out from the pain.

Matthew snarled at him in disgust, angered by his audacity to sleep when he was supposed to be suffering for his crimes. Reaching across, he wrenched the kitchen knife clean from the wood and began debating his next move.

At Craig's awkward side-slumped position, Matthew suddenly noticed something that he had failed to see before – a black furry hand protruding from the top of his scruffy chequered shirt. Matthew cocked his head and, with a frown of curiosity, studied the furry hand closer. He reached down and unbuttoned the shirt from the top down, slowly revealing more and more of the crude and faded tattoo upon his chest. The furry hand was quickly joined by a furry arm, then a furry body with a furry head. By the third shirt button down, the primitive ink was completely revealed; it was an ape, a gorilla, it was King Kong himself, baring his teeth and snarling up at Matthew from the saggy, wrinkled skin of the old man's chest. *You can call me King Kong for all I give a shit!* – Matthew immediately heard bouncing around in his head, soon joined by the bloody images of his dying parents.

"You see, Tammy! Here's your proof right here!" Matthew cried with a sense of immediate vindication, ripping the shirt wide open and sending the remaining buttons flying.

"What... what the hell are you talking about?" Tammy muttered in return, in a weak and weary voice.

Matthew smiled and twirled the knife in his hand, watching how the flickering cellar light twinkled and reflected upon the blade. He increased his grip and aimed the knife down at the old man's chest, gently teasing it over his skin as the beast began to purr at Matthew's bloody contemplations.

"Just... Just stop!" Tammy slurred, her voice sounding even weaker than before.

Matthew pressed the knife down gently into the skin, increasing the pressure slowly with small careful increments until the blade began to sink. The old man stirred and groaned, and the gargling of blood in his throat commenced again, but yet he failed to wake. Matthew dug the blade deeper and began to drag it, scraping it along the old man's ribs with a clackety stop and start.

Craig groaned again, louder, as he slowly started to regain consciousness to the realisation of what was happening to him. Matthew continued to drag the blade through the wrinkled skin with a firm hand, crudely tracing the faded tattoo with broad, round strokes, as blood oozed and trickle from the slumping gape.

Craig's eyes opened wide as he cried aloud in pain and terror, watching as the bloodied knife completed its wide circuit on his chest.

"Tammy, please! Please make this stop!" he whimpered in breathless desperation, as Matthew retracted the knife and stabbed it deep in the table beside his head once more. "Please!"

Matthew grinned widely as he leant down and gingerly fingered the edges of the scored flesh, gently teasing his fingers into the squelching gap as Craig released another deafening scream.

"No! God, no!" he bellowed with desperation.

Matthew slowly pulled back the top of the flap to the sound of gloopy ripping, and more tormented screams. He gripped the skin firmly in his hand, his fingernails sinking in to the soggy side as his knuckles turn white with strain. Then, with one single fluid motion, Matthew viciously ripped the tattooed flesh clean from the old man's body, exposing his bare pulsating muscles that twitched and gushed with blood.

The pitiful old man released a scream so intense that it carried no sound at all. The pain flooded him like white heat, engulfing every nerve and sense in his entire body and burning with such immensity that it consumed his entire being. The silent scream bellowed from his mortified, trembling face as it expelled every last molecule of air from his lungs, vibrating the pasting table with vigour, while his jaw locked open in twisted terror.

Matthew held up the dripping sheet of skin like some kind of ghastly award, maintaining the eerily proud grin upon his face as he felt the plumes that protruded from his back begin to grow. Reaching back into his father's toolbox, Matthew removed a hammer and nail. He slapped the sloppy sheet of skin against the wooden beams of the cellar, positioning it beside his most recent charcoal sketch of Craig Carlson, as he hammered in a nail to secure it.

Twitching with tremors of shock as his intense white pain continued, Craig finally gasped for air before projecting out another terrified scream. This time it was audible, high-pitched and harrowing, like a screaming cat being drowned in the bathtub.

THE DAMAGED

"Matthew? Matthew, please! I... I love you. Just stop this, stop now and we can be together," Tammy cried out in a weary slur.

The burning embers immediately faded from Matthew's eyes and the beast inside turned silent. He turned to Tammy with a stunned face, looking down at her as she panted and wept in the chair. The rain and wind battered the house from all directions as Tammy's words rolled around inside his head. *Was she sincere?*

Matthew opened his mouth to respond, but failed to formulate the right words. He sighed in torment as his mind ruminated through the plausibility of her sudden declaration. *Why say it now? A sudden realisation? The sleeping pills lowering her inhibitions? Deceit?*

"Please?" Tammy muttered again, her lips trembling and her head swaying wearily.

Craig's tortured screams slowly faded away from Matthew's focus as he gingerly stepped towards Tammy. He knelt down by her feet and tenderly placed his hands upon her knees.

"...Really? You really do love me?" he gingerly asked with an uplifted smile.

"Y...Yes... Matthew, I... I do. Just stop all this before it's too late," she mumbled like a drunk, seemingly losing her fight against the drugs running through her system.

Matthew's smile widened as he reached up and supported her floppy head with his hands, wiping away the tears from her face with his thumbs as he closed his eyes and visualised their life together.

"It's already too late, Darling," he whispered to her earnestly.

If Tammy's declaration had come sooner, long before he had embarked on his current path, then maybe things would have been different. What kind of life could they have together now? A life on the run? – Always looking over their shoulder for the police to recognise them? What kind of life was that?

Matthew leant forward and pressed his lips tenderly against hers. Tammy reciprocated, and their lips and tongues soon became entwined in the heat of passion as the storm grew louder and raged around them.

Although the sleeping pills had definitely taken a distinct toll upon Tammy, Matthew had failed to take into consideration the resilience that she had built up against them over the past six months of taking them, and had equally failed to recognise the exaggeration of her symptoms.

Still entwined in the lip-lock with Matthew, Tammy carefully slipped her right hand free from the stretched-out plastic that had previously restrained it. Reaching her hand behind her, she gripped upon the dusty neck of a bottle of 1970 'Chateauneuf du Pape' and carefully removed it from the shelf. Then, as she playfully nibbled upon Matthew's bottom lip, she suddenly bit down as hard as she could, preventing Matthew from retracting his head as she brought the glass bottle swinging. Too slow to realise the deceit, Matthew did not react in time. The bottle smashed against the side of his head, sending wine and shards of glass flying through the air as the remaining jagged neck section of the bottle sliced deep into the side of his face, cutting him wide open from temple to cheek.

Betrayal and surprise quickly twitched through Matthew's brief expressions, before his eyes rolled back in his head and consciousness rapidly departed him, leaving his body to slump down, seemingly lifelessly on the floor.

The divine smell of the vintage wine quickly filled the air as Tammy cried out in defiant triumph. Adrenaline pulsated rapidly though her tired body as she panted and dropped the neck of the bottle to the floor. Reaching up with her newly-liberated arm, she pulled the blindfold free from her face and gazed over to Craig Carlson upon the table, groaning and quickly bleeding to death.

"Tammy? Tammy, help me, please!" he pleaded in a desperate whimper.

"My God!" she mumbled in horror as she glanced upon the old man's ghastly inflictions. "I'm getting us out of here, Mr Carlson."

Tammy leant forward and stretched out her aching arm, removing the kitchen knife from the wooden pasting table and cutting herself free from her remaining restraints. She stood, light-headed and weak, feeling her knees wobbling like jelly and her heavy eyelids starting to drop. She quickly steadied her balance against the pasting table and took a deep breath, desperately trying to focus all her fleeting energy upon staying awake. Looking up to the top shelf of the wines, Tammy set her eyes upon her handbag.

"Tammy! Tammy, Hurry! Please!" Craig pleaded again.

She put down the knife and took a step forward, losing her balance once again and stumbling into the shelves of wine, sending various bottles tumbling free and smashing upon the ground around her. Securing the bag in her grip, Tammy immediately set her weary body back down in the chair. She took another long breath and rubbed her face, feeling her dizzy head slosh from side to side as her eyelids grew heavier and heavier. She removed her phone from her bag and turned it on, greeted by the chirpy jingle of the welcome logo as she fingered wearily down the numbers and pressed the nines.

"Emergency services, which service please?"

"I... I need the police..."

"Police, what's your emergency?"

"This is Tammy Atkins... I...I've been kidnapped. Please help!"

THE DAMAGED

"Okay, Tammy. Where are you now?"

"Number eight... Oak Street... We're in th-the cellar."

"Are you in any immediate danger?"

"YES!"

The phone then slipped from Tammy's feeble grip and splashed into a puddle of red wine. She cast her eyes down at it and groaned breathlessly as her heavy head slumped forward and her eyes fell shut.

"Tammy? Help me!" Craig howled in desperation, jolting Tammy back to consciousness again.

Tammy forced her head up and prised apart her sticky eyes as her swaying vision focused in on the pained desperation upon the old man's face. Reaching up with both hands, she gripped upon the bloody pasting table and hoisted her ungainly body upright, grimacing and reeling again from the grisly sight of the blood-drenched old man.

"Please!" he wailed despairingly. "I... I don't deserve this! It's not my fault!"

"Wha...What do you mean?" she slurred in drunken confusion, trying to focus her sights and her concentration.

"Help me, please Tammy! I'm sorry... I... I've paid for all my sins... I don't deserve this!"

Tammy frowned in bewilderment as she swayed back and forth on the spot, her head spinning like a merry-go-round while her weak body screamed at her for sleep. *What was he trying to say?* she wondered dizzily, as the rain and wind battered the house so fiercely that she could barely hear herself think. She turned her eyes to the wooden beam of the cellar and looked upon Matthew's charcoal sketches, studying them in detail for the first time. She looked at the eyes, the line of the jaw, and then to the bulbous brow and crook of the nose, and suddenly saw Craig Carlson looking back at her. *Was Matthew right?*

"You... You did it... didn't you?" she mumbled at him in a weak exhale.

"Please! Please help me, Tammy. It hurts so bad!" he replied, avoiding the question.

Tammy's jittering mind then turned bitter as her thoughts turned to Matthew's prolonged suffering at the hands of the callous man before her, and shame for depriving him of his long-sought revenge.

She summoned up all the remaining energy in her body and reached down for the kitchen knife, gripping it tight as she snarled down at the pitiful, whimpering old man.

"Tammy? What...What are you doing, Tammy?" Craig blubbered as the flickering cellar light glimmered on the blood-drenched blade.

Tammy shook her head solemnly as she held up the knife with both trembling hands and stumbled a step closer.

"Put down the knife, you crazy bitch!" he demanded in desperation, spraying blood at her from his battered gums.

Tammy shook her head again as tears streamed from her pale and tired face. Her eyelids began to fall and her arms shuddered with overwhelming fatigue. She felt herself starting to lose consciousness as she stood, but not before first slicing the knife through the air and burying it deep into Craig's bloody chest.

She lost her balance and fell back, landing awkwardly in the dining chair once again. Numb and completely exhausted from her final bout of exertion, Tammy could fight the drugs in her system no longer. She released a long sigh and sunk deep into the chair, her cloudy sights setting down upon Matthew who lay unconscious at her feet.

Her eyes closed and she began to gently drift away. Thinking of Matthew's tormented life as she slipped into a dream, her last conscious thought were *I'm sorry, Matthew. I love you, you crazy bastard.*

THE DAMAGED

THE HOUSE OF MIRRORS

The dark and menacing sky crackled and cracked as it flashed with lightning and howled with powerful gusts. PC Lang watched on with eerie trepidation as he sat parked in the car park of the local shops, eating a sausage roll and counting down the last few minutes of his long, monotonous shift. He remembered watching the weather report that morning, but no mention of a storm was ever made. The errors of '87 could easily be assigned to the poor technology of the time, but for an unpredicted storm of such magnitude to just appear today was completely unprecedented.

He mused over his unfruitful day with a sense of down-beaten melancholy, comforted mildly by the fact that his smug colleagues had made equally pitiful progress on the enviably juicy murder case. He finished off the last few bites of his sausage roll and brushed away the crumbs from his moustache, his thoughts briefly turning to the family he was eager to return to. PC Lang's radio then suddenly crackled into life, as an urgent voice from dispatch relayed the details of Tammy's panicked call.

In PC Lang's experience, the vast majority of missing person reports turned out to be nothing more than cases of impulsive runaways and drunken misadventures. So, for one to turn into a real-life kidnapping was almost as thrilling to him as the murder case was. He recognised the address read out to him immediately, his disconcerting suspicions of Matthew having lingered in his mind for the majority of the day. The nervousness and oddities of Matthew had stuck out to him like a sore thumb, and now he knew why.

"Two-zero-six to dispatch, en route now!" he immediately called into his collared radio, frantically revving up the engine of his patrol car and skidding away through the puddles of the car park.

SIMON LAW

Eager with anticipation, PC Lang flipped on the sirens and lights, squinting his eyes through the relentless rain as his wipers worked overtime to try and clear the twisted opaque view. Fighting through the remorseless battering of the wind, he hammered down the road as fast as the car could manage, blazing through red lights and forcing his way through the crawling evening traffic.

A deathly stillness had fallen upon the cellar of the house on Oak Street, interrupted only by the wind and rain as it rattled against the slanted rear cellar doors. Matthew and Tammy gently breathed in and out in peculiar symbiotic synchronicity, as they both drifted aimlessly through their own murky dream-worlds. Tammy dreamt of Jessica, reaching for her hand with a wide smile upon her face, giggling and dancing whimsically as past mistakes were all forgiven and forgotten. Matthew dreamt only of the raven, nudging its black rigid beak through his muscles and organs in a frantic attempt for freedom. His skin rippled and contorted, stretching and ripping until finally bursting open like a balloon. The raven croaked with glee, emerging from Matthew's bloody chest like a parasite bursting from its withered host.

The cold embrace of wakefulness tingled through Matthew's mind, jolting him to life with sudden flutters of anxiety. He peeled his face from the sticky puddle of blood and wine and rolled over to his back, feeling the pound of his head and the piercing throb of the bloody gouge that ripped him open from temple to cheek.

Distant mutterings in his fragile mind slowly began to gain momentum, filling his head with an incomprehensible cacophony of conflicting angry voices, all screaming down at him with nauseating, insistent demands. He released a low growl and slowly pulled apart his eyes, staring up at the spinning ceiling as the cellar light flickered and flashed at him like a mob of trigger-happy paparazzi.

"Get up, Matthew. Get up now!" screamed one of the anonymous voices in his head, as it rose high above the dissonance of the others.

"Quickly!" called another.

Matthew pulled himself forward and rubbed his bloody face, inadvertently ripping the deep gash open further and sending a fresh jolt of intense pain flooding through him. He reeled and took a deep breath, wearily casting his eyes around the blood-drenched room to assess the situation. His gaze then fell upon Tammy with confusion, gradually recalling their last embrace that had preceded the blunt force blow to his head. She had betrayed him, that much was clear, but to what end?

THE DAMAGED

"Sweetheart? Quickly, please! There's not much time left!" rose another voice insistently, a voice that could have been his mother's, but too muffled to say with certainty.

Matthew obeyed and forced his weary body to its feet, stumbling and swaying back and forth as his head continued to spin. It was then that Matthew's eyes were drawn down to the lifeless old man upon the pasting table, and to the knife now buried deep into his chest. The beast croaked with discontent that the terminal impaling had not been his, but Matthew quickly stifled it. A curious smile began to curl at the corners of his mouth as he turned back to Tammy once again, gazing down at her with perplexed intrigue and pride.

"You see, we're not too dissimilar after all, are we?" he told her as she continued to snooze before him.

Tammy's strange actions seemed to completely contradict her previous deceit, leaving Matthew's ailing mind whirling around in search of comprehension. *Maybe she had seen the light? Maybe she really did love me?* he pondered.

Matthew quickly realised that it really didn't matter either way. His quest of vengeance was now complete. He had finally reached the end of the long and winding road, and there was only one thing left to do. The idea of murder-suicide, setting Tammy and himself free from their arduous sorrowful lives so that they could finally be together, was his alone. As the intention now resurfaced in Matthew's mind, the beast squawked aloud with angry resistance to it. The beast wanted to live, to continue its rampage of wrath unimpeded, and wasn't prepared to relent without a fight. It flapped and croaked and pecked at Matthew's insides with vicious defiance, sending bolts of pain through his body and causing the protruding feathers on his back to elongate and multiply.

"Come with me, Matthew!" the beast growled in his ear. "Don't defy me now, we've only just begun!" it continued, clouding Matthew's mind with conflicting thoughts and reminding him again of the euphoria he'd felt at his first kill.

"No, leave me! I don't need you!" Matthew mumbled back in despair.

"You'd be nothing without me!"

"Leave!"

Matthew turned to the bloody corpse and wrenched the kitchen knife free, wiping it clean upon his trousers before then kneeling down at Tammy's feet.

"I love you, Tammy," he whispered with a smile, reaching up and running his fingers along the string of pearls around her neck.

He leant forward and kissed her, propping up her head tenderly with his hand as he brought up the knife and placed it tentatively against her throat. The thoughts and voices whirling through his head suddenly gained strength and volume, screaming opposing demands at him with frantic pressure and desperation. It was then that the angry beast from inside took full control of his hand, resisting against his force and pulling the knife away. The beast cared as little for Tammy's life as it did for the rest of Matthew's bloody victims, but it knew with certainty that once Tammy was dead Matthew's pending suicide would be completely unstoppable.

Matthew closed his eyes and took a breath. As he concentrated his utmost on regaining control of his mental upheaval, his senses became filled with the familiar scent of old floral perfume.

"Sweetheart?" cooed a voice, a voice not from inside his head, but from right in front of him.

Matthew opened up his eyes and gazed down at Tammy, but looking back at him was his mother, bright-eyed and smiling up reassuringly.

"Mother?"

"It's okay, Sweetheart. Just relax..." she told him, reaching up and tenderly grasping hold of his knife-wielding hand. "...We're all waiting for you here, Matthew. It's time to let go and join us now."

She gripped and forced Matthew's hand back towards her neck, smiling and nodding with warm, inviting eyes as the blade pressed gently against her skin.

A single trickle of blood ran down her neck as the blade slowly began to perforate the surface of the skin. Matthew gripped the knife tighter, ready to slice further into the skin, when his attention was suddenly alerted to the sound of a car engine. Matthew paused and lowered the knife, his befuddled mind immediately visualising the sight of his father's black Capri pulling onto the driveway.

"...Father?" he called out, strangely convinced in his unhinged mind that his father had somehow just returned from a long day in the office.

Matthew dropped the knife and stood. He leapt up the concrete cellar stairs and bounded towards the front door with excitement.

Switching off the sirens and lights as he drove down the street, PC Lang gently pulled up on the driveway and leant into his radio.

"Two-zero-six to dispatch, do you copy?"

"Dispatch, go ahead Two-zero-six."

"Have arrived at the property, please advise how to proceed."

"Proceed with caution, Two-zero-six. Armed response are en route too, ETA ten minutes, maybe more because of the storm."

"Ten-four."

PC Lang had just released the button on his radio when Matthew suddenly burst from the front door of the house, bare-chested and

THE DAMAGED

smothered in blood, his face gleaming with an odd euphoric smile. The rain and wind set upon him without mercy, blowing him backwards and stinging his vision to a murky blur. He held his hand to his eyes and gazed across to PC Lang, blinking and squinting away the blur until the patrol car finally came in to focus. His strange smile then swiftly changed to a fearful grimace, as terror and realisation flooded through him. PC Lang unbuckled his baton and quickly leapt from the car door, his eyes firmly fixed upon Matthew's as he flicked out the telescopic sections of the baton.

"Stay right where you are, Mr Mason!" he yelled at him through the deafening storm. "...I just want to talk to you!"

Matthew turned and dashed back into the house as PC Lang gave chase, pushing against the swinging door as Matthew tried to slam it closed. He swung the baton at him with all his might, striking it hard against the side of Matthew's right leg with a bone-shattering crack and sending Matthew flying face-first onto the lounge floor.

The chaotic voices swirling endlessly around Matthew's head were then joined by echoic, piercing laughter as the officer leapt onto his back, ramming his knee sharply between his shoulder blades and pinning him forcefully to the floor.

"Matthew Mason, I'm arresting you for suspicion of kidnapping..." the officer began to announce, dropping the baton to the floor as he reached back and pulled the handcuffs free from his belt. "You do not have to say anything..." he continued, wrenching Matthew's left hand awkwardly behind his back and securing the first cuff. "...But it may harm your defence if you do not mention something..." PC Lang was interrupted as Matthew began to struggle and fight back, wriggling and pushing against the floor with seemingly inhuman strength and sending the officer toppling off into his father's red leathered Chesterfield.

Matthew jumped to his feet and swung a fist, breaking PC Lang's nose and sending his helmet into the air. PC Lang quickly retaliated, grappling Matthew and trying to tackle him back down to the floor. Matthew's eyes exploded to amber as anger and fear started to fuel the raging beast, increasing his strength and ferocity as he sent the officer smashing into the grandfather clock. Shattered glass exploded across the room as a bolt of lightning lit up the night sky. Powerful gusts of wind bellowed through the house, howling and whistling and carrying the sadistic cackles of heavy-handed orderlies. Rising terror tingled icily across Matthew's trembling skin as Otis soon appeared at the window again, taunting him with a maniacal grin.

"We're coming for you, Matthew!" he chuckled as he tapped upon the glass.

SIMON LAW

With Matthew seemingly distracted, PC Lang saw his opportunity. He got to his feet, grabbed his fallen baton, and swiped it fiercely against Matthew's back. Matthew cried in agony, but remained on his feet, turning to the officer with a bitter snarl as he dived into him and smashed him against the flat-screen television. PC Lang clutched hold of Matthew, spinning him around with all his might and pinning him to the wall.

They were grappling and tussling back and forth, each struggling for supremacy over the other, when the wedding photograph suddenly fell from the mantle. It smashed against the floor to the sound of screams, as the broken glass cut deep into his parents' flesh and sent the loose pearls from around his mother's neck rolling aimlessly across the room.

Matthew roared with anger and adrenaline as he finally gained the upper hand, pulling the baton free from PC Lang's hand and throwing him crashing into the stereo system. The stereo fell from the stand and landed on the floor, knocking the 'Play' button upon the front of the machine and quickly filling the room with the sound of Vivaldi's 'Four Seasons'.

"Put it down, Matthew!" PC Lang demanded as he cowered in a ball with his hands shielding his face.

Matthew smiled as he listened to the sharp uplifting strings of the violin, feeling the baton in his grip while he debated PC Lang's fate.

The sound of distant sirens suddenly filled the air, and Matthew's confidence fell as Otis's menacing laugh quickly returned. Matthew snarled and shuddered, feeling his anxieties flutter up with the fear of his impending incarceration. His attention then returned to the pleading Officer at his feet, as he increased his grip upon the baton and brought it crashing through the air, savagely cracking PC Lang's head wide open and sending blood splattering all across the curling floral wallpaper.

PC Lang turned silent as Matthew began limping his way towards the cellar, desperate to finish what he'd started before the rest of the police arrived to take him away. He grit his teeth through the pain as he dragged his limp, broken leg through the lounge and into the kitchen, where he was met with a ghastly sight.

"Not today you don't, Buddy!" growled a stern American voice.

Matthew gazed in disbelief and horror, as James stood guarding the cellar door with Bronco loyally stood by his feet.

"You're dead! I killed you!" he cried in despair as he looked upon the man, his skin tarnished to a grisly zombified blue as his clothes dripped with the putrid slosh of the muddy swamp.

THE DAMAGED

Bronco barked and snarled with pent-up rage, baring his teeth as rabid foam dripped from his mouth, edging forward and scratching eagerly upon the floor as he awaited his master's commands.

Matthew's eyes flickered anxiously between Bronco and James as frantic panic quickly took full hold of his body, trembling through his fingers and racing through his heart and causing him to momentarily lose control of his bladder. He turned and fled as fast as his crippled leg would allow, the sound of Bronco's venomous barks bouncing around his head amidst the sea of muffled voices.

The sirens and lights grew louder and brighter as Matthew reached the open front door, looking out to the street to find himself completely surrounded by feral beady-eyed gun-wielding tramps.

"Now this won't hurt a bit!" Otis cackled with a sarcastic grin, suddenly appearing at the doorway with a loaded syringe of ominous green fluid.

Matthew stumbled backwards, attempting to regain his balance with his crippled leg, before feeling the bone snap completely. He shrieked in agony as he continued falling, landing upon the stairs behind him and gazing down in horror at his shattered shin bone protruding from his leg.

Otis laughed with glee as he stepped inside the house, looking down at Matthew with a patronising smile.

Matthew rolled onto his front and began desperately dragging himself up the stairs, watching the flowers upon the floral wallpaper as they began to wilt and decay before his eyes.

"Stop or we'll shoot!" screeched one of the feral tramps through a megaphone, quickly followed by the deafening sound of a gunshot.

"How about now, Matthew? Do you need me now?" taunted the beast as Matthew slowly reached the top of the stairs, leaving a crimson streaky trail of blood behind him.

Matthew did not respond.

Another shot fired, grazing passed Matthew's ribs and burying into the wall as he pulled himself upright and hobbled away on his good leg. He turned the corner and gazed down the hall, watching as it started to stretch and lengthen before him, twisting and winding away into the far distance to the sound of eerie, deranged screams and clanging metal.

Desperate spindly hands reached out from between the rusty iron bars of the padded isolation cells ahead, as Vivaldi's bright notes of spring transformed to summer and continued to bounce and distort against the walls.

"Welcome home, baby!" called Leila's twisted voice from within one of the cells, as she pressed her pale face between the bars and lapped at her lips with her long, pierced tongue. "Come closer, baby," she continued. "Come closer and let me suck your cock for old time's sake!"

Leila laughed and rattled on the bars, riling up the occupants of the other cells as they kicked and thumped upon their padded metal doors. The cell doors then suddenly all burst open in unison, crashing against the walls and releasing a mob of dribbling straitjacket-clad crazies into the hall. The fluorescent lights flickered and strobed as the deranged mob began closing in, following Leila's lead as she mimed silent blowjob gestures at Matthew with a disturbing crooked smile.

"I think it's time for your medication now, Matthew!" Otis cackled from behind the mob, teasing him again with the syringe of ominous green fluid. "Wouldn't you agree?"

Paralysing anxiety pulsated through Matthew with such vigour that he froze on the spot, his bladder muscles completely giving up resistance and drenching his trousers in urine. He closed his eyes and frantically tried to swim to the surface of the pickled stew of raging voices, begging for the confidence of the beast inside to return.

"Hey, Pissy-Pants? You didn't piss your pants now, Did you?" laughed the taunting voice of school bully Jason Selby. "-Do you need your nappy changed, little baby? Ha-Ha-Ha!"

The pain in Matthew's broken leg suddenly started to soar. He prised apart his weepy eyes and looked down, seeing the two blood-splattered white Persian cats ripping at his tattered flesh, lapping at the blood with their sandpaper tongues and gnawing upon his protruding shin bone with their pointy feline teeth.

"You filthy little cunt! You make me sick!" raged Aunt Julie, glaring down at him with pitiful disgust as maggots wriggled and fell from the bloody hole in the side of her head.

"Do you need me *now*?" asked the beast again, his voice shuddering through Matthew's ailing body like an icy cold breeze.

"YES!"

The familiar squawking and flapping of wings quickly returned to his gut, invigorating him and focussing him to face the sea of demons. His eyes instantly burnt back to amber as he croaked and lapped hysterically at the air with the forks of his slithering serpent tongue. He smiled and reaffirmed his grip upon the baton, snarling around at his aunt's grisly, deformed face as he loaded the baton back like a baseball bat and swung at her with rage.

He watched as Aunt Julie's decapitated head rolled awkwardly down the corridor, and then turned turned and fled, the anger and determination of the beast now providing him the strength to continue. Hobbling away and gritting his teeth through the pain of his broken leg,

THE DAMAGED

Matthew dropped the bloodied baton to the floor and burst through a set of double doors to the white sterile day room ahead.

The throbbing black plumes that protruded from his back began to grow and multiply further, as bony foreign masses wriggled disconcertingly from behind his shoulder muscles. The spiralling mixture of Vivaldi's strings and police sirens continued to whirl around the perpetual stew of echoic voices in his head, as the warm summer notes began phasing into autumn. Scanning across the room, Matthew noticed a fire escape in the distance and hobbled towards it as fast as he could, feeling the skin on each of his shoulder blades gradually ripping open as the developing bony appendages desperately fought to release themselves.

He leant upon the spring-loaded escape bar and pushed with all his might, fighting against the fierce resistance of the storm as it pushed back against the door like a herd of stampeding elephants. He growled and snarled as his biceps bulged and rippled under the immense strain; the icy wind now starting to invade the room through the gap and fluttering through his golden blonde hair. He leant in with his shoulder, leveraging against his good leg as he gave the door one final shove, finally toppling the resistance and sending the door flying around on its hinges. The raging gusts quickly filled the room, knocking Matthew back and taking away his breath as it spiralled and completely enveloped him.

Matthew caught his breath and gingerly stepped out onto the metal stairwell, quickly grasping a tight hold of the rail before the strong gusts could try to topple him again. Looking down upon the street below him, he gazed upon the blurry blue flashing lights through the rain and upon the hordes of people that stood watching the show, noticing that even frail old Edgar Brown from the house opposite had braved the storm for a front row seat.

Another echoic demand bellowed from the megaphone, but the fierce storm completely muffled the sound. Matthew watched as two laden stretchers emerged from the front door below, as PC Lang and Tammy were quickly transported into the back of a waiting ambulance.

The megaphone voice returned, quickly followed by the sound of gunfire. The bullets cut through the air and veered to the left, blown off course by the strength of the wind and sent blasting into the windows and bricks of the building. Matthew grinned down at their failings, as he turned and began slowly ascending the metal staircase, pulling his weight with his arms as his trailing broken leg dangled loosely behind him.

The pelting rain quickly drenched him to the bone before suddenly morphing to blood like it had before in his dream. It smothered him

SIMON LAW

crimson, battering him with relentless force as he fought through it and eventually reached the roof.

Matthew pulled himself up and steadied himself precariously against the chimney, feeling the fierce storm embracing him and feeling a strange sensation of calm flowing through him.

He cocked his head up to the angry sky, watching the circling conspiracy of ravens above longingly as they darted and meandered between the bright forks of lightning. He took a long inhale of air and flexed his muscles, rolling his shoulders in their joints and carefully unravelling his crumpled black appendages into fully-fledged wings. He felt the harsh wind ruffling bracingly through his thick black silky plumes, before croaking aloud into the night with pure exhilaration.

The faint sound of Vivaldi whispered out through the shattered window, as autumn then phased to winter with a series of dramatic icy sharp notes that pierced through the storm. Matthew smiled and stretched out his new wings in full, feeling the strong wind blowing against them and causing his feet to gently lift up off the roof. He flapped and hovered, feeling a sense of peace and belonging as the swarm of ravens swooped down and began to spiral around him, calling to him with tender allure and promises of freedom.

Relaxing his wings, Matthew gently landed back upon the roof, staring out into the dark night sky with confidence and certainty of the ravens' promises. Another strong gust then howled and bellowed, toppling an old oak tree in the street and sending it crashing upon a police car with an almighty crumpling thud. Matthew grinned at the sight, feeling the voices in his head now starting to die off and leaving him with a welcoming sense of clarity.

Another fierce gust of wind suddenly blew upon him, completely knocking him off his feet as the strong uplift sent him tumbling from the rooftop. Matthew quickly spread out his long black wings, catching the current and riding the powerful updraught as it ascended him far above the house. He flapped and squawked with glee, watching as the ant-like crowd below gazed up at him in awe and amazement, as he turned and flew away into the distance, soaring higher and higher into the sky with majestic care-free poise, until he completely disappeared.

THE DAMAGED

LEGACY

It was three days after the freak storm that had hit the small town in Sussex when Matthew's delusional flight of fancy finally came to an end. He landed with a graceful flutter and perched himself upon the roof of an old Victorian church, peering down over the peak of the vestibule like a Gothic stone gargoyle. He watched out with a confident sense of omnipotence as the people below went about their daily business, seemingly oblivious to his vigilant watching eyes.

It was at that moment when Matthew became aware of a distant series of beeping noises from all directions. The strange noises slowly grew louder and more defined, each beeping at him in a slightly different rhythm and pitch. His nose gradually filled with the repugnant scent of vomit and disinfectant, a scent that blew in on the waves of the breeze and started to linger and grow. Quiet whispering voices began speaking in Matthew's head, but not like before; the voices were not speaking to him, but with each other instead. He gazed out into the horizon, watching the fluffy white clouds gently drifting through the azure blue skies while praying that the disconcerting sensations would pass, but they didn't. Feeling fatigue suddenly overcome him, Matthew closed his eyes in mournful resignation, opening them back up a few moments later to find that the world he thought he knew had vanished.

Prising apart his sticky eyes, Matthew found himself lying in a dimly-lit room with his body encased in a web of plastic tubes. He tried to move, but his body did not react, instead replying to his request with a series of agonising jolts of pain. It was then that Matthew realised where he was, and that his life was hanging in the balance of the rhythm of the continued beeps that echoed all around him. He groaned in pain as a single tear rolled down his cheek. He motioned to speak but only one word left his weak, trembling lips; *Amon.*

SIMON LAW

The tabloids had described Matthew's last actions as 'The desperate psychotic suicide attempt of a crazed serial killer', having leapt from the roof of his family home to avoid capture and incarceration. Landing upon the ground with a bone-cracking thud, Matthew shattered his collarbone, broke his arm, his hip, and four ribs; one of which had perforated and deflated his right lung.

Five days after first waking, after forensics teams had dredged the swamp and recovered the black sacks of dismembered bodies, Matthew was transferred from the Intensive Care Unit to his own private police-guarded room down the hall; two doors down from PC Lang, who lay in a coma while consultants debated the severity of brain-damage that Matthew's fierce blow to the head had caused. Matthew was then officially charged with the murders of Craig Carlson, Samantha Jacobs, and five unidentified vagrants, along with the murder and cannibalism of Agnieszka Machowski, the kidnapping and false imprisonment of Tammy Atkins, and the aggravated assault of PC Patrick Lang.

One week later was the preliminary hearing of Matthew's case. After being wheeled into court by his lawyer, Matthew was to speak only to confirm his name and address, but immediately burst into a tirade of crazed ramblings. He confessed to all charges without contest, even confessing to the murder of Craig Carlson for the sake of upholding Tammy's good name, but claimed that his actions were coerced by a beast named 'Amon'. Matthew was immediately removed from court.

The courts later heard from an expert witness, who explained that Amon was a demon referred to in ancient demonology as one of the marquises of Hell; a demon with the power of possession, who either took the form of a wolf, or of a man with the head and wings of a raven. It was then that the court deemed Matthew mentally unfit to stand trial for his crimes, and instead sent him to Broadmoor Hospital – a high-security psychiatric hospital, for indefinite further treatment.

At the request of the courts, the police later investigated Matthew's allegations that Craig Carlson had been responsible for the deaths of his parents twenty-five years prior, but after a brief and somewhat lackadaisical investigation, concluded that there was insufficient evidence to support his claim.

After sleeping off the drugs circulating in her system, Tammy was released from hospital. Her statement was taken by police, and although her fingerprints were found upon the blade that killed Craig Carlson, she was never questioned further.

THE DAMAGED

Uncharacteristically sympathetic to her plight, Maureen granted Tammy a three-week period of paid leave to rest and recover, a period that Tammy spent mostly weeping and vomiting up into the toilet.

At one point, looking at her pale reflection in the bathroom mirror, Tammy gazed curiously at the small cut upon her throat, racking her brains for recollection of its occurrence whilst struggling to accept the most obvious explanation of them all. *Had Matthew really tried to kill me?*

By 16th October, the vomiting had become a daily occurrence, and in her mind Tammy knew its cause with absolute certainty. She had been back to work on light duties for a few weeks by this point, and life had somewhat returned to its depressing and lonely norm.

Stepping from the bus at the end of her shift, Tammy meandered lethargically back to her dark and empty flat. She picked up the mail from the doorstep and carried it through to the lounge, taking a seat upon the sofa and gazing down upon the sparse collection of letters with mournful disappointment. Slowly flicking through the various bills and pizza menus within her grip, the distinct lack of birthday cards was obvious. Tammy shrugged and sighed and rubbed her face forlornly, not entirely sure who she was expecting a birthday card from, but depressed nonetheless.

"Happy Birthday, Tammy!" she mumbled to herself sarcastically.

Tammy had hoped that maybe Keith might have sent a card on Jessica's behalf, or maybe Matthew would have sent one from the hospital, (if he was even allowed to send cards, that was) but there was nothing at all.

Tammy ripped up the menus and had begun to sift through the bills when an ominous brown envelope caught her attention. She immediately opened it and started reading.

"Dear Miss Atkins," the formal letter began. "Despite our best efforts, I'm sorry to inform you that Mr K Sampson has declined your request for family mediation in regards to your daughter, Jessica Sampson. My recommendation to you is...."

Tammy stopped reading and threw the letter angrily to the floor, feeling her eyes well up as the lure of the beckoning razorblade began niggling in her mind. She had expected her traumatic ordeal to invoke a certain degree of sympathy from Keith, or at least a degree of lenience, but that was clearly not the case.

"Happy Birthday Tammy indeed!" she repeated.

Tammy reached into her bag and removed an unopened packet of cigarettes, the same packet that had been in her bag for the past six weeks now. She gazed down at them longingly, chewing on her bottom lip as she fingered the plastic seal and began to tease it away. She gulped and grit her teeth, turning her hand to a fist and burying her long nails into her palm as she fought to overturn her burning cravings. Releasing a slow, agitated breath, Tammy stuffed the cigarettes back into her bag and removed the pink cupcake that one of her old ladies had given her that morning, placing it down upon the coffee table and staring at it with a faint crooked smile. *At least someone remembered,* she thought.

Tammy then delved back into the bag again and removed a small, long box with the chemist's logo upon it. She gazed down at the box in contemplation, rotating it slowly between her fingers while her mind drifted off into an anxious pondering daze. Peculiar thoughts and possibilities drifted in and out of her mind for a few moments until she finally composed herself and stood up decisively, taking the small box and disappearing off into the bathroom.

Returning a few minutes later, her face was flushed with ambivalent feelings of panic and unexpected joy. She placed the urine-soaked stick upon the table and sat, placing her head in her hands while trying to calm her racing heart. She was pregnant, and the pregnancy test had proved it. It seemed amazing to her that such a thing was even possible, with all the trauma that she had been through, not to mention her eating disorder and her alcoholism, but the facts were now undeniable.

Tammy picked up her cupcake and left the flat to take a walk, thinking that the fresh air might aid in clearing her head. She sat down at the bus stop where she and James would often sit for a chat, and took a big bite of the pink sugary cupcake, smearing buttercream and icing sugar all around the corners of her lips. Her thoughts quickly turned to Matthew, the father of her unborn baby, as her mind span around inside her head in an attempt to reconcile her conflicting feelings for him.

The sun slowly began to set and so Tammy retreated back to the flat once again. She turned on the television and gazed numbly at the nightly news. The news was then followed by some inane reality show on a beach, followed by a documentary on the twenty-fifth anniversary of the storm of eighty-seven, where Michael Fish desperately tried to defend his infamous misinformed forecast once again.

Her thoughts then inevitably returned to Matthew, as it suddenly occurred to her what a poignant day it must have been for him too, being the twenty-fifth anniversary of his parents' murder. Though confused and clouded in her muddled mind, her love for him was still true, that much Tammy couldn't deny. She started wondering how he was, how well he was recovering from his horrific injuries, if he was in any pain. She wondered how he would be coping, all alone on a day

THE DAMAGED

when he would desperately need a comforting shoulder to cry upon. The contemplation of visiting him then entered her mind, despite the strong advice from the police not to, to ask him face to face about the gash upon her throat, to tell him about their unborn child growing inside of her, and to gaze deep into the endless oceans of his azure blue eyes one more time.

Tammy felt herself overcome with emotions once again and so dragged herself to bed, snuggling into the duvet with Jessica's stuffed giraffe toy tightly in her grasp, and gently cried herself to sleep.

In the midst of a dream, Tammy woke abruptly with a cold shiver tingling its way down her spine. The display on her bedside clock read three o'clock, though she could scarcely believe it as she now felt fully rested. Tammy frowned in confusion and lay back down, and that was when the tapping started from across the hall, from within Jessica's bedroom. She sat bolt upright and tuned her ears into the strange sound, tap-tap tapping upon Jessica's bedroom door. Tammy rubbed her face and picked out the sleep sediment from her eyes with her fingernails, and then she saw it, laying at the end of her bed like a ghostly calling card, still and ominous, a single silky black plume.

Her heart skipped a beat then started to race within her as paralysing terror flooded through her mind. The tapping then grew louder, echoing through the flat like thunder and beckoning her out, into the hall, into Jessica's bedroom where the beast would be lying in wait for her.

Tap. Tap. Tap.

THE END

Made in the USA
San Bernardino, CA
10 January 2016